DATE DUE

PRINTED IN U.S.A.

ONI PRESS

AN ONI PRESS PUBLICATION

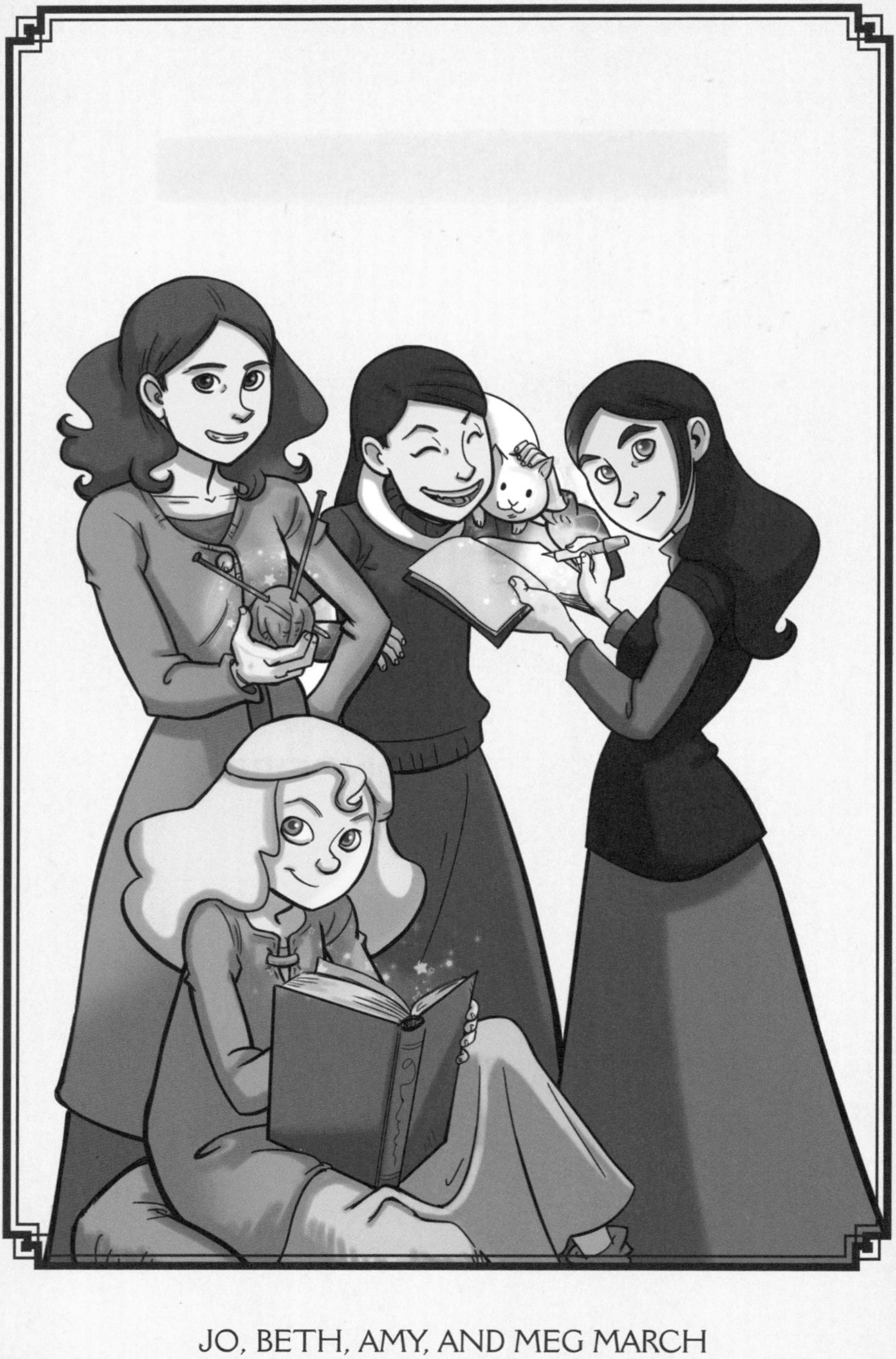

JO, BETH, AMY, AND MEG MARCH

Little Witches

MAGIC IN CONCORD

BY
LEIGH DRAGOON

WITH ILLUSTRATIONS BY
LEIGH DRAGOON

&

LETTERS BY
HASSAN OTSMANE-ELHAOU

EDITED BY
ROBIN HERRERA

DESIGNED BY
SONJA SYNAK

PORTLAND
ONI PRESS
2020

PUBLISHED BY ONI-LION FORGE PUBLISHING GROUP, LLC

ONI PRESS

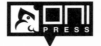

James Lucas Jones, *president & publisher*
Sarah Gaydos, *editor in chief*
Charlie Chu, *e.v.p. of creative & business development*
Brad Rooks, *director of operations*
Amber O'Neill, *special projects manager*
Harris Fish, *events manager*
Margot Wood, *director of marketing & sales*
Devin Funches, *sales & marketing manager*
Katie Sainz, *marketing manager*
Tara Lehmann, *publicist*
Troy Look, *director of design & production*
Kate Z. Stone, *senior graphic designer*
Sonja Synak, *graphic designer*
Hilary Thompson, *graphic designer*
Sarah Rockwell, *junior graphic designer*
Angie Knowles, *digital prepress lead*
Vincent Kukua, *digital prepress technician*
Jasmine Amiri, *senior editor*
Shawna Gore, *senior editor*
Amanda Meadows, *senior editor*
Robert Meyers, *senior editor, licensing*
Grace Bornhoft, *editor*
Zack Soto, *editor*
Chris Cerasi, *editorial coordinator*
Steve Ellis, *vice president of games*
Ben Eisner, *game developer*
Michelle Nguyen, *executive assistant*
Jung Lee, *logistics coordinator*

Joe Nozemack, *publisher emeritus*

onipress.com
lionforge.com
facebook.com/onipress
facebook.com/lionforge
twitter.com/onipress
twitter.com/lionforge
instagram.com/onipress
instagram.com/lionforge

leighdragoon.com

First Edition: August 2020

ISBN 978-1-62010-721-8
eISBN 978-1-62010-649-5

LITTLE WITCHES: MAGIC IN CONCORD, August 2020. Published by Oni-Lion Forge Publishing Group, LLC. 1319 SE Martin Luther King Jr. Blvd., Suite 240, Portland, OR 97214.

Printed in Printed in South Korea through Four Colour Print Group, Louisville, KY.

Library of Congress Control Number: 2019931468

2468109753 1

To everyone who helped.
And to my own favorite Amy, Alice.

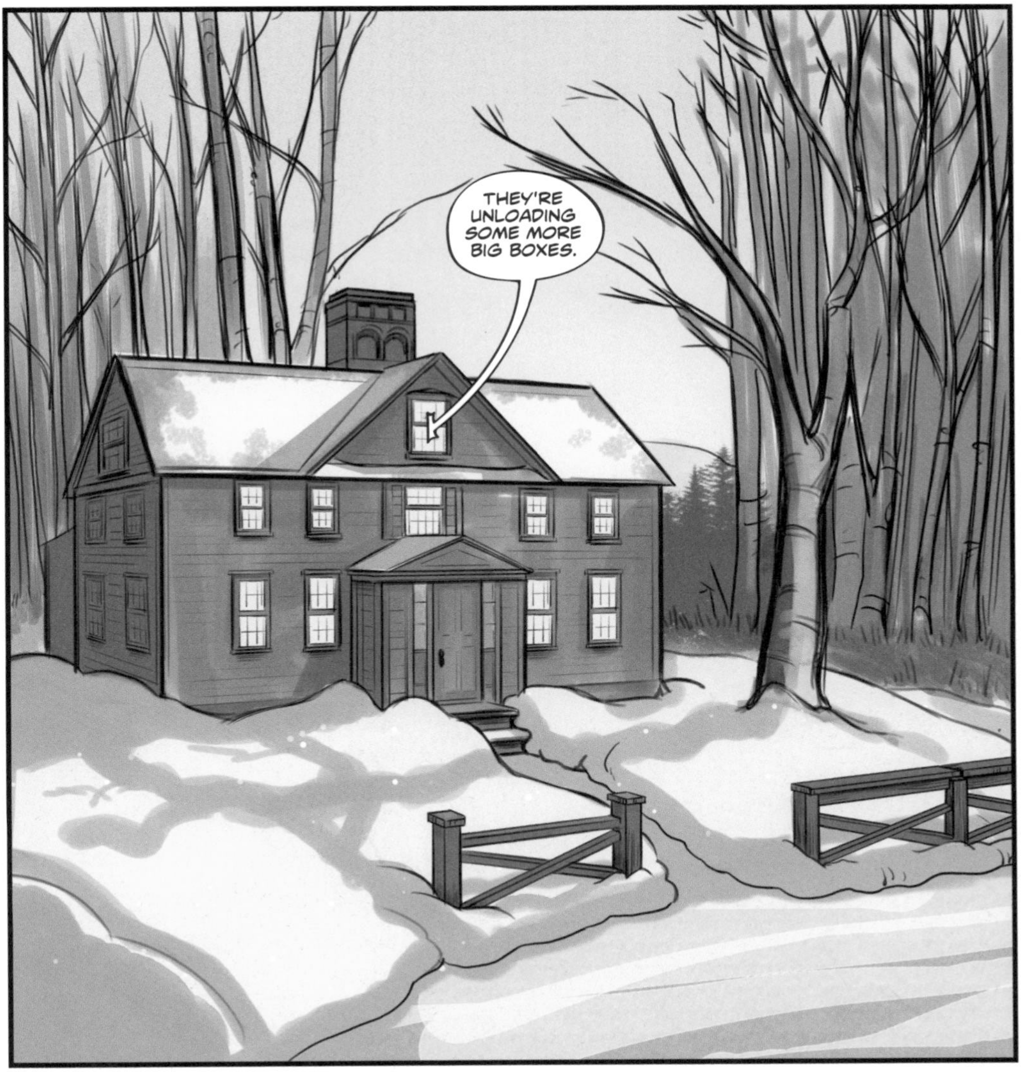
THEY'RE UNLOADING SOME MORE BIG BOXES.

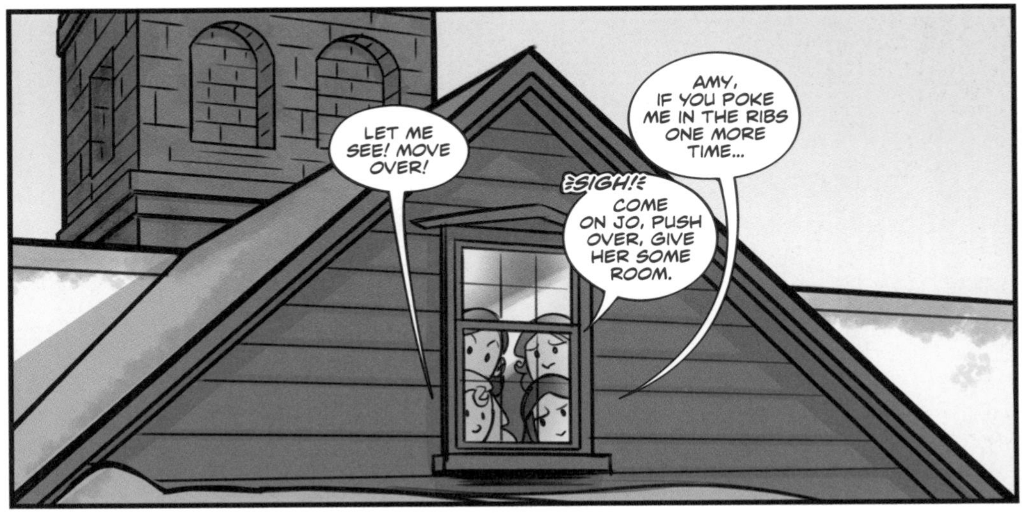
LET ME SEE! MOVE OVER!
AMY, IF YOU POKE ME IN THE RIBS ONE MORE TIME...
SIGH!
COME ON JO, PUSH OVER, GIVE HER SOME ROOM.

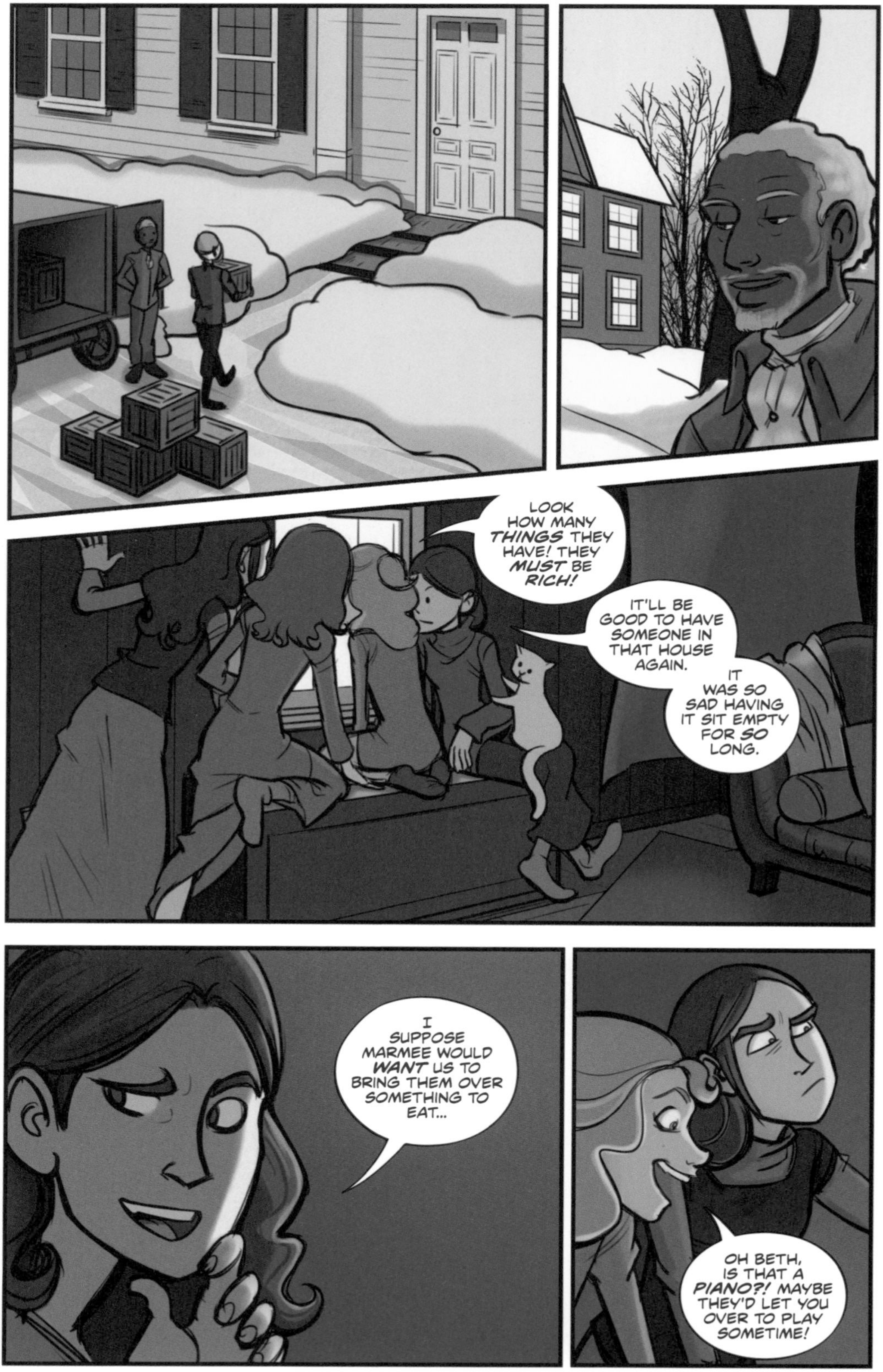
LOOK HOW MANY THINGS THEY HAVE! THEY MUST BE RICH!
IT'LL BE GOOD TO HAVE SOMEONE IN THAT HOUSE AGAIN.
IT WAS SO SAD HAVING IT SIT EMPTY FOR SO LONG.
I SUPPOSE MARMEE WOULD WANT US TO BRING THEM OVER SOMETHING TO EAT...
OH BETH, IS THAT A PIANO?! MAYBE THEY'D LET YOU OVER TO PLAY SOMETIME!

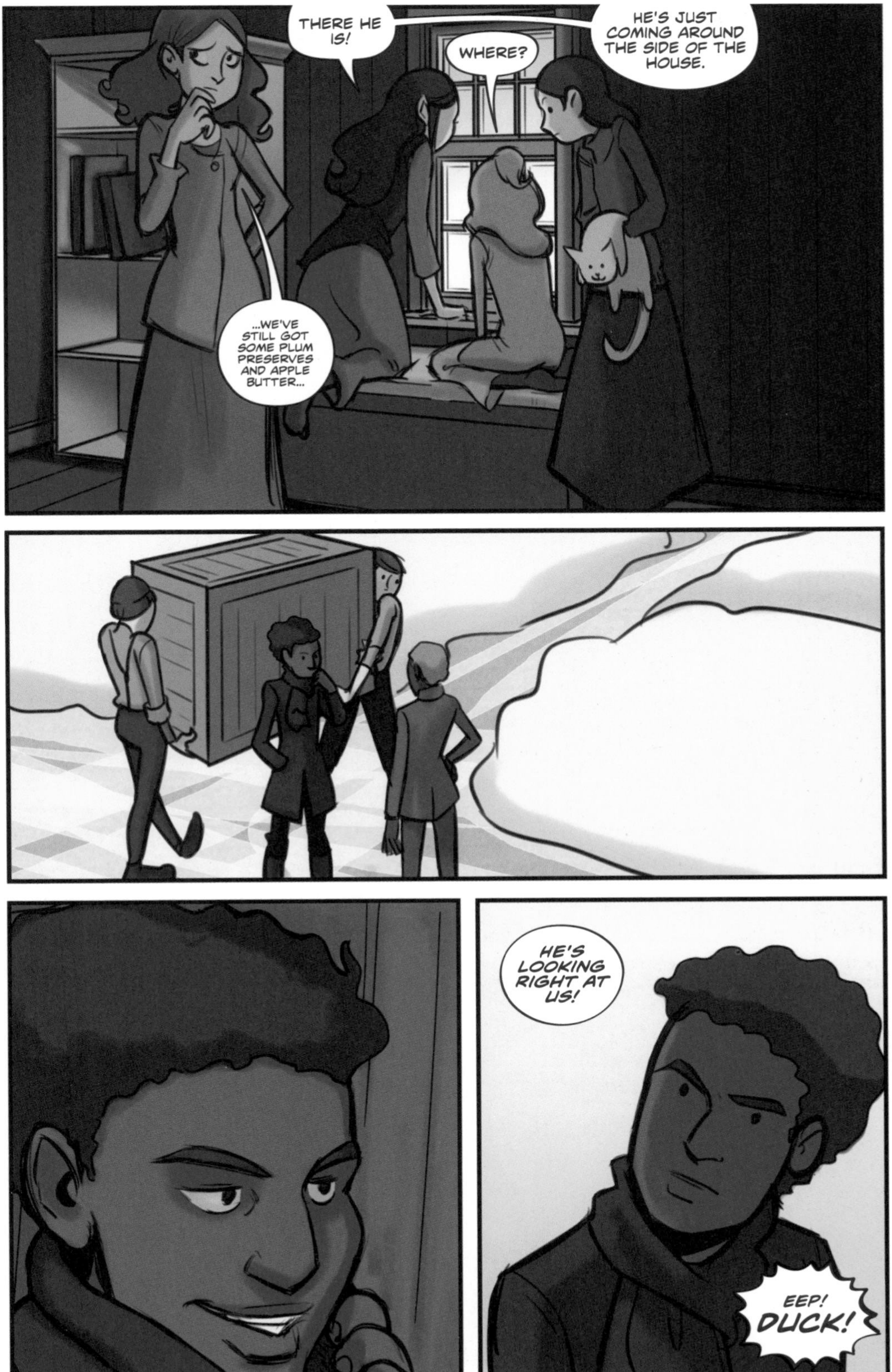
THERE HE IS!
WHERE?
HE'S JUST COMING AROUND THE SIDE OF THE HOUSE.
...WE'VE STILL GOT SOME PLUM PRESERVES AND APPLE BUTTER...
HE'S LOOKING RIGHT AT US!
EEP! DUCK!

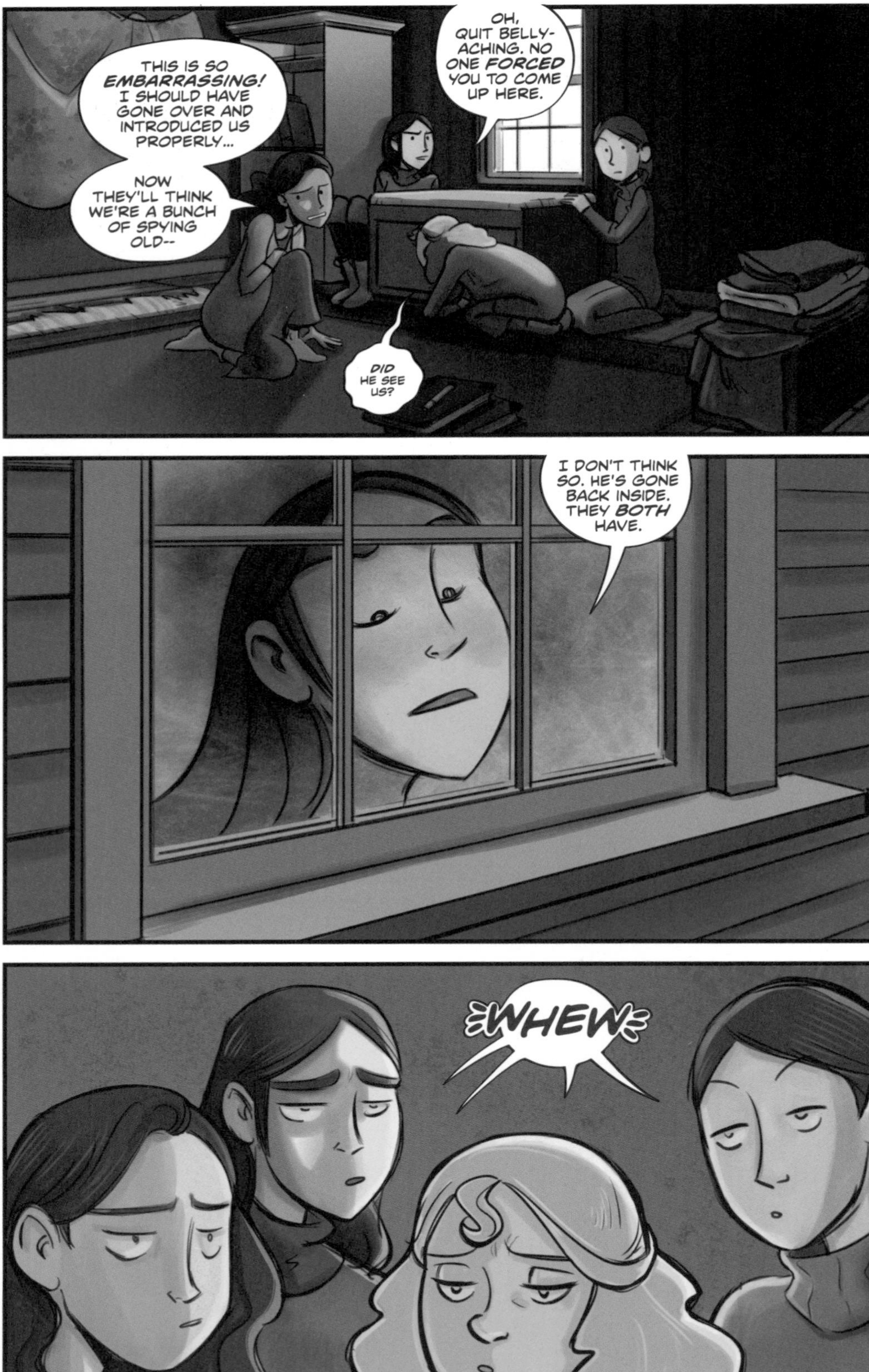
THIS IS SO EMBARRASSING! I SHOULD HAVE GONE OVER AND INTRODUCED US PROPERLY...
NOW THEY'LL THINK WE'RE A BUNCH OF SPYING OLD--
OH, QUIT BELLY-ACHING. NO ONE FORCED YOU TO COME UP HERE.
DID HE SEE US?
I DON'T THINK SO. HE'S GONE BACK INSIDE. THEY BOTH HAVE.
WHEW

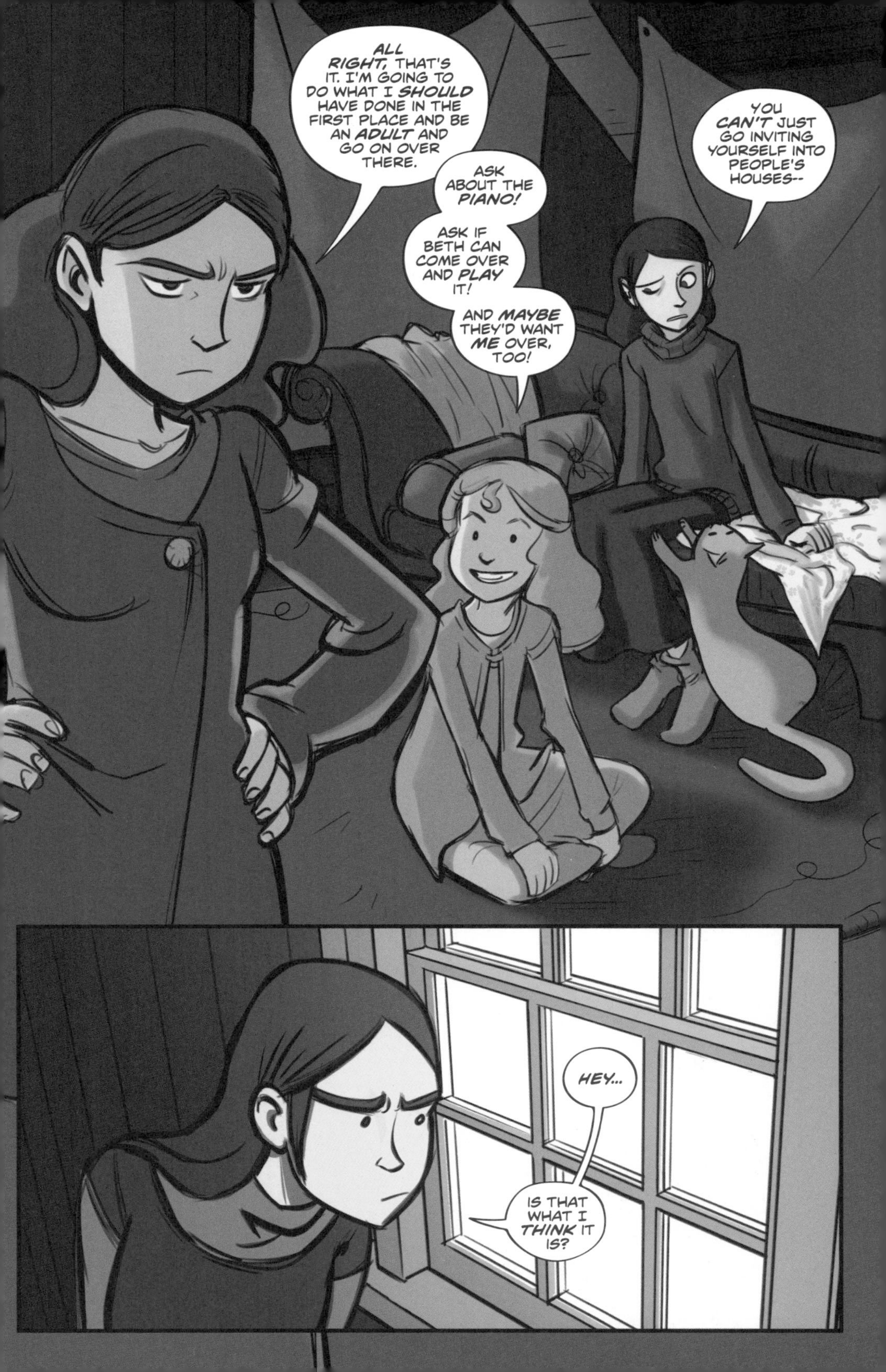
ALL RIGHT, THAT'S IT. I'M GOING TO DO WHAT I SHOULD HAVE DONE IN THE FIRST PLACE AND BE AN ADULT AND GO ON OVER THERE.
ASK ABOUT THE PIANO!
ASK IF BETH CAN COME OVER AND PLAY IT!
AND MAYBE THEY'D WANT ME OVER, TOO!
YOU CAN'T JUST GO INVITING YOURSELF INTO PEOPLE'S HOUSES--
HEY...
IS THAT WHAT I THINK IT IS?

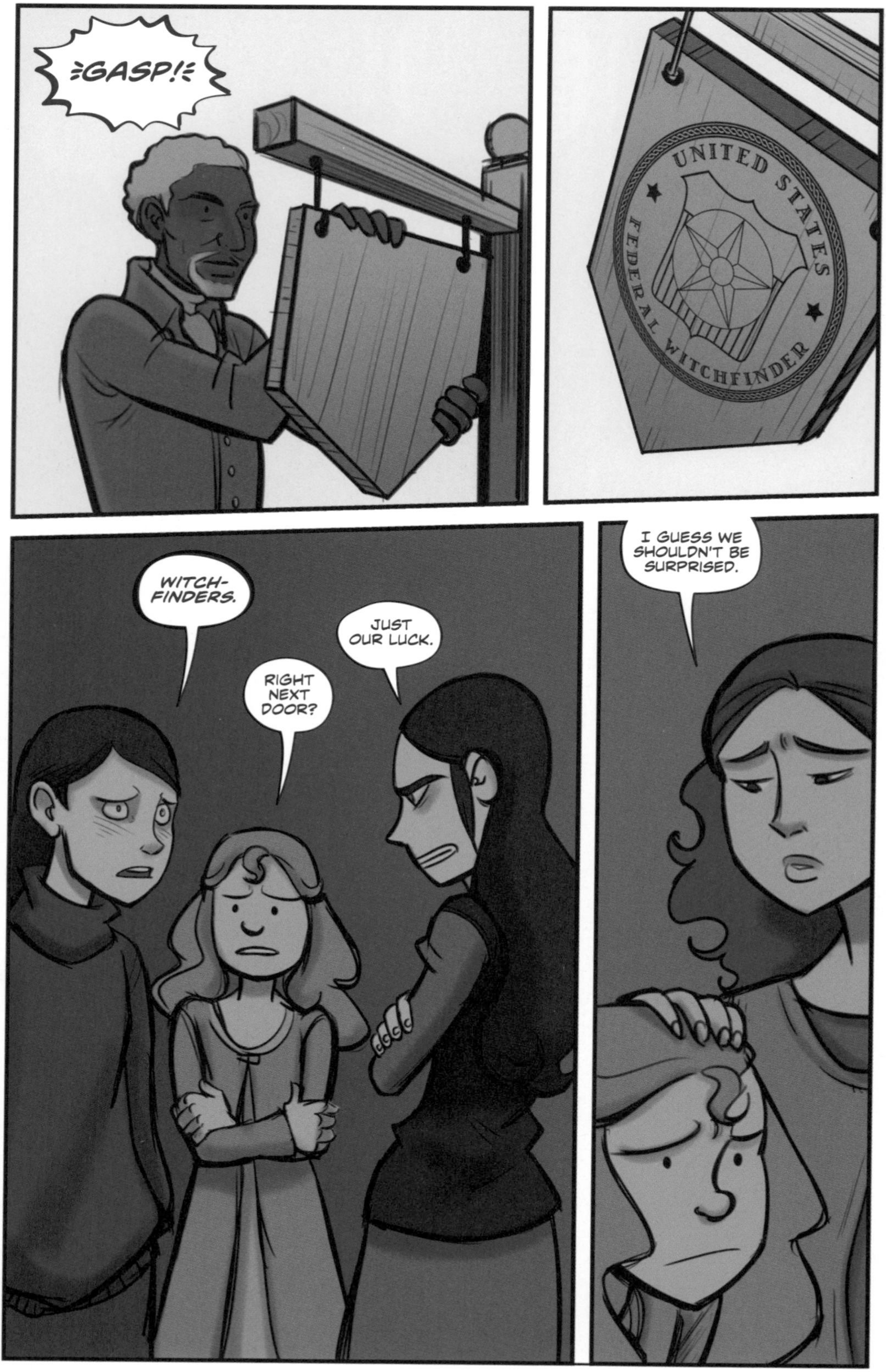
GASP!
UNITED STATES FEDERAL WITCHFINDER
WITCH-FINDERS.
RIGHT NEXT DOOR?
JUST OUR LUCK.
I GUESS WE SHOULDN'T BE SURPRISED.

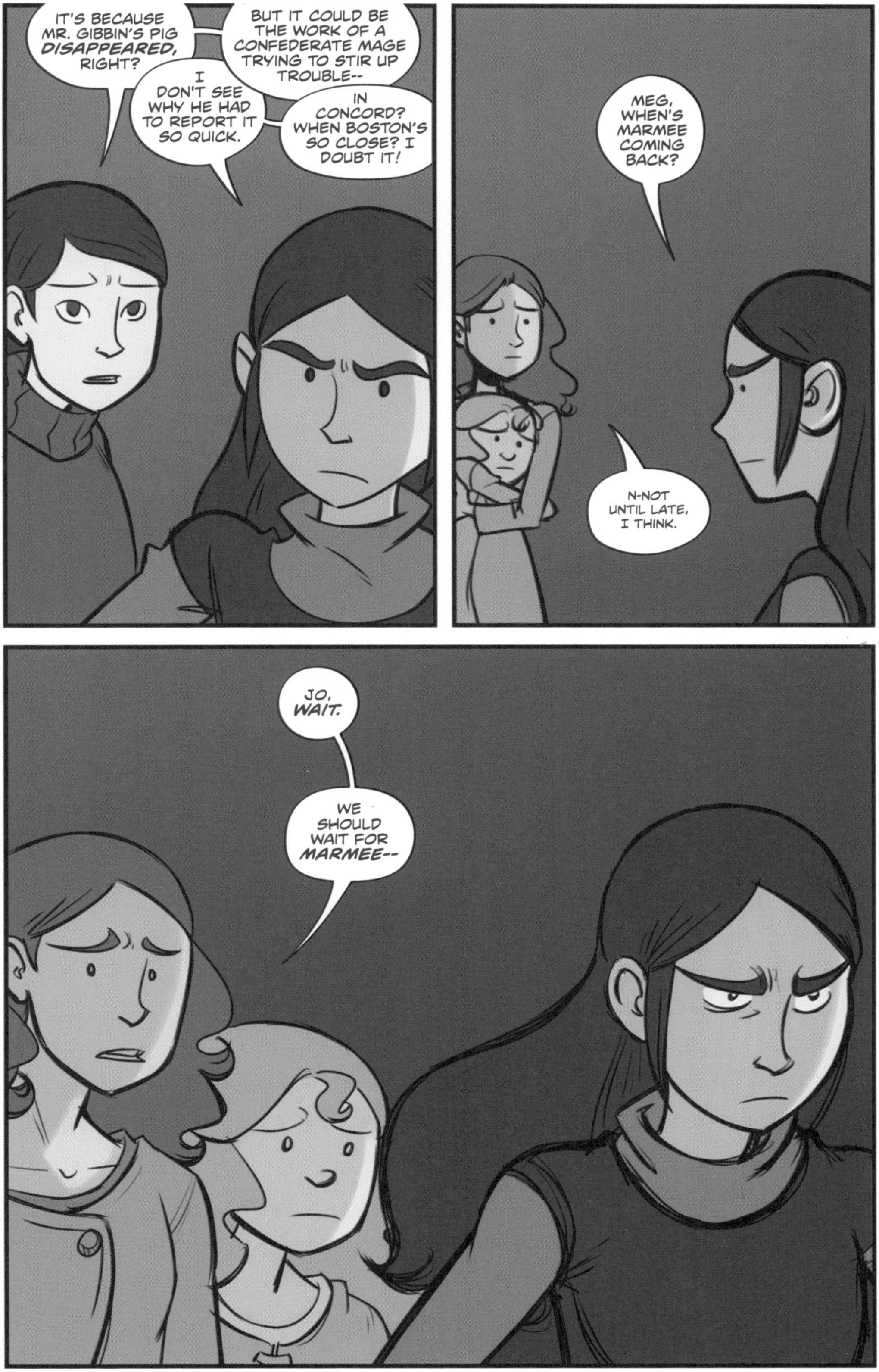
IT'S BECAUSE MR. GIBBIN'S PIG *DISAPPEARED,* RIGHT?
BUT IT COULD BE THE WORK OF A CONFEDERATE MAGE TRYING TO STIR UP TROUBLE--
I DON'T SEE WHY HE HAD TO REPORT IT SO QUICK.
IN CONCORD? WHEN BOSTON'S SO CLOSE? I DOUBT IT!
MEG, WHEN'S MARMEE COMING BACK?
N-NOT UNTIL LATE, I THINK.
JO, *WAIT.*
WE SHOULD WAIT FOR *MARMEE--*

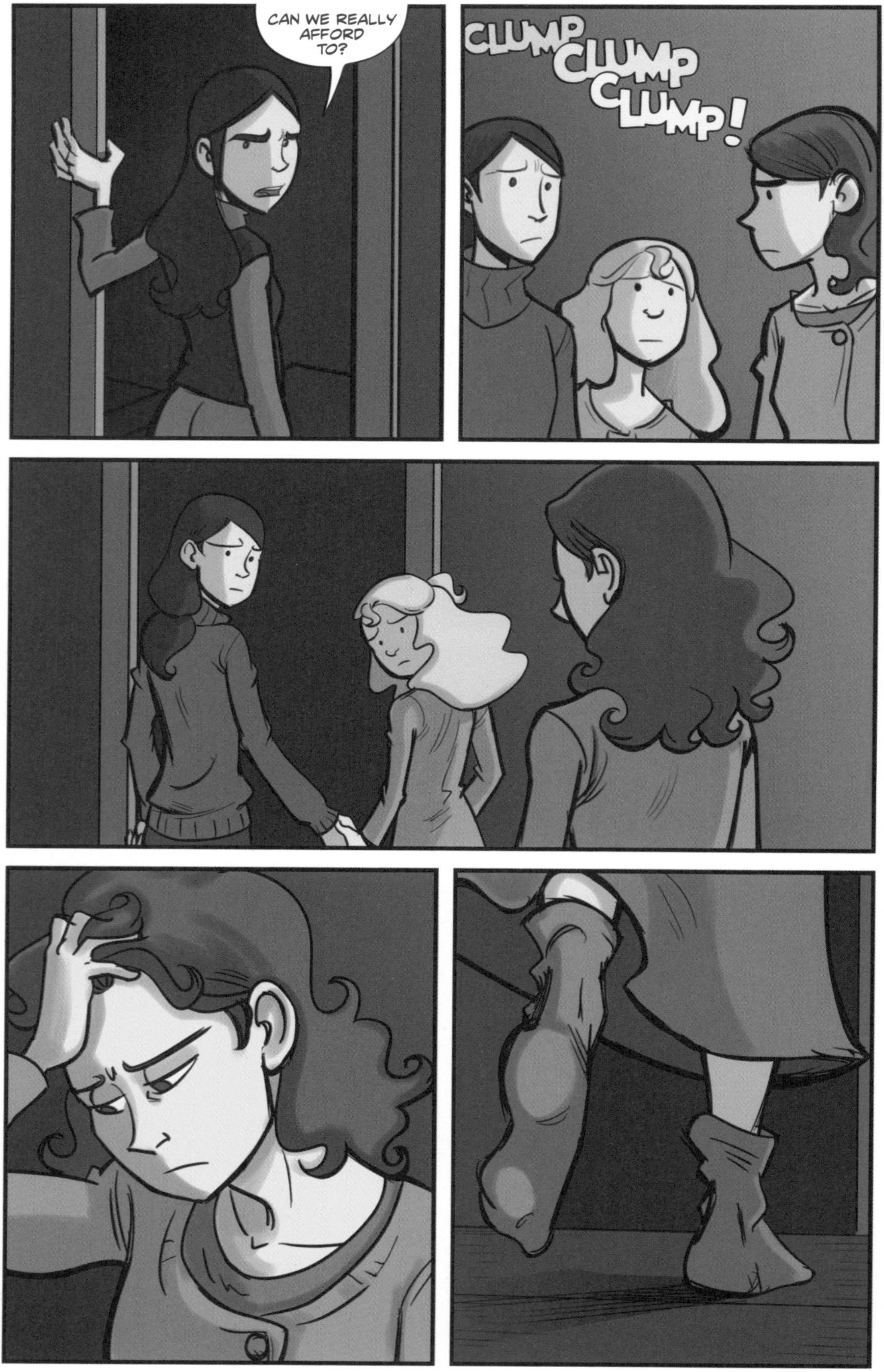
CAN WE REALLY AFFORD TO?
CLUMP CLUMP CLUMP!

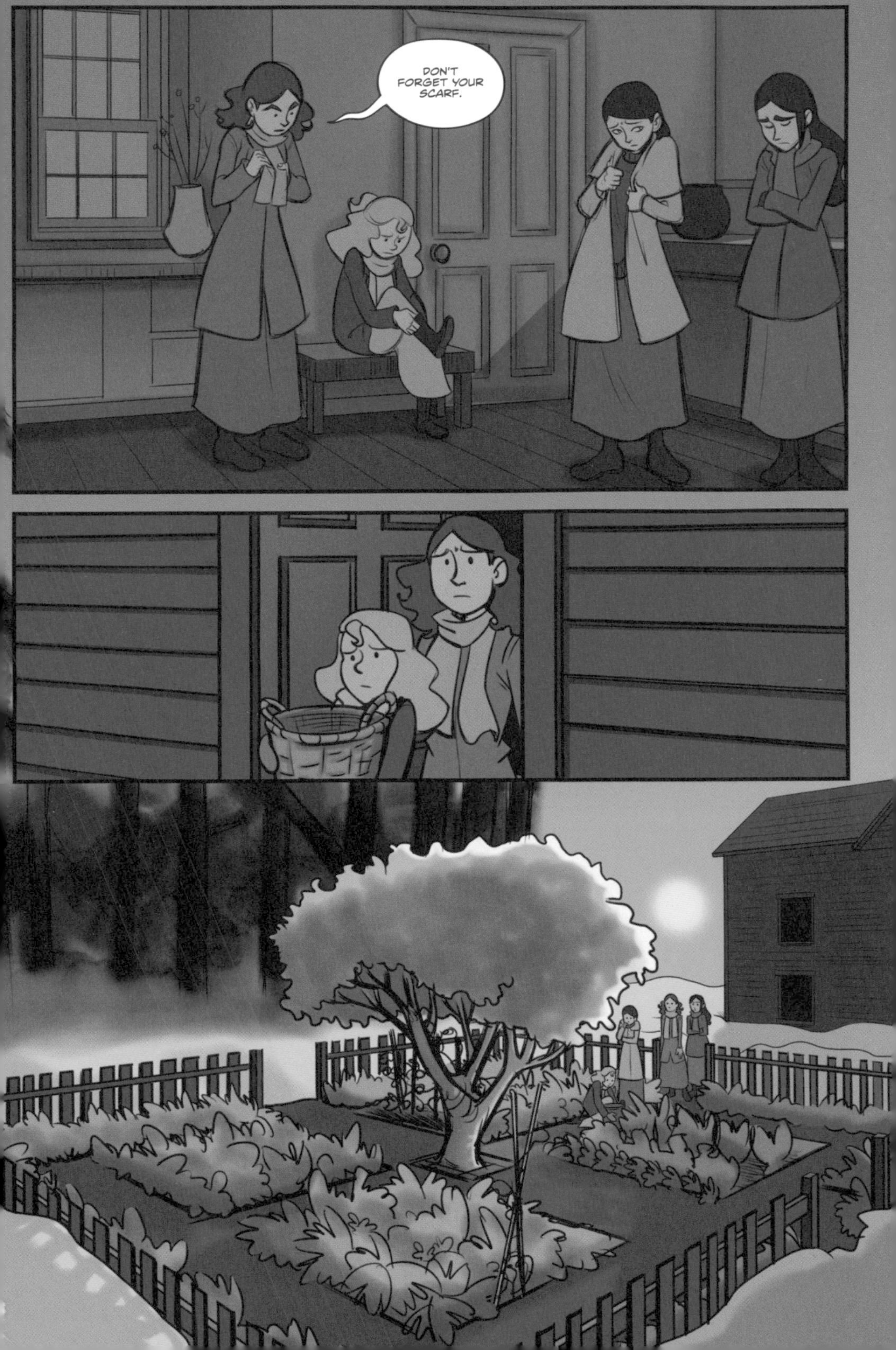
DON'T FORGET YOUR SCARF.

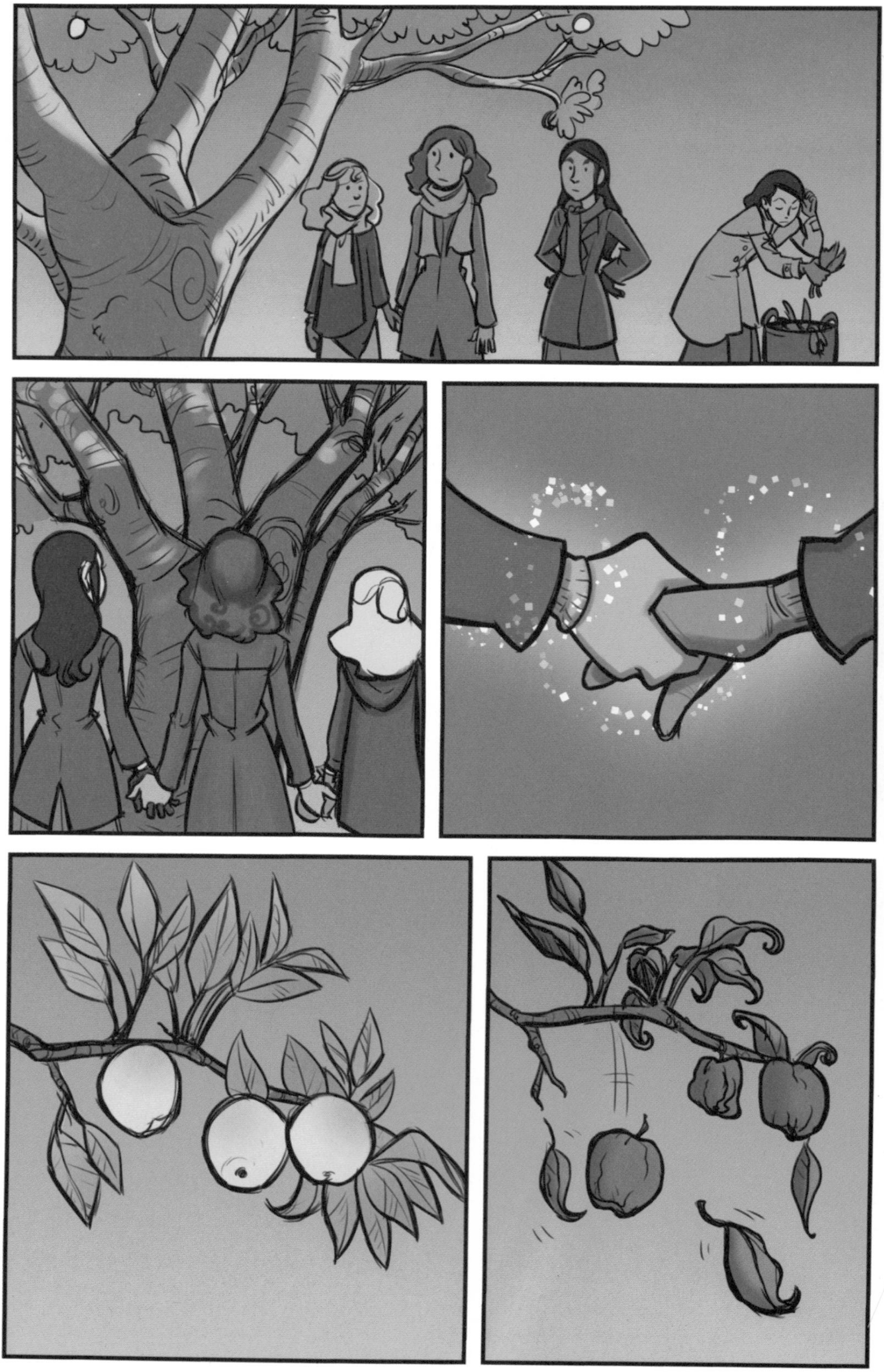

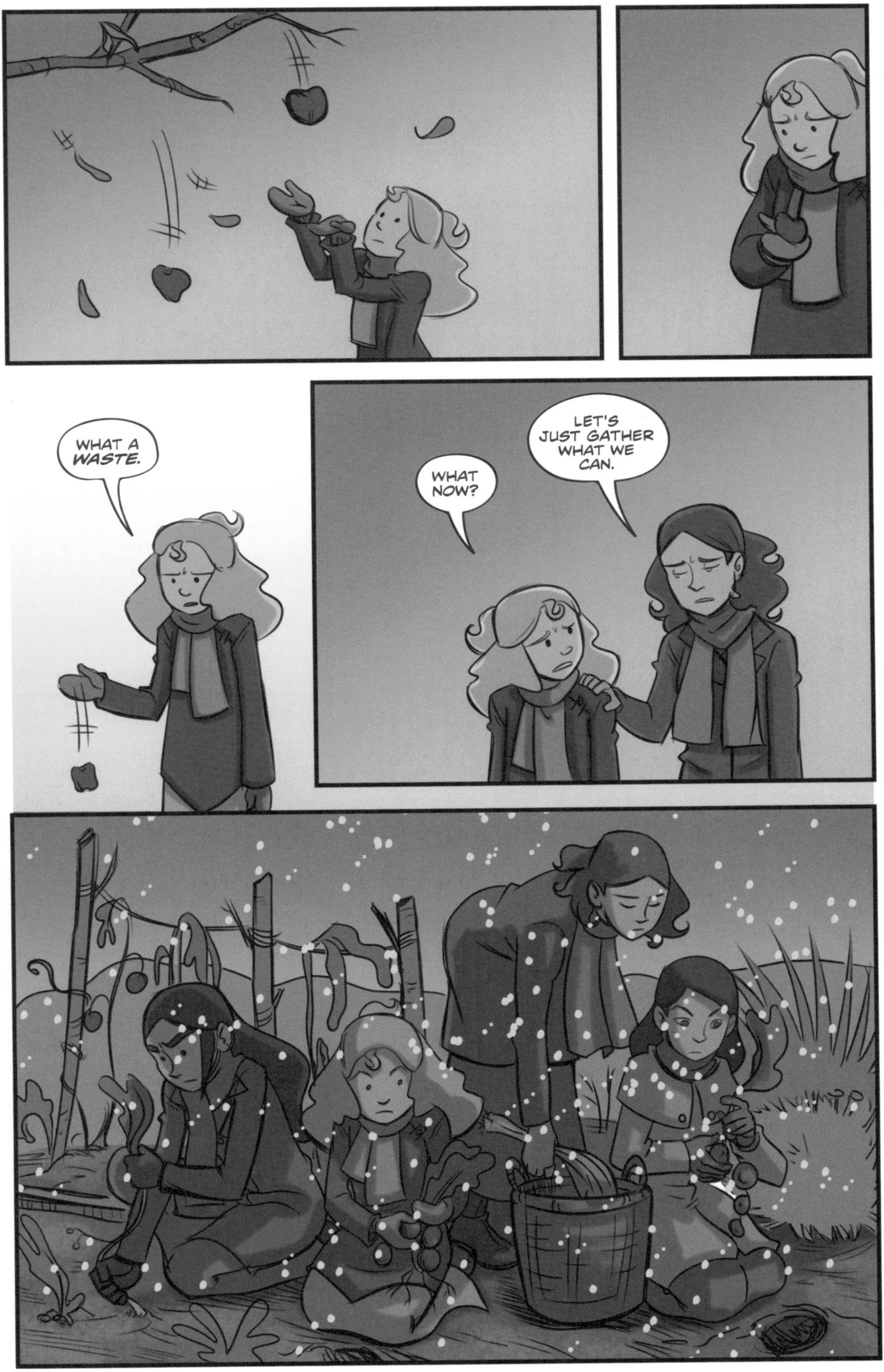
WHAT A *WASTE.*
WHAT NOW?
LET'S JUST GATHER WHAT WE CAN.

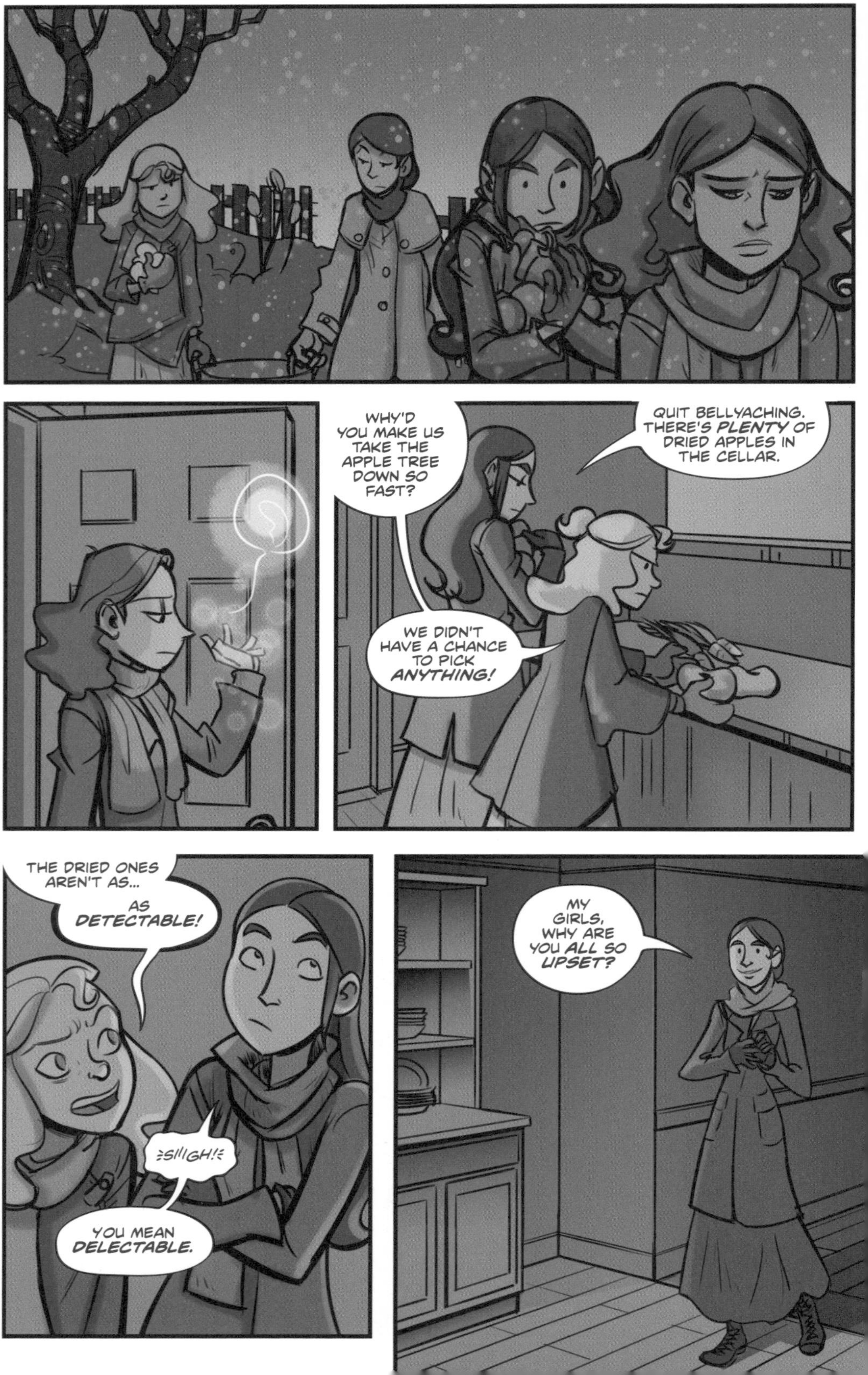
WHY'D YOU MAKE US TAKE THE APPLE TREE DOWN SO FAST?
QUIT BELLYACHING. THERE'S PLENTY OF DRIED APPLES IN THE CELLAR.
WE DIDN'T HAVE A CHANCE TO PICK ANYTHING!
THE DRIED ONES AREN'T AS...
AS DETECTABLE!
SIIIGH!
YOU MEAN DELECTABLE.
MY GIRLS, WHY ARE YOU ALL SO UPSET?

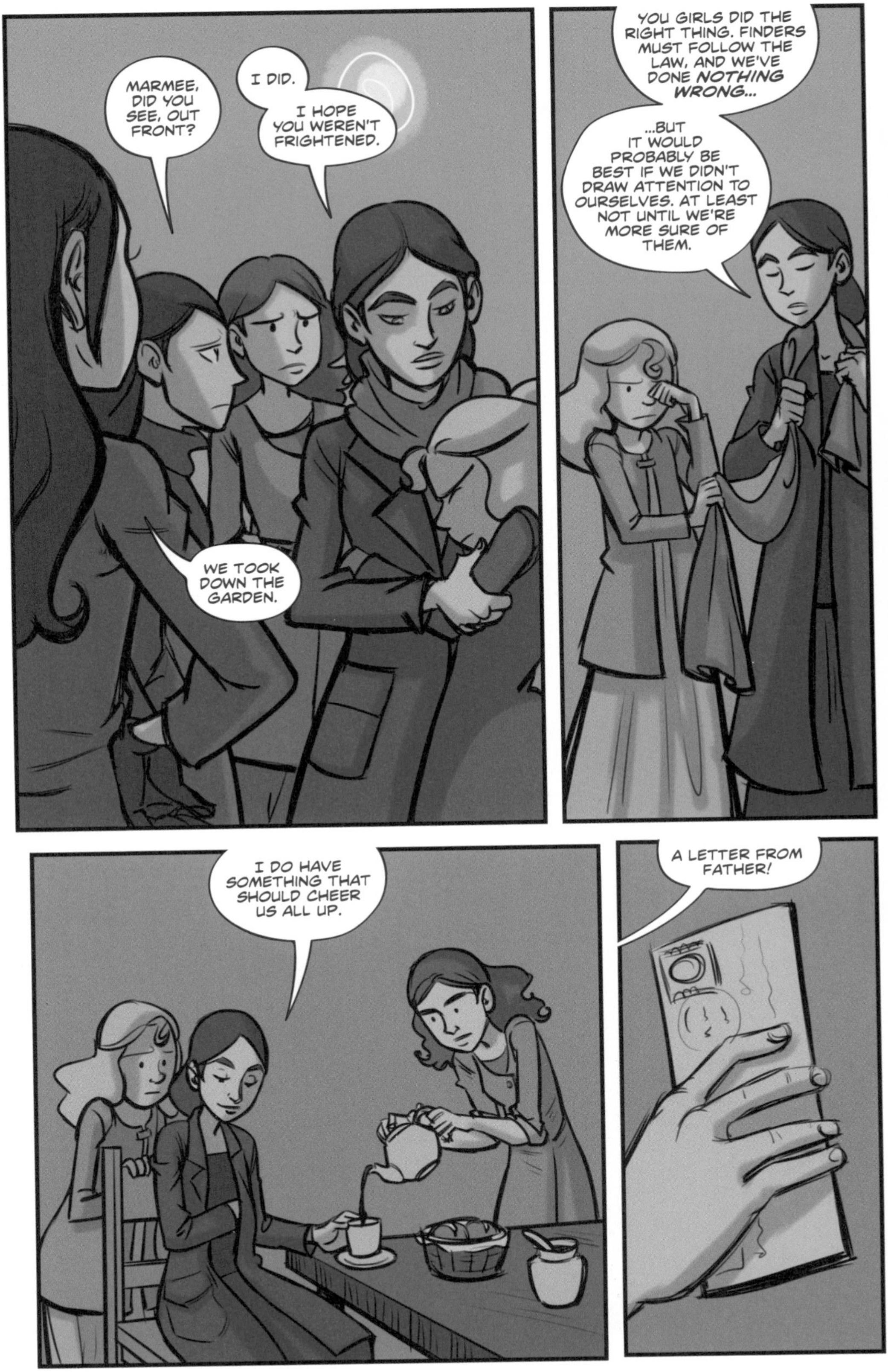
MARMEE, DID YOU SEE, OUT FRONT?
I DID.
I HOPE YOU WEREN'T FRIGHTENED.
WE TOOK DOWN THE GARDEN.
YOU GIRLS DID THE RIGHT THING. FINDERS MUST FOLLOW THE LAW, AND WE'VE DONE *NOTHING WRONG...*
...BUT IT WOULD PROBABLY BE BEST IF WE DIDN'T DRAW ATTENTION TO OURSELVES. AT LEAST NOT UNTIL WE'RE MORE SURE OF THEM.
I DO HAVE SOMETHING THAT SHOULD CHEER US ALL UP.
A LETTER FROM FATHER!

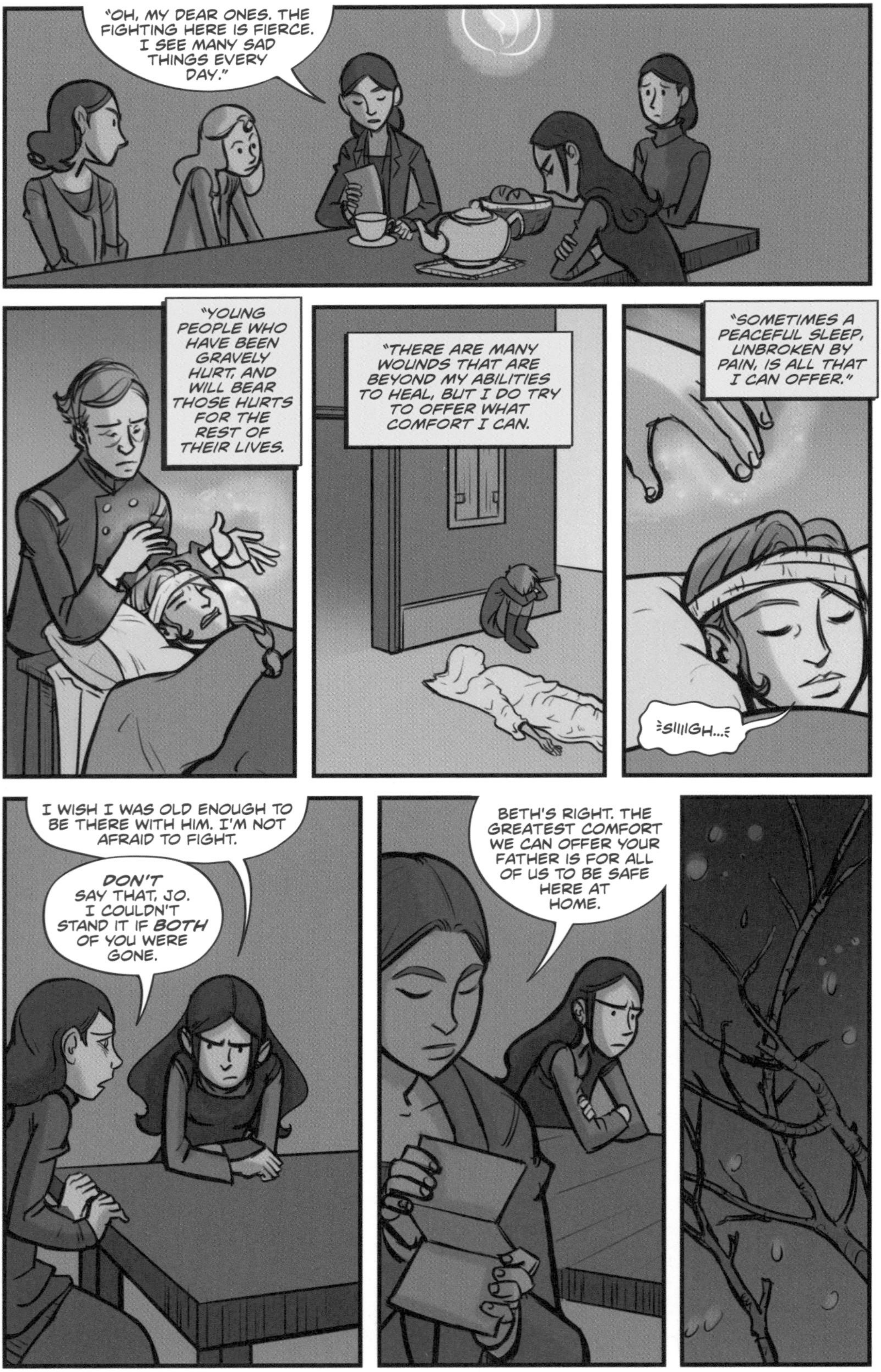
"OH, MY DEAR ONES. THE FIGHTING HERE IS FIERCE. I SEE MANY SAD THINGS EVERY DAY."
"YOUNG PEOPLE WHO HAVE BEEN GRAVELY HURT, AND WILL BEAR THOSE HURTS FOR THE REST OF THEIR LIVES.
"THERE ARE MANY WOUNDS THAT ARE BEYOND MY ABILITIES TO HEAL, BUT I DO TRY TO OFFER WHAT COMFORT I CAN.
"SOMETIMES A PEACEFUL SLEEP, UNBROKEN BY PAIN, IS ALL THAT I CAN OFFER."
SIIIIGH...
I WISH I WAS OLD ENOUGH TO BE THERE WITH HIM. I'M NOT AFRAID TO FIGHT.
DON'T SAY THAT, JO. I COULDN'T STAND IT IF *BOTH* OF YOU WERE GONE.
BETH'S RIGHT. THE GREATEST COMFORT WE CAN OFFER YOUR FATHER IS FOR ALL OF US TO BE SAFE HERE AT HOME.

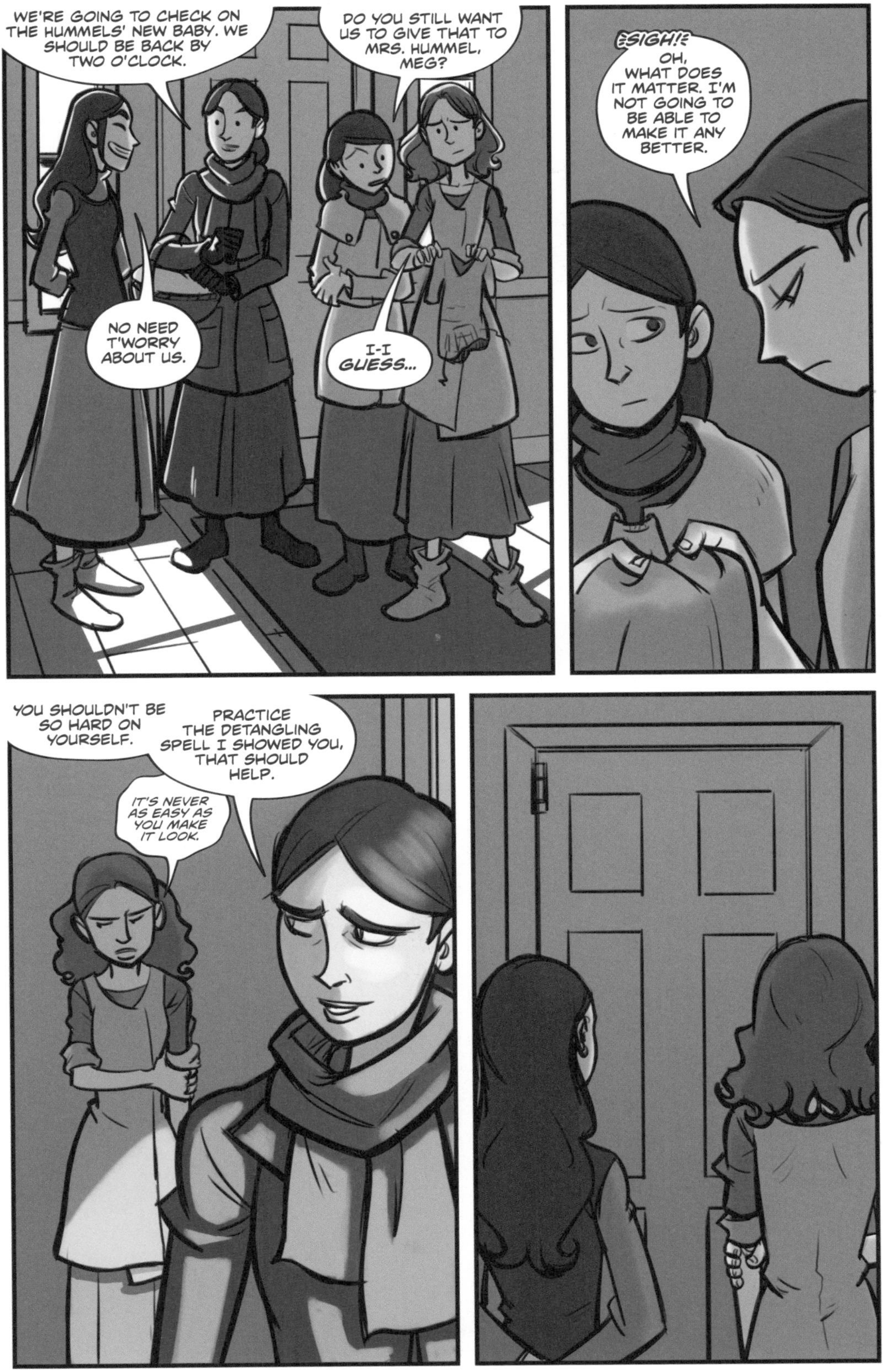
WE'RE GOING TO CHECK ON THE HUMMELS' NEW BABY. WE SHOULD BE BACK BY TWO O'CLOCK.
NO NEED T'WORRY ABOUT US.
DO YOU STILL WANT US TO GIVE THAT TO MRS. HUMMEL, MEG?
I-I GUESS...
SIGH!
OH, WHAT DOES IT MATTER. I'M NOT GOING TO BE ABLE TO MAKE IT ANY BETTER.
YOU SHOULDN'T BE SO HARD ON YOURSELF.
PRACTICE THE DETANGLING SPELL I SHOWED YOU, THAT SHOULD HELP.
IT'S NEVER AS EASY AS YOU MAKE IT LOOK.

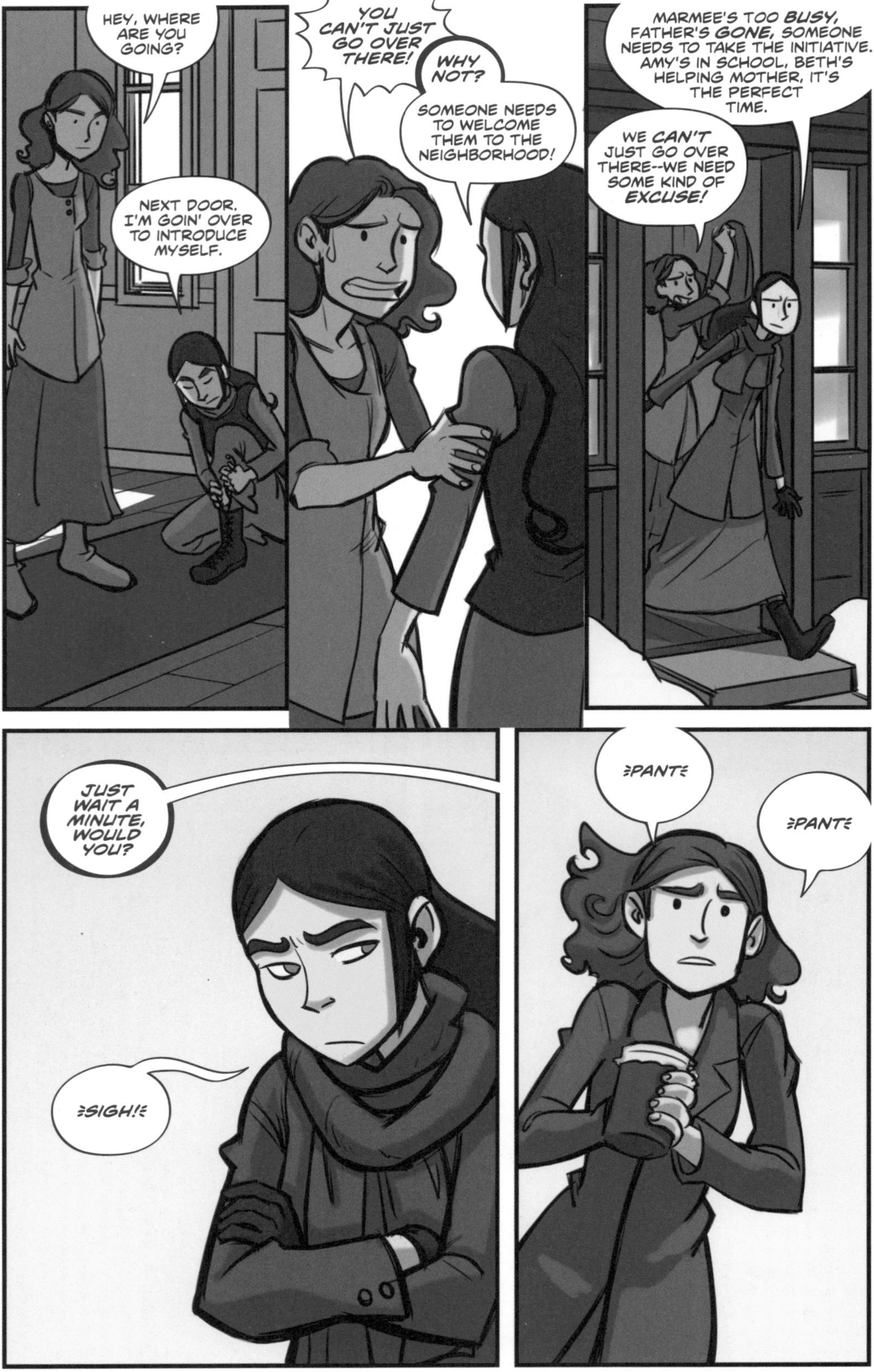
HEY, WHERE ARE YOU GOING?
NEXT DOOR. I'M GOIN' OVER TO INTRODUCE MYSELF.
YOU CAN'T JUST GO OVER THERE!
WHY NOT?
SOMEONE NEEDS TO WELCOME THEM TO THE NEIGHBORHOOD!
MARMEE'S TOO BUSY, FATHER'S GONE, SOMEONE NEEDS TO TAKE THE INITIATIVE. AMY'S IN SCHOOL, BETH'S HELPING MOTHER, IT'S THE PERFECT TIME.
WE CAN'T JUST GO OVER THERE--WE NEED SOME KIND OF EXCUSE!
JUST WAIT A MINUTE, WOULD YOU?
SIGH!
PANT
PANT

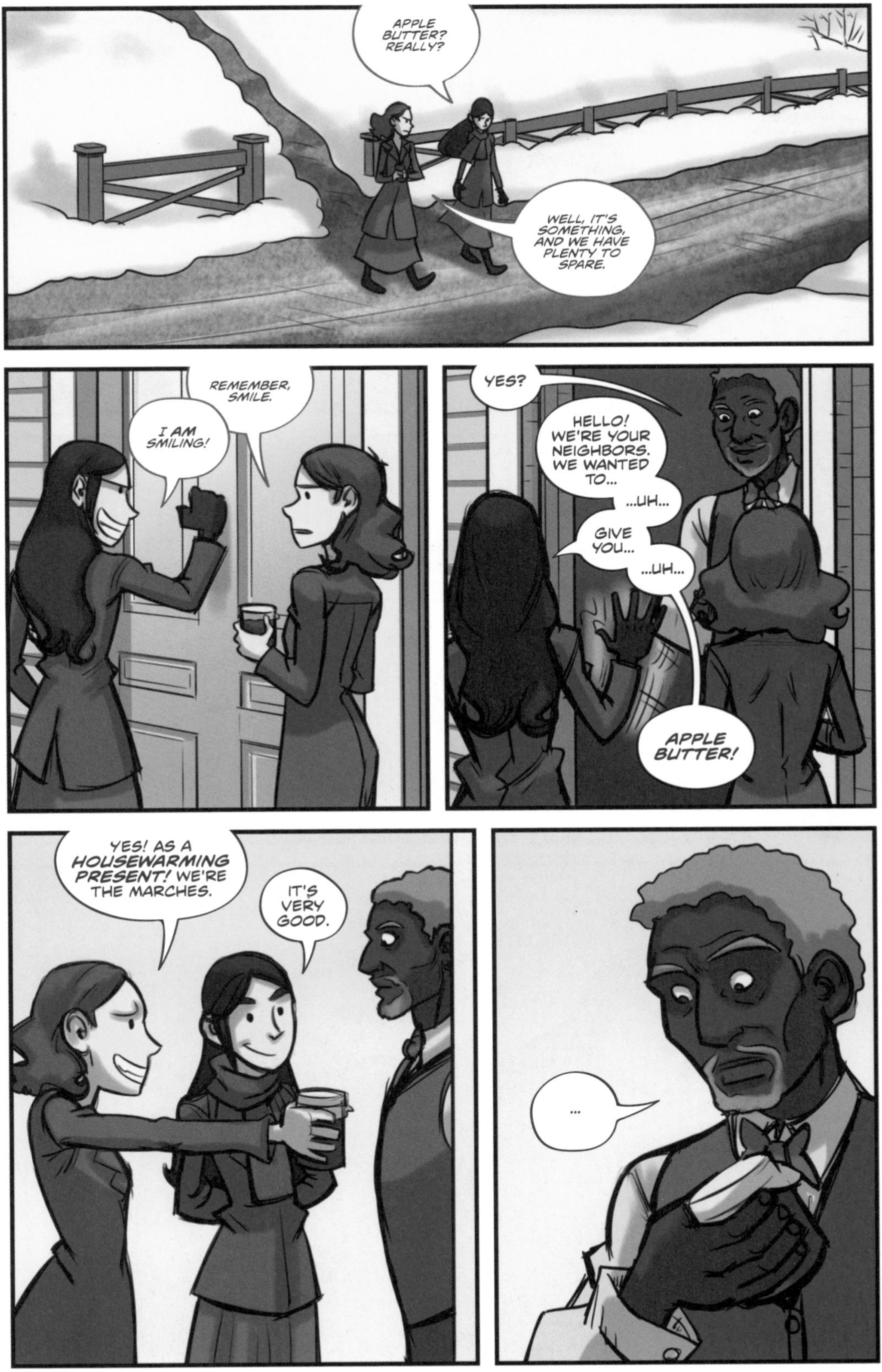
APPLE BUTTER? REALLY?
WELL, IT'S SOMETHING, AND WE HAVE PLENTY TO SPARE.
REMEMBER, SMILE.
I AM SMILING!
YES?
HELLO! WE'RE YOUR NEIGHBORS. WE WANTED TO...
...UH...
GIVE YOU...
...UH...
APPLE BUTTER!
YES! AS A HOUSEWARMING PRESENT! WE'RE THE MARCHES.
IT'S VERY GOOD.
...

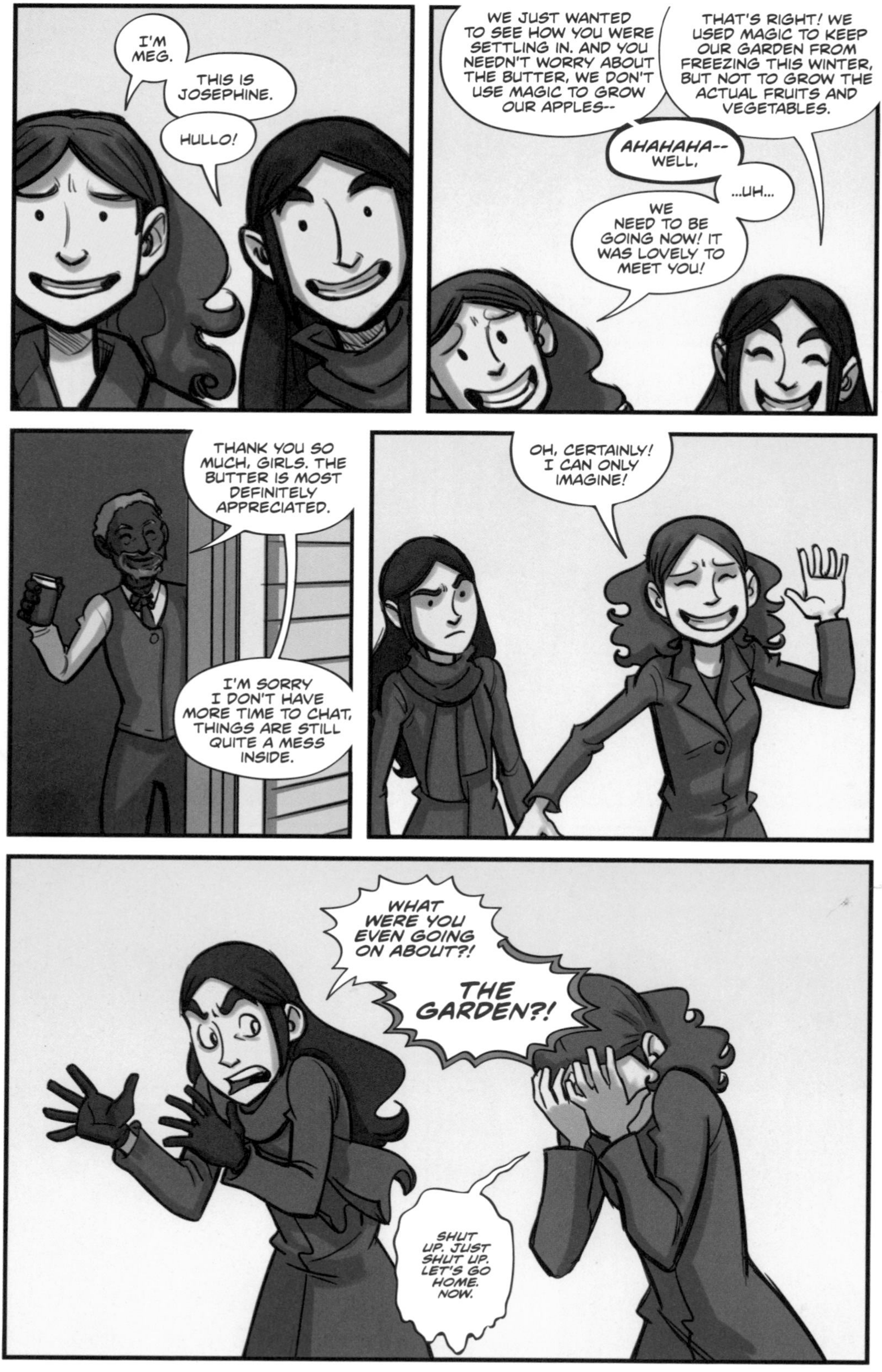
I'M MEG.
THIS IS JOSEPHINE.
HULLO!
WE JUST WANTED TO SEE HOW YOU WERE SETTLING IN. AND YOU NEEDN'T WORRY ABOUT THE BUTTER, WE DON'T USE MAGIC TO GROW OUR APPLES--
THAT'S RIGHT! WE USED MAGIC TO KEEP OUR GARDEN FROM FREEZING THIS WINTER, BUT NOT TO GROW THE ACTUAL FRUITS AND VEGETABLES.
AHAHAHA-- WELL,
...UH...
WE NEED TO BE GOING NOW! IT WAS LOVELY TO MEET YOU!
THANK YOU SO MUCH, GIRLS. THE BUTTER IS MOST DEFINITELY APPRECIATED.
I'M SORRY I DON'T HAVE MORE TIME TO CHAT, THINGS ARE STILL QUITE A MESS INSIDE.
OH, CERTAINLY! I CAN ONLY IMAGINE!
WHAT WERE YOU EVEN GOING ON ABOUT?!
THE GARDEN?!
SHUT UP. JUST SHUT UP. LET'S GO HOME. NOW.

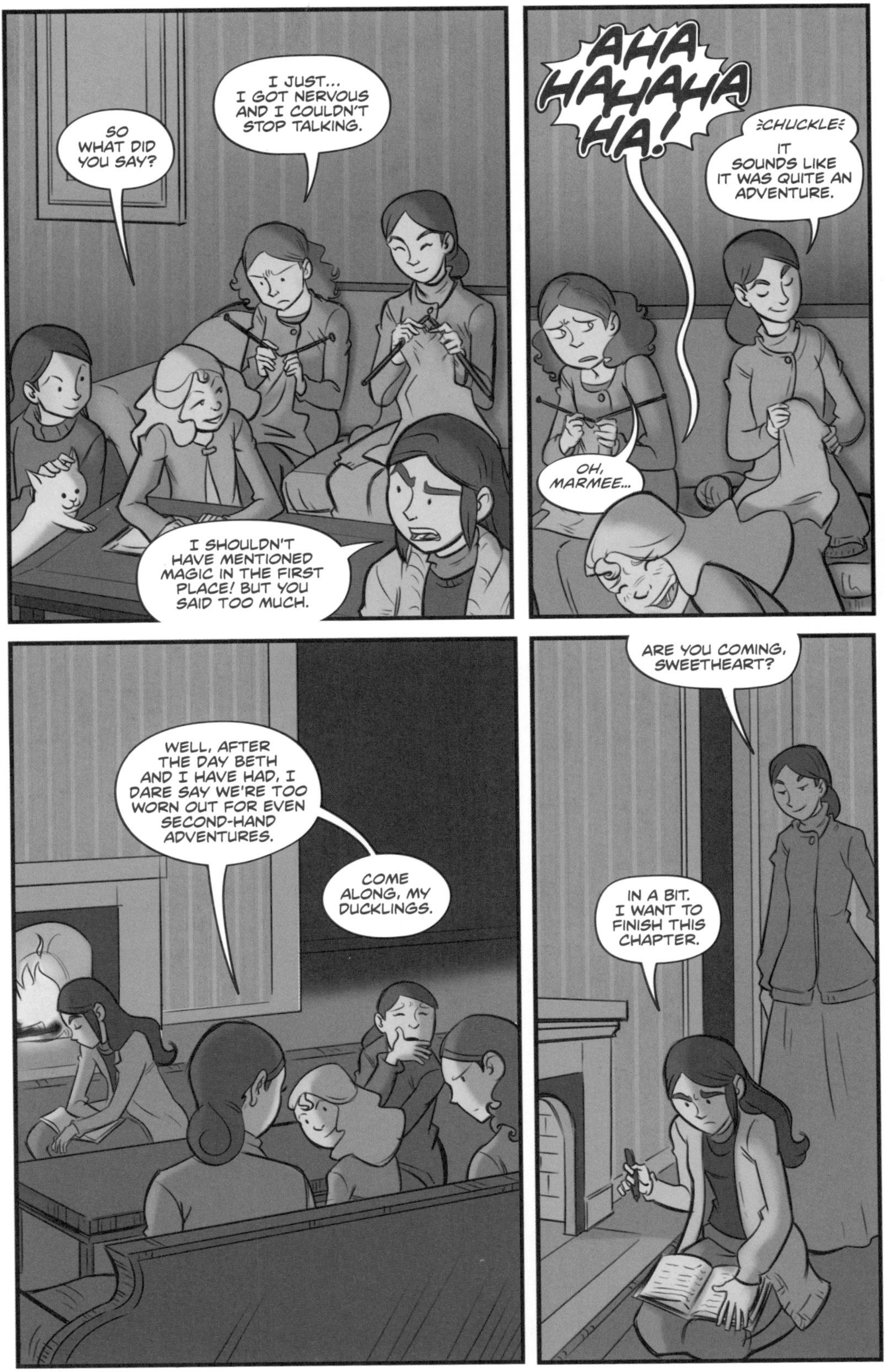

SO WHAT DID YOU SAY?
I JUST... I GOT NERVOUS AND I COULDN'T STOP TALKING.
I SHOULDN'T HAVE MENTIONED MAGIC IN THE FIRST PLACE! BUT YOU SAID TOO MUCH.
AHA HAHAHA HA!
CHUCKLE
IT SOUNDS LIKE IT WAS QUITE AN ADVENTURE.
OH, MARMEE...
WELL, AFTER THE DAY BETH AND I HAVE HAD, I DARE SAY WE'RE TOO WORN OUT FOR EVEN SECOND-HAND ADVENTURES.
COME ALONG, MY DUCKLINGS.
ARE YOU COMING, SWEETHEART?
IN A BIT. I WANT TO FINISH THIS CHAPTER.

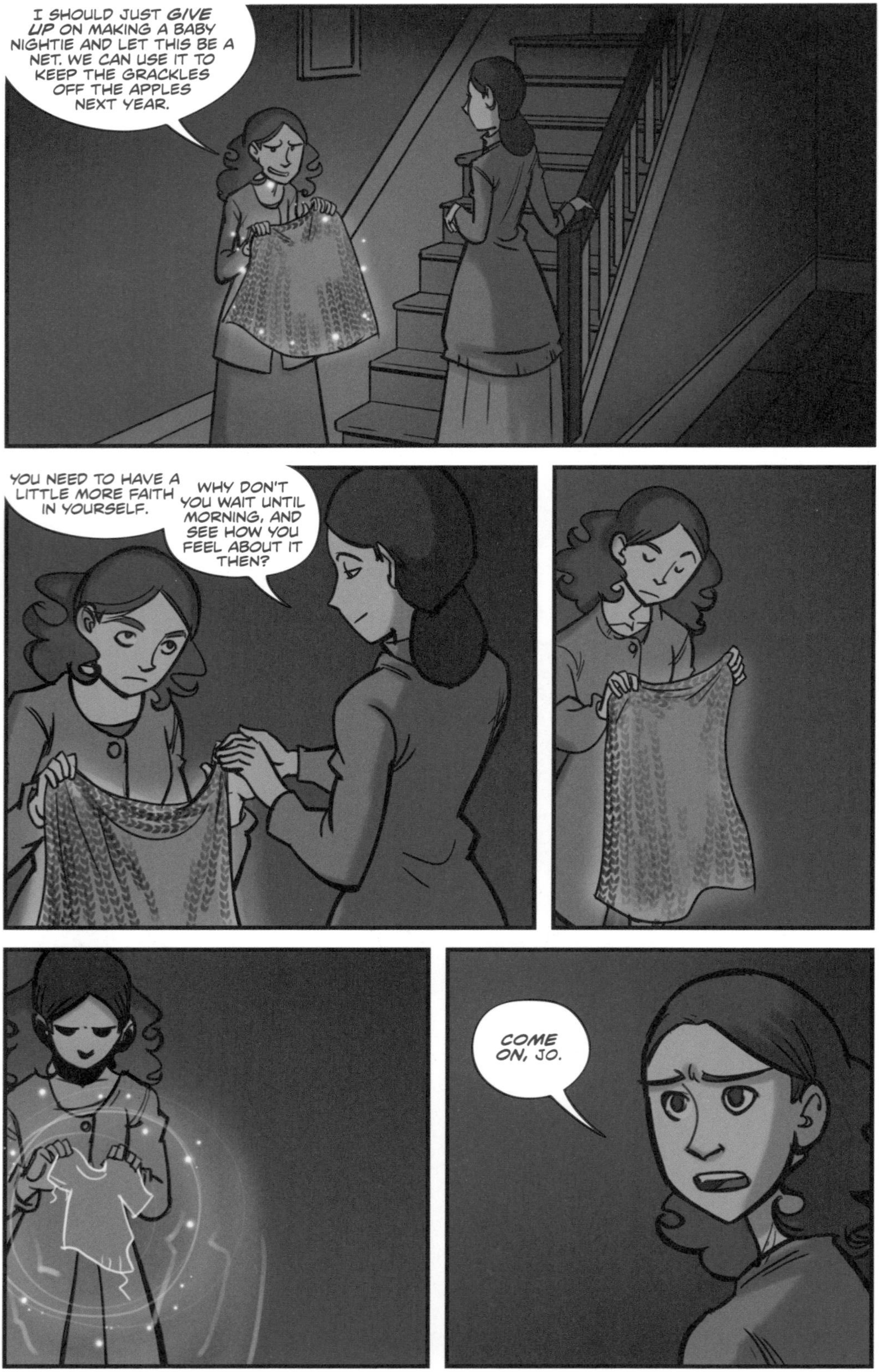
I SHOULD JUST *GIVE UP* ON MAKING A BABY NIGHTIE AND LET THIS BE A NET. WE CAN USE IT TO KEEP THE GRACKLES OFF THE APPLES NEXT YEAR.
YOU NEED TO HAVE A LITTLE MORE FAITH IN YOURSELF.
WHY DON'T YOU WAIT UNTIL MORNING, AND SEE HOW YOU FEEL ABOUT IT THEN?
COME ON, JO.

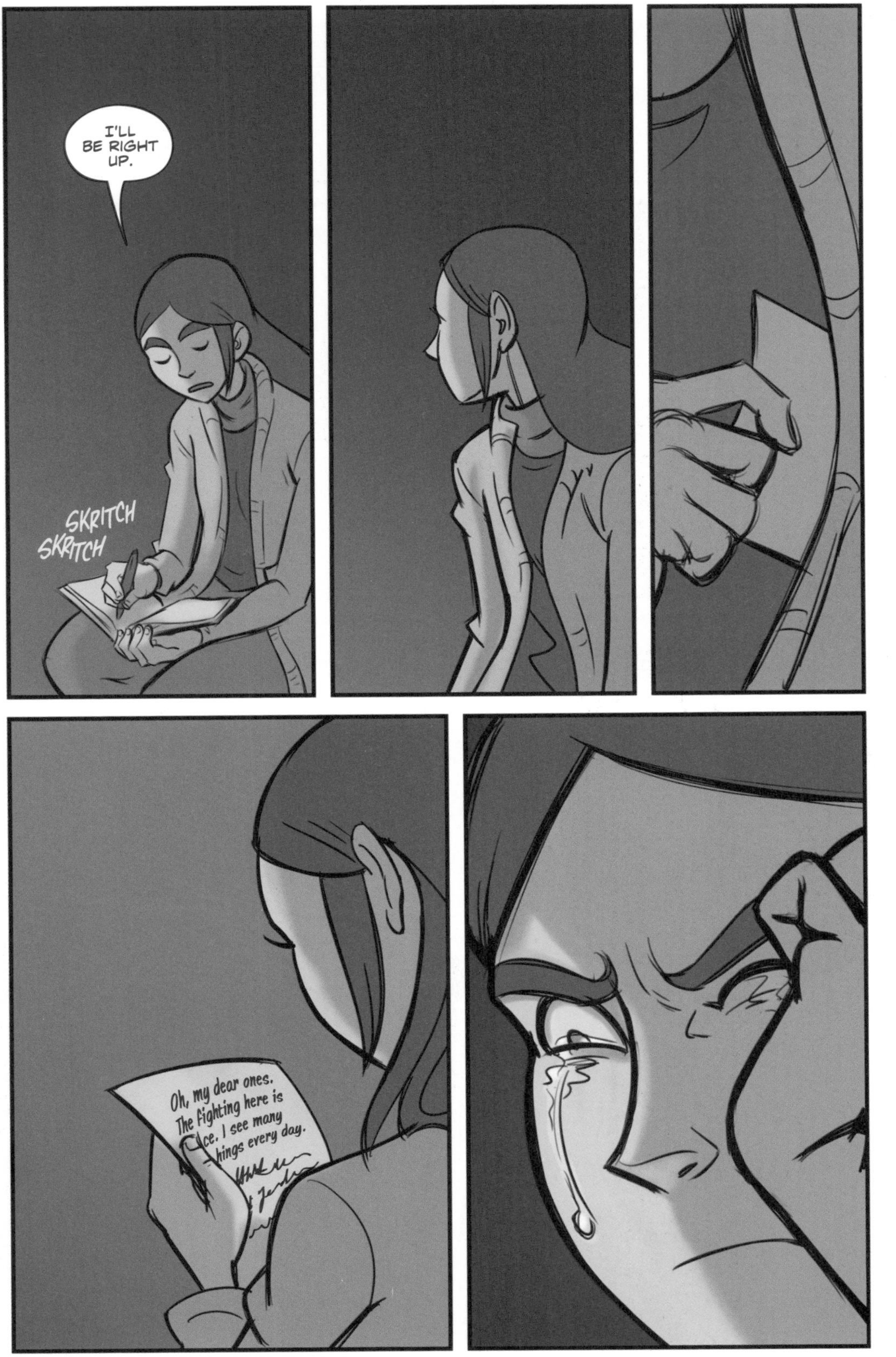
I'LL BE RIGHT UP.
SKRITCH
SKRITCH
Oh, my dear ones.
The fighting here is
ce. I see many
hings every day.

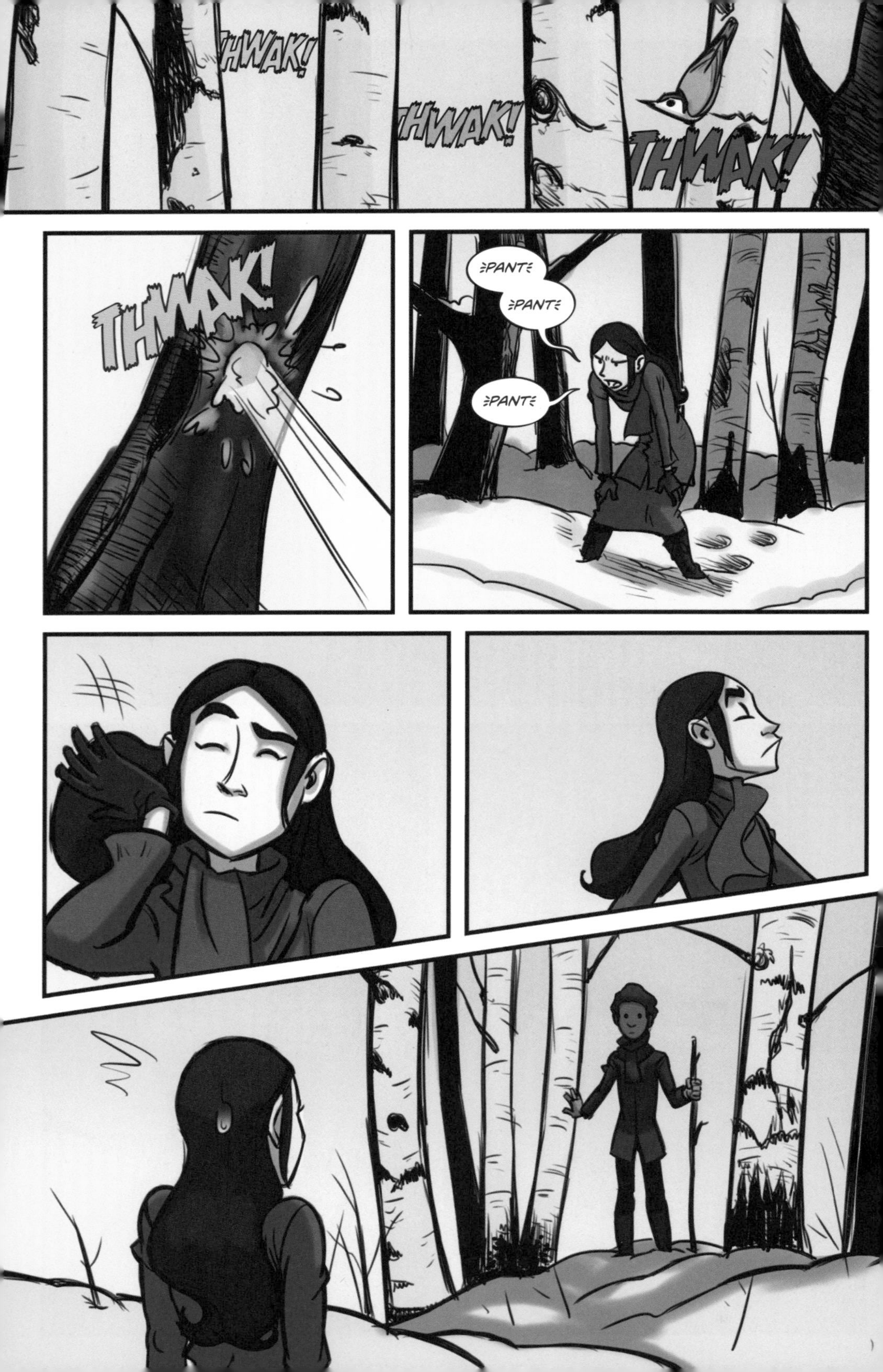

THWAK!
THWAK!
THWAK!
THWAK!
PANT
PANT
PANT

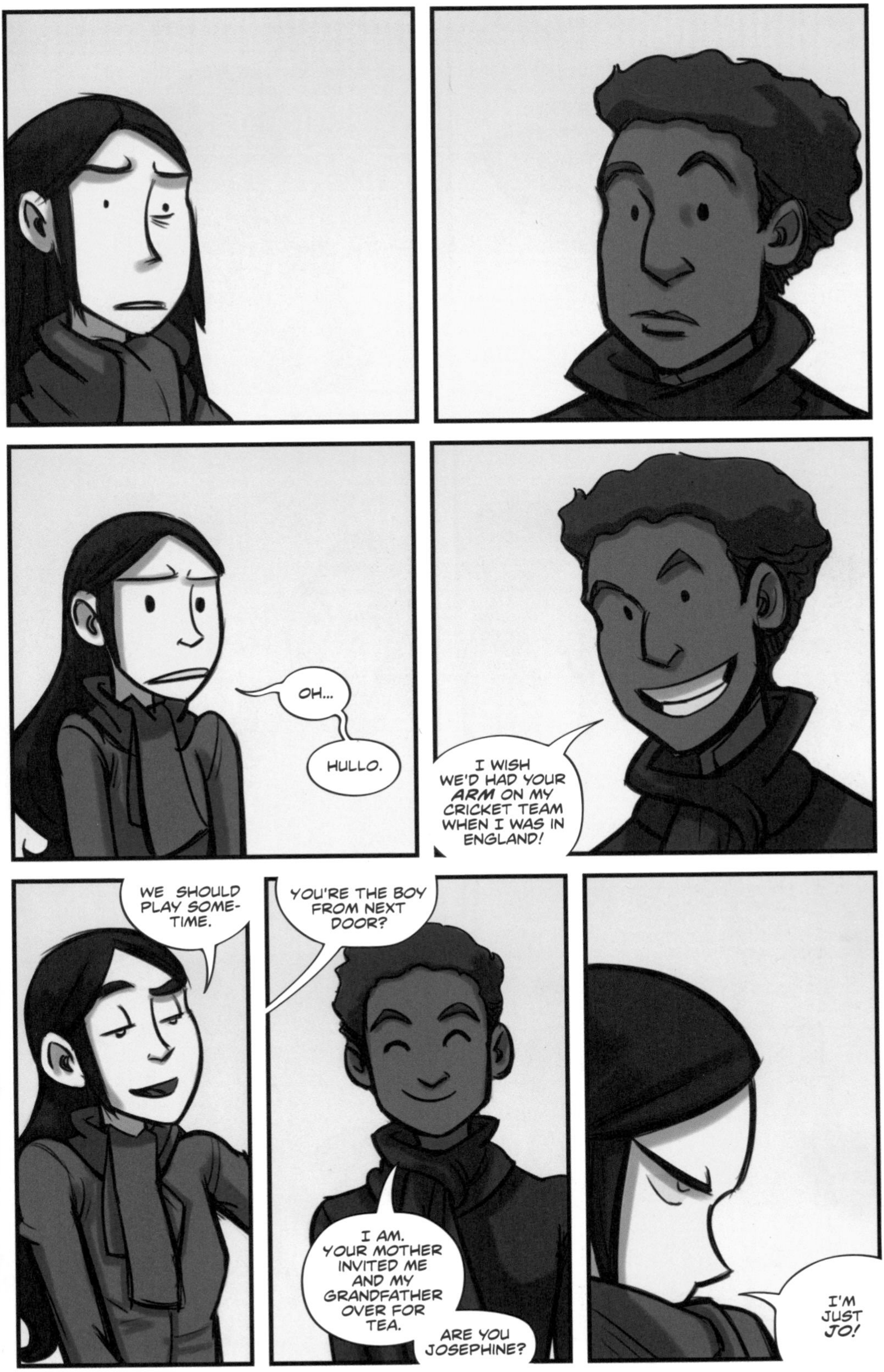
OH...
HULLO.
I WISH WE'D HAD YOUR ARM ON MY CRICKET TEAM WHEN I WAS IN ENGLAND!
WE SHOULD PLAY SOME-TIME.
YOU'RE THE BOY FROM NEXT DOOR?
I AM. YOUR MOTHER INVITED ME AND MY GRANDFATHER OVER FOR TEA.
ARE YOU JOSEPHINE?
I'M JUST JO!

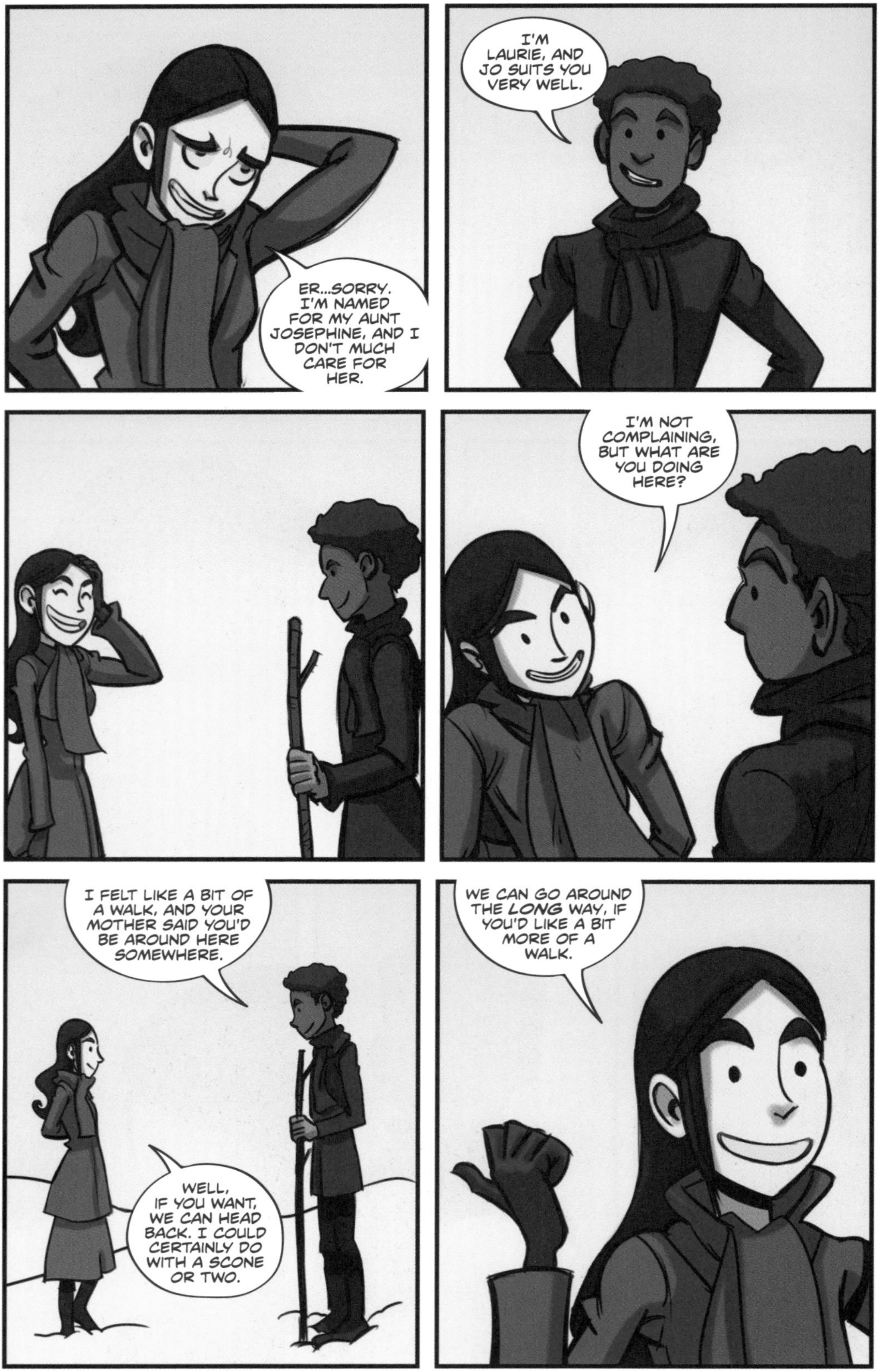
ER...SORRY. I'M NAMED FOR MY AUNT JOSEPHINE, AND I DON'T MUCH CARE FOR HER.
I'M LAURIE, AND JO SUITS YOU VERY WELL.
I'M NOT COMPLAINING, BUT WHAT ARE YOU DOING HERE?
I FELT LIKE A BIT OF A WALK, AND YOUR MOTHER SAID YOU'D BE AROUND HERE SOMEWHERE.
WELL, IF YOU WANT, WE CAN HEAD BACK. I COULD CERTAINLY DO WITH A SCONE OR TWO.
WE CAN GO AROUND THE *LONG* WAY, IF YOU'D LIKE A BIT MORE OF A WALK.

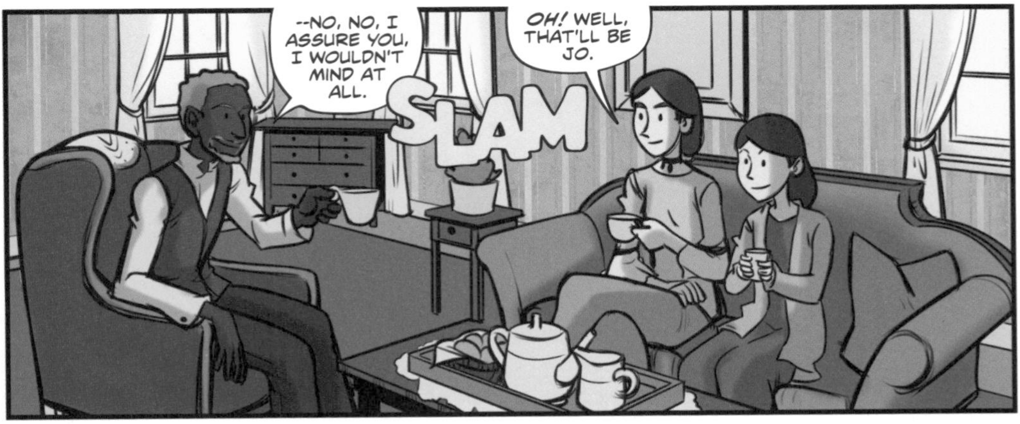
--NO, NO, I ASSURE YOU, I WOULDN'T MIND AT ALL.
SLAM
OH! WELL, THAT'LL BE JO.

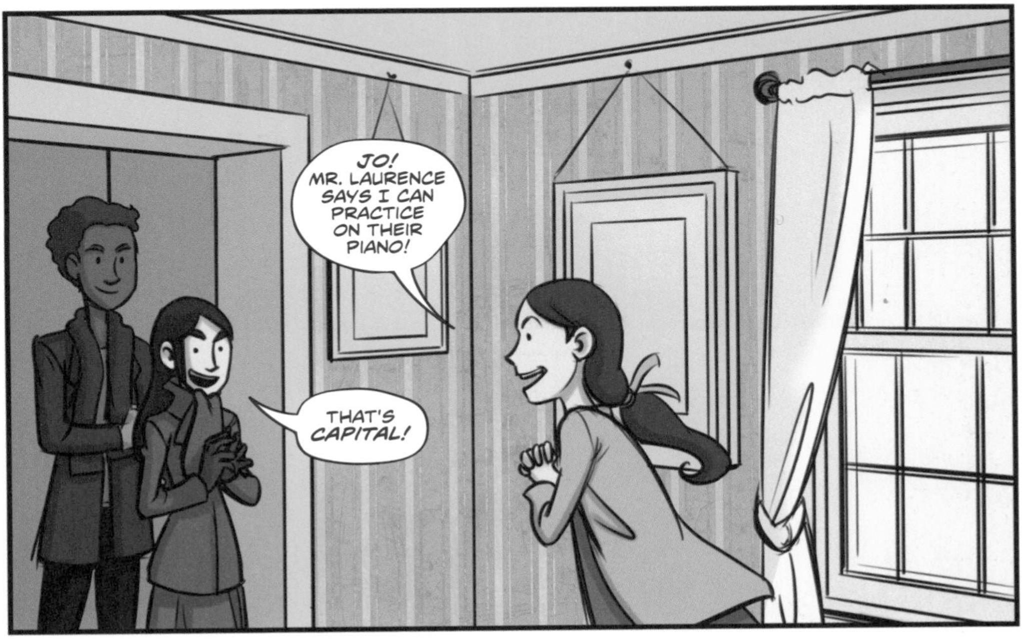
JO! MR. LAURENCE SAYS I CAN PRACTICE ON THEIR PIANO!
THAT'S *CAPITAL!*

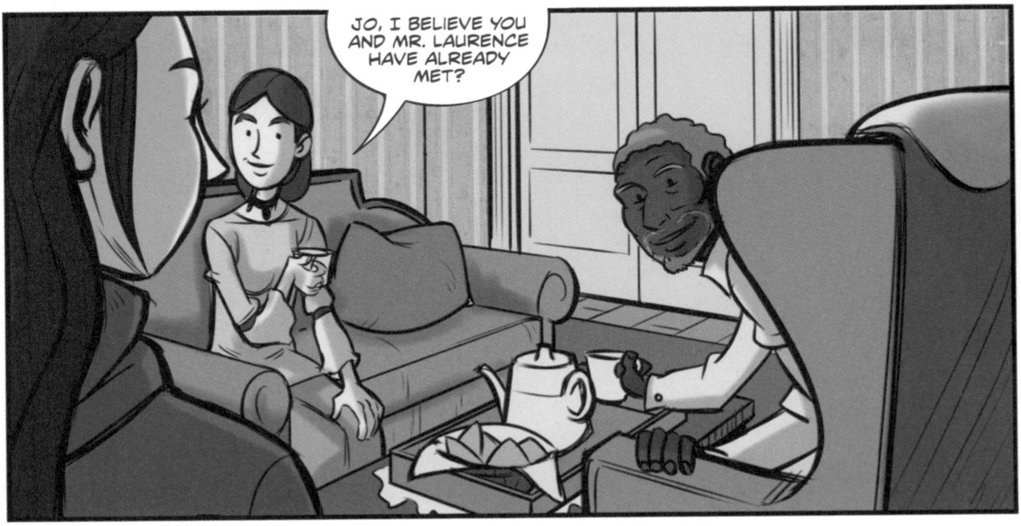
JO, I BELIEVE YOU AND MR. LAURENCE HAVE ALREADY MET?

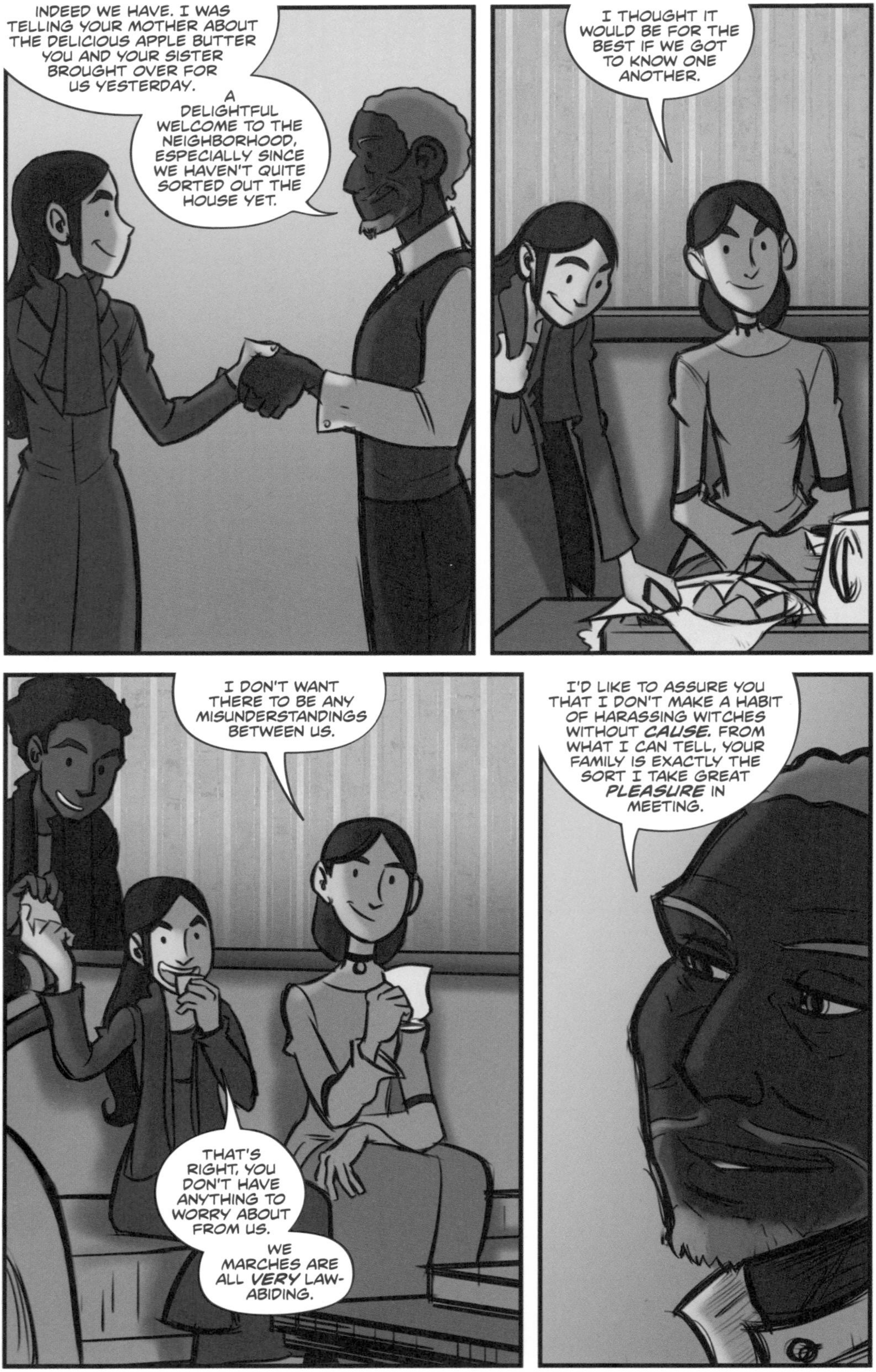

INDEED WE HAVE. I WAS TELLING YOUR MOTHER ABOUT THE DELICIOUS APPLE BUTTER YOU AND YOUR SISTER BROUGHT OVER FOR US YESTERDAY.
A DELIGHTFUL WELCOME TO THE NEIGHBORHOOD, ESPECIALLY SINCE WE HAVEN'T QUITE SORTED OUT THE HOUSE YET.
I THOUGHT IT WOULD BE FOR THE BEST IF WE GOT TO KNOW ONE ANOTHER.
I DON'T WANT THERE TO BE ANY MISUNDERSTANDINGS BETWEEN US.
THAT'S RIGHT, YOU DON'T HAVE ANYTHING TO WORRY ABOUT FROM US.
WE MARCHES ARE ALL *VERY* LAW-ABIDING.
I'D LIKE TO ASSURE YOU THAT I DON'T MAKE A HABIT OF HARASSING WITCHES WITHOUT *CAUSE.* FROM WHAT I CAN TELL, YOUR FAMILY IS EXACTLY THE SORT I TAKE GREAT *PLEASURE* IN MEETING.

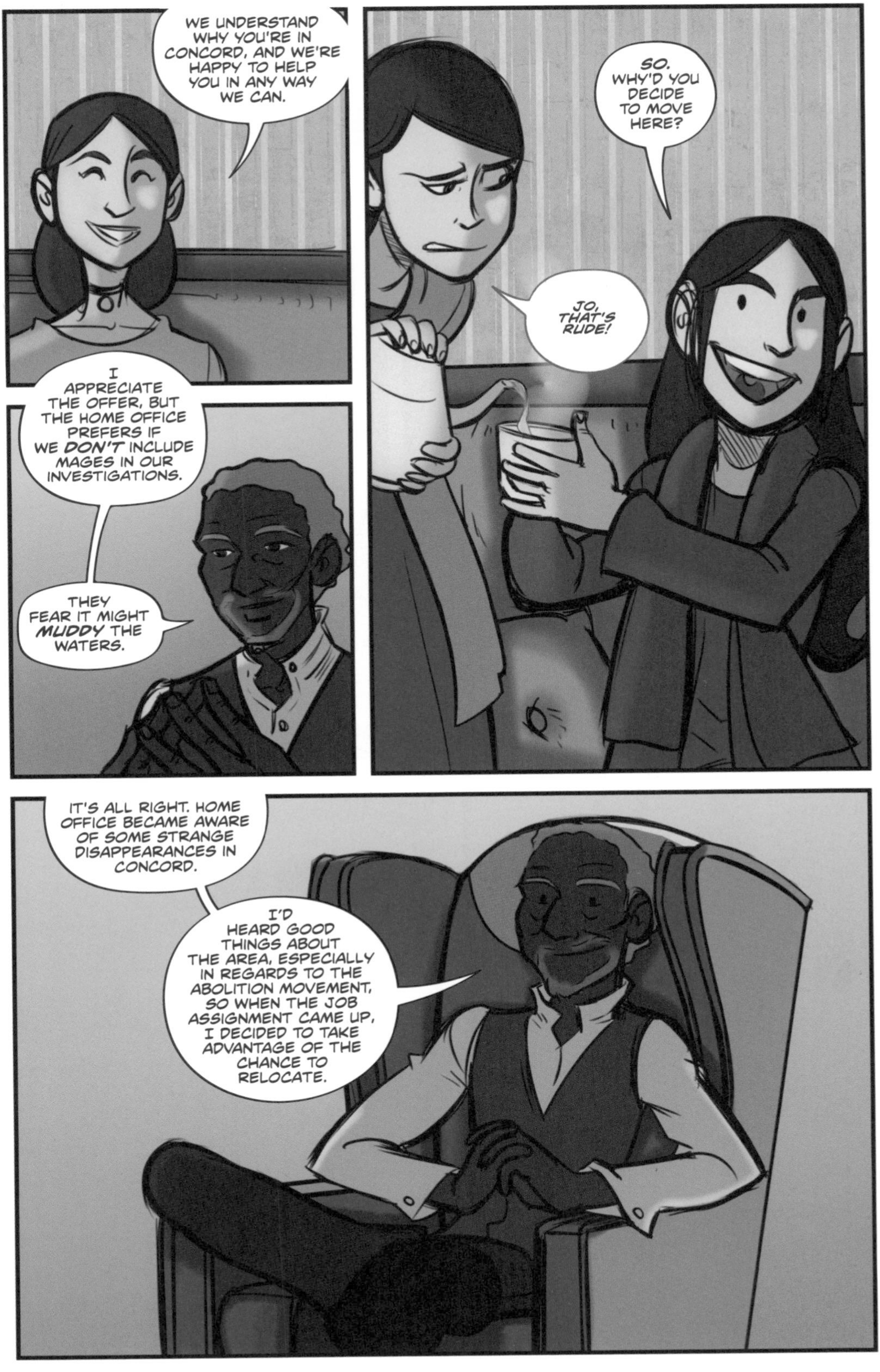
WE UNDERSTAND WHY YOU'RE IN CONCORD, AND WE'RE HAPPY TO HELP YOU IN ANY WAY WE CAN.
SO. WHY'D YOU DECIDE TO MOVE HERE?
JO, THAT'S RUDE!
I APPRECIATE THE OFFER, BUT THE HOME OFFICE PREFERS IF WE DON'T INCLUDE MAGES IN OUR INVESTIGATIONS.
THEY FEAR IT MIGHT MUDDY THE WATERS.
IT'S ALL RIGHT. HOME OFFICE BECAME AWARE OF SOME STRANGE DISAPPEARANCES IN CONCORD.
I'D HEARD GOOD THINGS ABOUT THE AREA, ESPECIALLY IN REGARDS TO THE ABOLITION MOVEMENT, SO WHEN THE JOB ASSIGNMENT CAME UP, I DECIDED TO TAKE ADVANTAGE OF THE CHANCE TO RELOCATE.

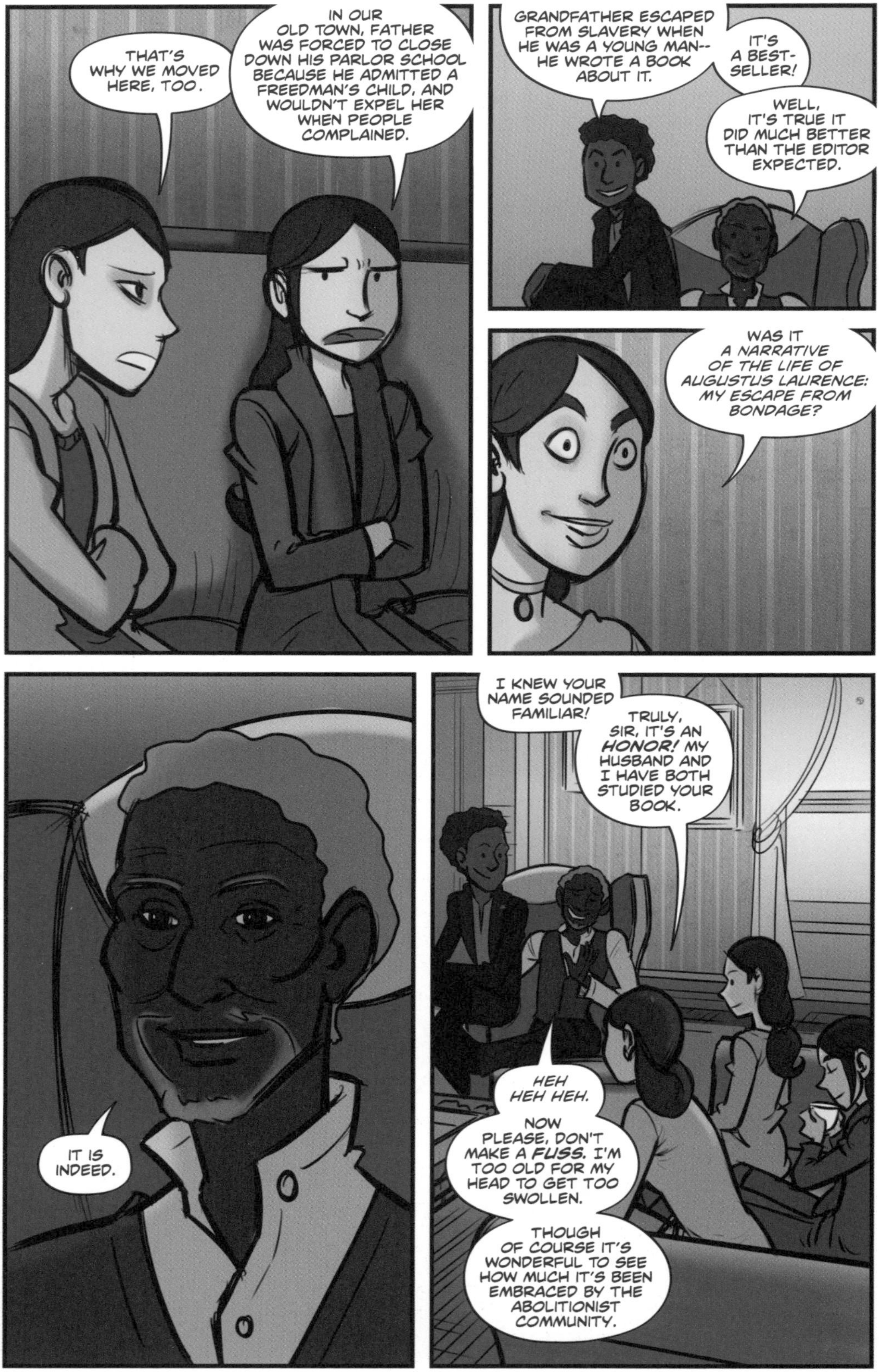
THAT'S WHY WE MOVED HERE, TOO.
IN OUR OLD TOWN, FATHER WAS FORCED TO CLOSE DOWN HIS PARLOR SCHOOL BECAUSE HE ADMITTED A FREEDMAN'S CHILD, AND WOULDN'T EXPEL HER WHEN PEOPLE COMPLAINED.
GRANDFATHER ESCAPED FROM SLAVERY WHEN HE WAS A YOUNG MAN-- HE WROTE A BOOK ABOUT IT.
IT'S A BEST-SELLER!
WELL, IT'S TRUE IT DID MUCH BETTER THAN THE EDITOR EXPECTED.
WAS IT *A NARRATIVE OF THE LIFE OF AUGUSTUS LAURENCE: MY ESCAPE FROM BONDAGE*?
IT IS INDEED.
I KNEW YOUR NAME SOUNDED FAMILIAR!
TRULY, SIR, IT'S AN ***HONOR!*** MY HUSBAND AND I HAVE BOTH STUDIED YOUR BOOK.
HEH HEH HEH.
NOW PLEASE, DON'T MAKE A ***FUSS.*** I'M TOO OLD FOR MY HEAD TO GET TOO SWOLLEN.
THOUGH OF COURSE IT'S WONDERFUL TO SEE HOW MUCH IT'S BEEN EMBRACED BY THE ABOLITIONIST COMMUNITY.

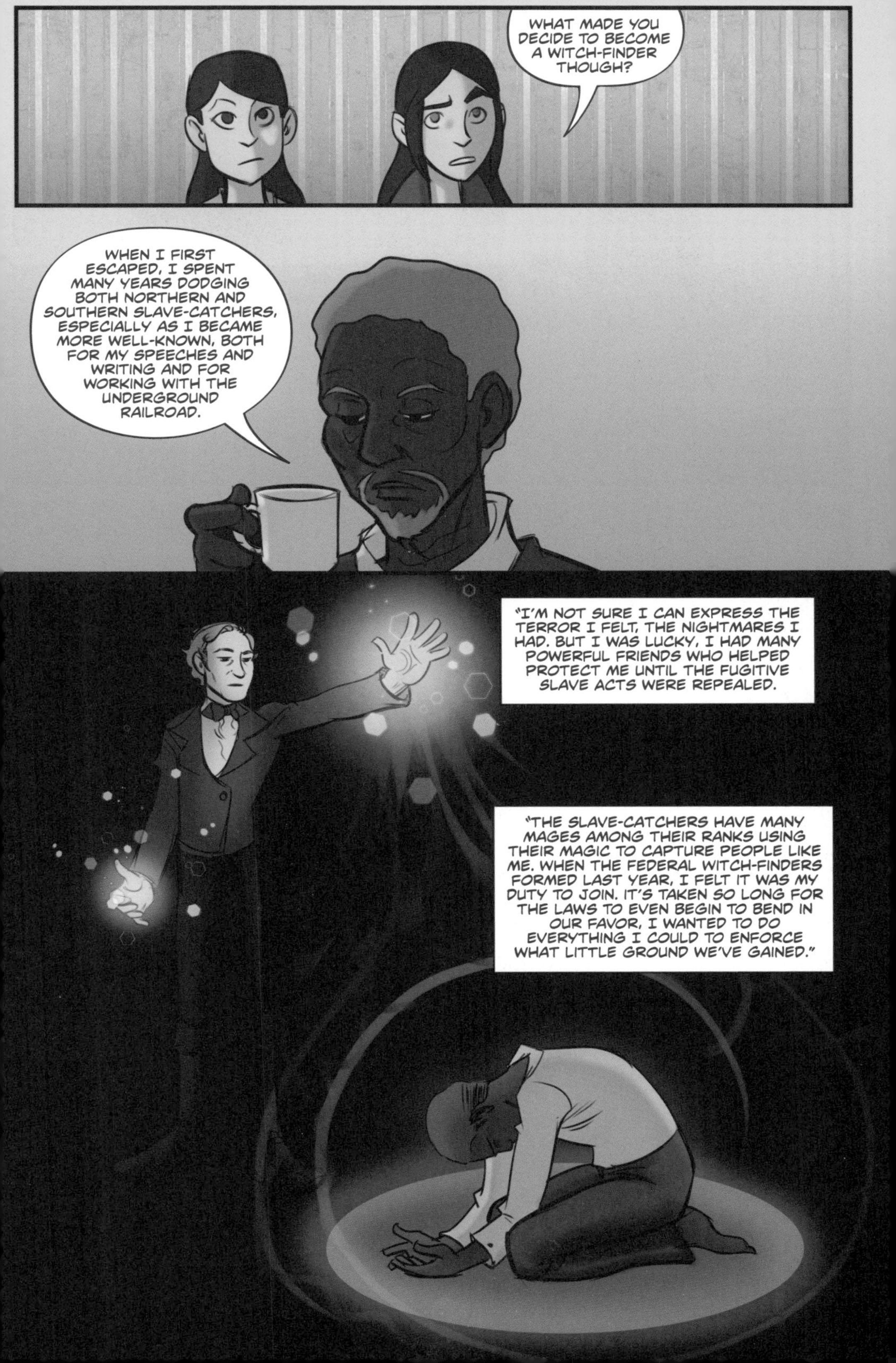
WHAT MADE YOU DECIDE TO BECOME A WITCH-FINDER THOUGH?
WHEN I FIRST ESCAPED, I SPENT MANY YEARS DODGING BOTH NORTHERN AND SOUTHERN SLAVE-CATCHERS, ESPECIALLY AS I BECAME MORE WELL-KNOWN, BOTH FOR MY SPEECHES AND WRITING AND FOR WORKING WITH THE UNDERGROUND RAILROAD.
"I'M NOT SURE I CAN EXPRESS THE TERROR I FELT, THE NIGHTMARES I HAD. BUT I WAS LUCKY, I HAD MANY POWERFUL FRIENDS WHO HELPED PROTECT ME UNTIL THE FUGITIVE SLAVE ACTS WERE REPEALED.
"THE SLAVE-CATCHERS HAVE MANY MAGES AMONG THEIR RANKS USING THEIR MAGIC TO CAPTURE PEOPLE LIKE ME. WHEN THE FEDERAL WITCH-FINDERS FORMED LAST YEAR, I FELT IT WAS MY DUTY TO JOIN. IT'S TAKEN SO LONG FOR THE LAWS TO EVEN BEGIN TO BEND IN OUR FAVOR, I WANTED TO DO EVERYTHING I COULD TO ENFORCE WHAT LITTLE GROUND WE'VE GAINED."

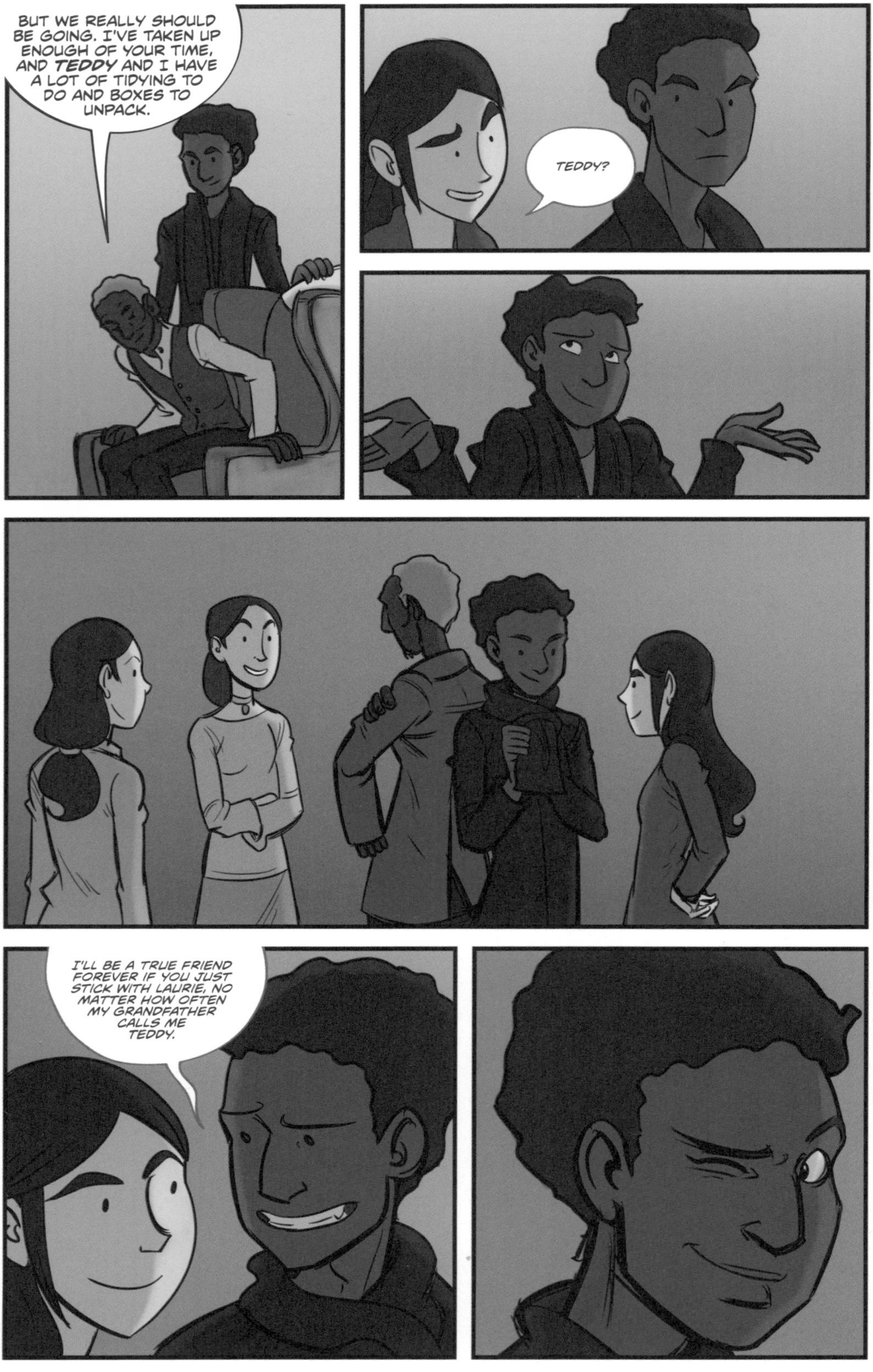
BUT WE REALLY SHOULD BE GOING. I'VE TAKEN UP ENOUGH OF YOUR TIME, AND *TEDDY* AND I HAVE A LOT OF TIDYING TO DO AND BOXES TO UNPACK.
TEDDY?
I'LL BE A TRUE FRIEND FOREVER IF YOU JUST STICK WITH LAURIE, NO MATTER HOW OFTEN MY GRANDFATHER CALLS ME TEDDY.

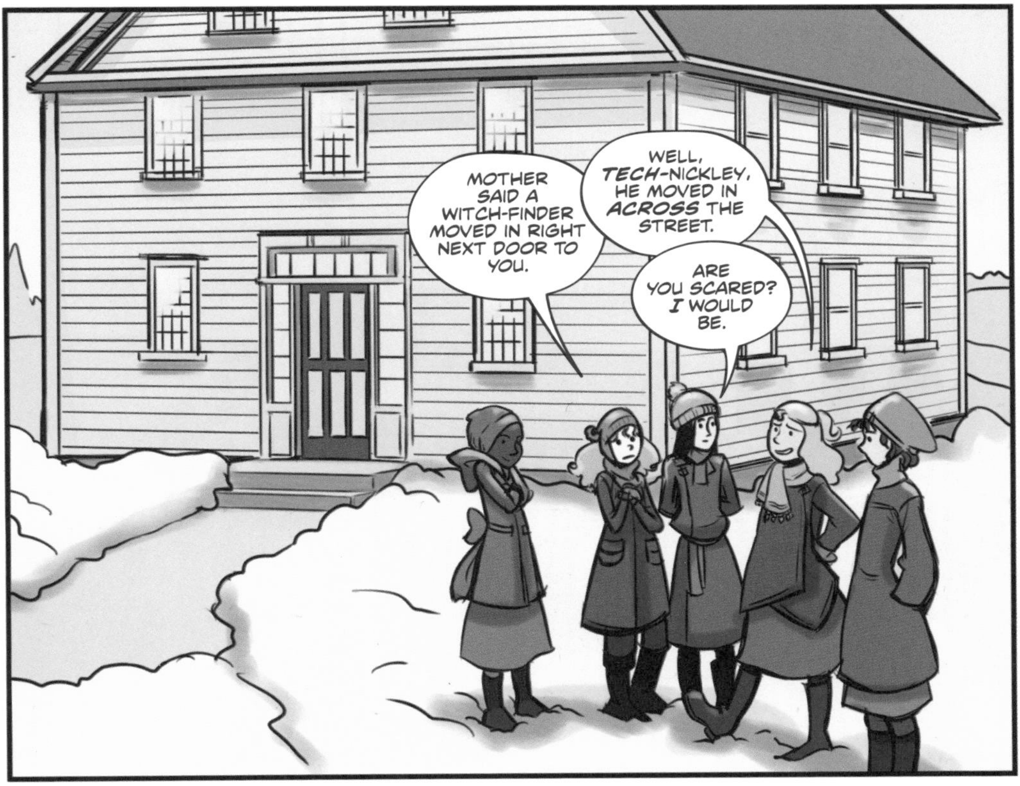
MOTHER SAID A WITCH-FINDER MOVED IN RIGHT NEXT DOOR TO YOU.
WELL, *TECH*-NICKLEY, HE MOVED IN *ACROSS* THE STREET.
ARE YOU SCARED? *I* WOULD BE.

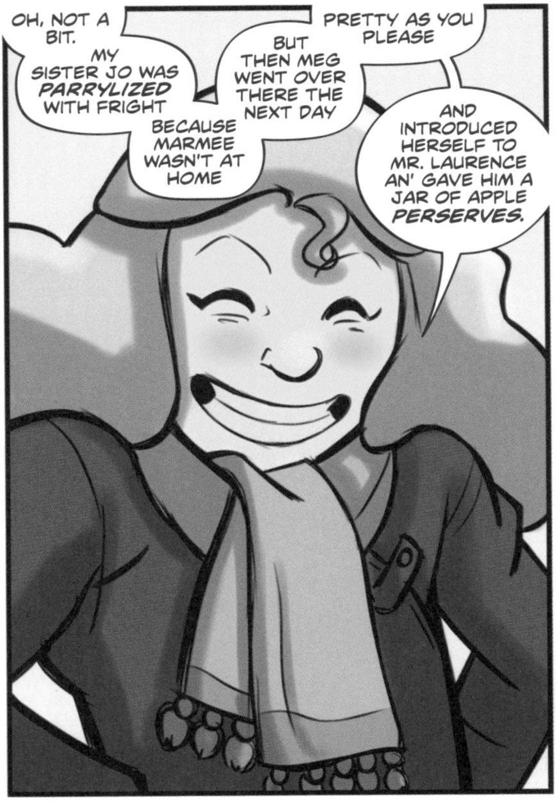
OH, NOT A BIT.
MY SISTER JO WAS *PARRYLIZED* WITH FRIGHT
BECAUSE MARMEE WASN'T AT HOME
BUT THEN MEG WENT OVER THERE THE NEXT DAY
PRETTY AS YOU PLEASE
AND INTRODUCED HERSELF TO MR. LAURENCE AN' GAVE HIM A JAR OF APPLE *PERSERVES.*

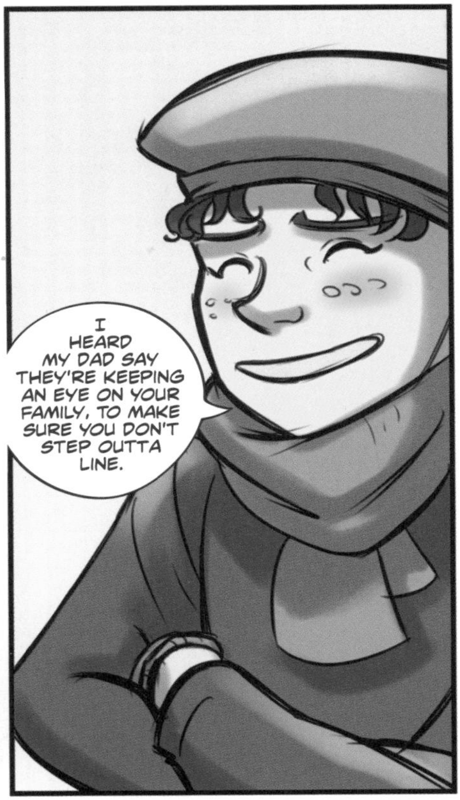
I HEARD MY DAD SAY THEY'RE KEEPING AN EYE ON YOUR FAMILY, TO MAKE SURE YOU DON'T STEP OUTTA LINE.

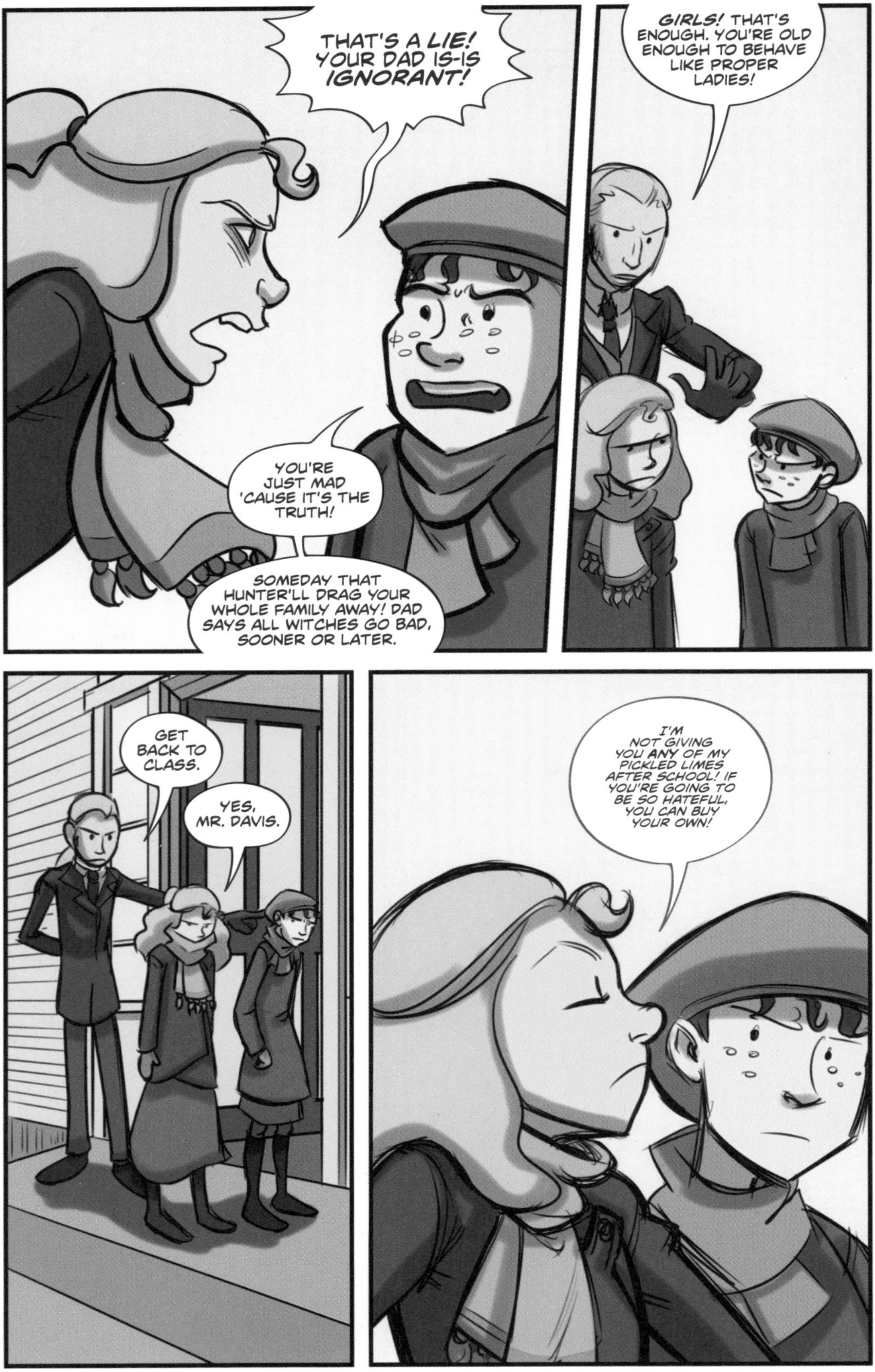
THAT'S A LIE! YOUR DAD IS-IS IGNORANT!
YOU'RE JUST MAD 'CAUSE IT'S THE TRUTH!
SOMEDAY THAT HUNTER'LL DRAG YOUR WHOLE FAMILY AWAY! DAD SAYS ALL WITCHES GO BAD, SOONER OR LATER.
GIRLS! THAT'S ENOUGH. YOU'RE OLD ENOUGH TO BEHAVE LIKE PROPER LADIES!
GET BACK TO CLASS.
YES, MR. DAVIS.
I'M NOT GIVING YOU ANY OF MY PICKLED LIMES AFTER SCHOOL! IF YOU'RE GOING TO BE SO HATEFUL, YOU CAN BUY YOUR OWN!

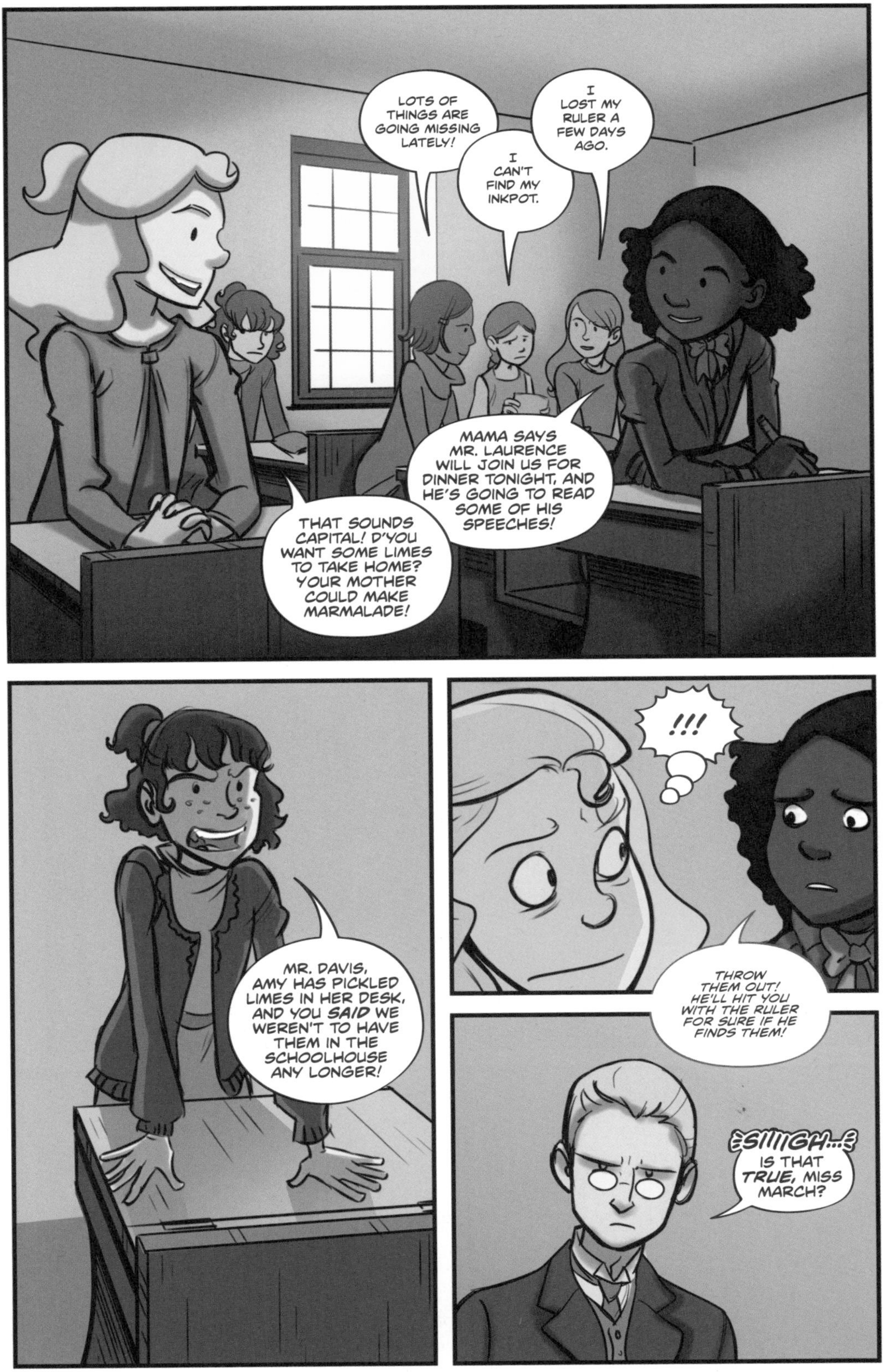

LOTS OF THINGS ARE GOING MISSING LATELY!
I CAN'T FIND MY INKPOT.
I LOST MY RULER A FEW DAYS AGO.
MAMA SAYS MR. LAURENCE WILL JOIN US FOR DINNER TONIGHT, AND HE'S GOING TO READ SOME OF HIS SPEECHES!
THAT SOUNDS CAPITAL! D'YOU WANT SOME LIMES TO TAKE HOME? YOUR MOTHER COULD MAKE MARMALADE!
MR. DAVIS, AMY HAS PICKLED LIMES IN HER DESK, AND YOU *SAID* WE WEREN'T TO HAVE THEM IN THE SCHOOLHOUSE ANY LONGER!
!!!
THROW THEM OUT! HE'LL HIT YOU WITH THE RULER FOR SURE IF HE FINDS THEM!
SIIIIGH...
IS THAT *TRUE*, MISS MARCH?

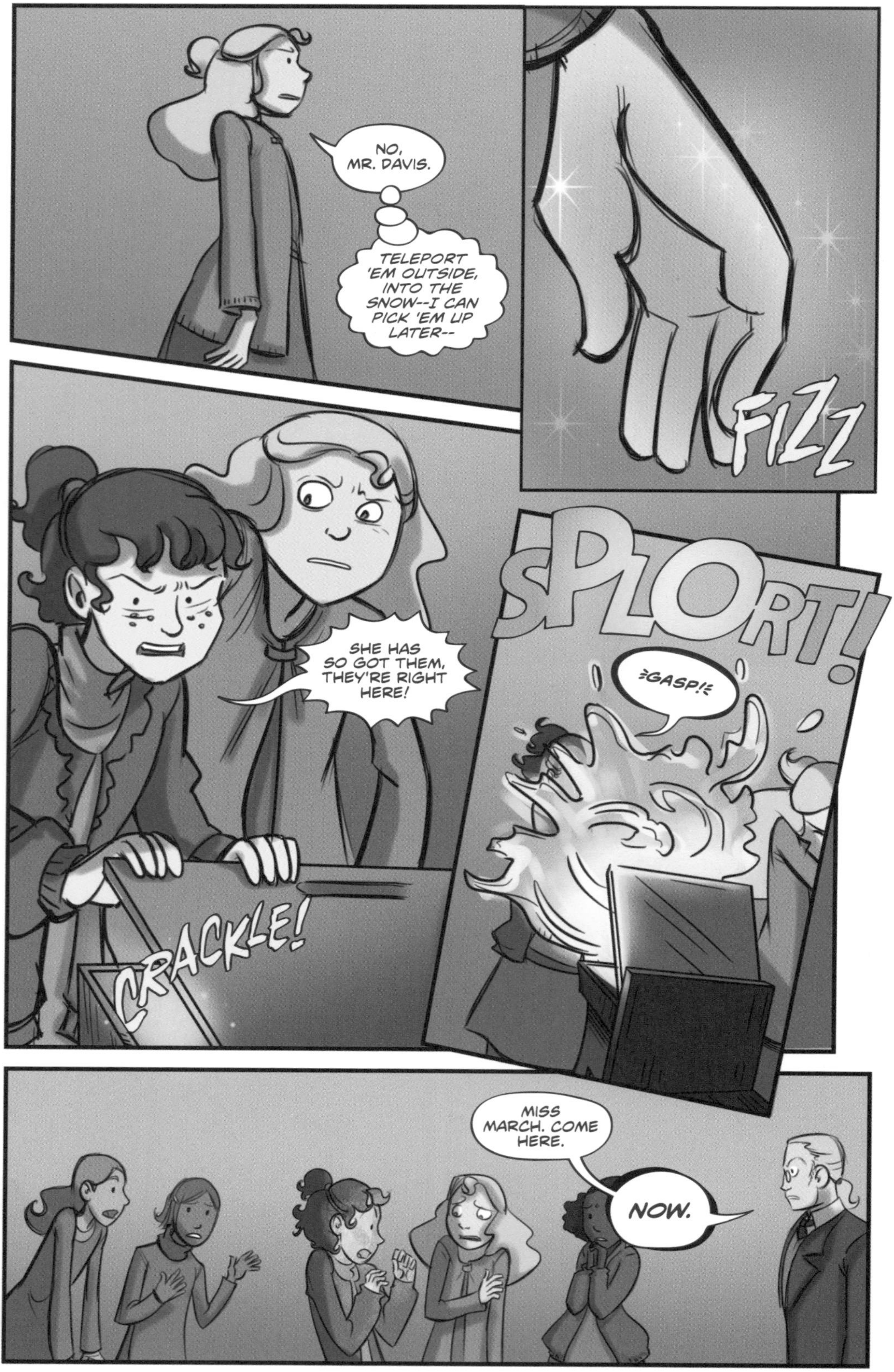
NO, MR. DAVIS.
TELEPORT 'EM OUTSIDE, INTO THE SNOW--I CAN PICK 'EM UP LATER--
FIZZ
SHE HAS SO GOT THEM, THEY'RE RIGHT HERE!
CRACKLE!
SPLORT!
GASP!
MISS MARCH. COME HERE.
NOW.

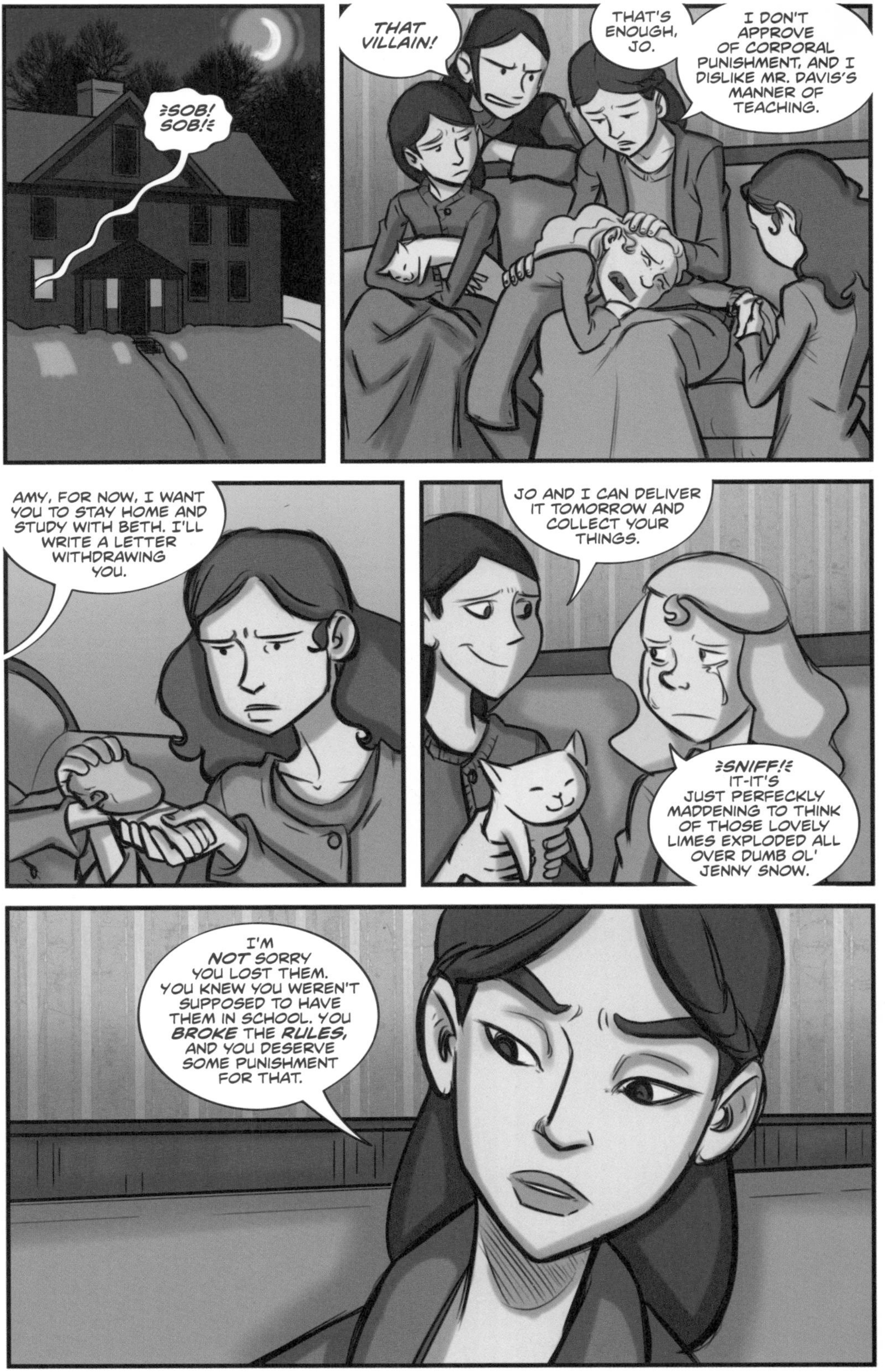
≈SOB! SOB!≈
THAT VILLAIN!
THAT'S ENOUGH, JO.
I DON'T APPROVE OF CORPORAL PUNISHMENT, AND I DISLIKE MR. DAVIS'S MANNER OF TEACHING.
AMY, FOR NOW, I WANT YOU TO STAY HOME AND STUDY WITH BETH. I'LL WRITE A LETTER WITHDRAWING YOU.
JO AND I CAN DELIVER IT TOMORROW AND COLLECT YOUR THINGS.
≈SNIFF!≈ IT-IT'S JUST PERFECKLY MADDENING TO THINK OF THOSE LOVELY LIMES EXPLODED ALL OVER DUMB OL' JENNY SNOW.
I'M NOT SORRY YOU LOST THEM. YOU KNEW YOU WEREN'T SUPPOSED TO HAVE THEM IN SCHOOL. YOU BROKE THE RULES, AND YOU DESERVE SOME PUNISHMENT FOR THAT.

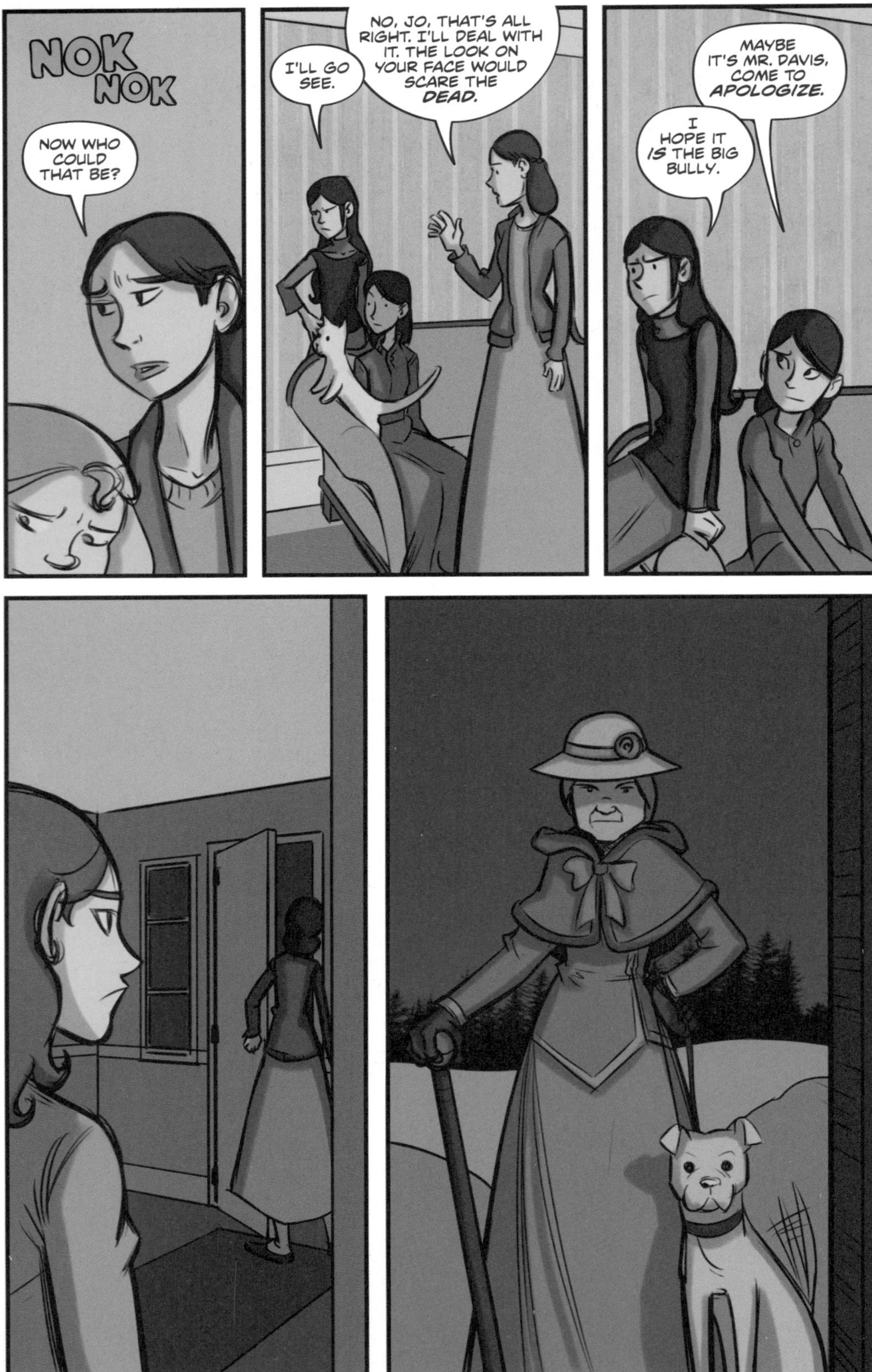
NOK NOK
NOW WHO COULD THAT BE?
I'LL GO SEE.
NO, JO, THAT'S ALL RIGHT. I'LL DEAL WITH IT. THE LOOK ON YOUR FACE WOULD SCARE THE *DEAD.*
MAYBE IT'S MR. DAVIS, COME TO *APOLOGIZE.*
I HOPE IT *IS* THE BIG BULLY.

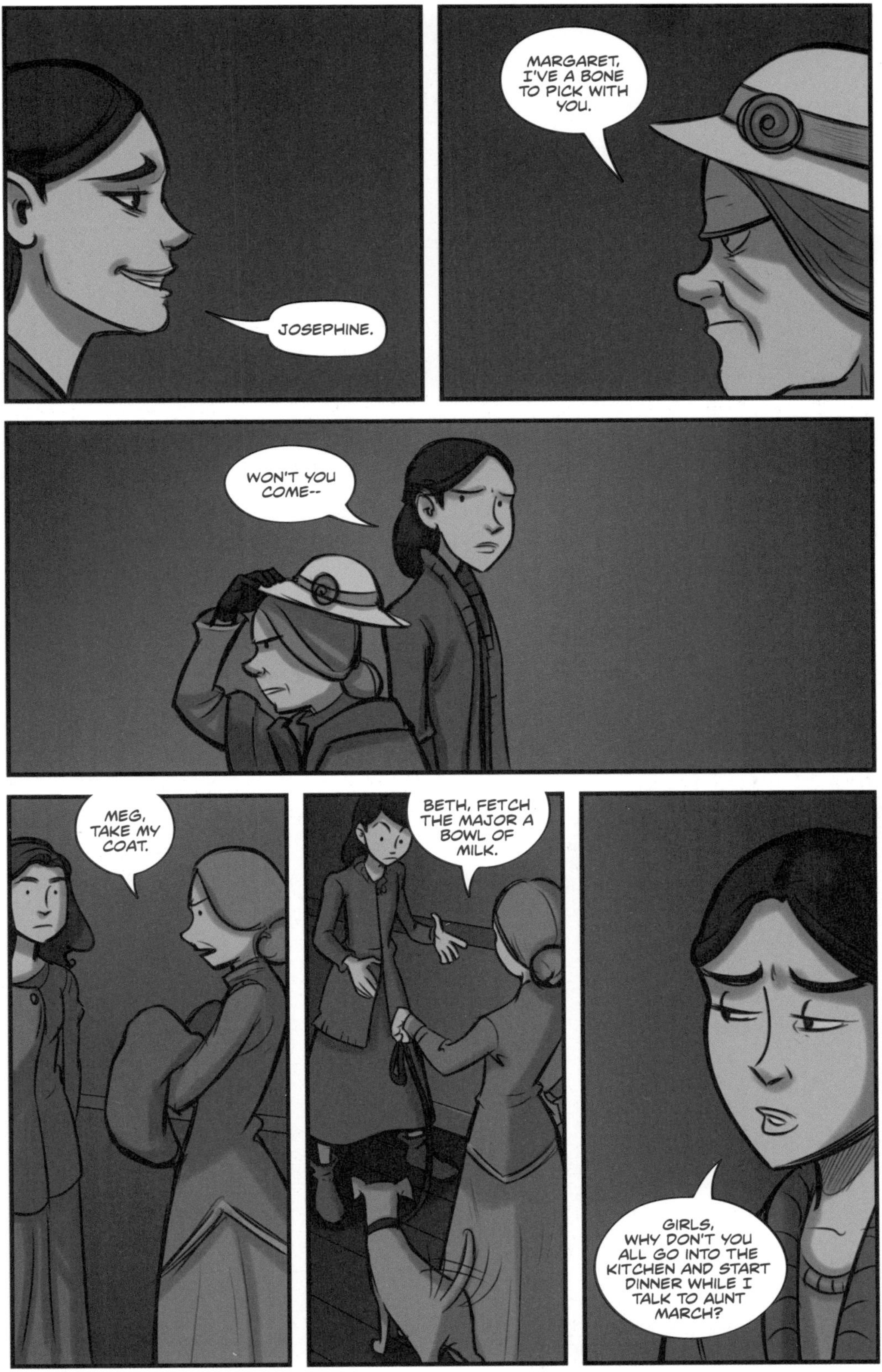
JOSEPHINE.
MARGARET, I'VE A BONE TO PICK WITH YOU.
WON'T YOU COME--
MEG, TAKE MY COAT.
BETH, FETCH THE MAJOR A BOWL OF MILK.
GIRLS, WHY DON'T YOU ALL GO INTO THE KITCHEN AND START DINNER WHILE I TALK TO AUNT MARCH?

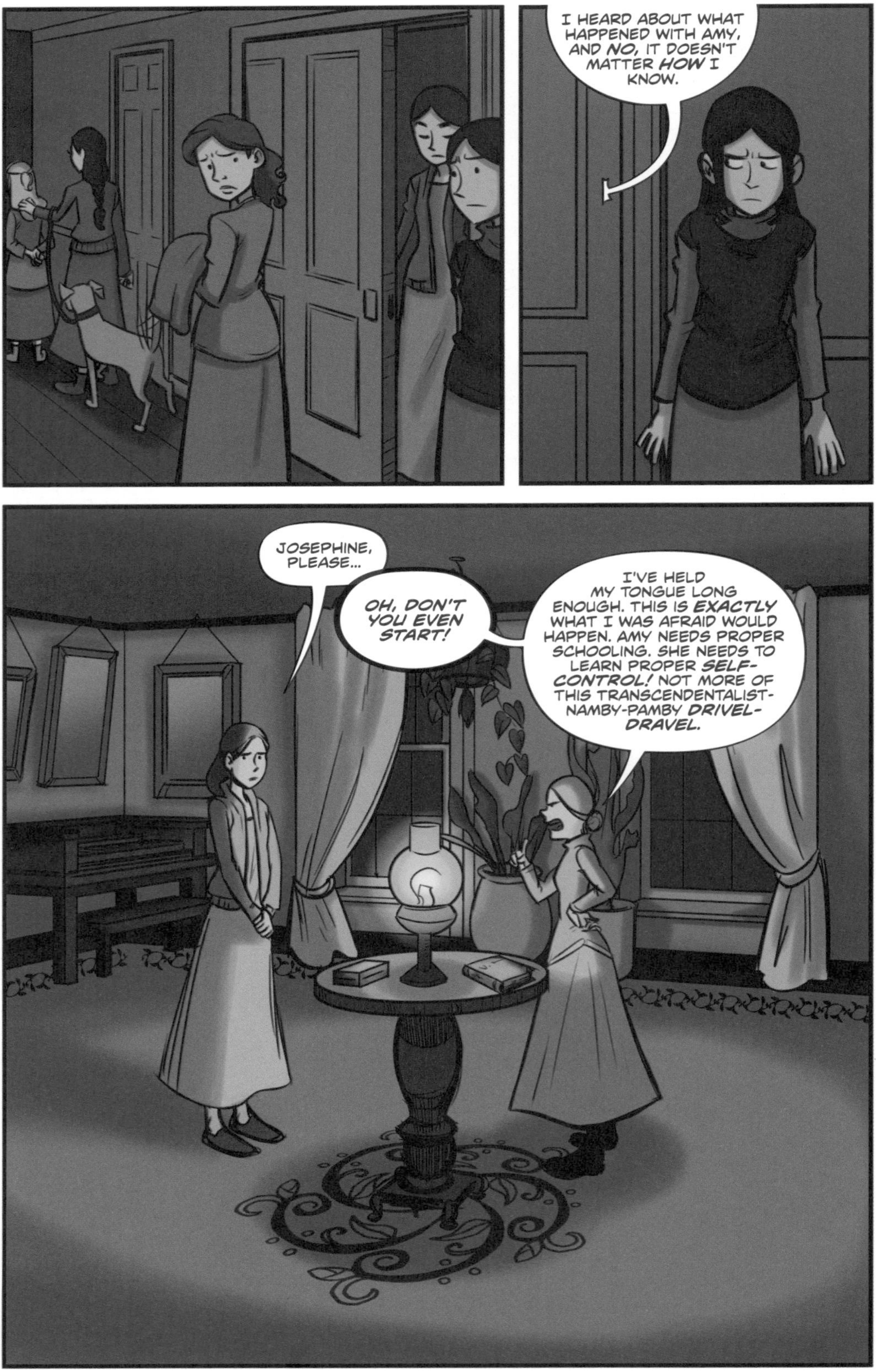
I HEARD ABOUT WHAT HAPPENED WITH AMY, AND NO, IT DOESN'T MATTER HOW I KNOW.
JOSEPHINE, PLEASE...
OH, DON'T YOU EVEN START!
I'VE HELD MY TONGUE LONG ENOUGH. THIS IS EXACTLY WHAT I WAS AFRAID WOULD HAPPEN. AMY NEEDS PROPER SCHOOLING. SHE NEEDS TO LEARN PROPER SELF-CONTROL! NOT MORE OF THIS TRANSCENDENTALIST-NAMBY-PAMBY DRIVEL-DRAVEL.

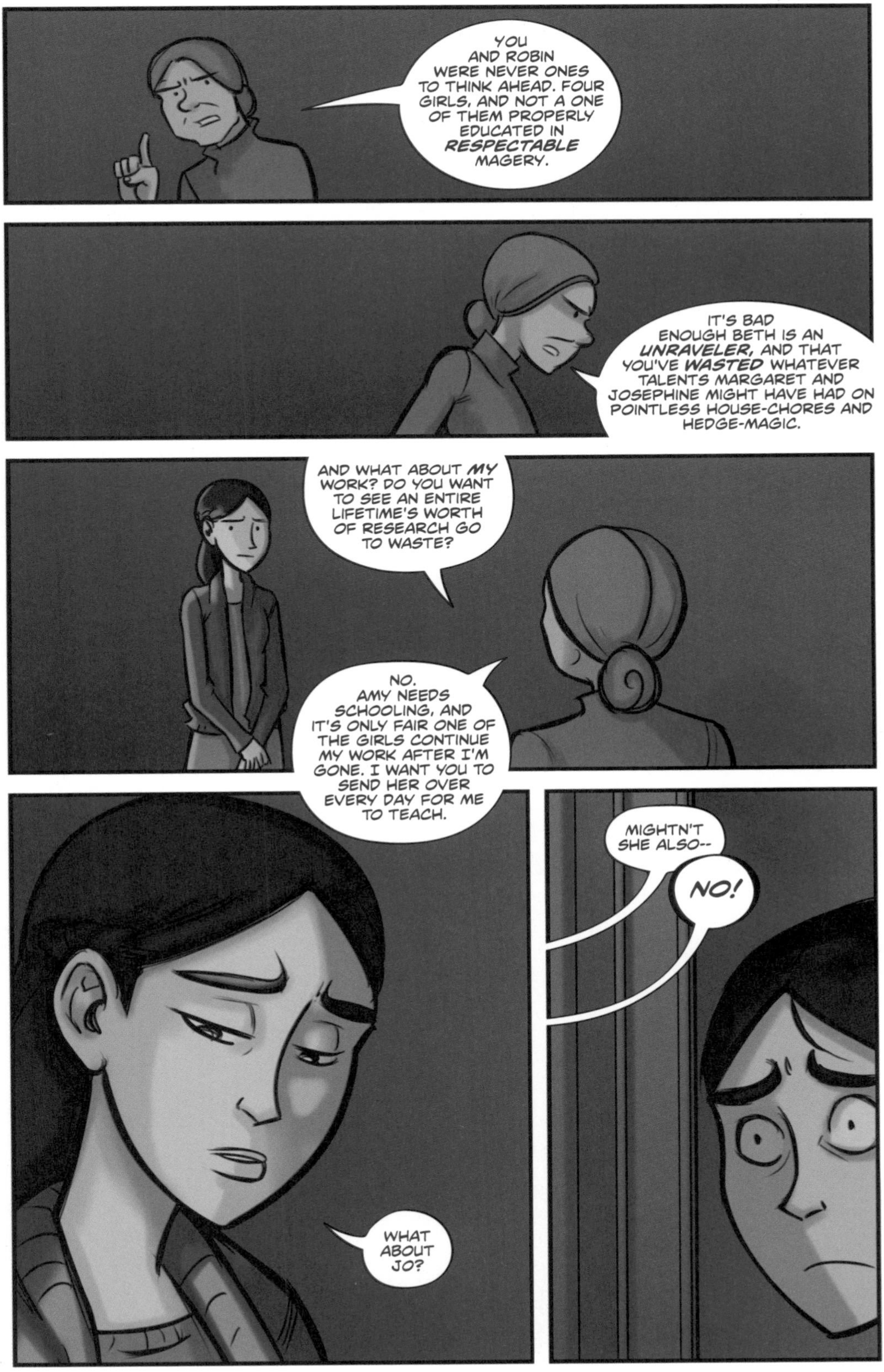
YOU AND ROBIN WERE NEVER ONES TO THINK AHEAD. FOUR GIRLS, AND NOT A ONE OF THEM PROPERLY EDUCATED IN RESPECTABLE MAGERY.
IT'S BAD ENOUGH BETH IS AN UNRAVELER, AND THAT YOU'VE WASTED WHATEVER TALENTS MARGARET AND JOSEPHINE MIGHT HAVE HAD ON POINTLESS HOUSE-CHORES AND HEDGE-MAGIC.
AND WHAT ABOUT MY WORK? DO YOU WANT TO SEE AN ENTIRE LIFETIME'S WORTH OF RESEARCH GO TO WASTE?
NO. AMY NEEDS SCHOOLING, AND IT'S ONLY FAIR ONE OF THE GIRLS CONTINUE MY WORK AFTER I'M GONE. I WANT YOU TO SEND HER OVER EVERY DAY FOR ME TO TEACH.
WHAT ABOUT JO?
MIGHTN'T SHE ALSO--
NO!

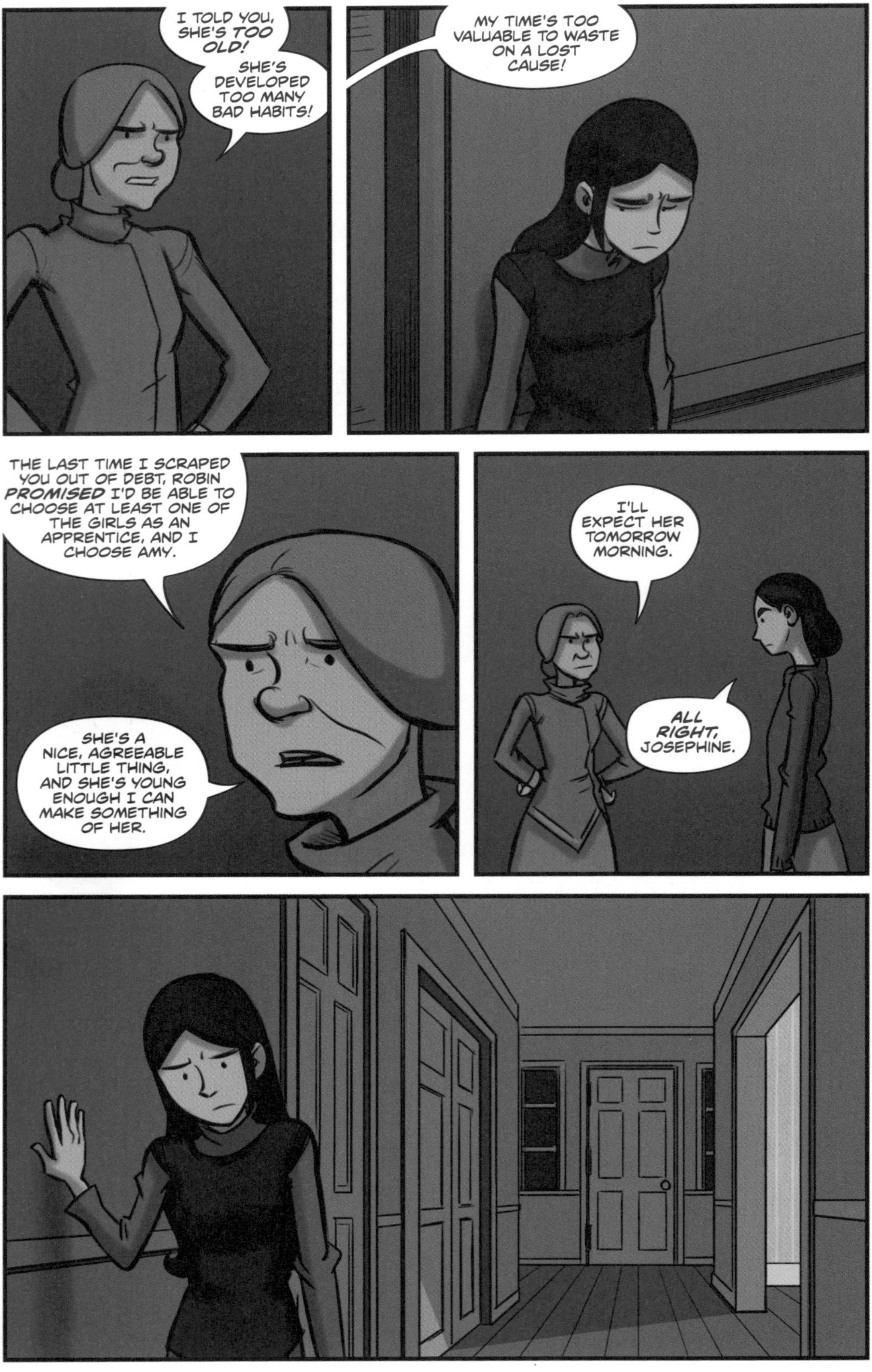
I TOLD YOU, SHE'S *TOO OLD!*
SHE'S DEVELOPED TOO MANY BAD HABITS!
MY TIME'S TOO VALUABLE TO WASTE ON A LOST CAUSE!
THE LAST TIME I SCRAPED YOU OUT OF DEBT, ROBIN ***PROMISED*** I'D BE ABLE TO CHOOSE AT LEAST ONE OF THE GIRLS AS AN APPRENTICE, AND I CHOOSE AMY.
SHE'S A NICE, AGREEABLE LITTLE THING, AND SHE'S YOUNG ENOUGH I CAN MAKE SOMETHING OF HER.
I'LL EXPECT HER TOMORROW MORNING.
ALL RIGHT, JOSEPHINE.

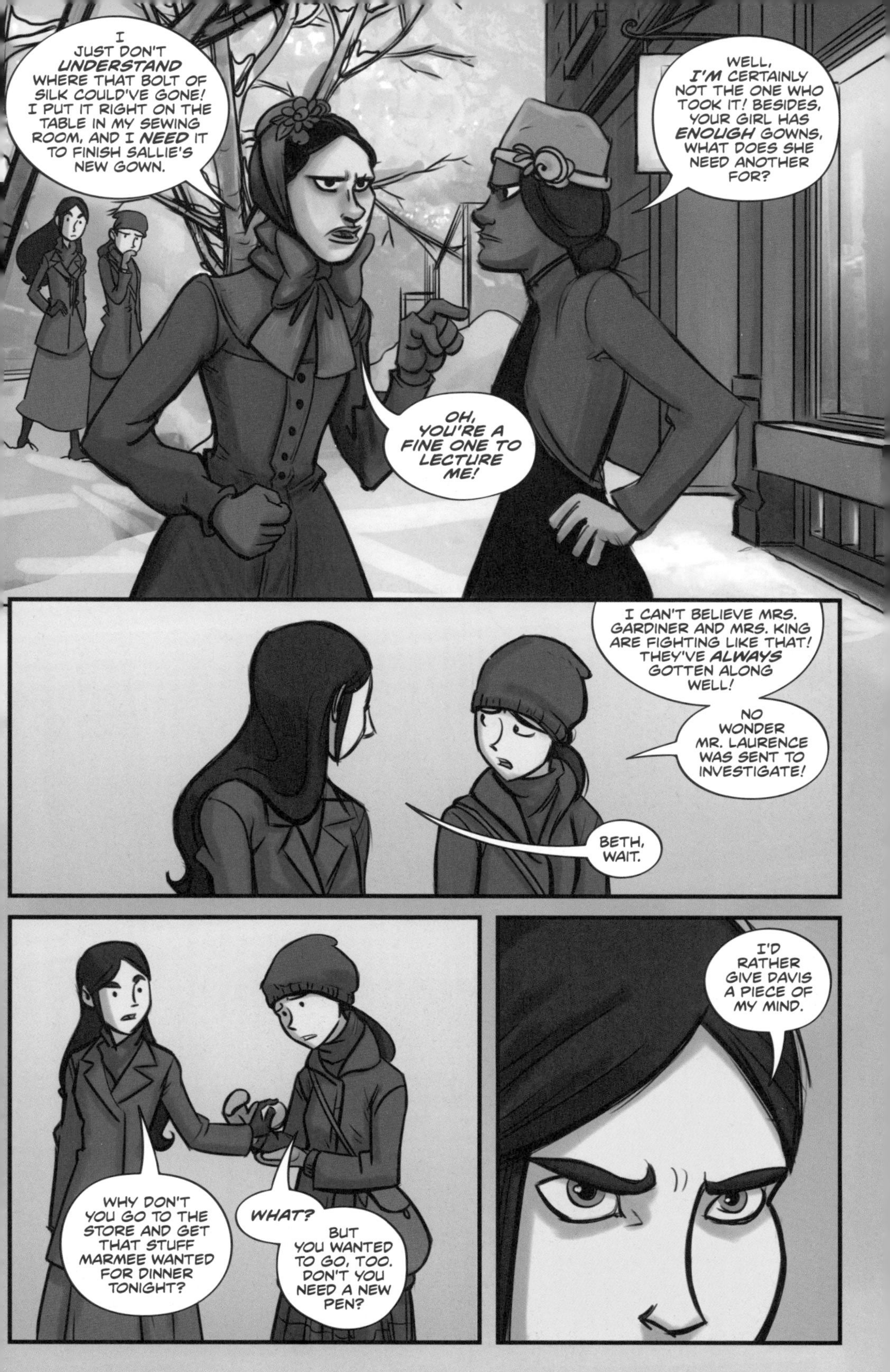
I JUST DON'T UNDERSTAND WHERE THAT BOLT OF SILK COULD'VE GONE! I PUT IT RIGHT ON THE TABLE IN MY SEWING ROOM, AND I NEED IT TO FINISH SALLIE'S NEW GOWN.
WELL, I'M CERTAINLY NOT THE ONE WHO TOOK IT! BESIDES, YOUR GIRL HAS ENOUGH GOWNS. WHAT DOES SHE NEED ANOTHER FOR?
OH, YOU'RE A FINE ONE TO LECTURE ME!
I CAN'T BELIEVE MRS. GARDINER AND MRS. KING ARE FIGHTING LIKE THAT! THEY'VE ALWAYS GOTTEN ALONG WELL!
NO WONDER MR. LAURENCE WAS SENT TO INVESTIGATE!
BETH, WAIT.
WHY DON'T YOU GO TO THE STORE AND GET THAT STUFF MARMEE WANTED FOR DINNER TONIGHT?
WHAT?
BUT YOU WANTED TO GO, TOO. DON'T YOU NEED A NEW PEN?
I'D RATHER GIVE DAVIS A PIECE OF MY MIND.

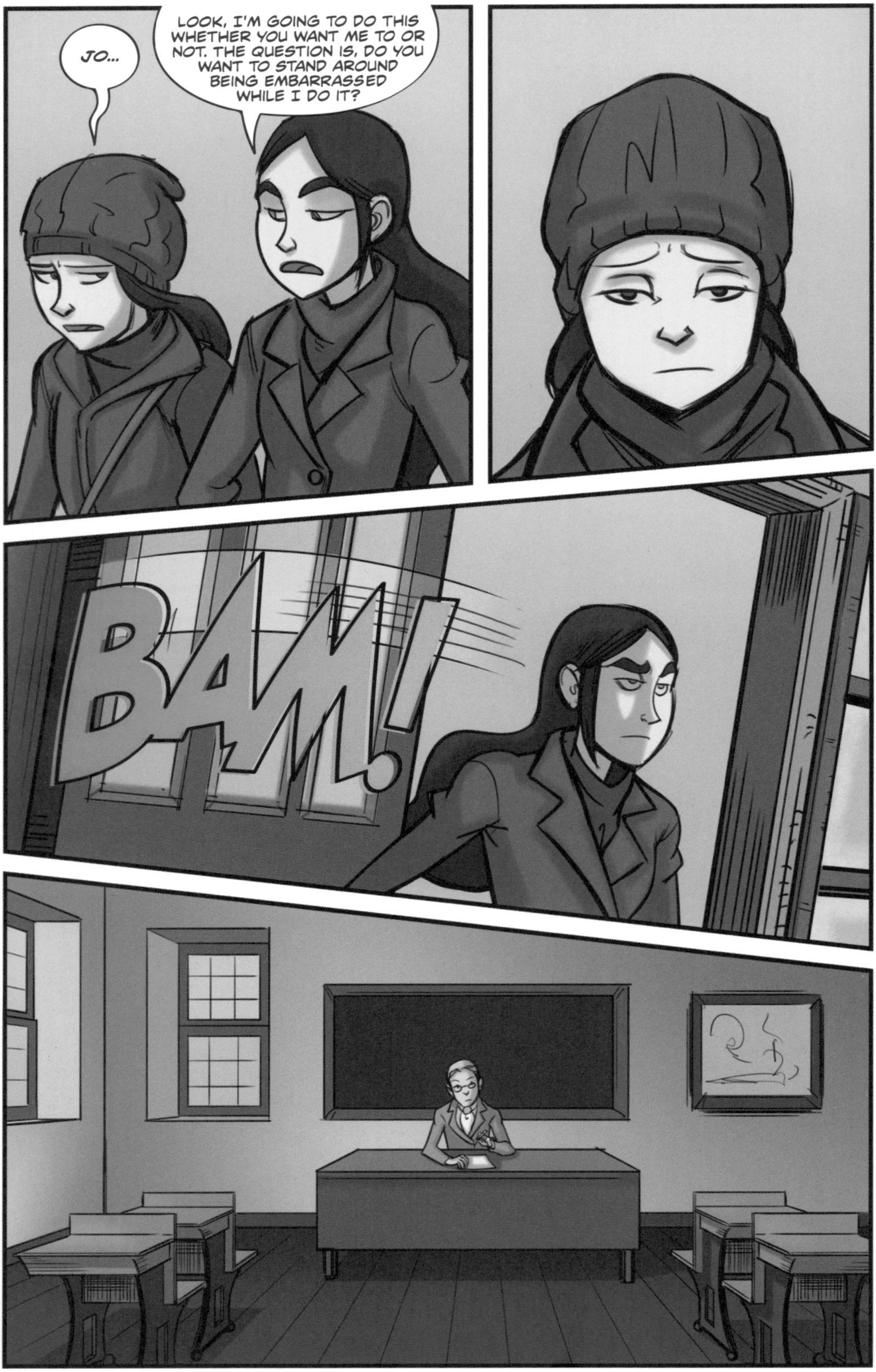
JO...
LOOK, I'M GOING TO DO THIS WHETHER YOU WANT ME TO OR NOT. THE QUESTION IS, DO YOU WANT TO STAND AROUND BEING EMBARRASSED WHILE I DO IT?
BAM!

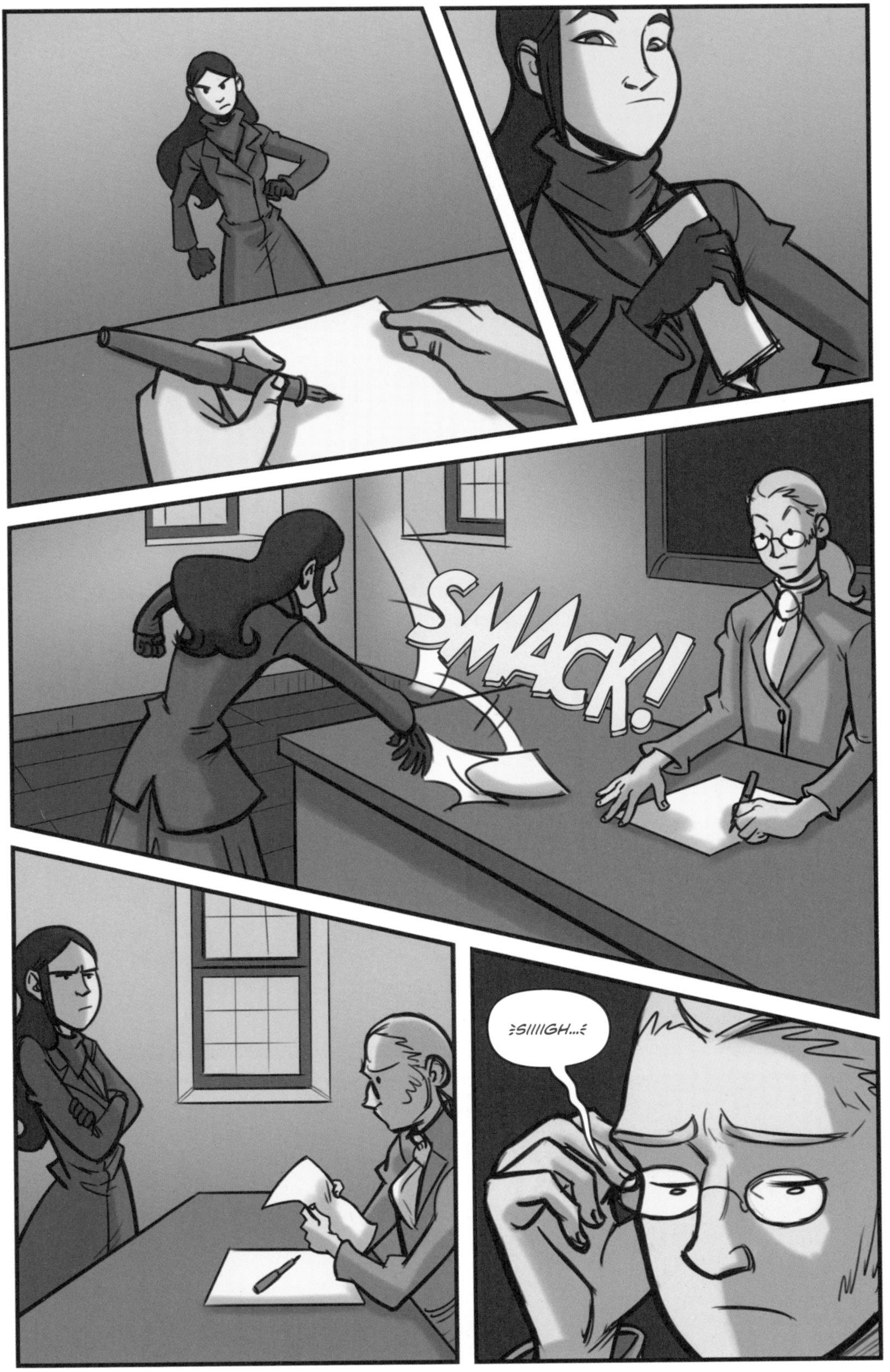
SMACK!
SIIIIGH...

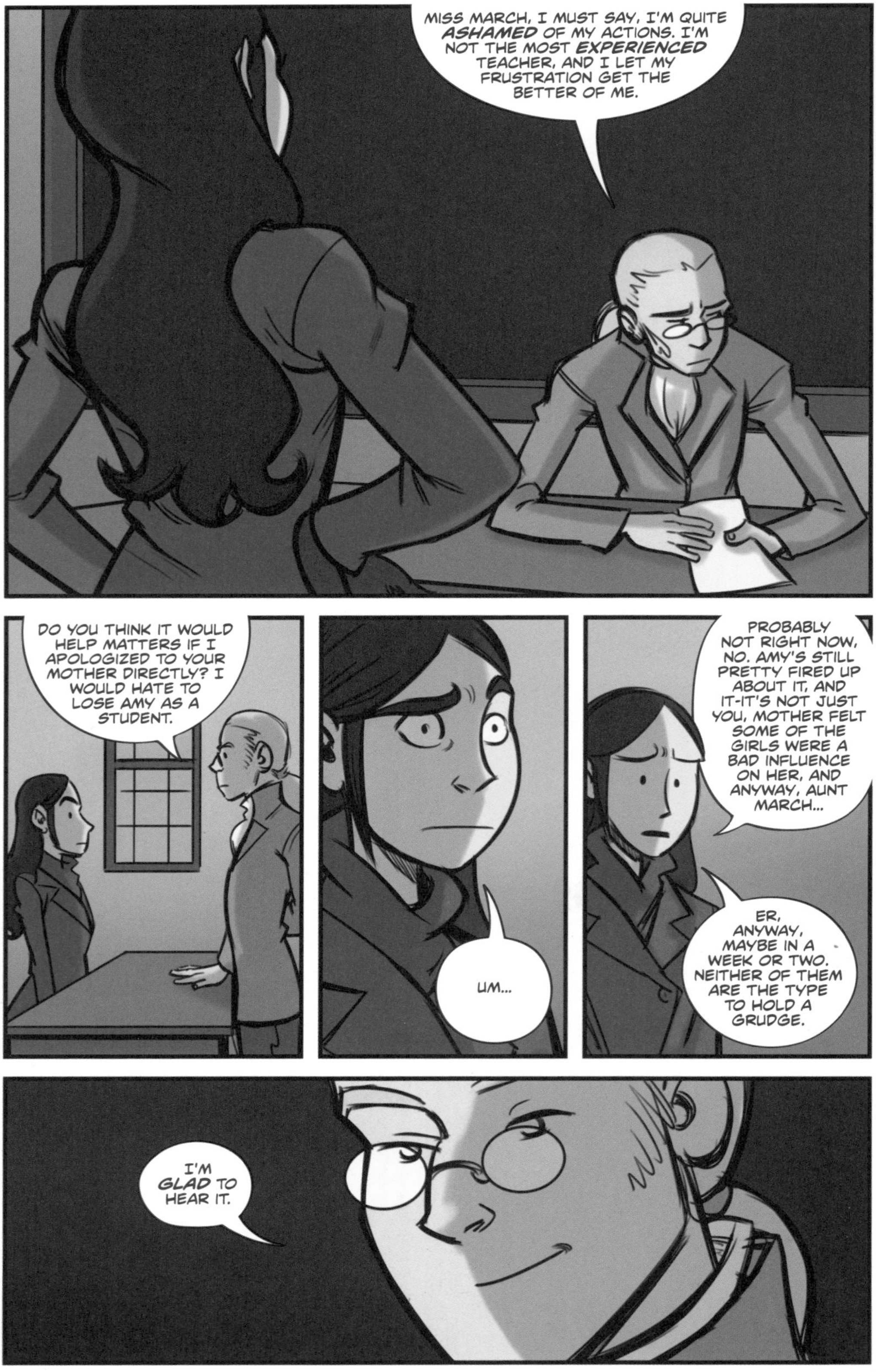
MISS MARCH, I MUST SAY, I'M QUITE ASHAMED OF MY ACTIONS. I'M NOT THE MOST EXPERIENCED TEACHER, AND I LET MY FRUSTRATION GET THE BETTER OF ME.
DO YOU THINK IT WOULD HELP MATTERS IF I APOLOGIZED TO YOUR MOTHER DIRECTLY? I WOULD HATE TO LOSE AMY AS A STUDENT.
UM...
PROBABLY NOT RIGHT NOW, NO. AMY'S STILL PRETTY FIRED UP ABOUT IT, AND IT-IT'S NOT JUST YOU, MOTHER FELT SOME OF THE GIRLS WERE A BAD INFLUENCE ON HER, AND ANYWAY, AUNT MARCH...
ER, ANYWAY, MAYBE IN A WEEK OR TWO. NEITHER OF THEM ARE THE TYPE TO HOLD A GRUDGE.
I'M GLAD TO HEAR IT.

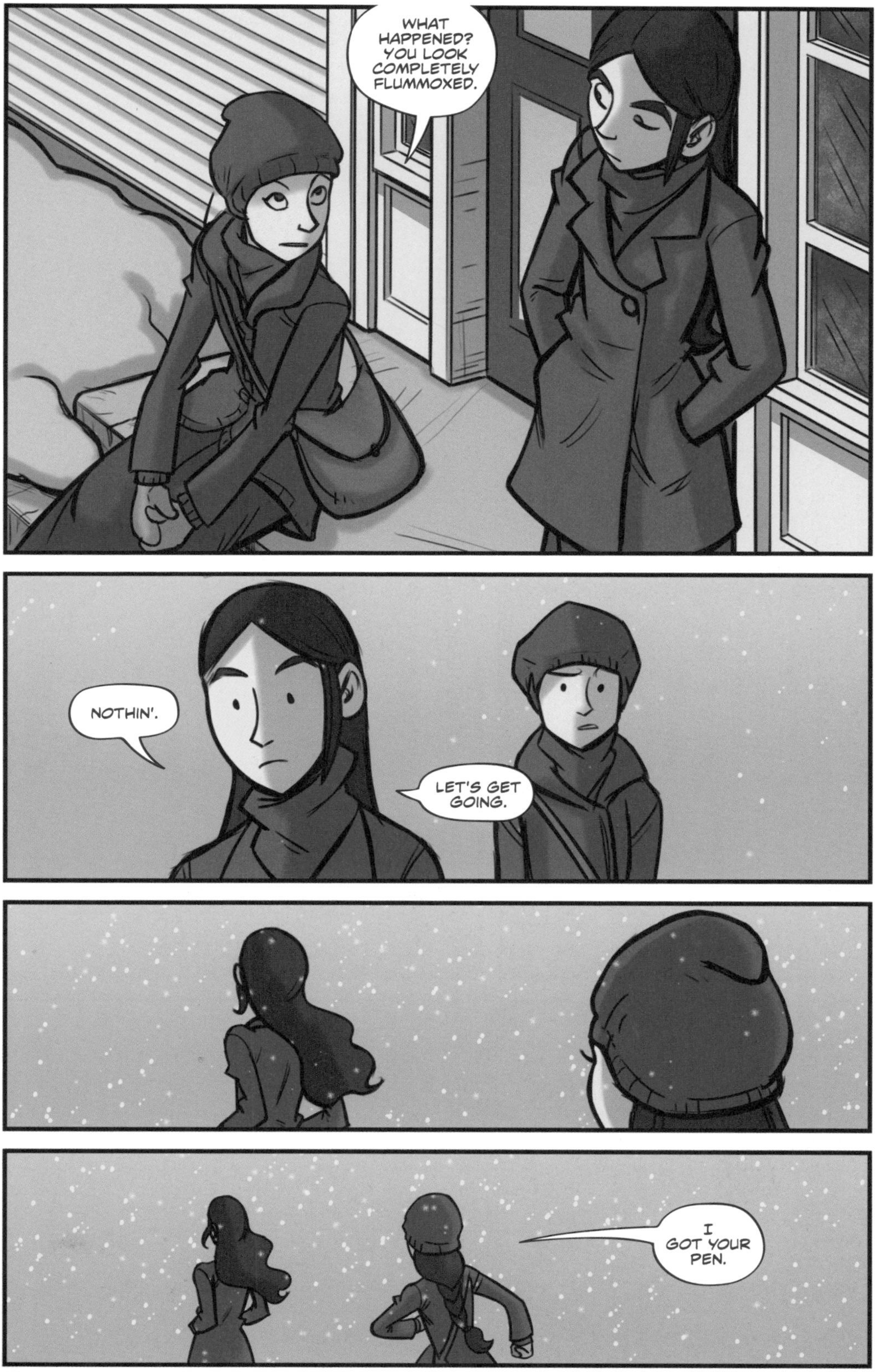
WHAT HAPPENED? YOU LOOK COMPLETELY FLUMMOXED.
NOTHIN'.
LET'S GET GOING.
I GOT YOUR PEN.

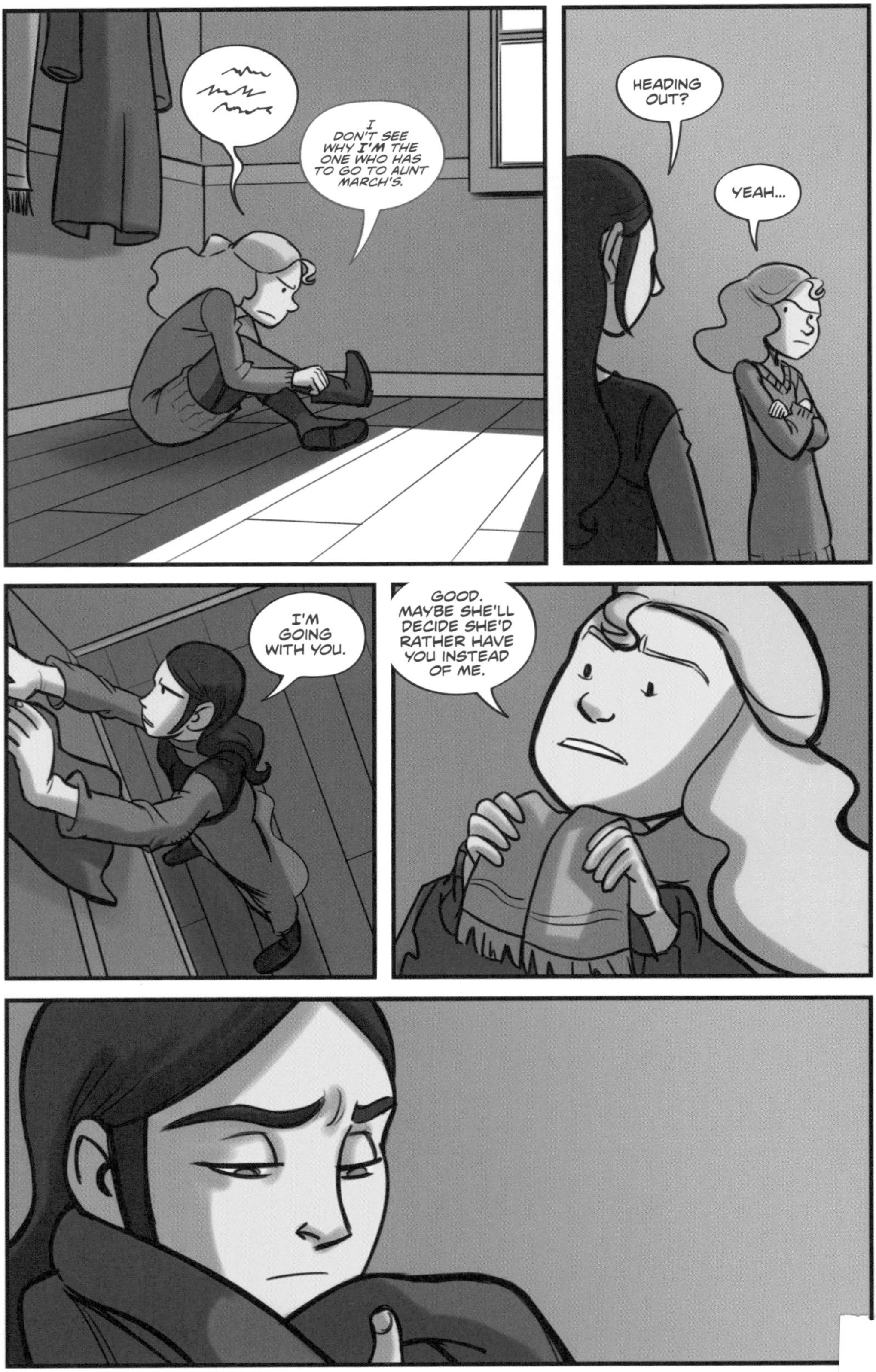
I DON'T SEE WHY I'M THE ONE WHO HAS TO GO TO AUNT MARCH'S.
HEADING OUT?
YEAH...
I'M GOING WITH YOU.
GOOD. MAYBE SHE'LL DECIDE SHE'D RATHER HAVE YOU INSTEAD OF ME.

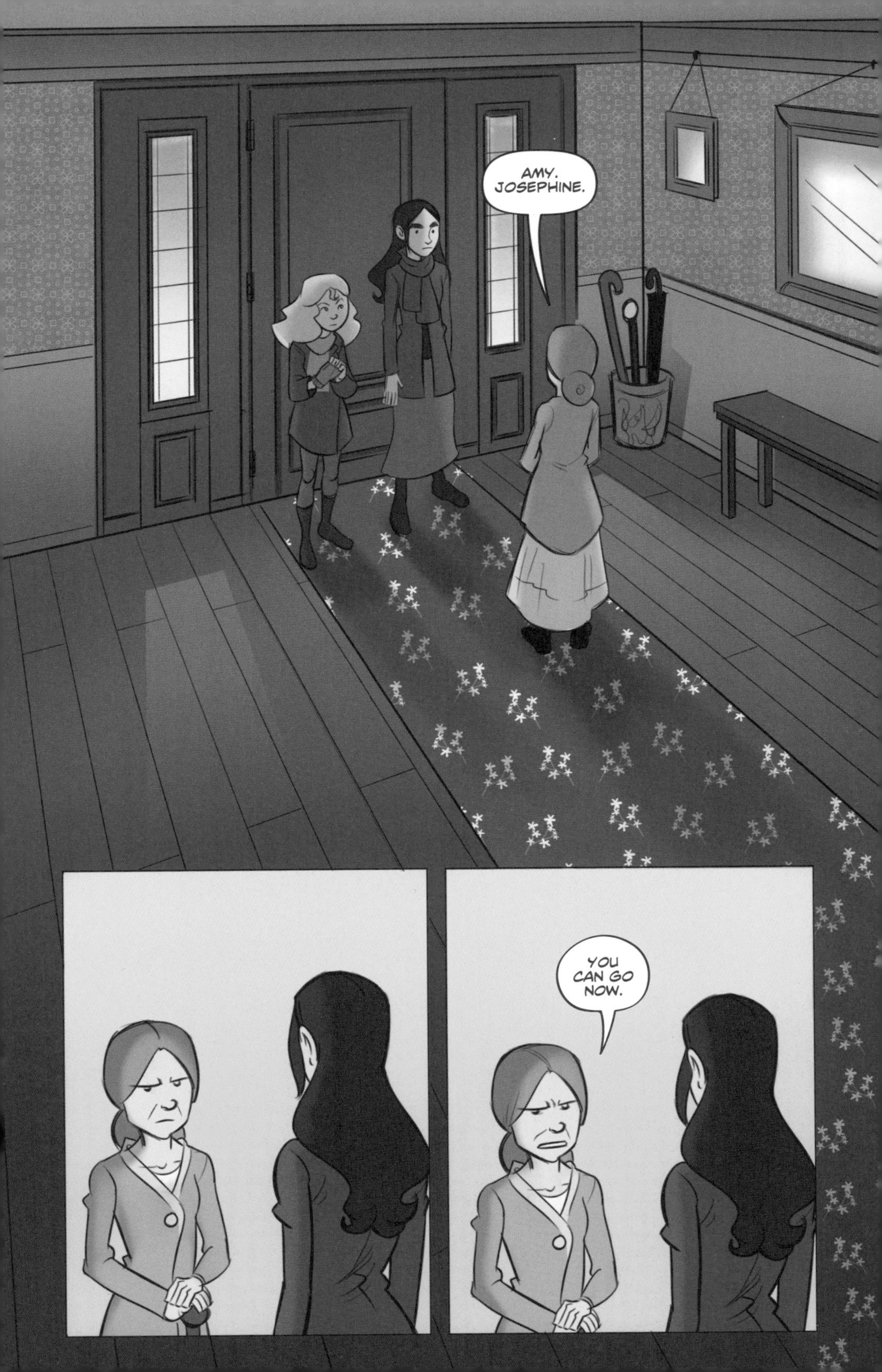
AMY. JOSEPHINE.
YOU CAN GO NOW.

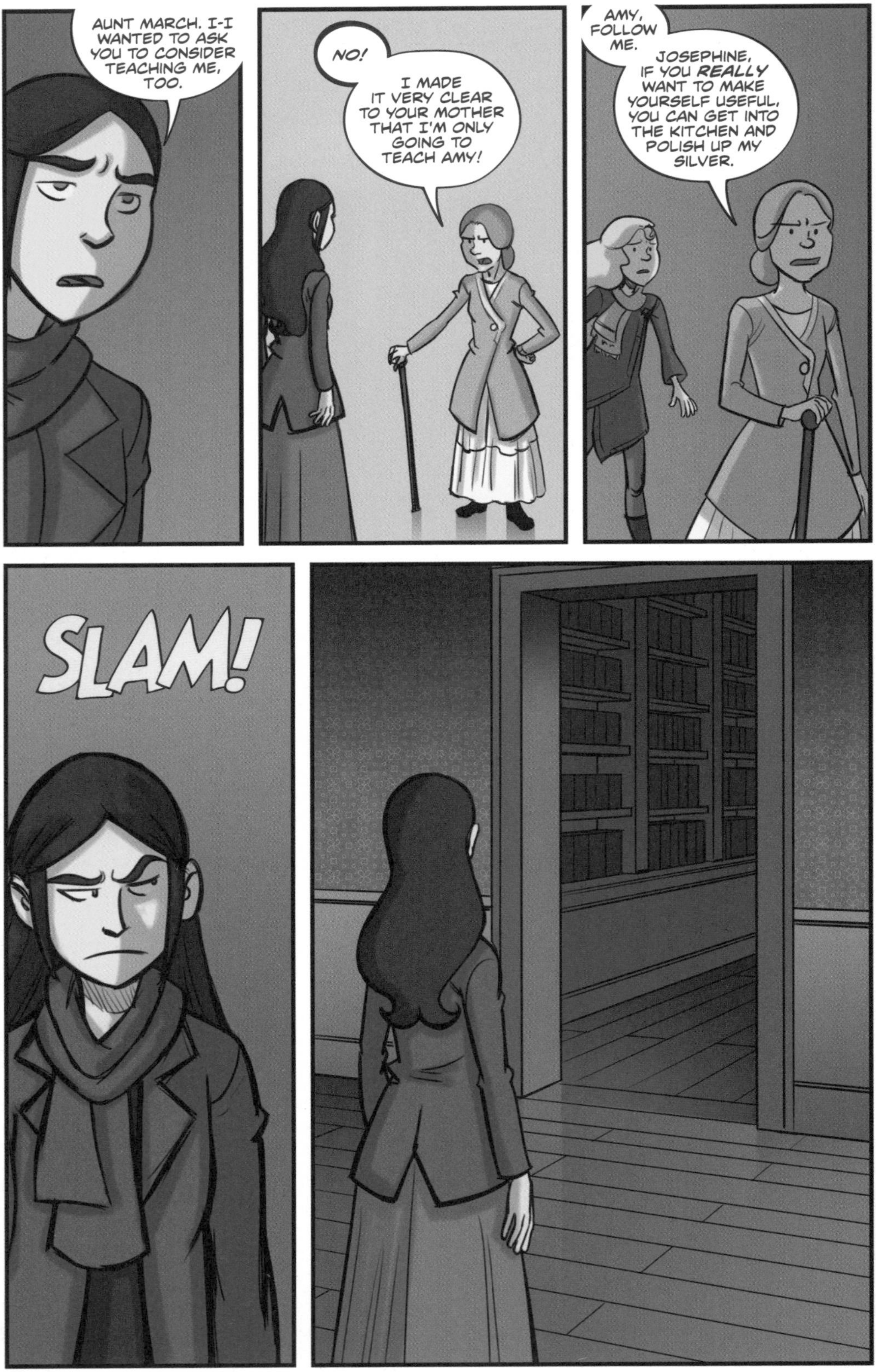
AUNT MARCH. I-I WANTED TO ASK YOU TO CONSIDER TEACHING ME, TOO.
NO!
I MADE IT VERY CLEAR TO YOUR MOTHER THAT I'M ONLY GOING TO TEACH AMY!
AMY, FOLLOW ME.
JOSEPHINE, IF YOU **REALLY** WANT TO MAKE YOURSELF USEFUL, YOU CAN GET INTO THE KITCHEN AND POLISH UP MY SILVER.
SLAM!

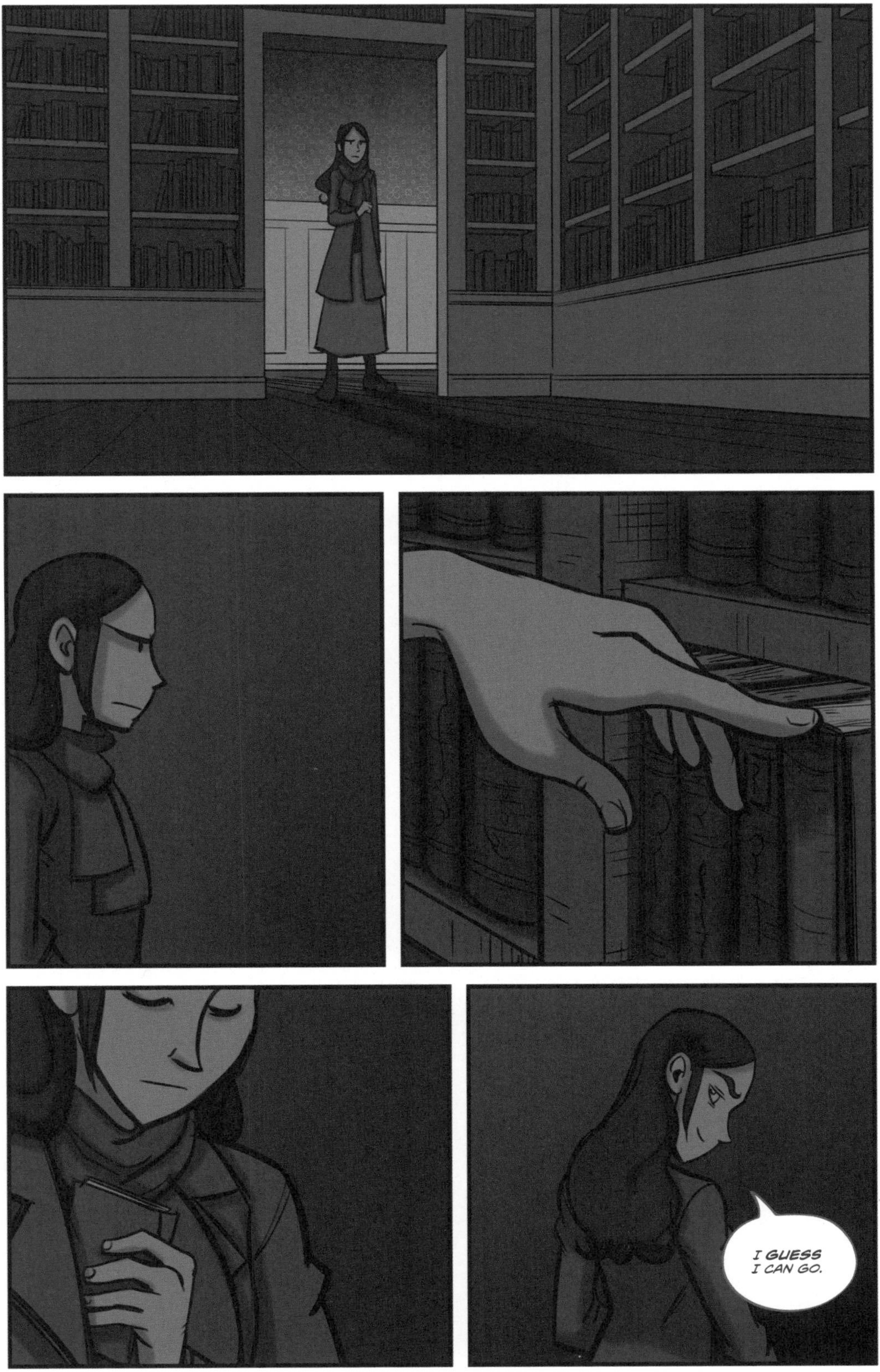
I GUESS
I CAN GO.

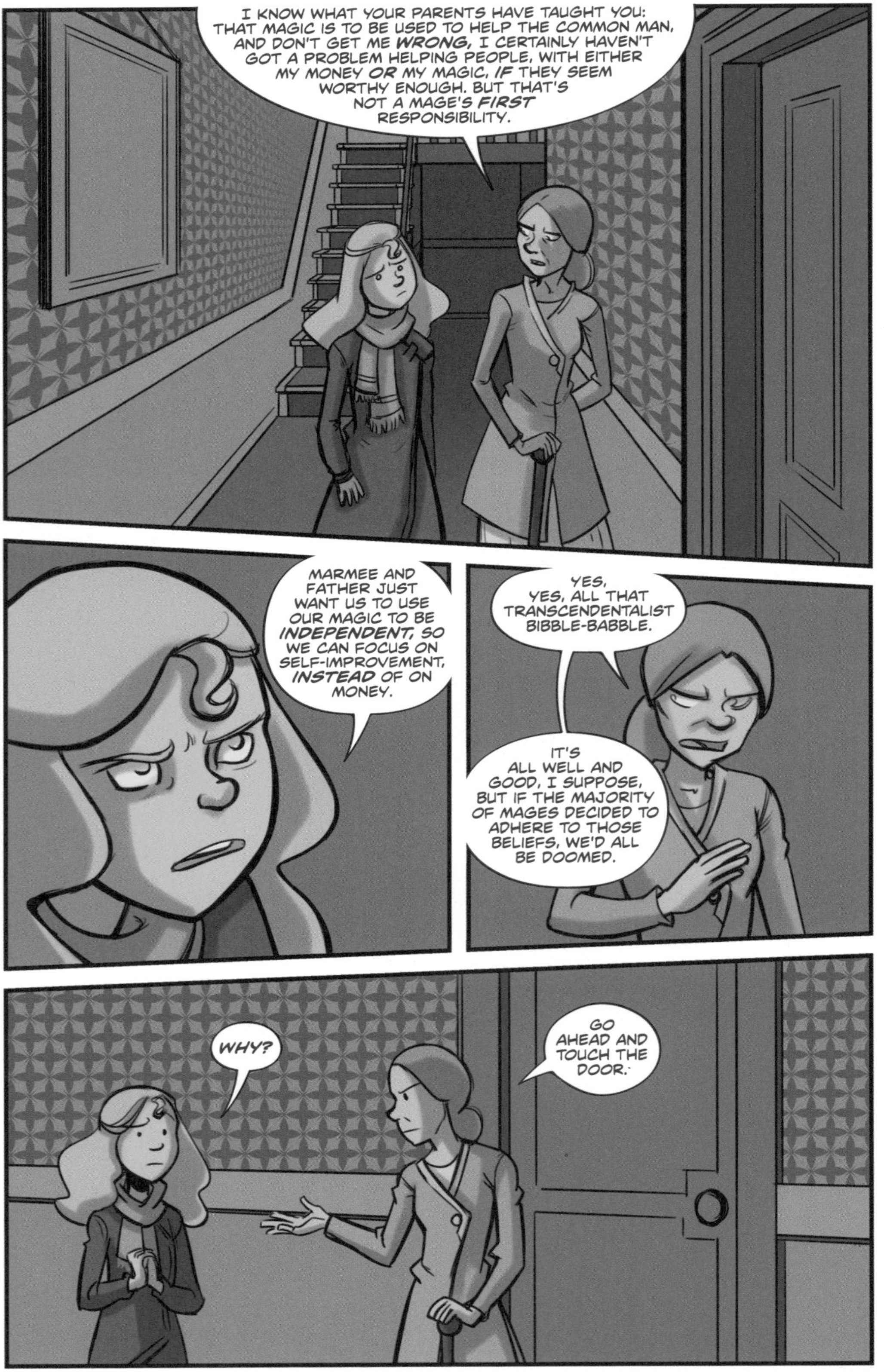
I KNOW WHAT YOUR PARENTS HAVE TAUGHT YOU: THAT MAGIC IS TO BE USED TO HELP THE COMMON MAN, AND DON'T GET ME WRONG, I CERTAINLY HAVEN'T GOT A PROBLEM HELPING PEOPLE, WITH EITHER MY MONEY OR MY MAGIC, IF THEY SEEM WORTHY ENOUGH. BUT THAT'S NOT A MAGE'S FIRST RESPONSIBILITY.
MARMEE AND FATHER JUST WANT US TO USE OUR MAGIC TO BE INDEPENDENT, SO WE CAN FOCUS ON SELF-IMPROVEMENT, INSTEAD OF ON MONEY.
YES, YES, ALL THAT TRANSCENDENTALIST BIBBLE-BABBLE.
IT'S ALL WELL AND GOOD, I SUPPOSE, BUT IF THE MAJORITY OF MAGES DECIDED TO ADHERE TO THOSE BELIEFS, WE'D ALL BE DOOMED.
GO AHEAD AND TOUCH THE DOOR.
WHY?

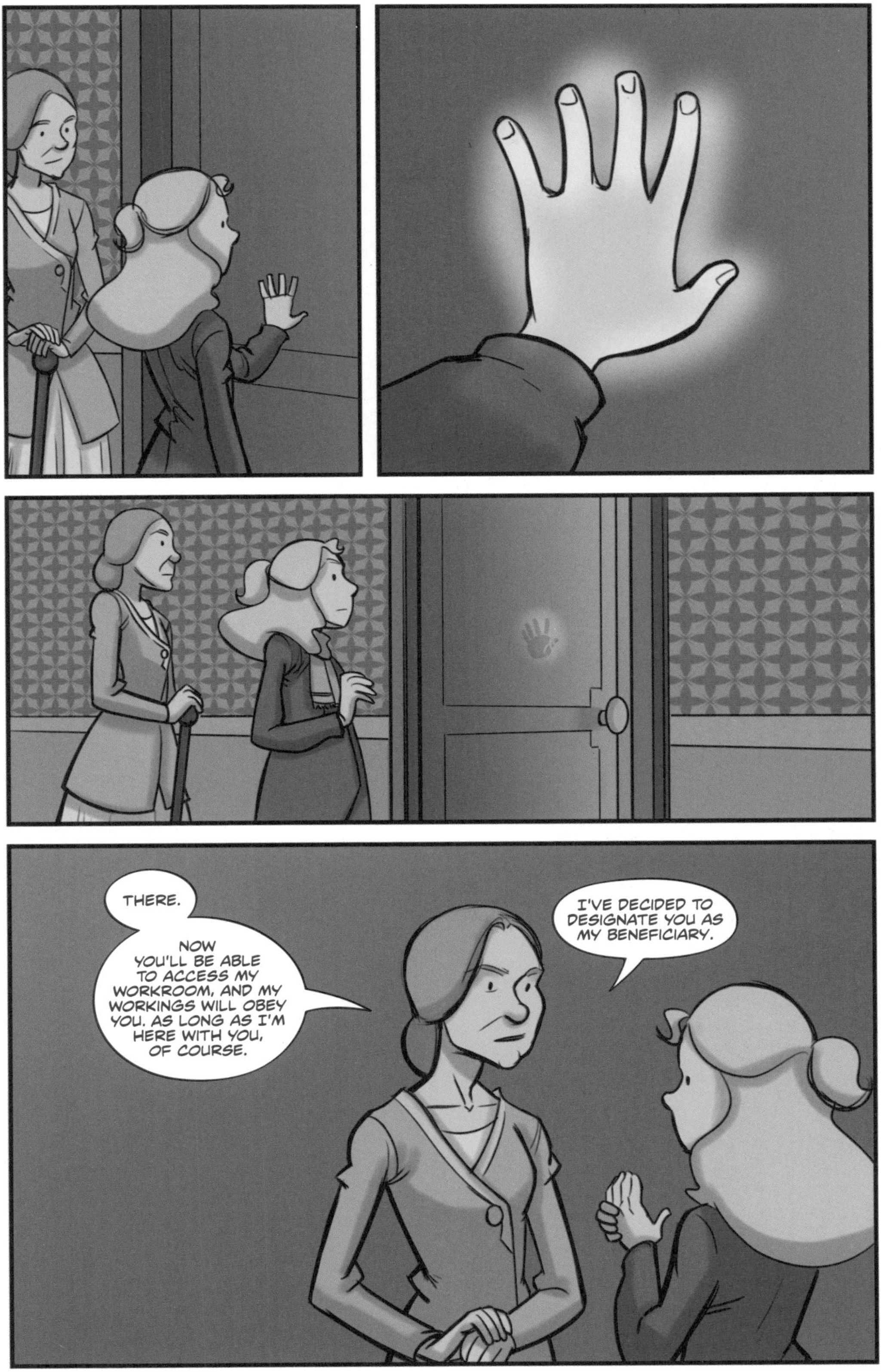
THERE.
NOW YOU'LL BE ABLE TO ACCESS MY WORKROOM, AND MY WORKINGS WILL OBEY YOU. AS LONG AS I'M HERE WITH YOU, OF COURSE.
I'VE DECIDED TO DESIGNATE YOU AS MY BENEFICIARY.

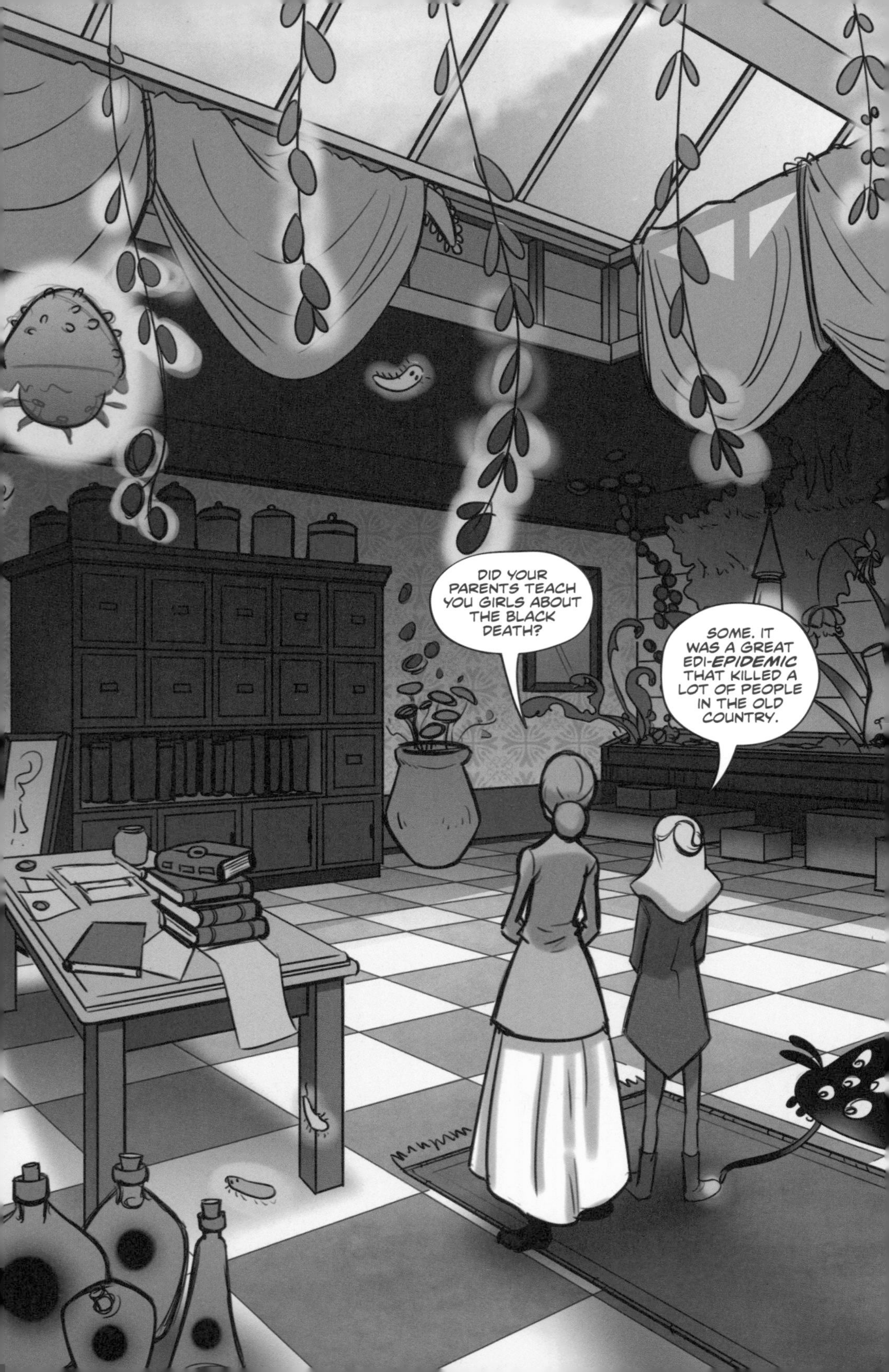
DID YOUR PARENTS TEACH YOU GIRLS ABOUT THE BLACK DEATH?
SOME. IT WAS A GREAT EDI-EPIDEMIC THAT KILLED A LOT OF PEOPLE IN THE OLD COUNTRY.

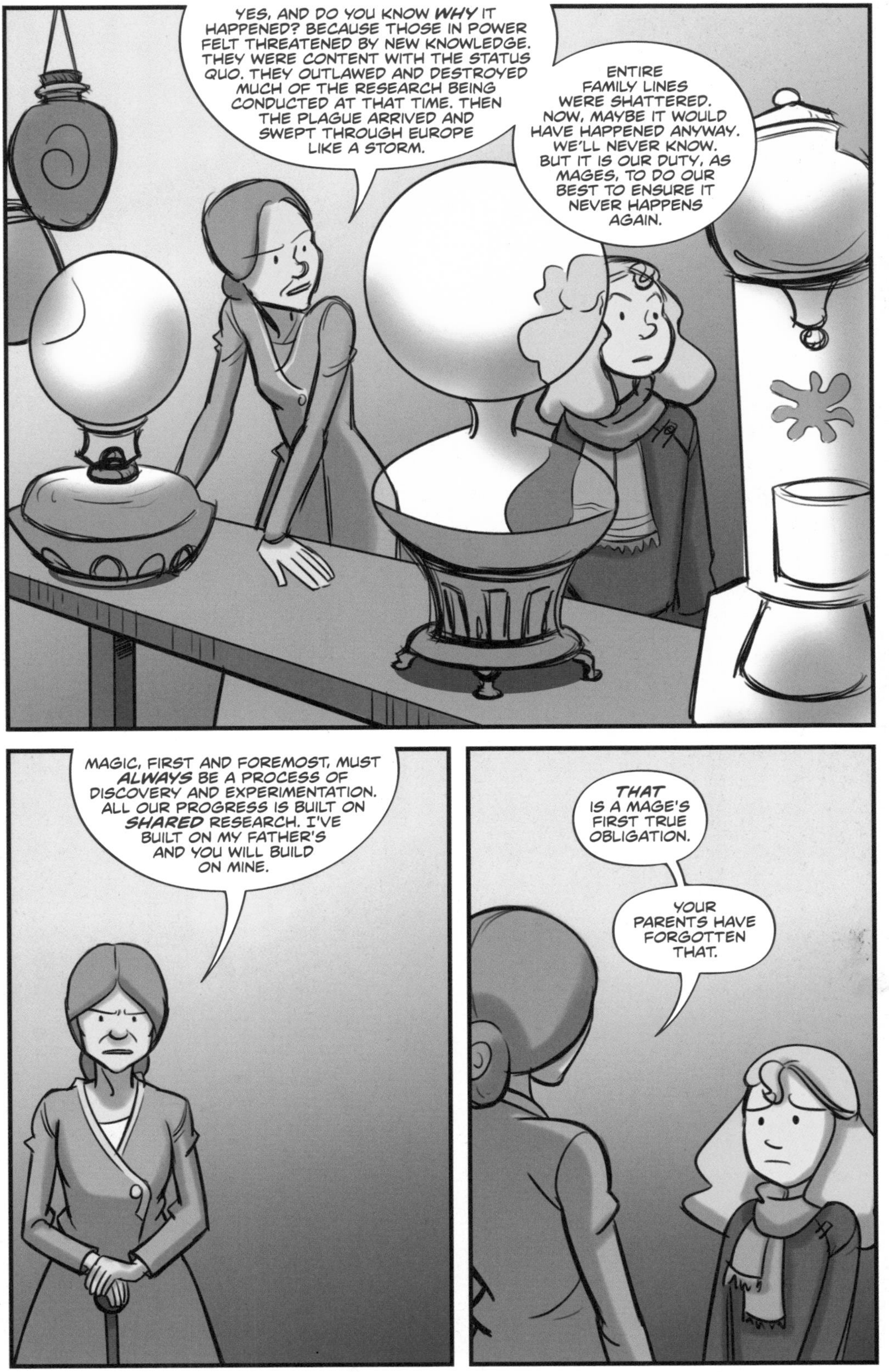
YES, AND DO YOU KNOW WHY IT HAPPENED? BECAUSE THOSE IN POWER FELT THREATENED BY NEW KNOWLEDGE. THEY WERE CONTENT WITH THE STATUS QUO. THEY OUTLAWED AND DESTROYED MUCH OF THE RESEARCH BEING CONDUCTED AT THAT TIME. THEN THE PLAGUE ARRIVED AND SWEPT THROUGH EUROPE LIKE A STORM.
ENTIRE FAMILY LINES WERE SHATTERED. NOW, MAYBE IT WOULD HAVE HAPPENED ANYWAY. WE'LL NEVER KNOW. BUT IT IS OUR DUTY, AS MAGES, TO DO OUR BEST TO ENSURE IT NEVER HAPPENS AGAIN.
MAGIC, FIRST AND FOREMOST, MUST ALWAYS BE A PROCESS OF DISCOVERY AND EXPERIMENTATION. ALL OUR PROGRESS IS BUILT ON SHARED RESEARCH. I'VE BUILT ON MY FATHER'S AND YOU WILL BUILD ON MINE.
THAT IS A MAGE'S FIRST TRUE OBLIGATION.
YOUR PARENTS HAVE FORGOTTEN THAT.

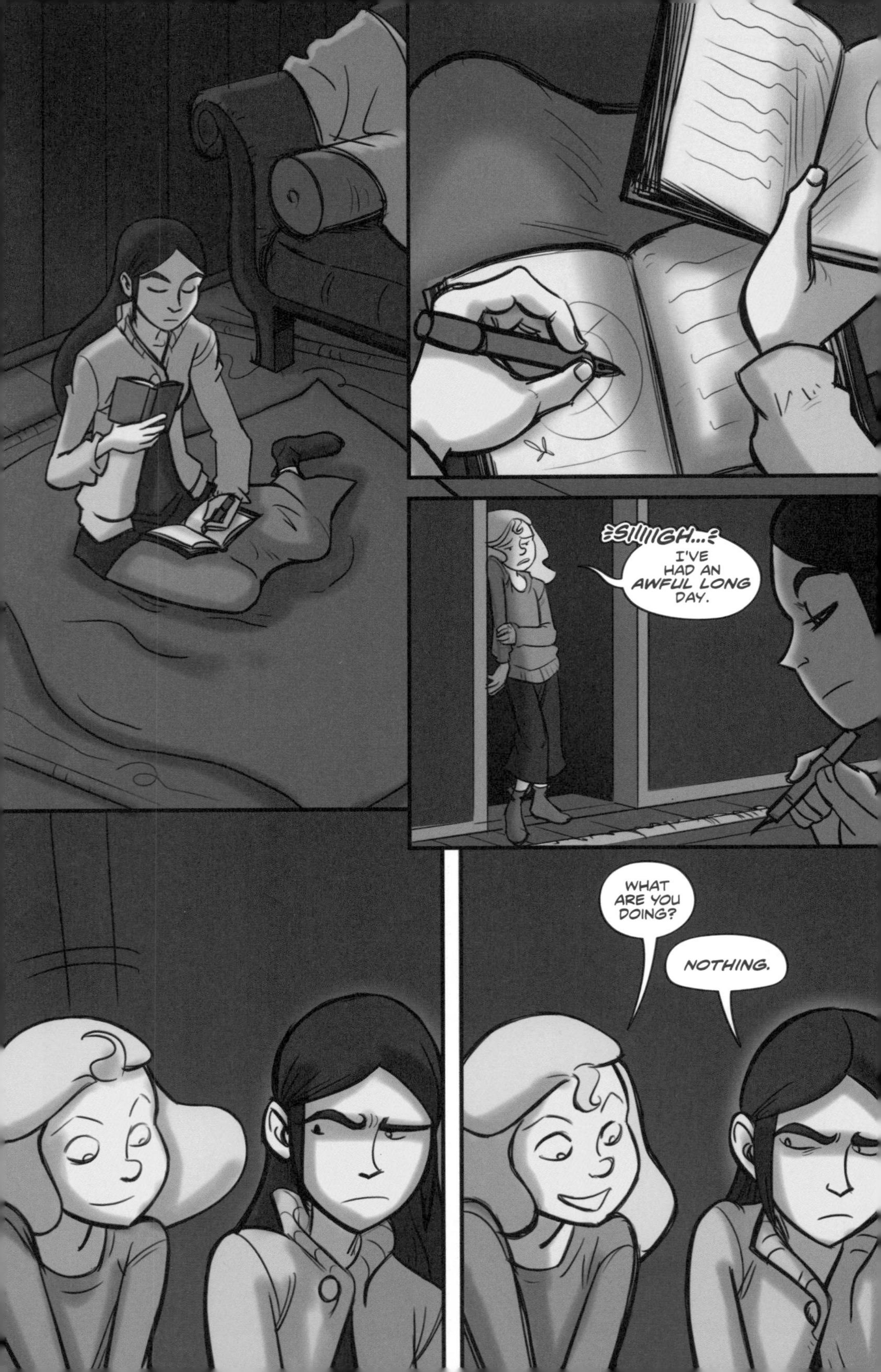
SIIIIGH...
I'VE HAD AN AWFUL LONG DAY.
WHAT ARE YOU DOING?
NOTHING.

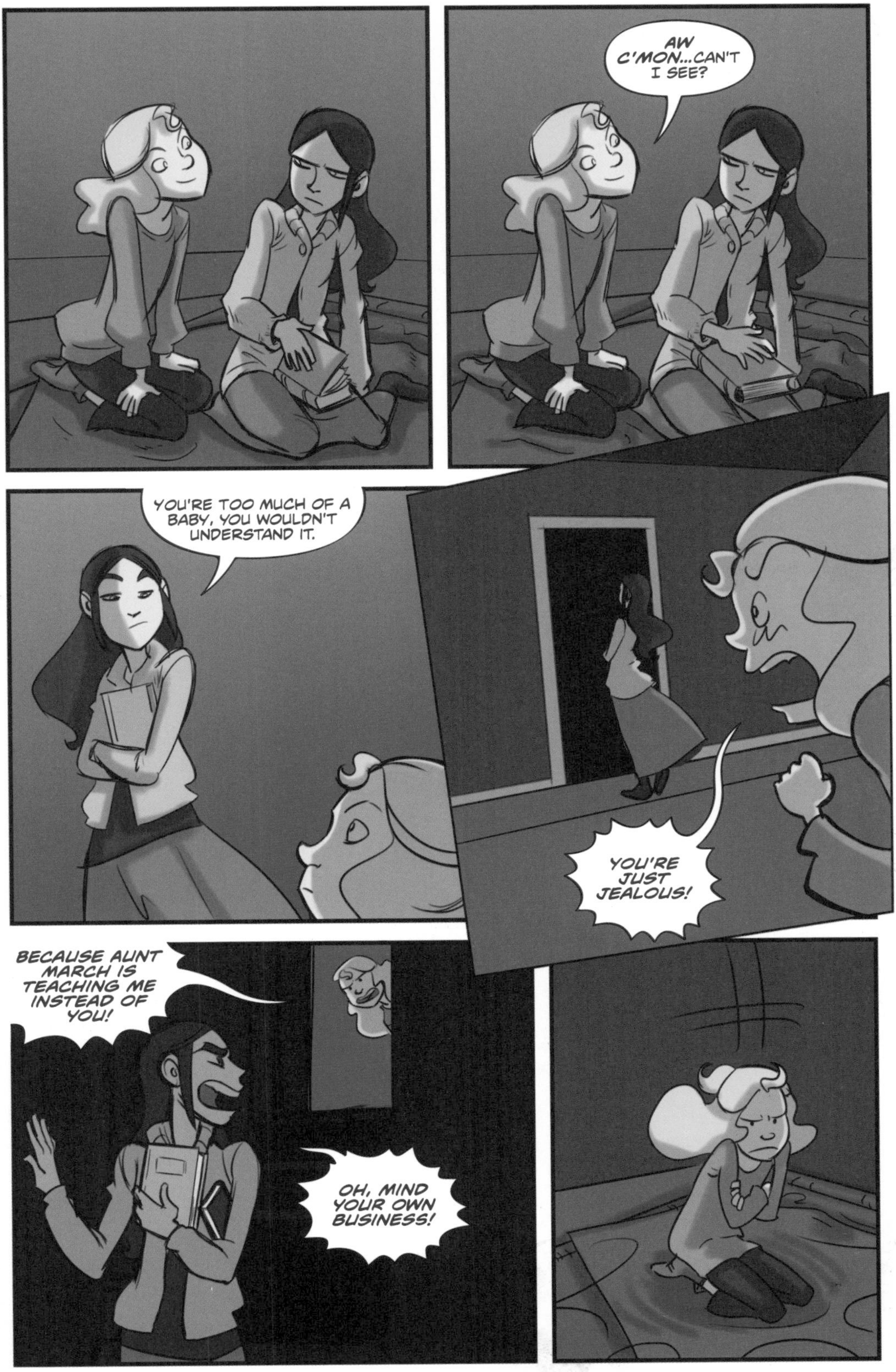
AW C'MON...CAN'T I SEE?
YOU'RE TOO MUCH OF A BABY, YOU WOULDN'T UNDERSTAND IT.
YOU'RE JUST JEALOUS!
BECAUSE AUNT MARCH IS TEACHING ME INSTEAD OF YOU!
OH, MIND YOUR OWN BUSINESS!

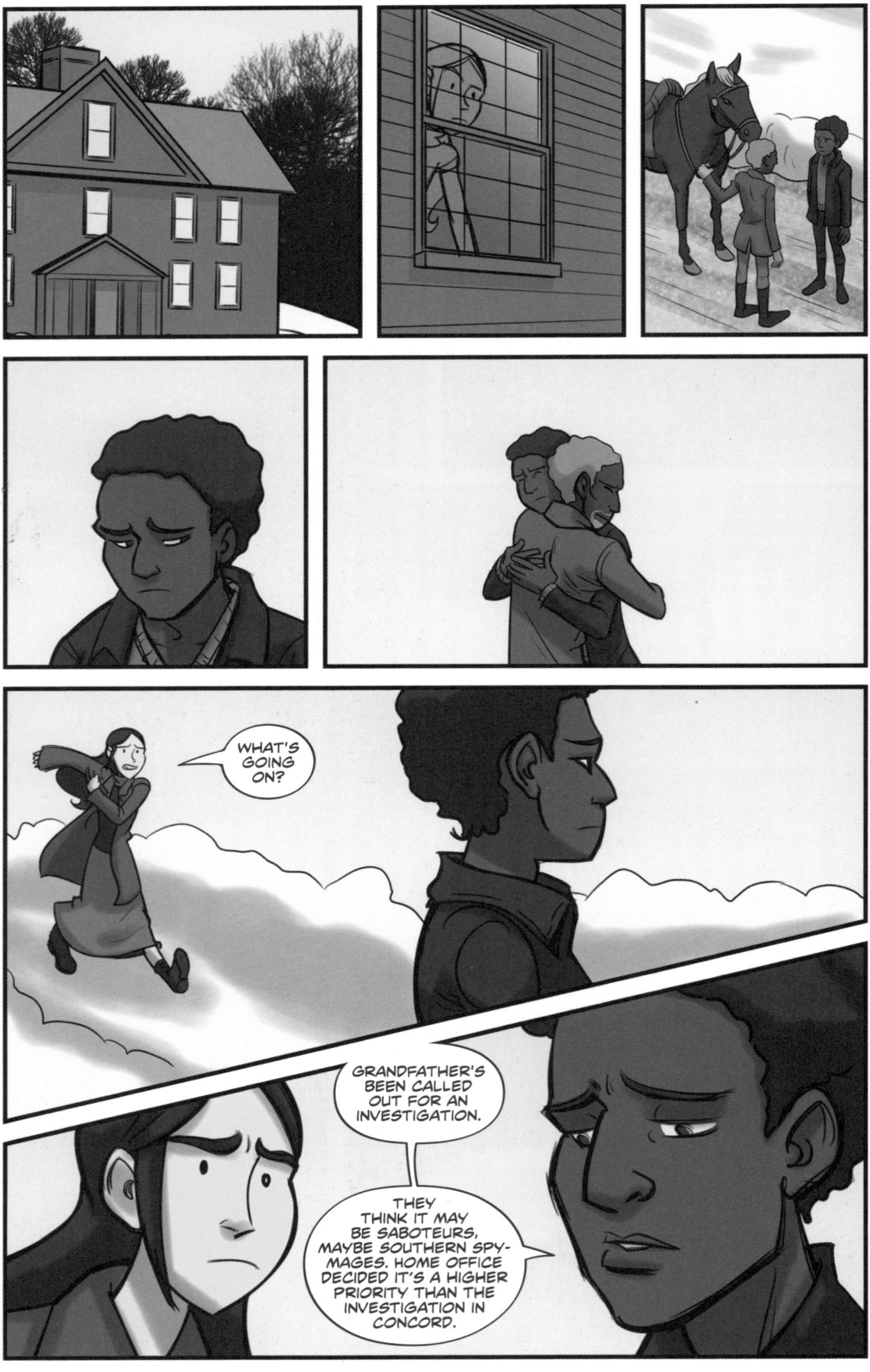
WHAT'S GOING ON?
GRANDFATHER'S BEEN CALLED OUT FOR AN INVESTIGATION.
THEY THINK IT MAY BE SABOTEURS, MAYBE SOUTHERN SPY-MAGES. HOME OFFICE DECIDED IT'S A HIGHER PRIORITY THAN THE INVESTIGATION IN CONCORD.

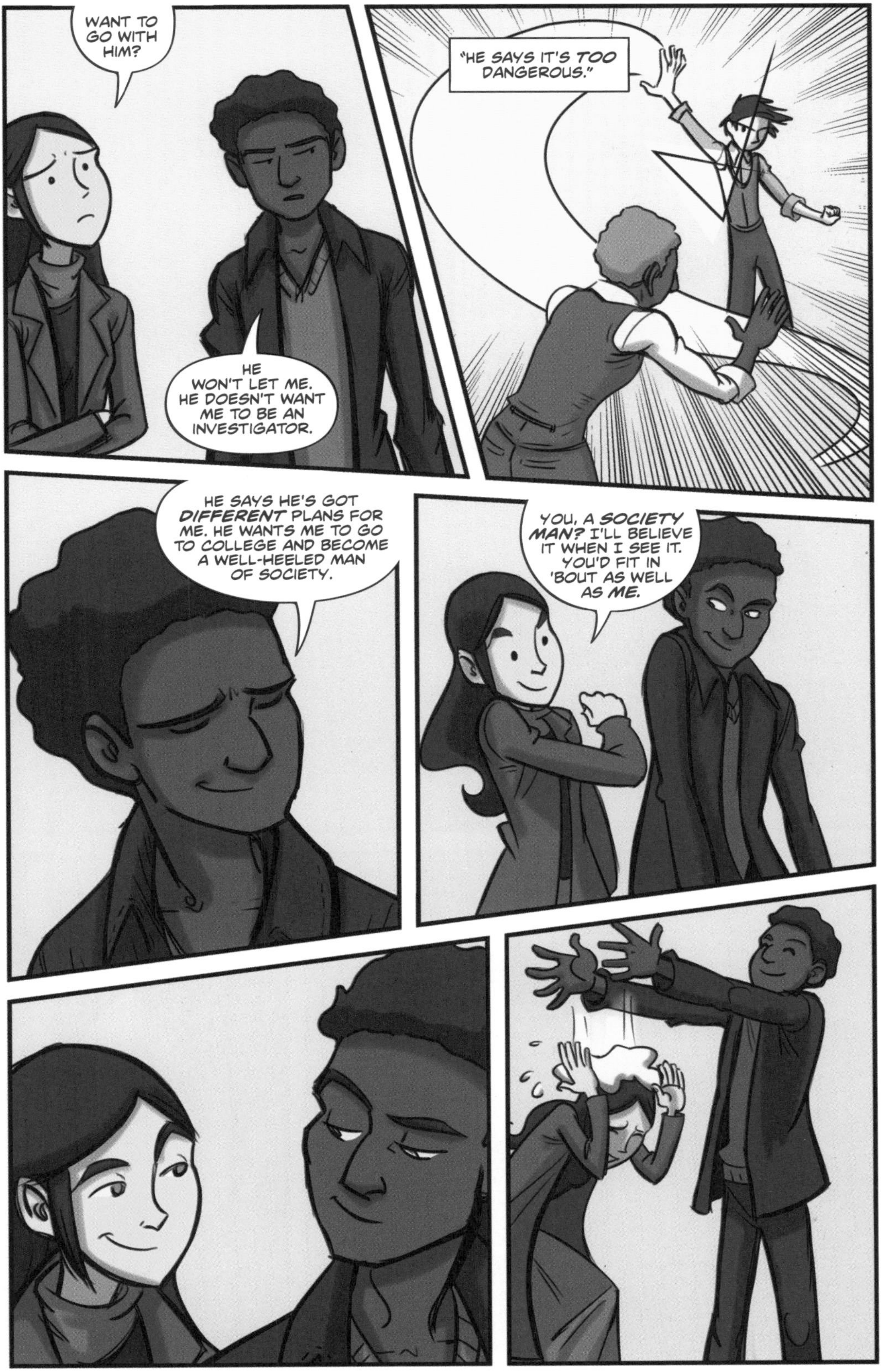
WANT TO GO WITH HIM?
HE WON'T LET ME. HE DOESN'T WANT ME TO BE AN INVESTIGATOR.
"HE SAYS IT'S TOO DANGEROUS."
HE SAYS HE'S GOT DIFFERENT PLANS FOR ME. HE WANTS ME TO GO TO COLLEGE AND BECOME A WELL-HEELED MAN OF SOCIETY.
YOU, A SOCIETY MAN? I'LL BELIEVE IT WHEN I SEE IT. YOU'D FIT IN 'BOUT AS WELL AS ME.

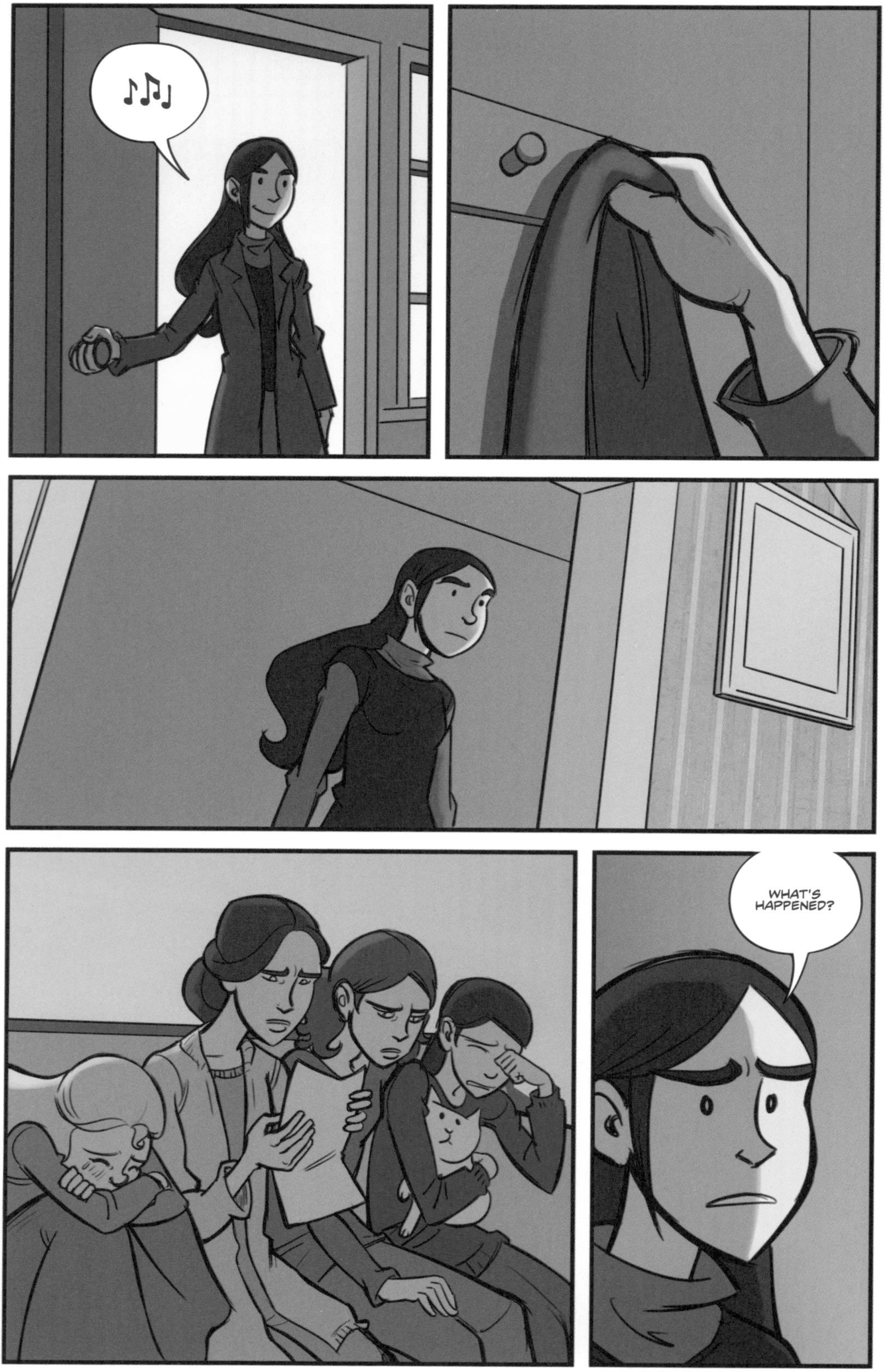
WHAT'S HAPPENED?

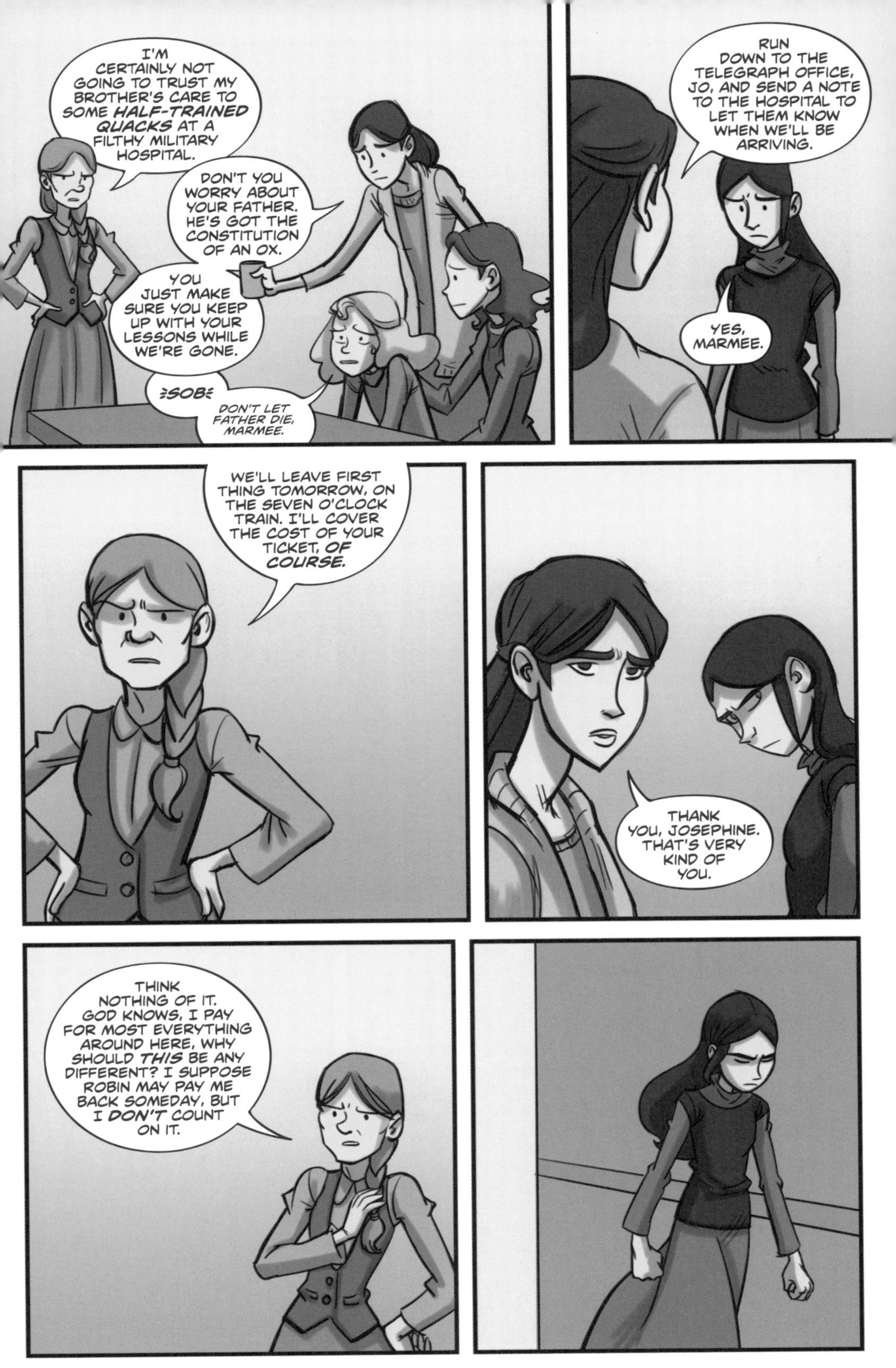
I'M CERTAINLY NOT GOING TO TRUST MY BROTHER'S CARE TO SOME HALF-TRAINED QUACKS AT A FILTHY MILITARY HOSPITAL.
DON'T YOU WORRY ABOUT YOUR FATHER. HE'S GOT THE CONSTITUTION OF AN OX.
YOU JUST MAKE SURE YOU KEEP UP WITH YOUR LESSONS WHILE WE'RE GONE.
SOB
DON'T LET FATHER DIE, MARMEE.
RUN DOWN TO THE TELEGRAPH OFFICE, JO, AND SEND A NOTE TO THE HOSPITAL TO LET THEM KNOW WHEN WE'LL BE ARRIVING.
YES, MARMEE.
WE'LL LEAVE FIRST THING TOMORROW, ON THE SEVEN O'CLOCK TRAIN. I'LL COVER THE COST OF YOUR TICKET, OF COURSE.
THANK YOU, JOSEPHINE. THAT'S VERY KIND OF YOU.
THINK NOTHING OF IT. GOD KNOWS, I PAY FOR MOST EVERYTHING AROUND HERE, WHY SHOULD THIS BE ANY DIFFERENT? I SUPPOSE ROBIN MAY PAY ME BACK SOMEDAY, BUT I DON'T COUNT ON IT.

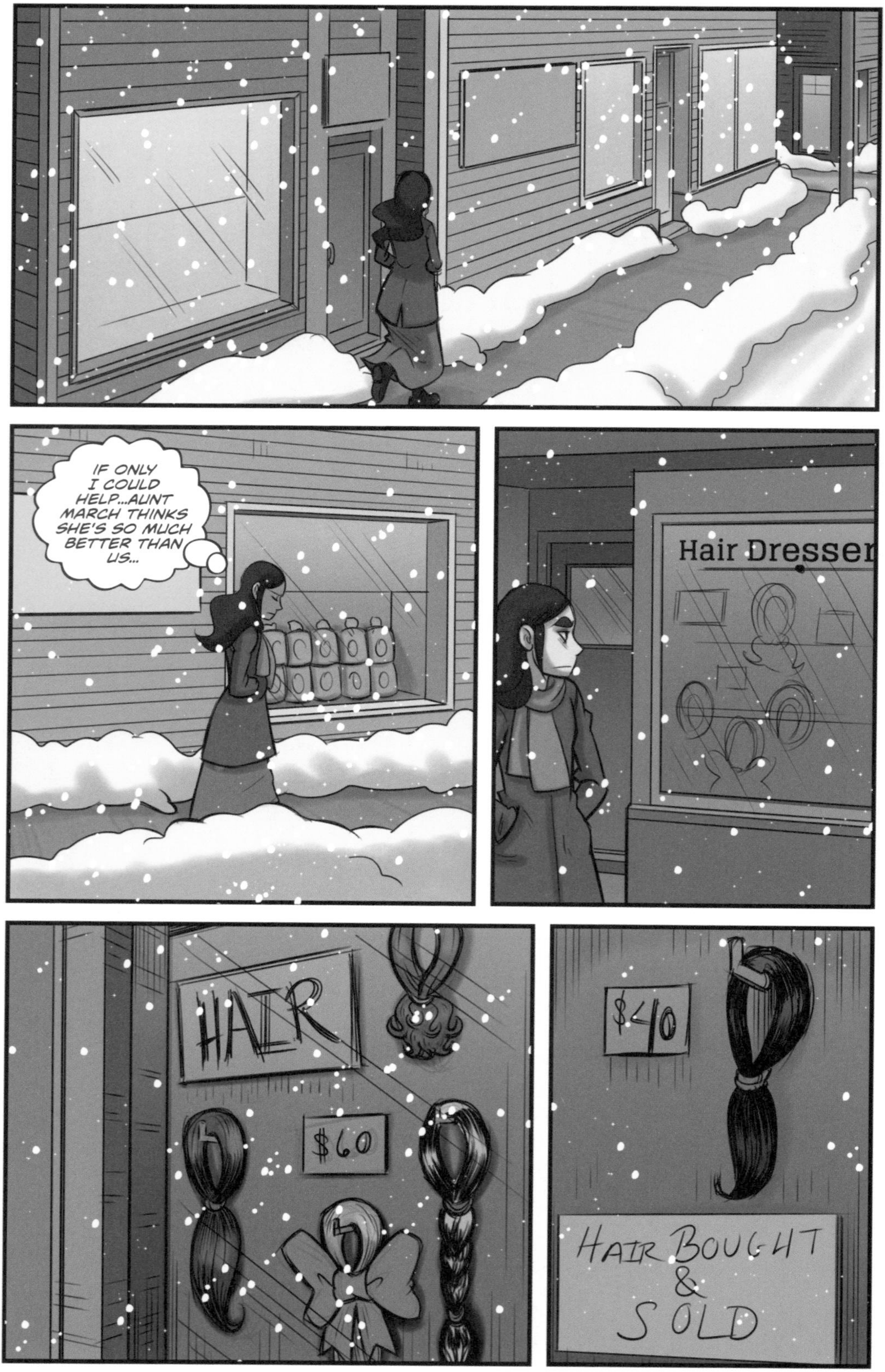
IF ONLY I COULD HELP...AUNT MARCH THINKS SHE'S SO MUCH BETTER THAN US...
Hair Dresser
HAIR
$60
$40
HAIR BOUGHT & SOLD

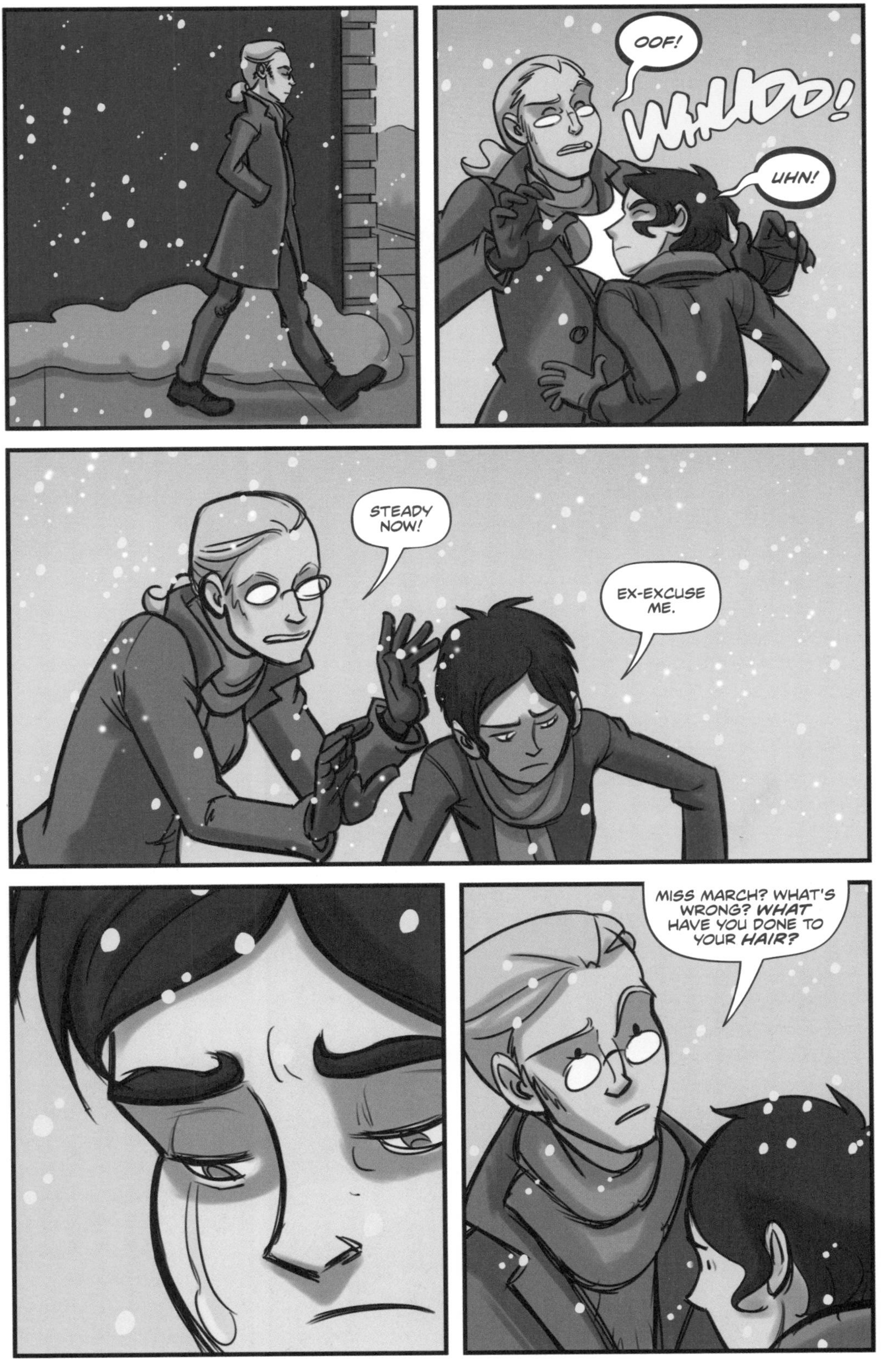
OOF!
WHUDD!
UHN!
STEADY NOW!
EX-EXCUSE ME.
MISS MARCH? WHAT'S WRONG? *WHAT* HAVE YOU DONE TO YOUR *HAIR?*

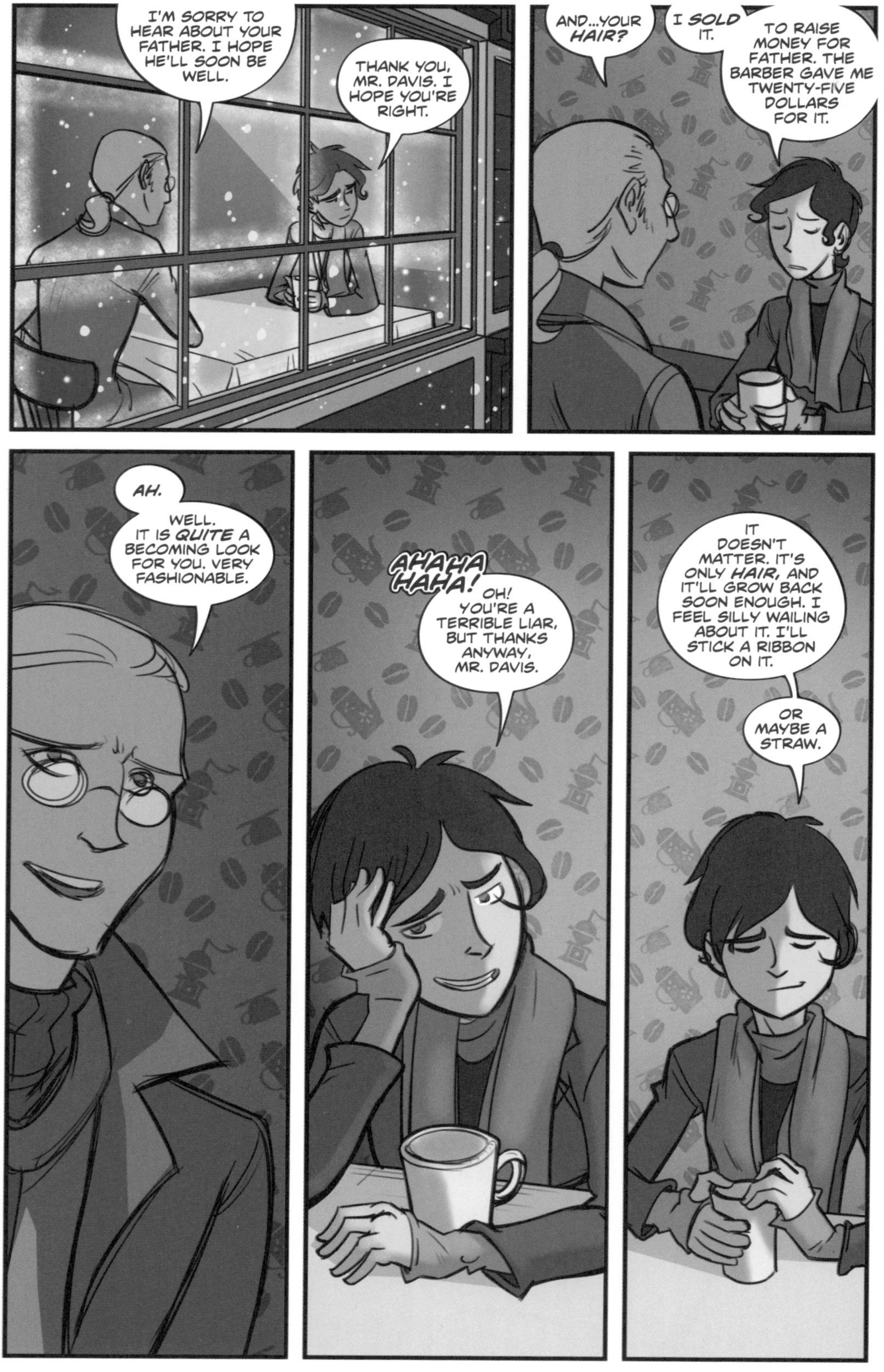
I'M SORRY TO HEAR ABOUT YOUR FATHER. I HOPE HE'LL SOON BE WELL.
THANK YOU, MR. DAVIS. I HOPE YOU'RE RIGHT.
AND...YOUR HAIR?
I SOLD IT.
TO RAISE MONEY FOR FATHER. THE BARBER GAVE ME TWENTY-FIVE DOLLARS FOR IT.
AH.
WELL. IT IS QUITE A BECOMING LOOK FOR YOU. VERY FASHIONABLE.
AHAHA HAHA!
OH! YOU'RE A TERRIBLE LIAR, BUT THANKS ANYWAY, MR. DAVIS.
IT DOESN'T MATTER. IT'S ONLY HAIR, AND IT'LL GROW BACK SOON ENOUGH. I FEEL SILLY WAILING ABOUT IT. I'LL STICK A RIBBON ON IT.
OR MAYBE A STRAW.

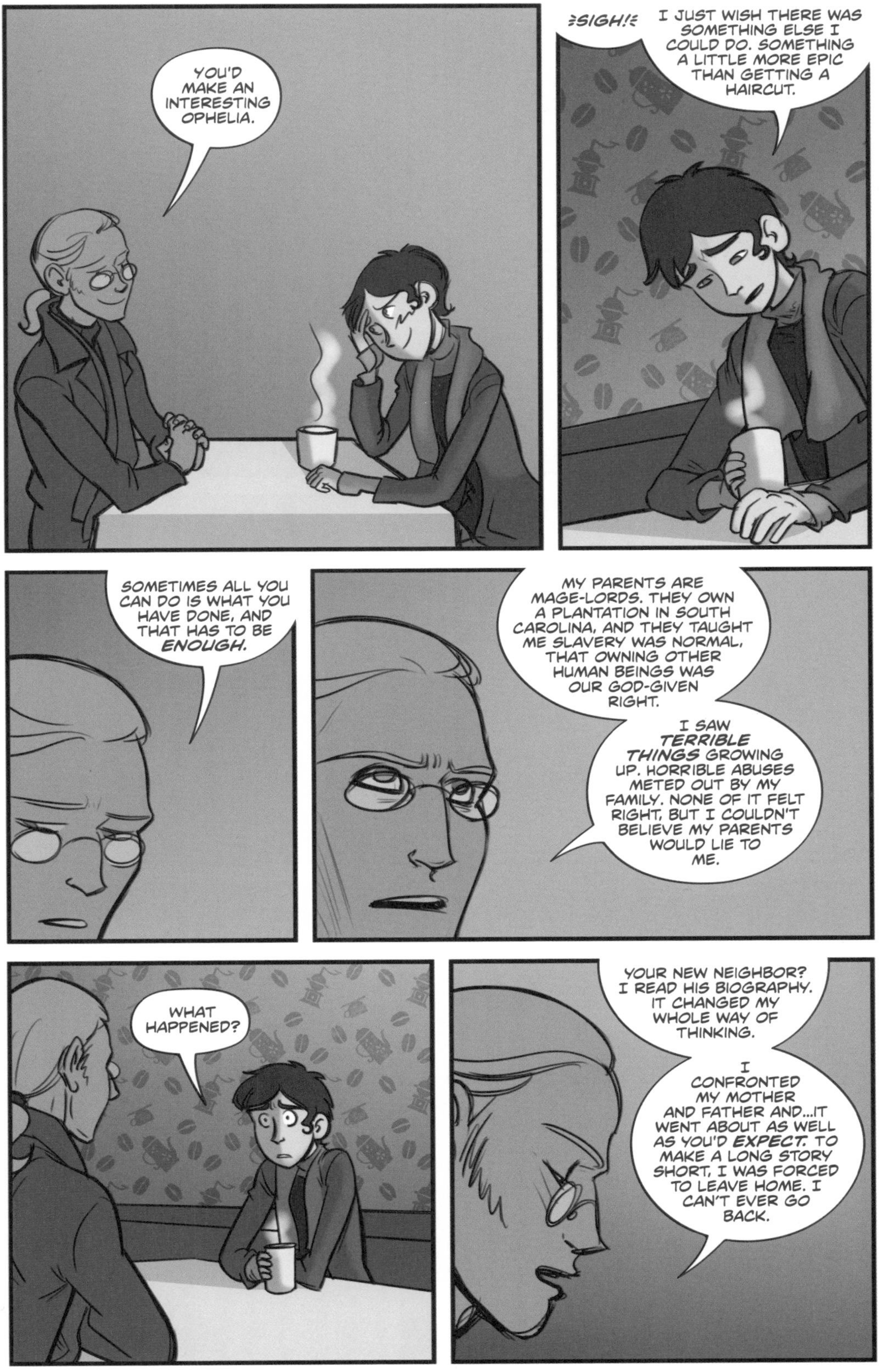
YOU'D MAKE AN INTERESTING OPHELIA.
SIGH!
I JUST WISH THERE WAS SOMETHING ELSE I COULD DO. SOMETHING A LITTLE MORE EPIC THAN GETTING A HAIRCUT.
SOMETIMES ALL YOU CAN DO IS WHAT YOU HAVE DONE, AND THAT HAS TO BE ENOUGH.
MY PARENTS ARE MAGE-LORDS. THEY OWN A PLANTATION IN SOUTH CAROLINA, AND THEY TAUGHT ME SLAVERY WAS NORMAL, THAT OWNING OTHER HUMAN BEINGS WAS OUR GOD-GIVEN RIGHT.
I SAW TERRIBLE THINGS GROWING UP. HORRIBLE ABUSES METED OUT BY MY FAMILY. NONE OF IT FELT RIGHT, BUT I COULDN'T BELIEVE MY PARENTS WOULD LIE TO ME.
WHAT HAPPENED?
YOUR NEW NEIGHBOR? I READ HIS BIOGRAPHY. IT CHANGED MY WHOLE WAY OF THINKING.
I CONFRONTED MY MOTHER AND FATHER AND...IT WENT ABOUT AS WELL AS YOU'D EXPECT. TO MAKE A LONG STORY SHORT, I WAS FORCED TO LEAVE HOME. I CAN'T EVER GO BACK.

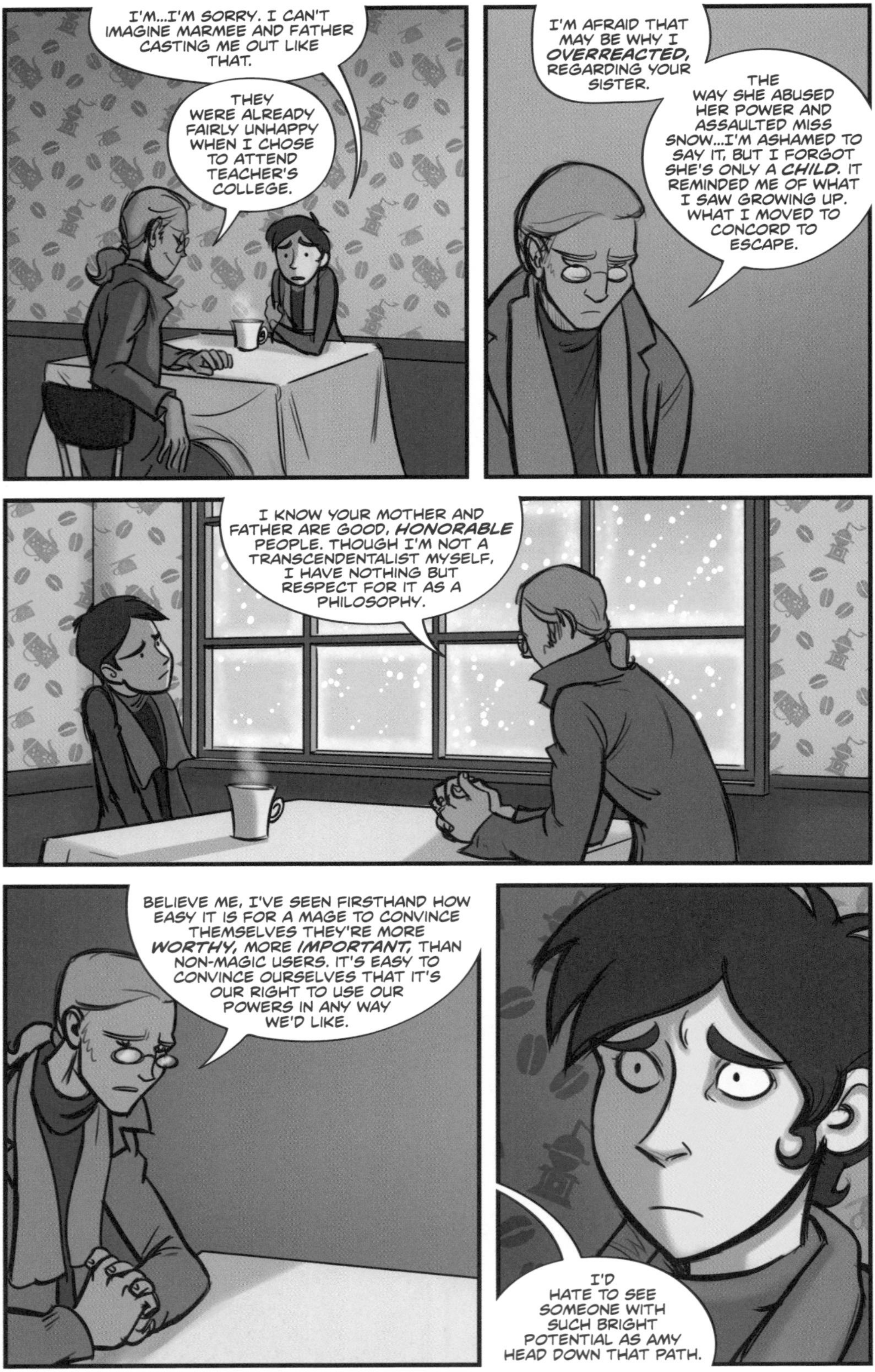
I'M...I'M SORRY. I CAN'T IMAGINE MARMEE AND FATHER CASTING ME OUT LIKE THAT.
THEY WERE ALREADY FAIRLY UNHAPPY WHEN I CHOSE TO ATTEND TEACHER'S COLLEGE.
I'M AFRAID THAT MAY BE WHY I *OVERREACTED,* REGARDING YOUR SISTER.
THE WAY SHE ABUSED HER POWER AND ASSAULTED MISS SNOW...I'M ASHAMED TO SAY IT, BUT I FORGOT SHE'S ONLY A *CHILD.* IT REMINDED ME OF WHAT I SAW GROWING UP. WHAT I MOVED TO CONCORD TO ESCAPE.
I KNOW YOUR MOTHER AND FATHER ARE GOOD, *HONORABLE* PEOPLE. THOUGH I'M NOT A TRANSCENDENTALIST MYSELF, I HAVE NOTHING BUT RESPECT FOR IT AS A PHILOSOPHY.
BELIEVE ME, I'VE SEEN FIRSTHAND HOW EASY IT IS FOR A MAGE TO CONVINCE THEMSELVES THEY'RE MORE *WORTHY,* MORE *IMPORTANT,* THAN NON-MAGIC USERS. IT'S EASY TO CONVINCE OURSELVES THAT IT'S OUR RIGHT TO USE OUR POWERS IN ANY WAY WE'D LIKE.
I'D HATE TO SEE SOMEONE WITH SUCH BRIGHT POTENTIAL AS AMY HEAD DOWN THAT PATH.

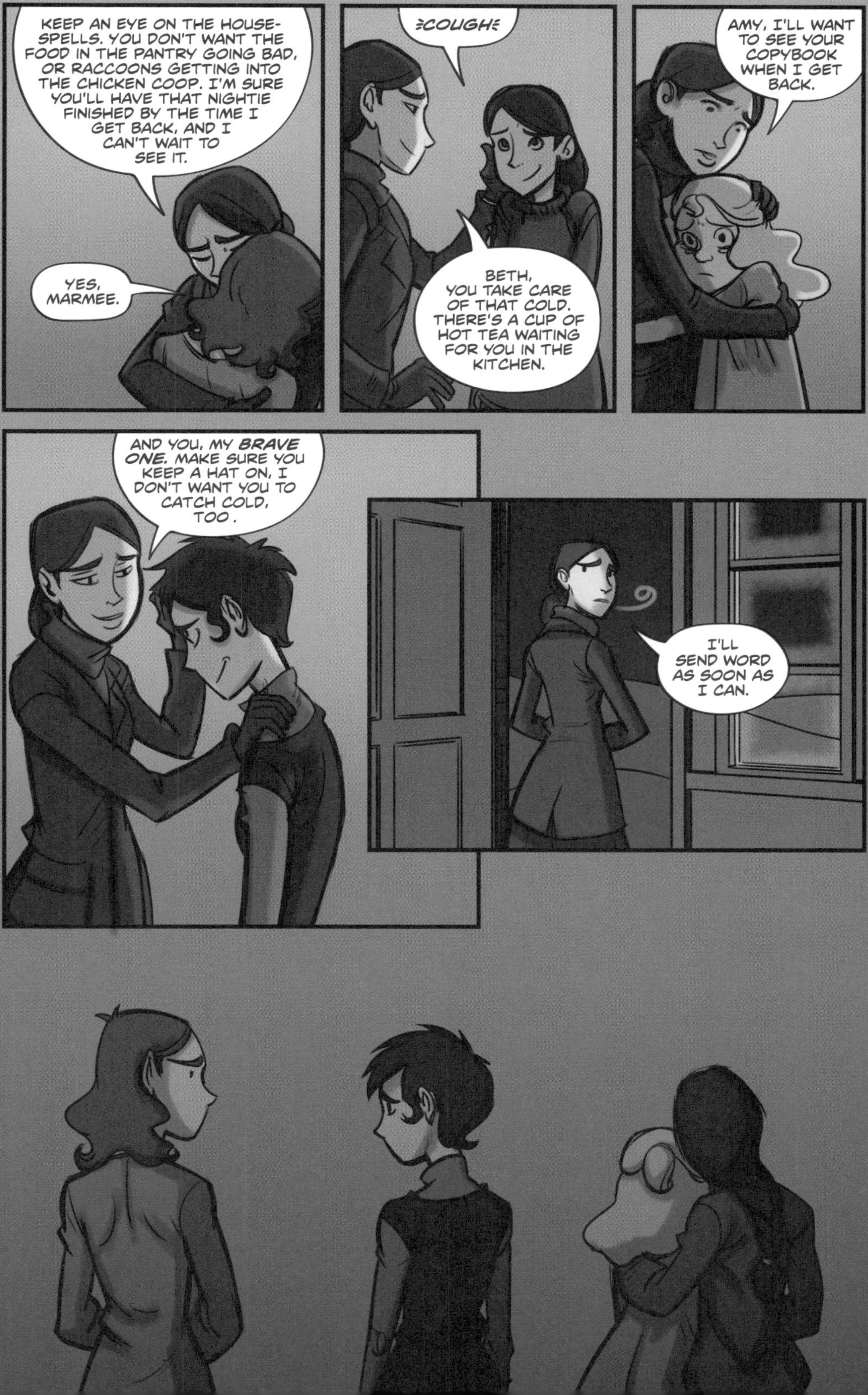
KEEP AN EYE ON THE HOUSE-SPELLS. YOU DON'T WANT THE FOOD IN THE PANTRY GOING BAD, OR RACCOONS GETTING INTO THE CHICKEN COOP. I'M SURE YOU'LL HAVE THAT NIGHTIE FINISHED BY THE TIME I GET BACK, AND I CAN'T WAIT TO SEE IT.
YES, MARMEE.
COUGH
BETH, YOU TAKE CARE OF THAT COLD. THERE'S A CUP OF HOT TEA WAITING FOR YOU IN THE KITCHEN.
AMY, I'LL WANT TO SEE YOUR COPYBOOK WHEN I GET BACK.
AND YOU, MY *BRAVE ONE.* MAKE SURE YOU KEEP A HAT ON, I DON'T WANT YOU TO CATCH COLD, TOO.
I'LL SEND WORD AS SOON AS I CAN.

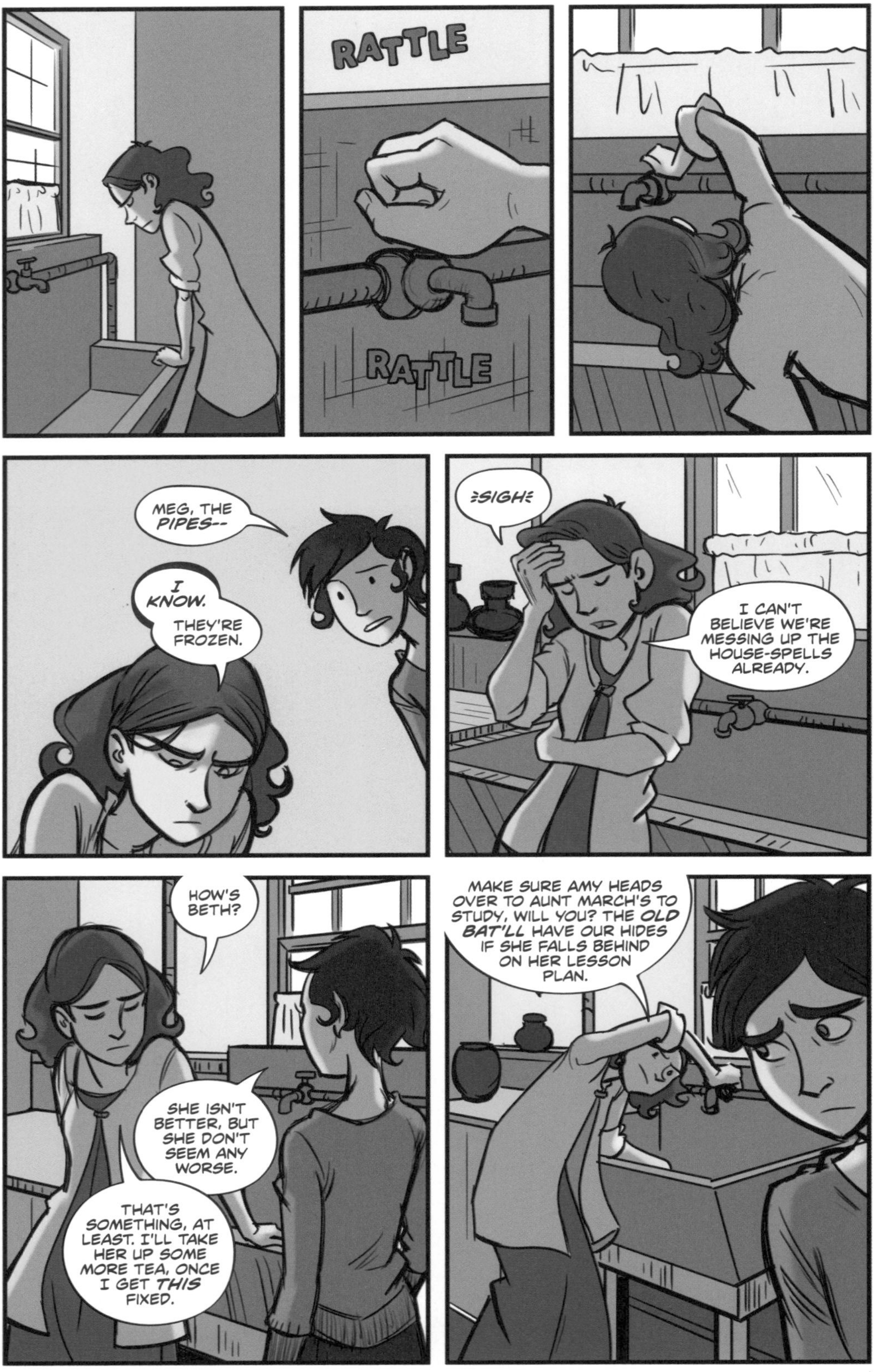
RATTLE
RATTLE
MEG, THE PIPES--
I KNOW. THEY'RE FROZEN.
SIGH
I CAN'T BELIEVE WE'RE MESSING UP THE HOUSE-SPELLS ALREADY.
HOW'S BETH?
SHE ISN'T BETTER, BUT SHE DON'T SEEM ANY WORSE.
THAT'S SOMETHING, AT LEAST. I'LL TAKE HER UP SOME MORE TEA, ONCE I GET THIS FIXED.
MAKE SURE AMY HEADS OVER TO AUNT MARCH'S TO STUDY, WILL YOU? THE OLD BAT'LL HAVE OUR HIDES IF SHE FALLS BEHIND ON HER LESSON PLAN.

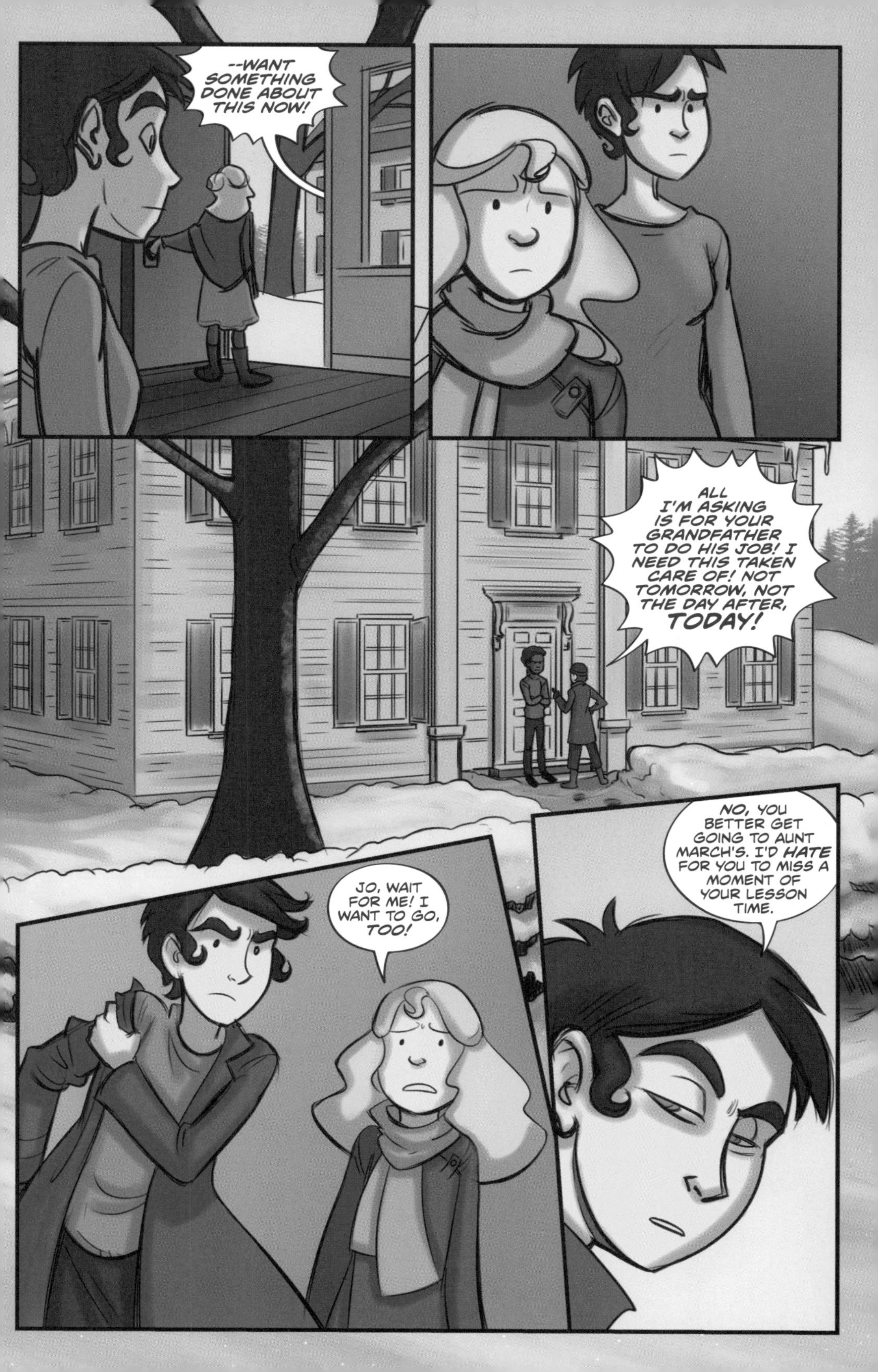
--WANT SOMETHING DONE ABOUT THIS NOW!
ALL I'M ASKING IS FOR YOUR GRANDFATHER TO DO HIS JOB! I NEED THIS TAKEN CARE OF! NOT TOMORROW, NOT THE DAY AFTER, TODAY!
JO, WAIT FOR ME! I WANT TO GO, TOO!
NO, YOU BETTER GET GOING TO AUNT MARCH'S. I'D HATE FOR YOU TO MISS A MOMENT OF YOUR LESSON TIME.

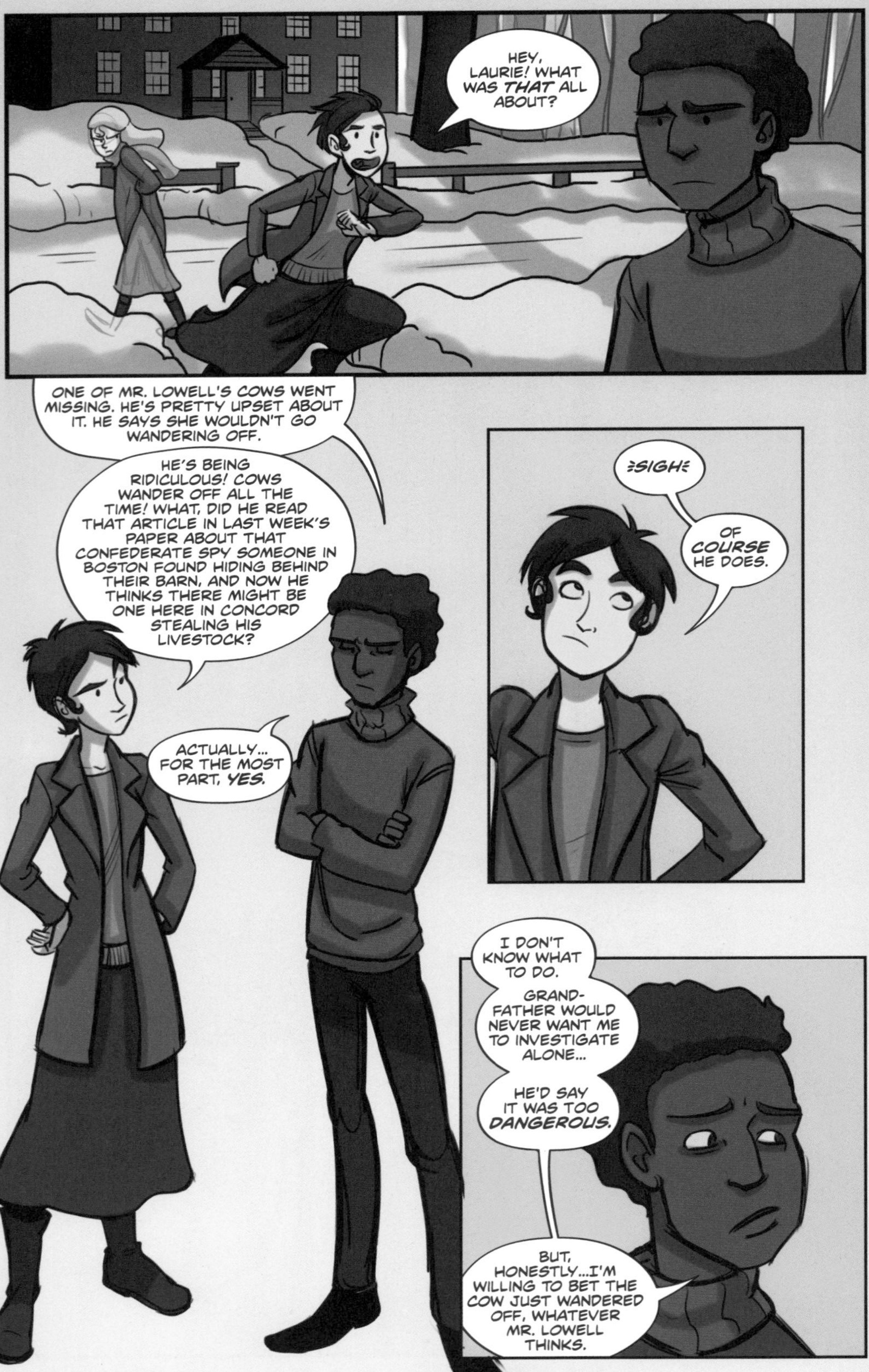
HEY, LAURIE! WHAT WAS THAT ALL ABOUT?
ONE OF MR. LOWELL'S COWS WENT MISSING. HE'S PRETTY UPSET ABOUT IT. HE SAYS SHE WOULDN'T GO WANDERING OFF.
HE'S BEING RIDICULOUS! COWS WANDER OFF ALL THE TIME! WHAT, DID HE READ THAT ARTICLE IN LAST WEEK'S PAPER ABOUT THAT CONFEDERATE SPY SOMEONE IN BOSTON FOUND HIDING BEHIND THEIR BARN, AND NOW HE THINKS THERE MIGHT BE ONE HERE IN CONCORD STEALING HIS LIVESTOCK?
ACTUALLY... FOR THE MOST PART, YES.
SIGH
OF COURSE HE DOES.
I DON'T KNOW WHAT TO DO.
GRAND-FATHER WOULD NEVER WANT ME TO INVESTIGATE ALONE...
HE'D SAY IT WAS TOO DANGEROUS.
BUT, HONESTLY...I'M WILLING TO BET THE COW JUST WANDERED OFF, WHATEVER MR. LOWELL THINKS.

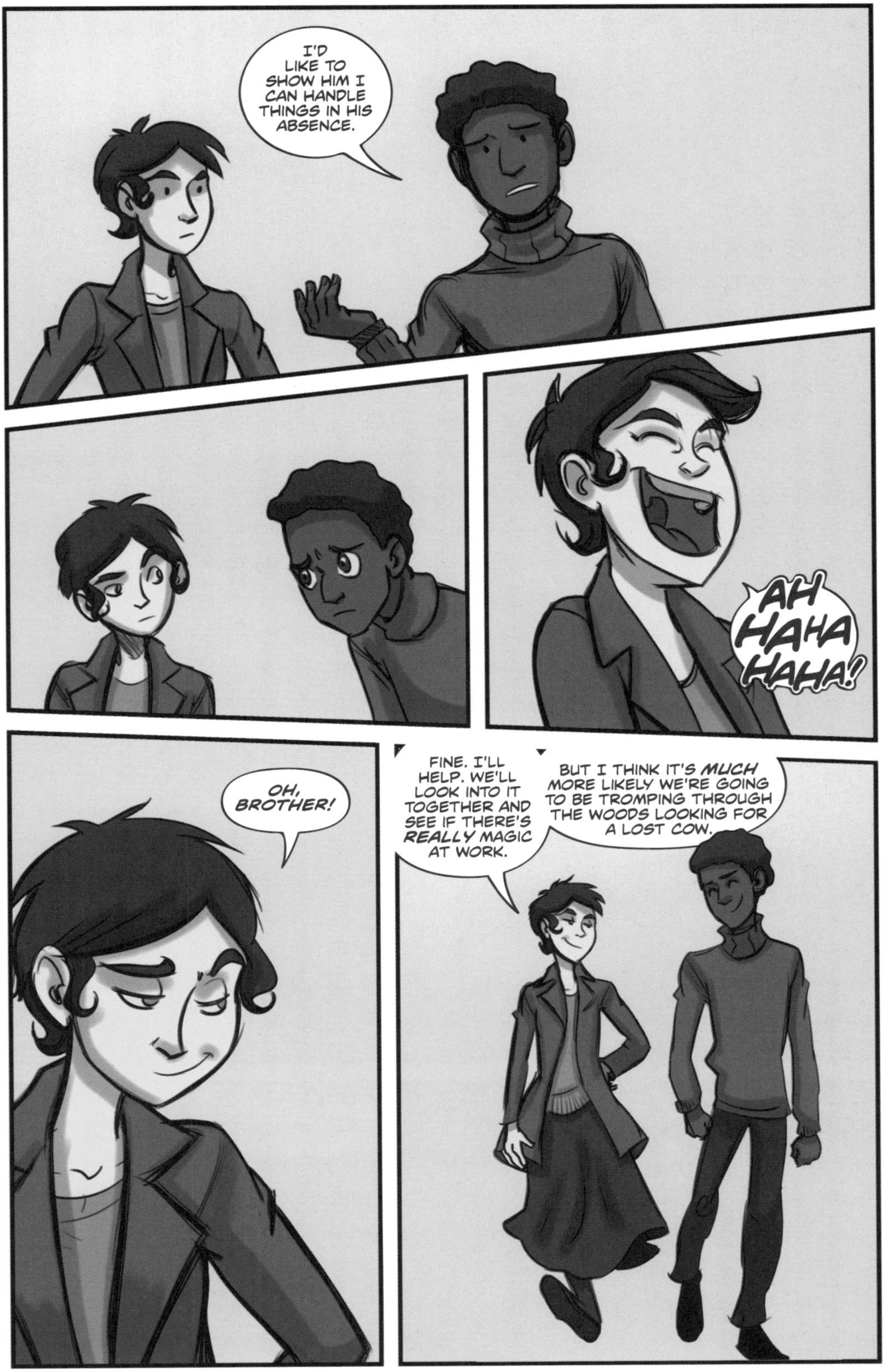
I'D LIKE TO SHOW HIM I CAN HANDLE THINGS IN HIS ABSENCE.
AH HAHA HAHA!
OH, BROTHER!
FINE. I'LL HELP. WE'LL LOOK INTO IT TOGETHER AND SEE IF THERE'S *REALLY* MAGIC AT WORK.
BUT I THINK IT'S *MUCH* MORE LIKELY WE'RE GOING TO BE TROMPING THROUGH THE WOODS LOOKING FOR A LOST COW.

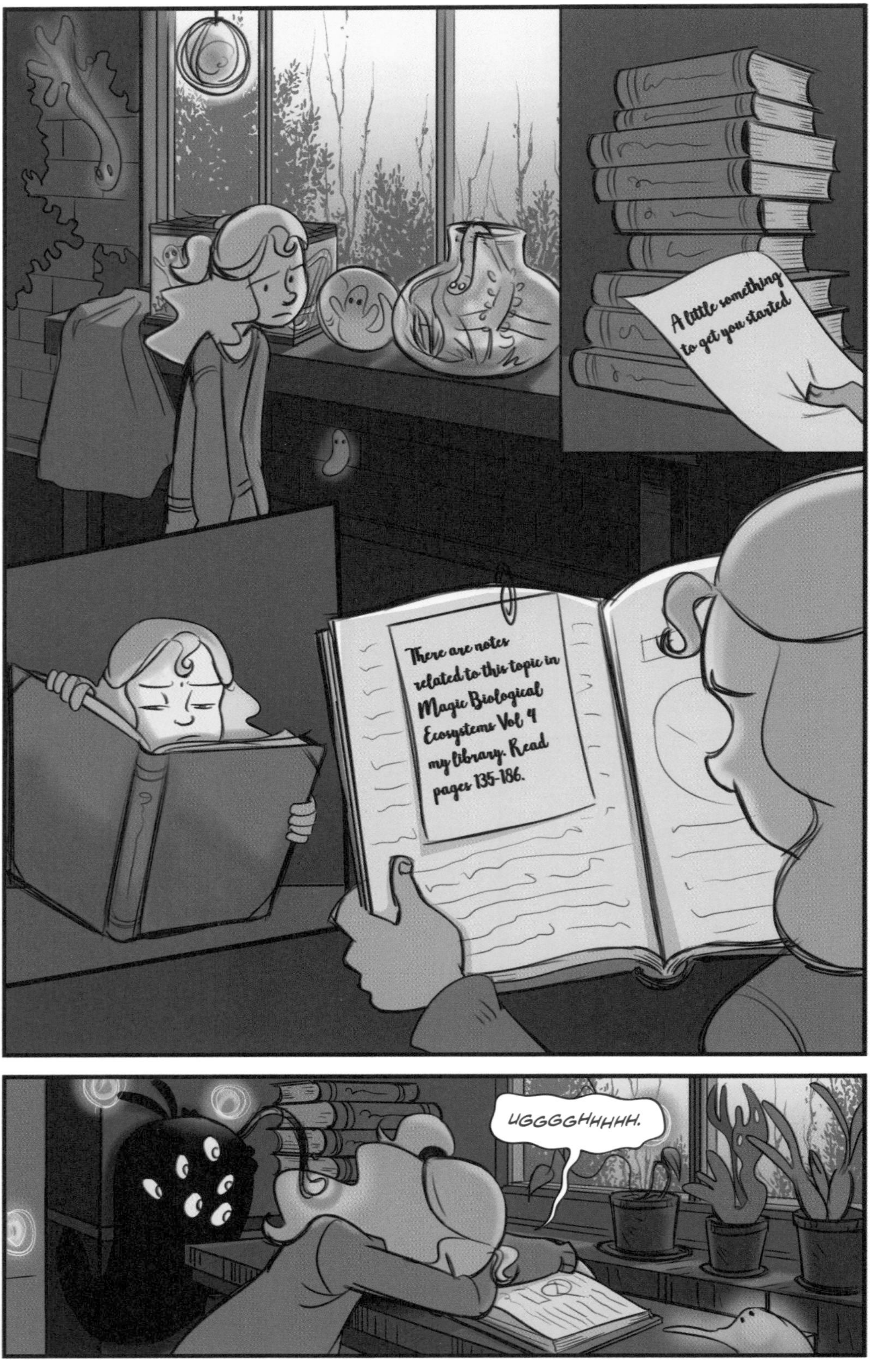
A little something
to get you started
There are notes related to this topic in Magic Biological Ecosystems Vol 4 my library. Read pages 135-186.
UGGGGHHHHH.

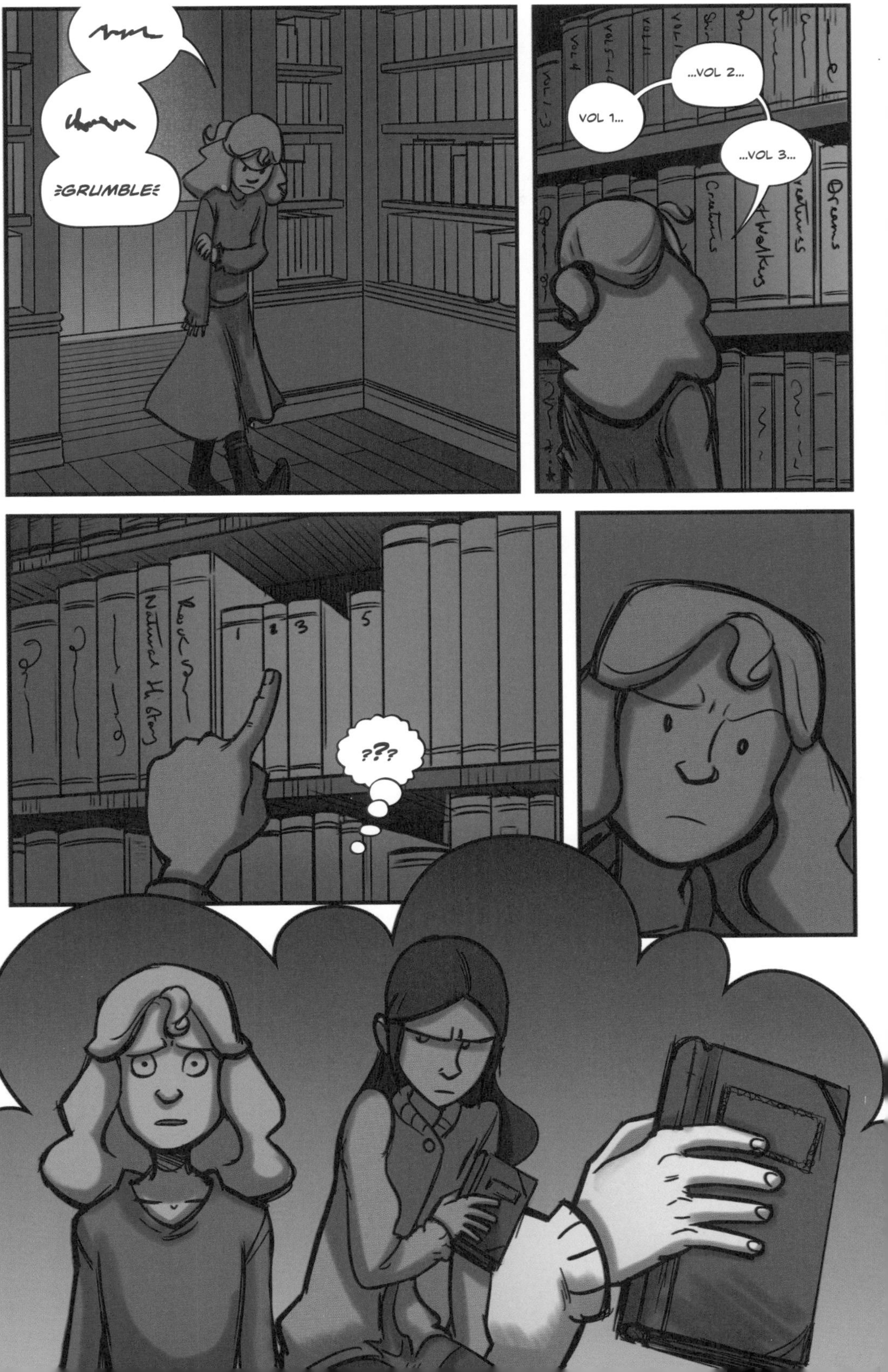

GRUMBLE
VOL 1...
...VOL 2...
...VOL 3...
???

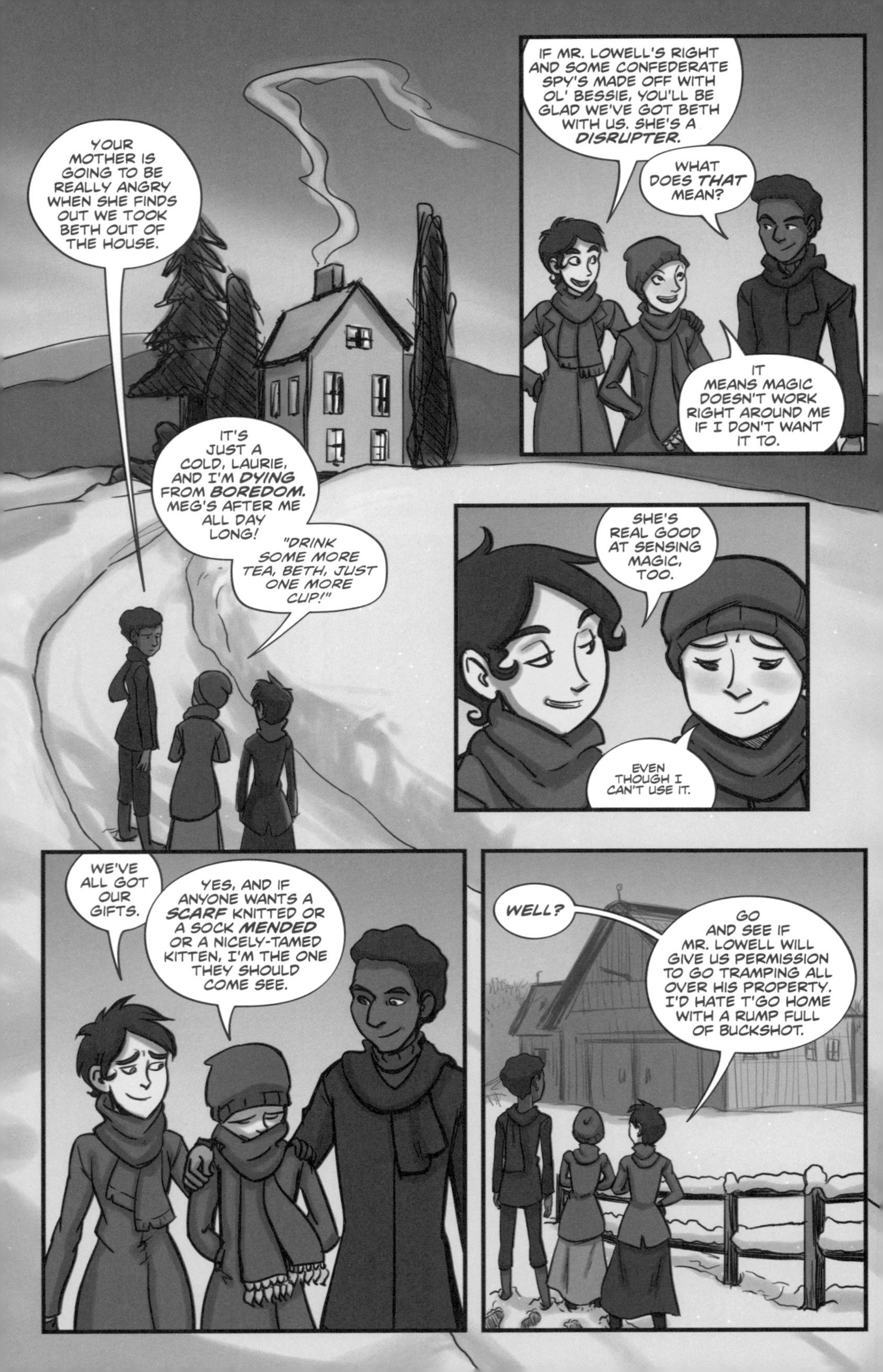
YOUR MOTHER IS GOING TO BE REALLY ANGRY WHEN SHE FINDS OUT WE TOOK BETH OUT OF THE HOUSE.
IT'S JUST A COLD, LAURIE, AND I'M DYING FROM BOREDOM. MEG'S AFTER ME ALL DAY LONG!
"DRINK SOME MORE TEA, BETH, JUST ONE MORE CUP!"
IF MR. LOWELL'S RIGHT AND SOME CONFEDERATE SPY'S MADE OFF WITH OL' BESSIE, YOU'LL BE GLAD WE'VE GOT BETH WITH US. SHE'S A DISRUPTER.
WHAT DOES THAT MEAN?
IT MEANS MAGIC DOESN'T WORK RIGHT AROUND ME IF I DON'T WANT IT TO.
SHE'S REAL GOOD AT SENSING MAGIC, TOO.
EVEN THOUGH I CAN'T USE IT.
WE'VE ALL GOT OUR GIFTS.
YES, AND IF ANYONE WANTS A SCARF KNITTED OR A SOCK MENDED OR A NICELY-TAMED KITTEN, I'M THE ONE THEY SHOULD COME SEE.
WELL?
GO AND SEE IF MR. LOWELL WILL GIVE US PERMISSION TO GO TRAMPING ALL OVER HIS PROPERTY. I'D HATE T'GO HOME WITH A RUMP FULL OF BUCKSHOT.

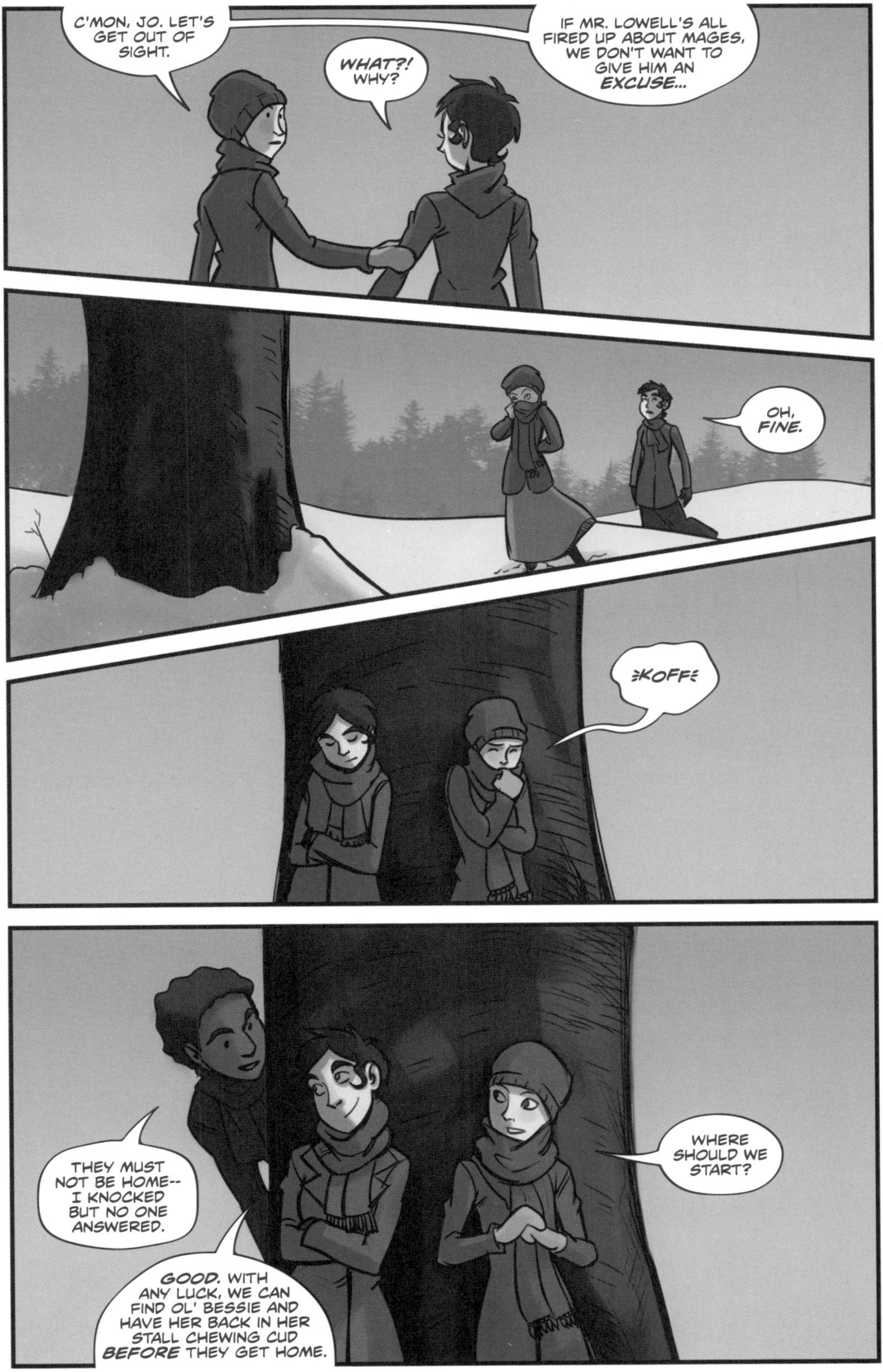
C'MON, JO. LET'S GET OUT OF SIGHT.
WHAT?! WHY?
IF MR. LOWELL'S ALL FIRED UP ABOUT MAGES, WE DON'T WANT TO GIVE HIM AN EXCUSE...
OH, FINE.
KOFF
THEY MUST NOT BE HOME-- I KNOCKED BUT NO ONE ANSWERED.
GOOD. WITH ANY LUCK, WE CAN FIND OL' BESSIE AND HAVE HER BACK IN HER STALL CHEWING CUD BEFORE THEY GET HOME.
WHERE SHOULD WE START?

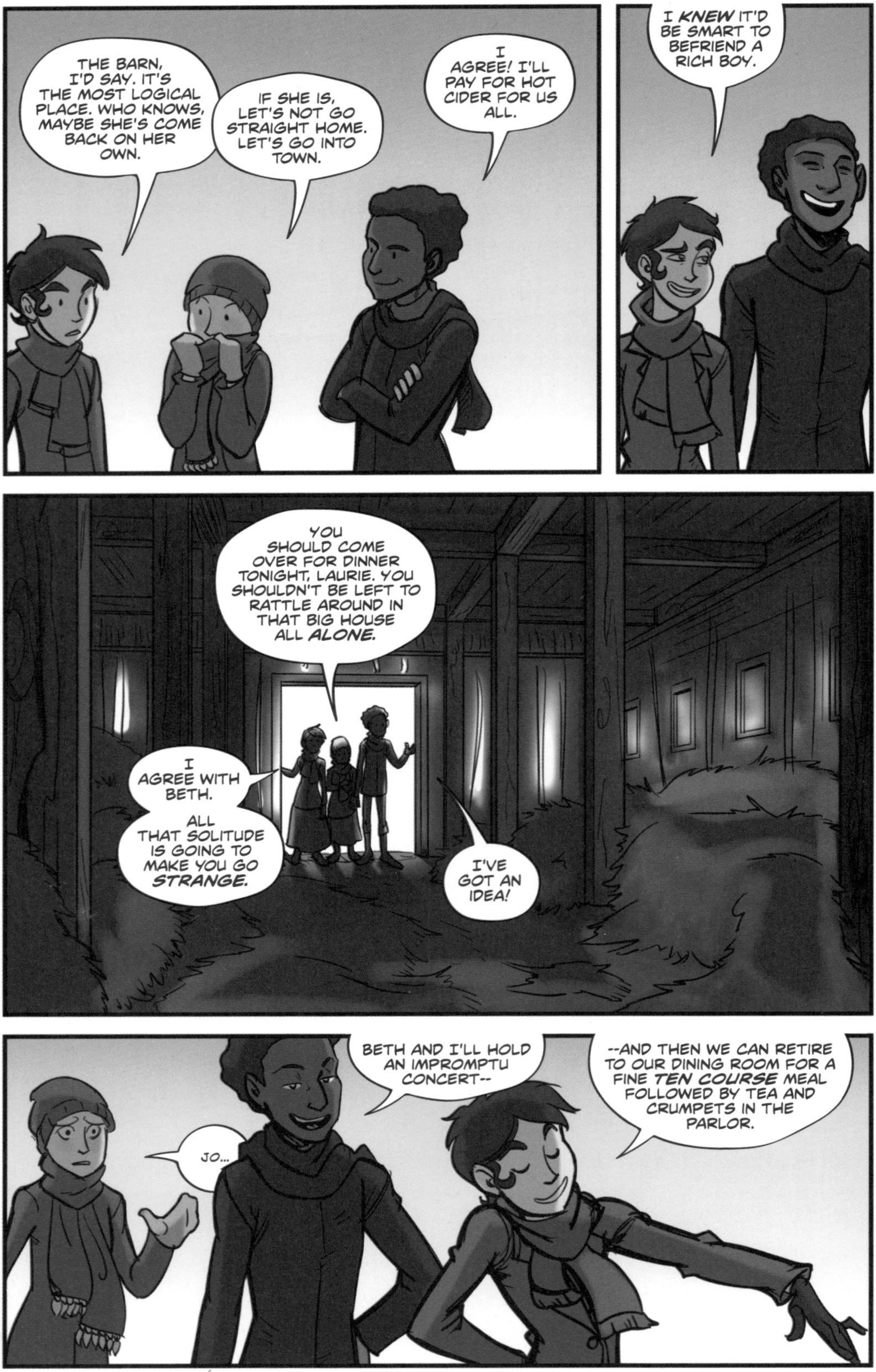
THE BARN, I'D SAY. IT'S THE MOST LOGICAL PLACE. WHO KNOWS, MAYBE SHE'S COME BACK ON HER OWN.
IF SHE IS, LET'S NOT GO STRAIGHT HOME. LET'S GO INTO TOWN.
I AGREE! I'LL PAY FOR HOT CIDER FOR US ALL.
I *KNEW* IT'D BE SMART TO BEFRIEND A RICH BOY.
YOU SHOULD COME OVER FOR DINNER TONIGHT, LAURIE. YOU SHOULDN'T BE LEFT TO RATTLE AROUND IN THAT BIG HOUSE ALL *ALONE.*
I AGREE WITH BETH.
ALL THAT SOLITUDE IS GOING TO MAKE YOU GO *STRANGE.*
I'VE GOT AN IDEA!
BETH AND I'LL HOLD AN IMPROMPTU CONCERT--
--AND THEN WE CAN RETIRE TO OUR DINING ROOM FOR A FINE *TEN COURSE* MEAL FOLLOWED BY TEA AND CRUMPETS IN THE PARLOR.
JO...

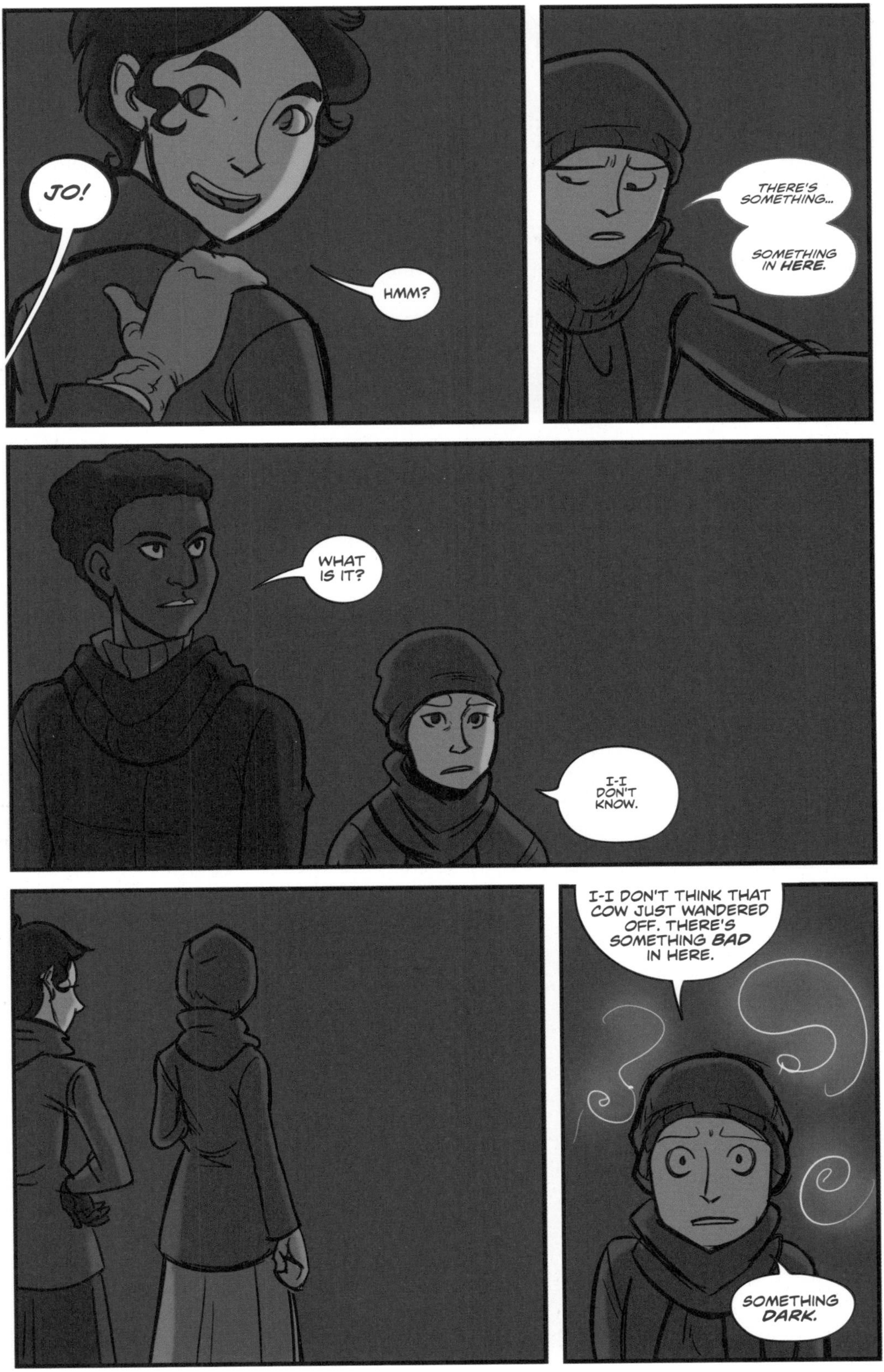
JO!
HMM?
THERE'S SOMETHING...
SOMETHING IN HERE.
WHAT IS IT?
I-I DON'T KNOW.
I-I DON'T THINK THAT COW JUST WANDERED OFF. THERE'S SOMETHING BAD IN HERE.
SOMETHING DARK.

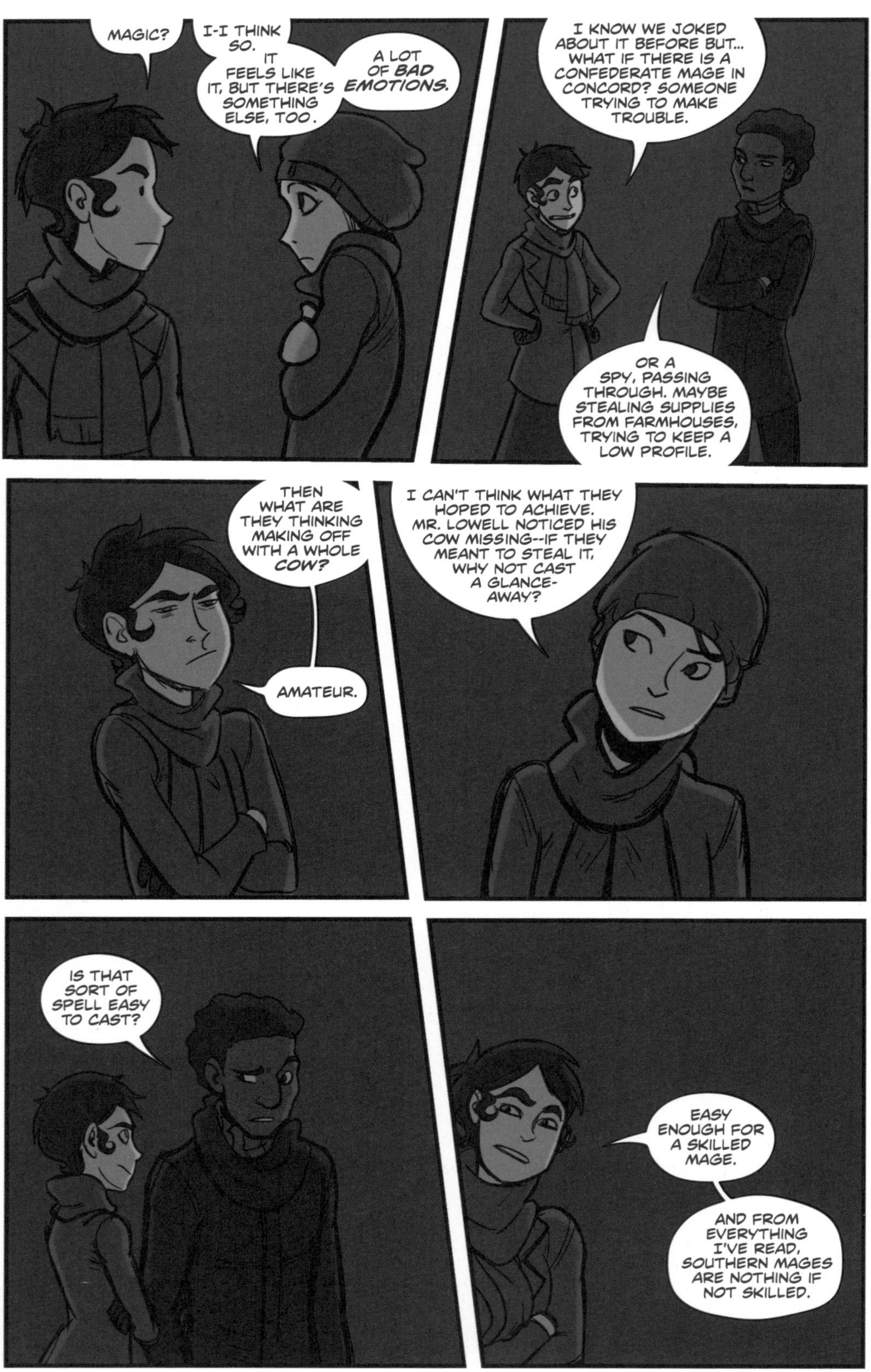
MAGIC?
I-I THINK SO.
IT FEELS LIKE IT, BUT THERE'S SOMETHING ELSE, TOO.
A LOT OF *BAD EMOTIONS.*
I KNOW WE JOKED ABOUT IT BEFORE BUT... WHAT IF THERE IS A CONFEDERATE MAGE IN CONCORD? SOMEONE TRYING TO MAKE TROUBLE.
OR A SPY, PASSING THROUGH. MAYBE STEALING SUPPLIES FROM FARMHOUSES, TRYING TO KEEP A LOW PROFILE.
THEN WHAT ARE THEY THINKING MAKING OFF WITH A WHOLE *COW?*
AMATEUR.
I CAN'T THINK WHAT THEY HOPED TO ACHIEVE. MR. LOWELL NOTICED HIS COW MISSING--IF THEY MEANT TO STEAL IT, WHY NOT CAST A GLANCE-AWAY?
IS THAT SORT OF SPELL EASY TO CAST?
EASY ENOUGH FOR A SKILLED MAGE.
AND FROM EVERYTHING I'VE READ, SOUTHERN MAGES ARE NOTHING IF NOT SKILLED.

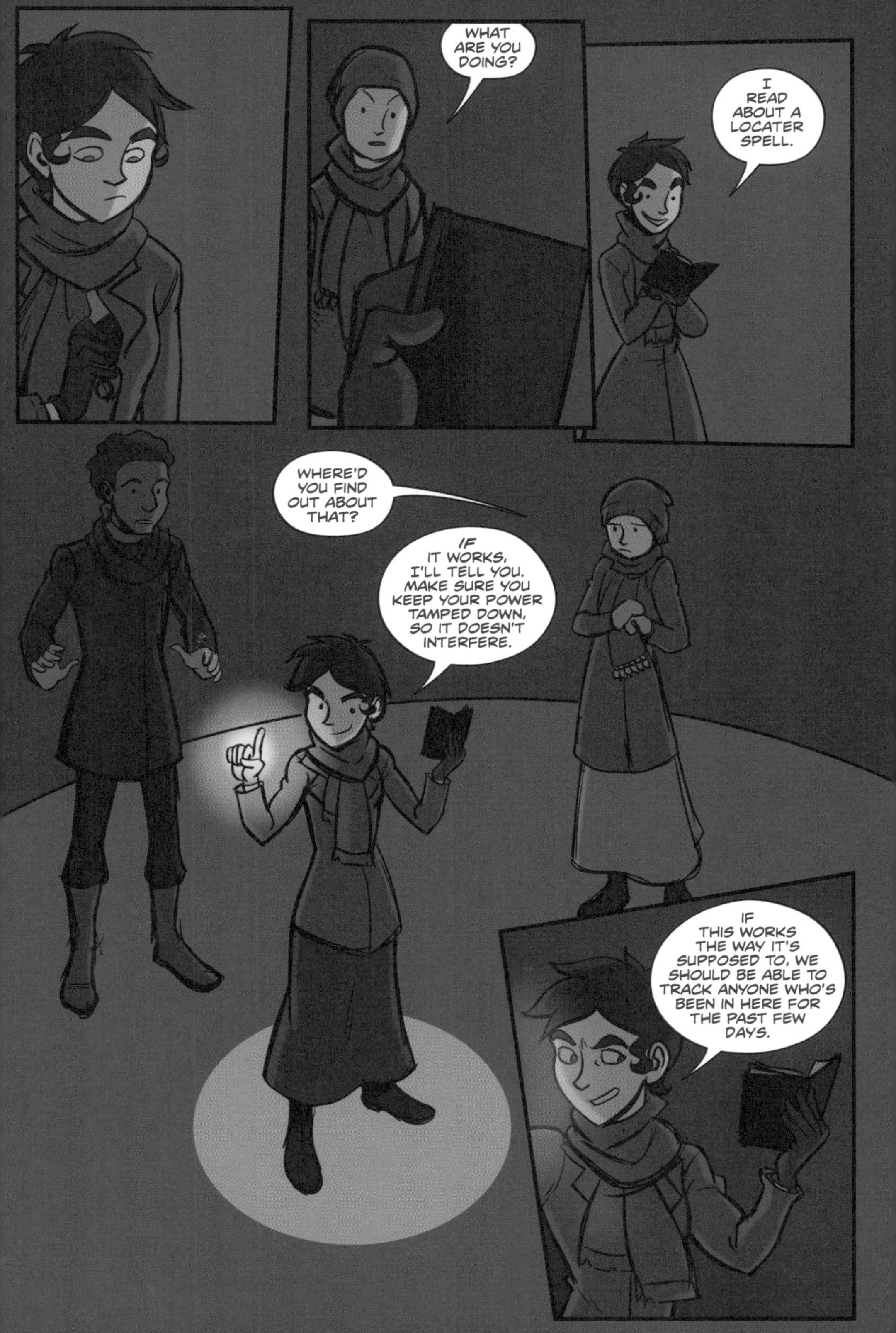
WHAT ARE YOU DOING?
I READ ABOUT A LOCATER SPELL.
WHERE'D YOU FIND OUT ABOUT THAT?
IF IT WORKS, I'LL TELL YOU. MAKE SURE YOU KEEP YOUR POWER TAMPED DOWN, SO IT DOESN'T INTERFERE.
IF THIS WORKS THE WAY IT'S SUPPOSED TO, WE SHOULD BE ABLE TO TRACK ANYONE WHO'S BEEN IN HERE FOR THE PAST FEW DAYS.

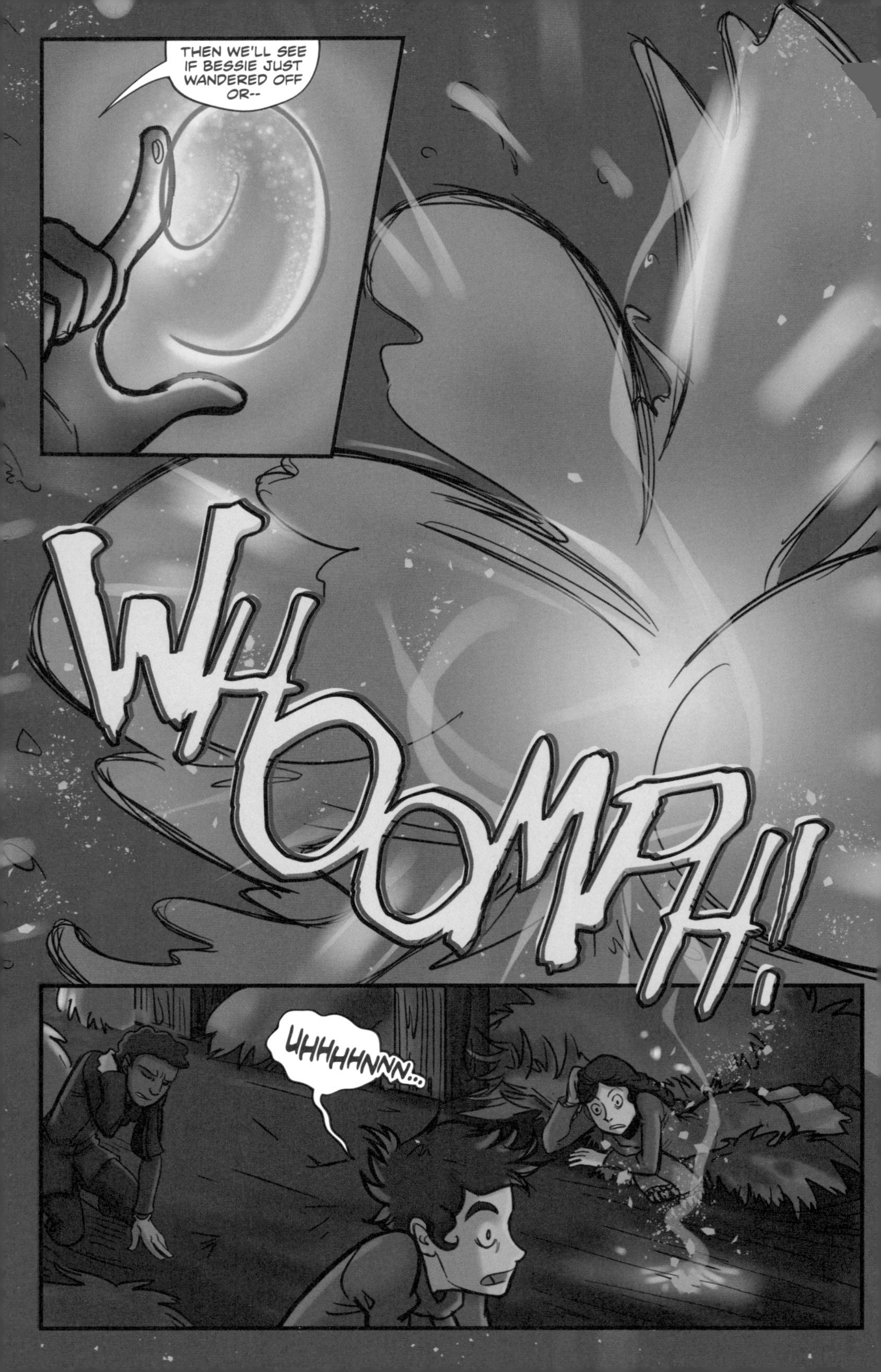
THEN WE'LL SEE IF BESSIE JUST WANDERED OFF OR--
WHOOMPH!
UHHHHNNN...

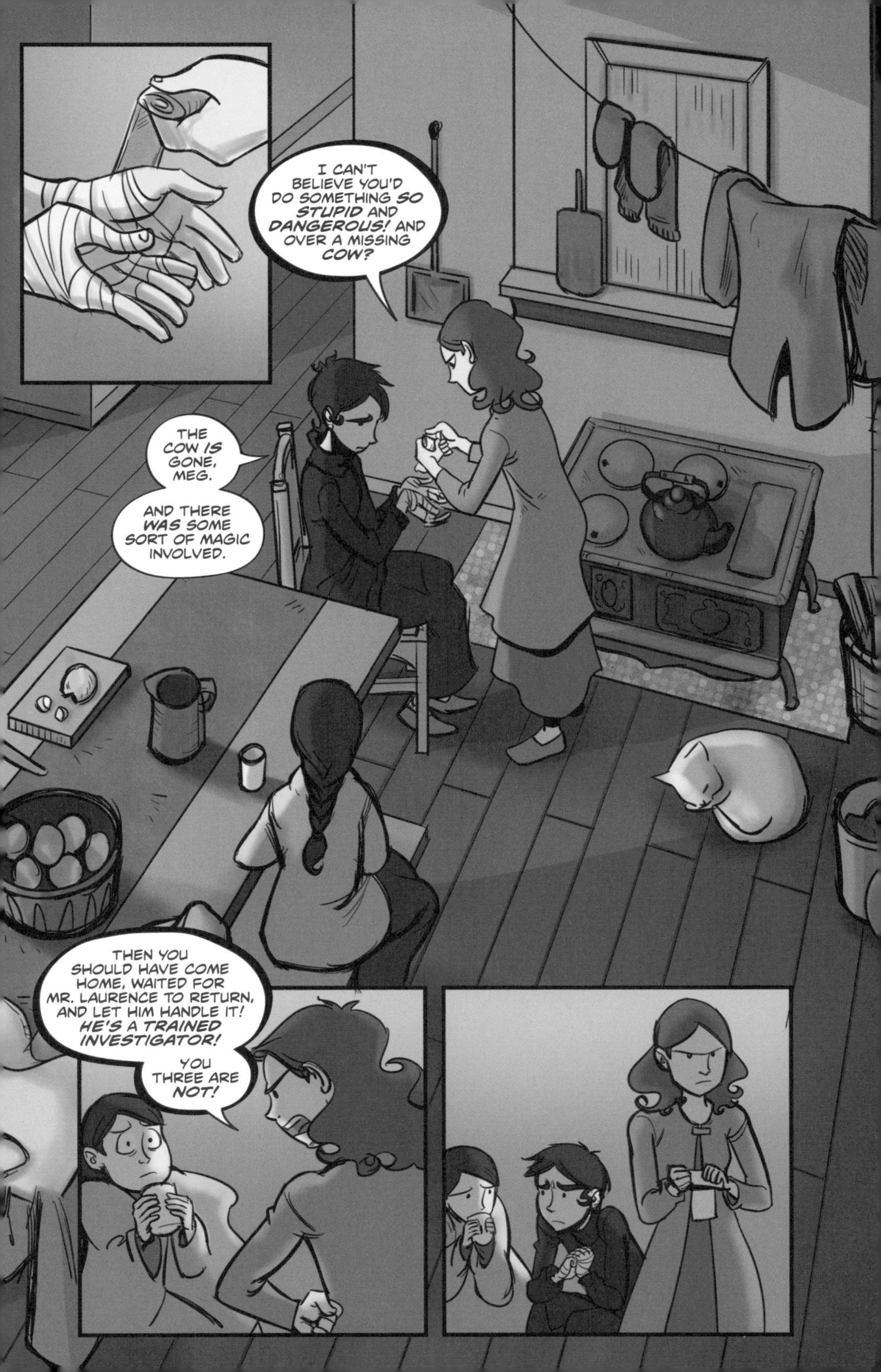
I CAN'T BELIEVE YOU'D DO SOMETHING SO STUPID AND DANGEROUS! AND OVER A MISSING COW?
THE COW IS GONE, MEG.
AND THERE WAS SOME SORT OF MAGIC INVOLVED.
THEN YOU SHOULD HAVE COME HOME, WAITED FOR MR. LAURENCE TO RETURN, AND LET HIM HANDLE IT! HE'S A TRAINED INVESTIGATOR!
YOU THREE ARE NOT!

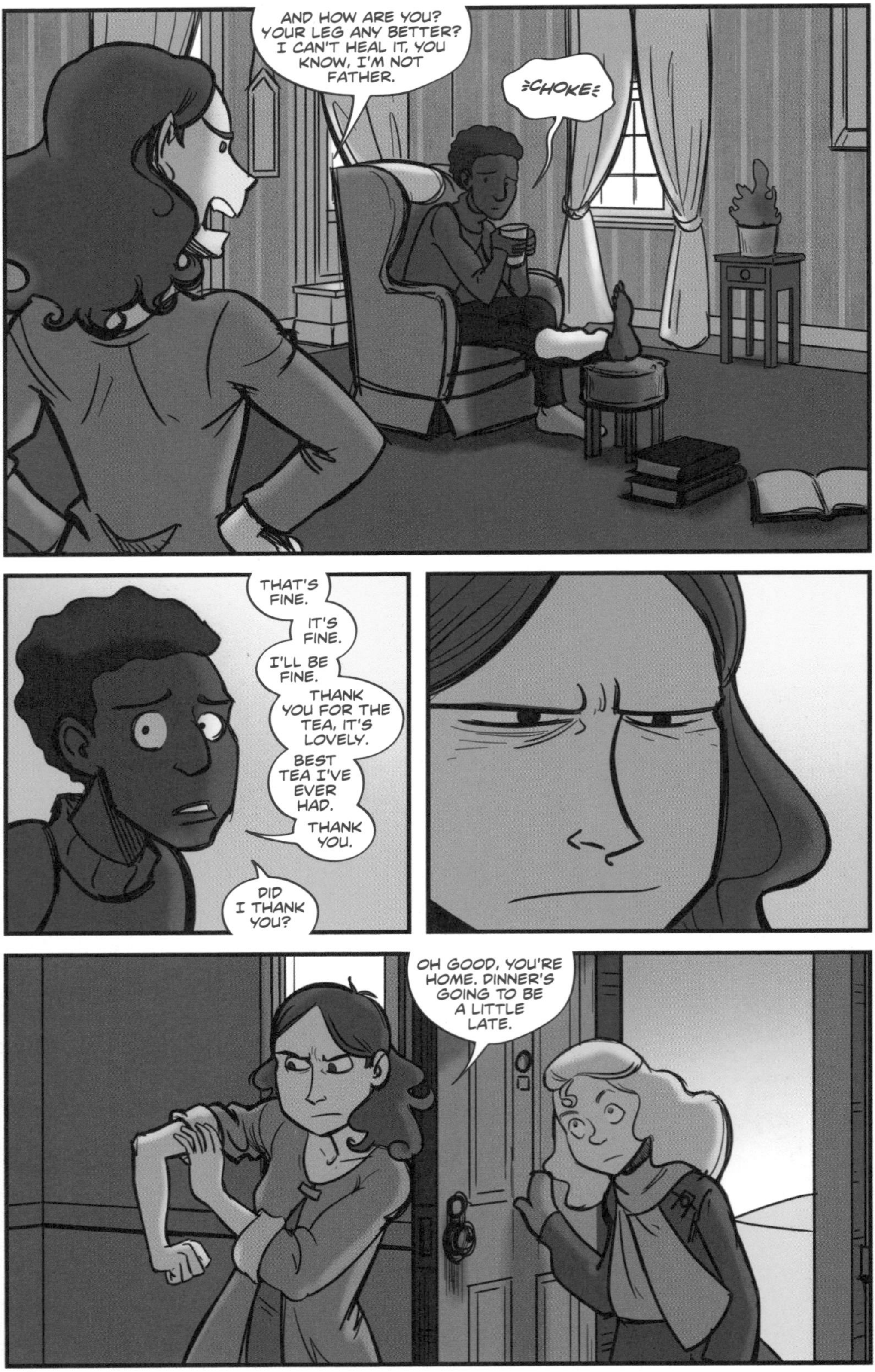
AND HOW ARE YOU? YOUR LEG ANY BETTER? I CAN'T HEAL IT, YOU KNOW, I'M NOT FATHER.
CHOKE
THAT'S FINE.
IT'S FINE.
I'LL BE FINE.
THANK YOU FOR THE TEA, IT'S LOVELY.
BEST TEA I'VE EVER HAD.
THANK YOU.
DID I THANK YOU?
OH GOOD, YOU'RE HOME. DINNER'S GOING TO BE A LITTLE LATE.

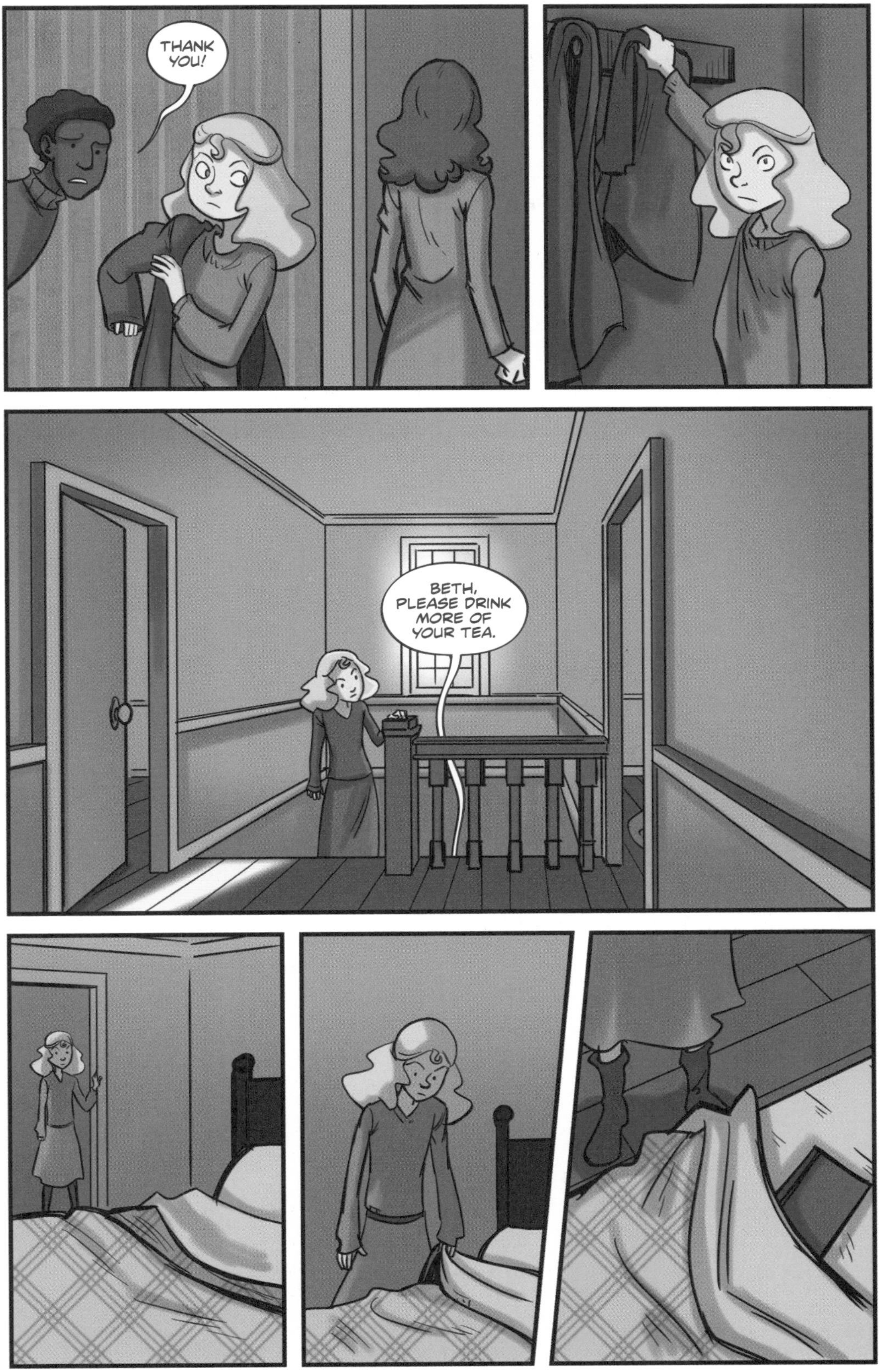
THANK YOU!
BETH, PLEASE DRINK MORE OF YOUR TEA.

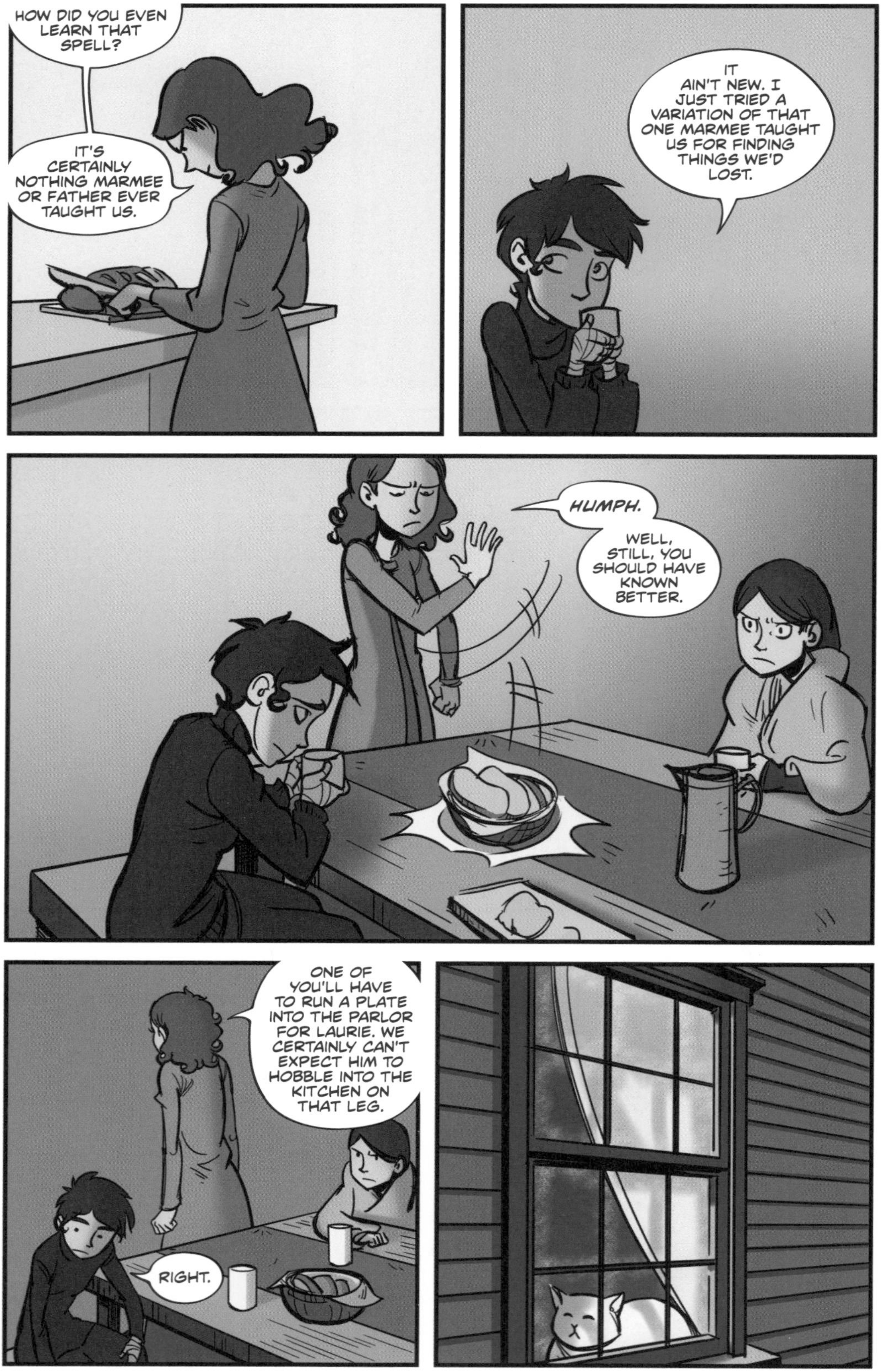
HOW DID YOU EVEN LEARN THAT SPELL?
IT'S CERTAINLY NOTHING MARMEE OR FATHER EVER TAUGHT US.
IT AIN'T NEW. I JUST TRIED A VARIATION OF THAT ONE MARMEE TAUGHT US FOR FINDING THINGS WE'D LOST.
HUMPH.
WELL, STILL, YOU SHOULD HAVE KNOWN BETTER.
ONE OF YOU'LL HAVE TO RUN A PLATE INTO THE PARLOR FOR LAURIE. WE CERTAINLY CAN'T EXPECT HIM TO HOBBLE INTO THE KITCHEN ON THAT LEG.
RIGHT.

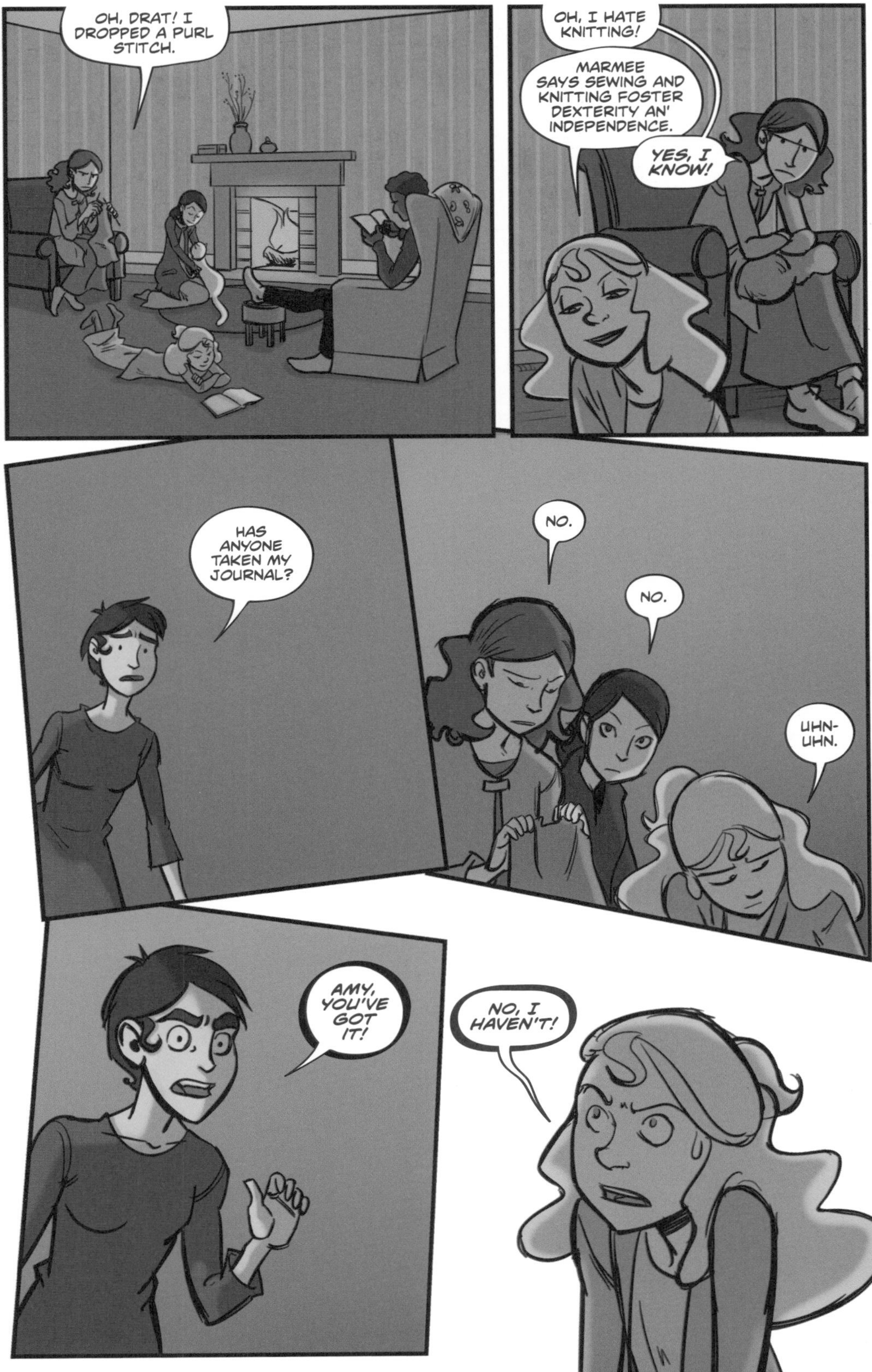
OH, DRAT! I DROPPED A PURL STITCH.
OH, I HATE KNITTING!
MARMEE SAYS SEWING AND KNITTING FOSTER DEXTERITY AN' INDEPENDENCE.
YES, I KNOW!
HAS ANYONE TAKEN MY JOURNAL?
NO.
NO.
UHN-UHN.
AMY, YOU'VE GOT IT!
NO, I HAVEN'T!

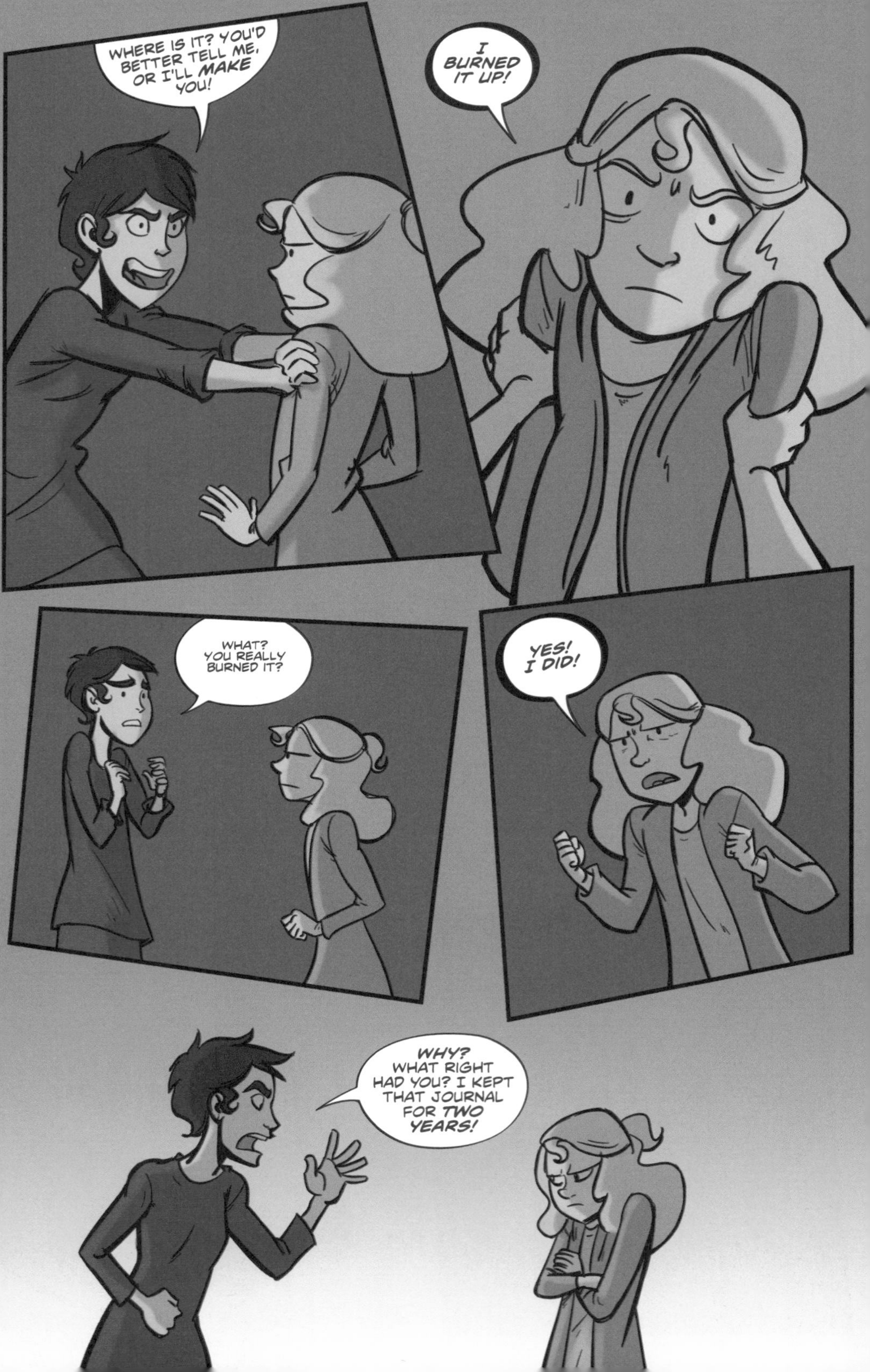
WHERE IS IT? YOU'D BETTER TELL ME, OR I'LL MAKE YOU!
I BURNED IT UP!
WHAT? YOU REALLY BURNED IT?
YES! I DID!
WHY? WHAT RIGHT HAD YOU? I KEPT THAT JOURNAL FOR TWO YEARS!

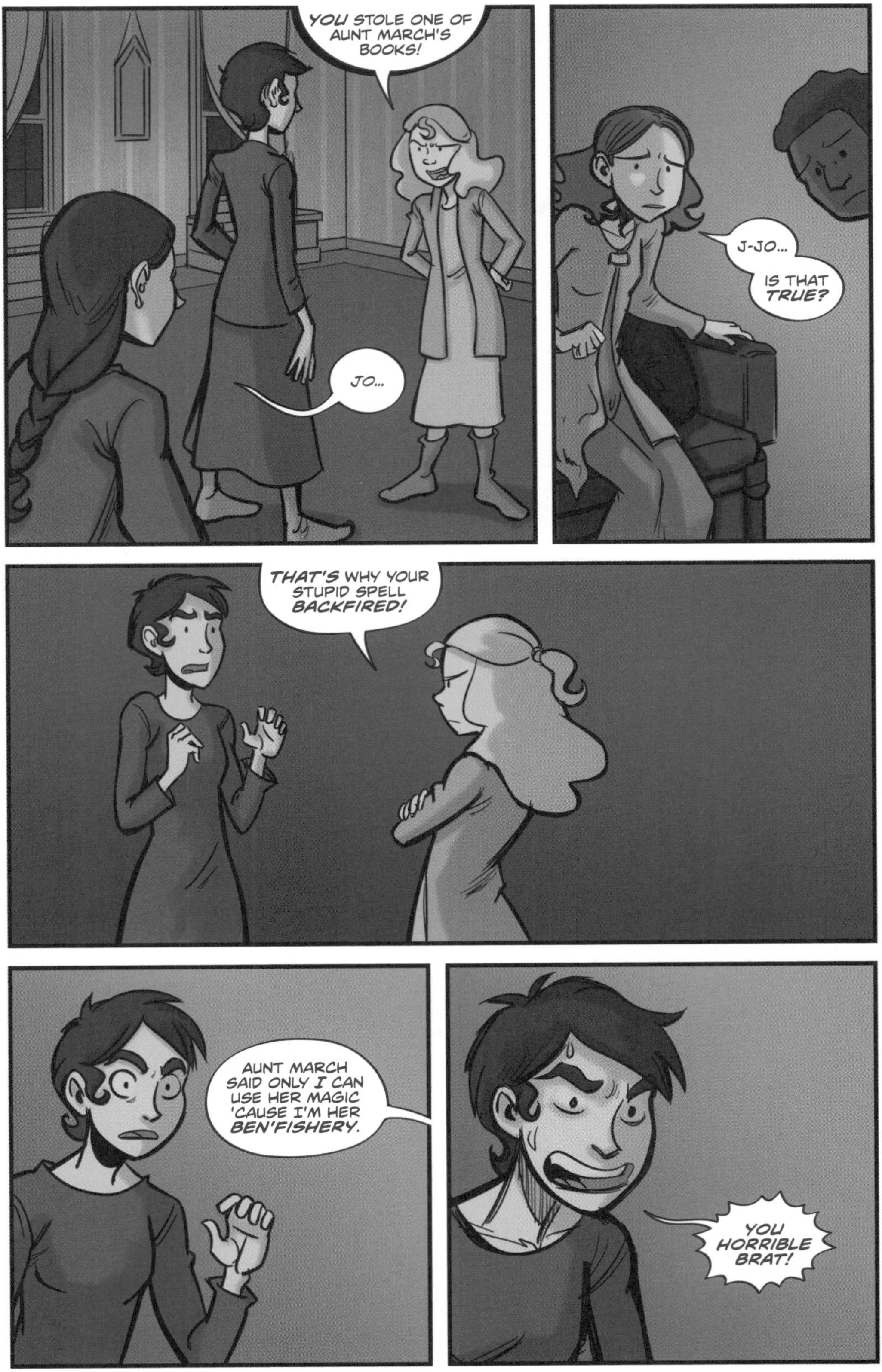
YOU STOLE ONE OF AUNT MARCH'S BOOKS!
JO...
J-JO...
IS THAT TRUE?
THAT'S WHY YOUR STUPID SPELL BACKFIRED!
AUNT MARCH SAID ONLY I CAN USE HER MAGIC 'CAUSE I'M HER BEN'FISHERY.
YOU HORRIBLE BRAT!

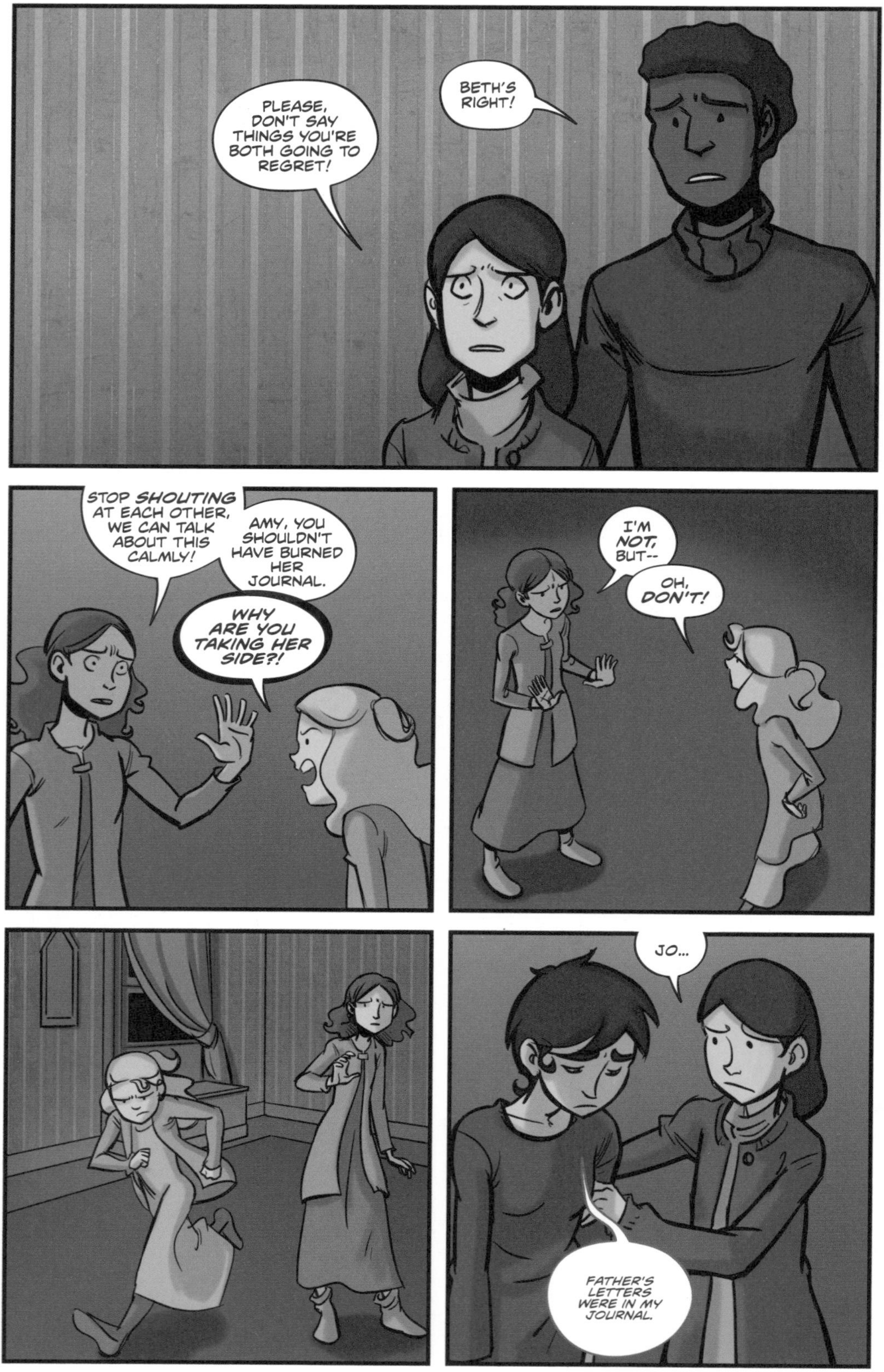
PLEASE, DON'T SAY THINGS YOU'RE BOTH GOING TO REGRET!
BETH'S RIGHT!
STOP *SHOUTING* AT EACH OTHER, WE CAN TALK ABOUT THIS CALMLY!
AMY, YOU SHOULDN'T HAVE BURNED HER JOURNAL.
WHY ARE YOU TAKING HER SIDE?!
I'M *NOT,* BUT--
OH, *DON'T!*
JO...
FATHER'S LETTERS WERE IN MY JOURNAL.

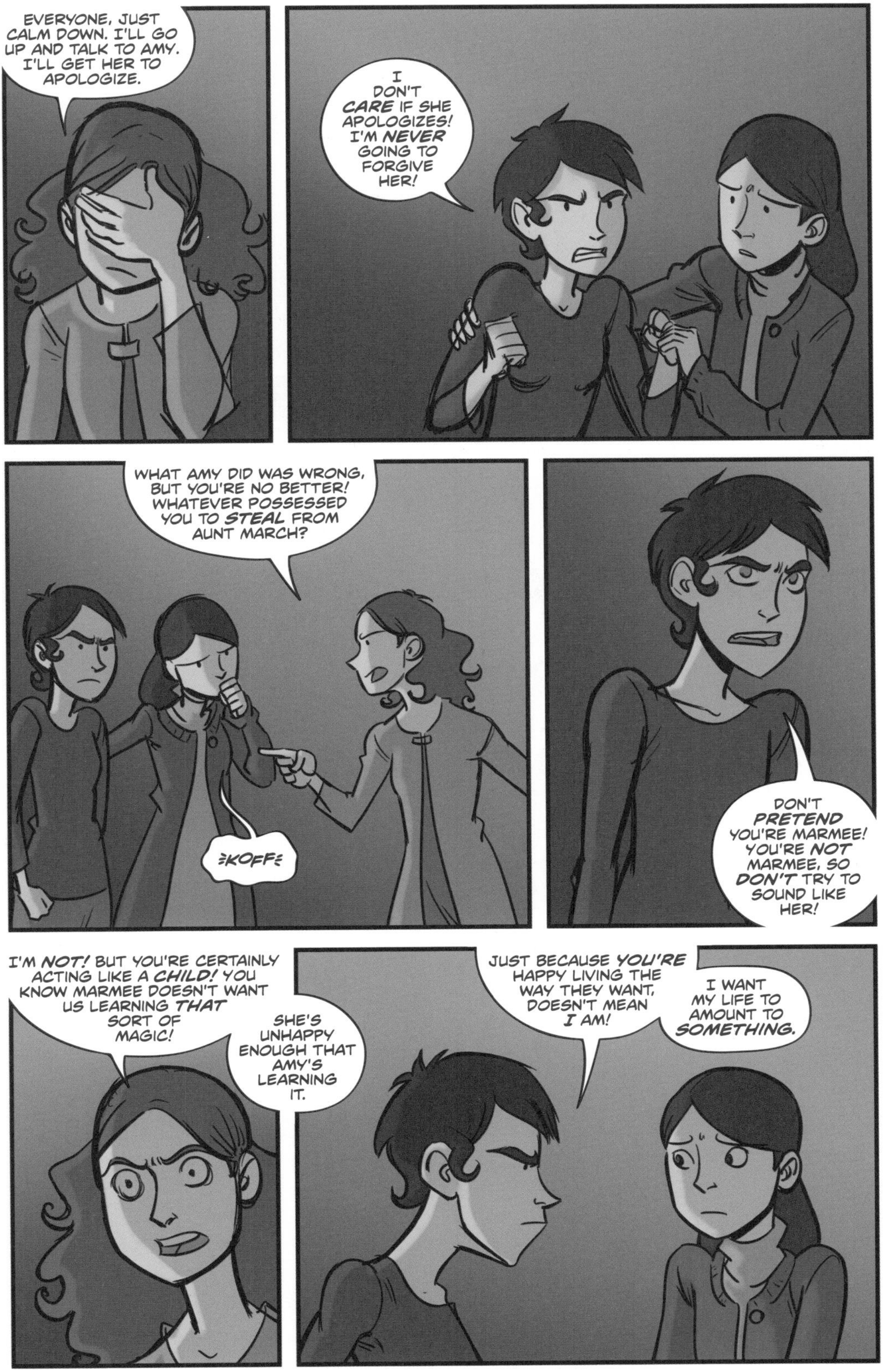
EVERYONE, JUST CALM DOWN. I'LL GO UP AND TALK TO AMY. I'LL GET HER TO APOLOGIZE.
I DON'T CARE IF SHE APOLOGIZES! I'M NEVER GOING TO FORGIVE HER!
WHAT AMY DID WAS WRONG, BUT YOU'RE NO BETTER! WHATEVER POSSESSED YOU TO STEAL FROM AUNT MARCH?
KOFF
DON'T PRETEND YOU'RE MARMEE! YOU'RE NOT MARMEE, SO DON'T TRY TO SOUND LIKE HER!
I'M NOT! BUT YOU'RE CERTAINLY ACTING LIKE A CHILD! YOU KNOW MARMEE DOESN'T WANT US LEARNING THAT SORT OF MAGIC!
SHE'S UNHAPPY ENOUGH THAT AMY'S LEARNING IT.
JUST BECAUSE YOU'RE HAPPY LIVING THE WAY THEY WANT, DOESN'T MEAN I AM!
I WANT MY LIFE TO AMOUNT TO SOMETHING.

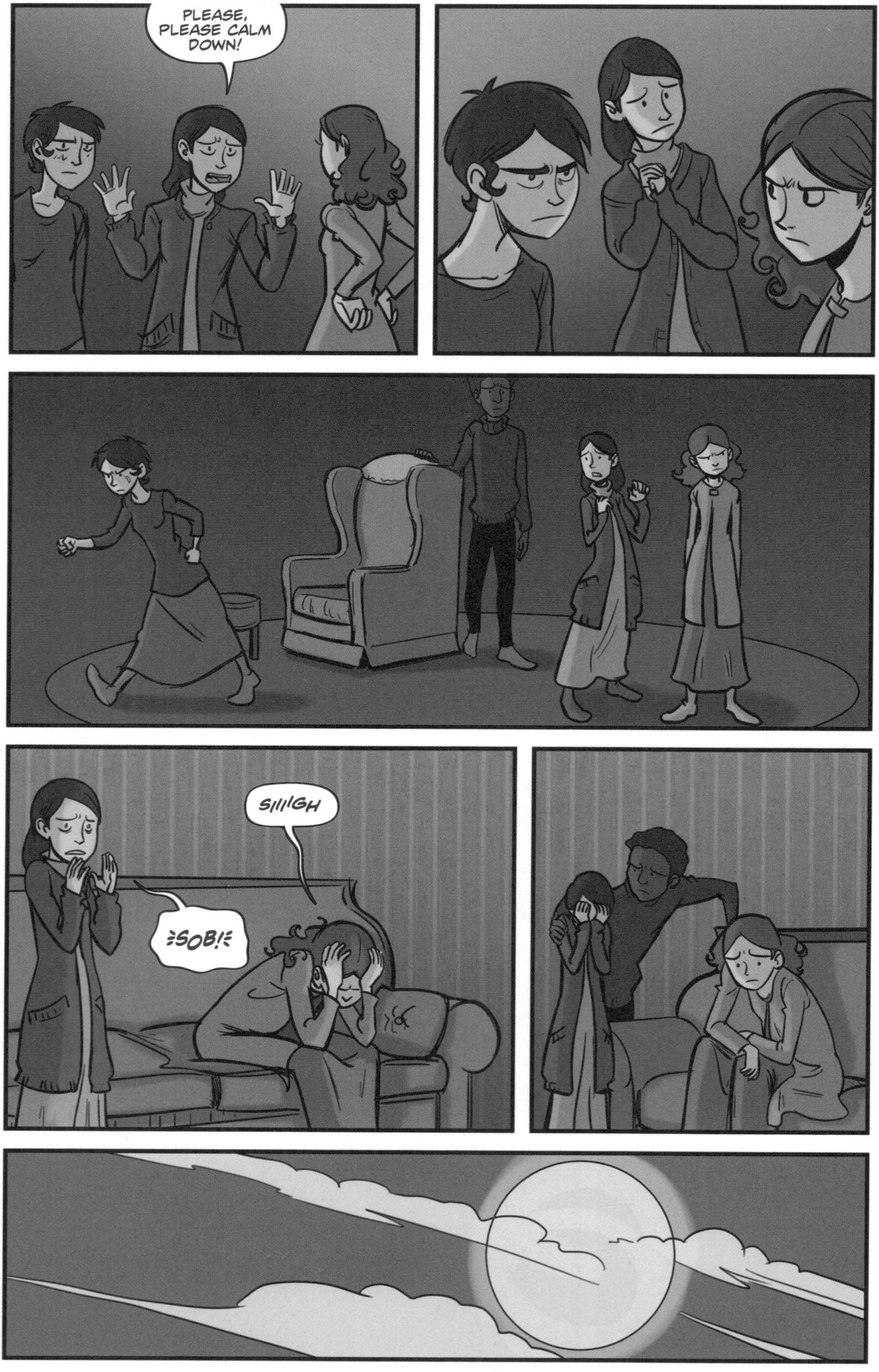
PLEASE, PLEASE CALM DOWN!
SIIIGH
SOB!

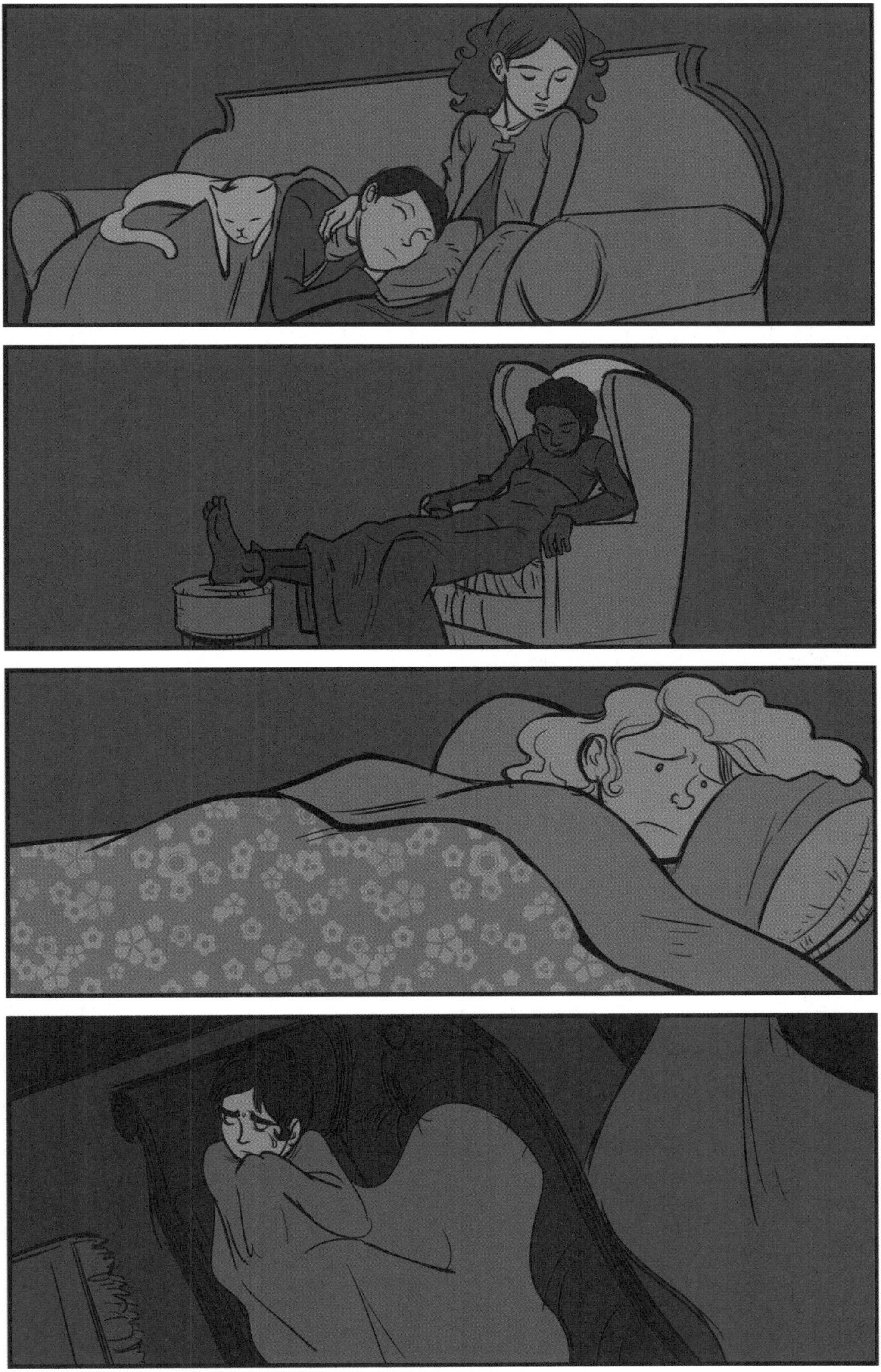

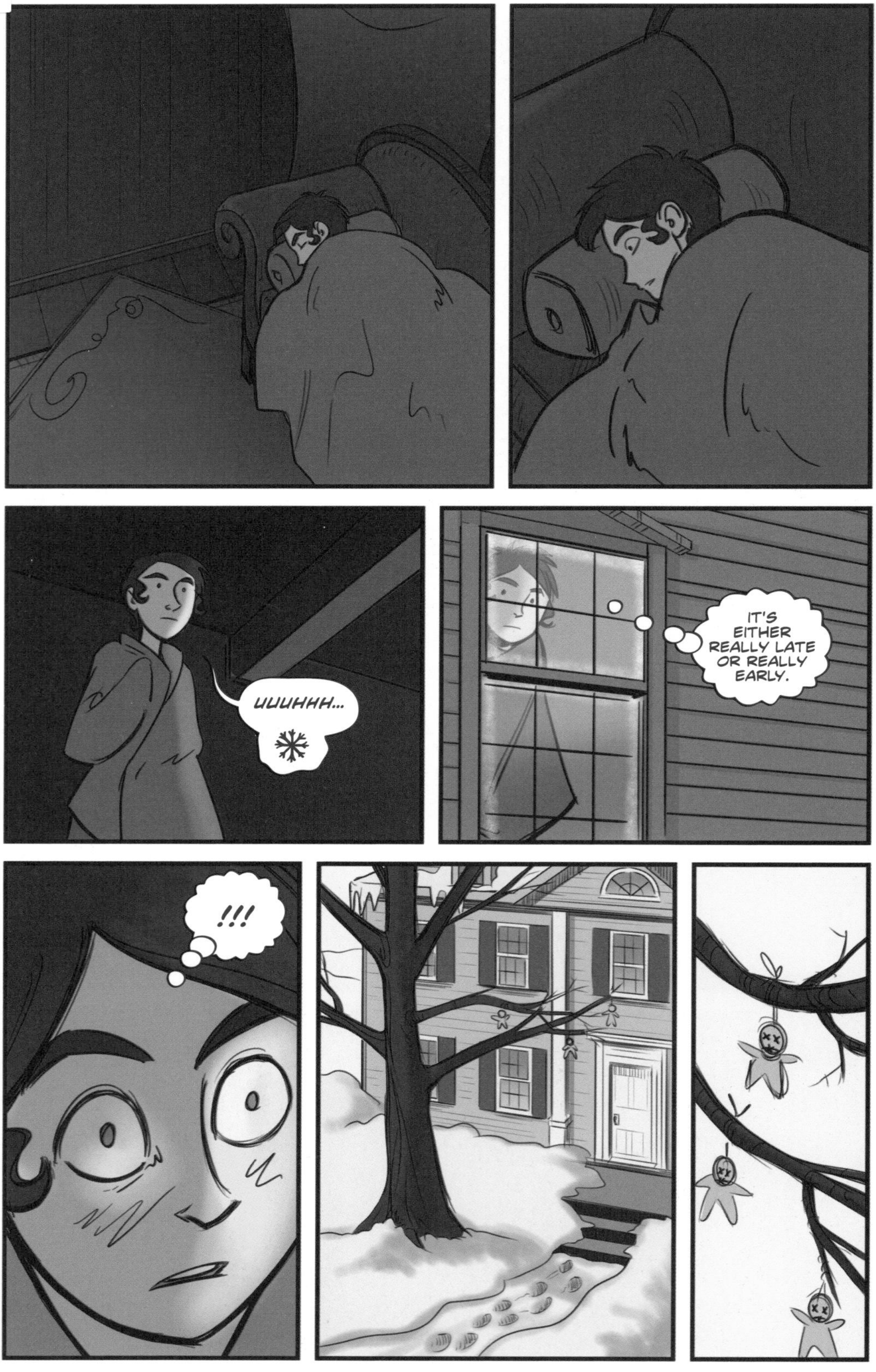
UUUHHH...
IT'S EITHER REALLY LATE OR REALLY EARLY.
!!!

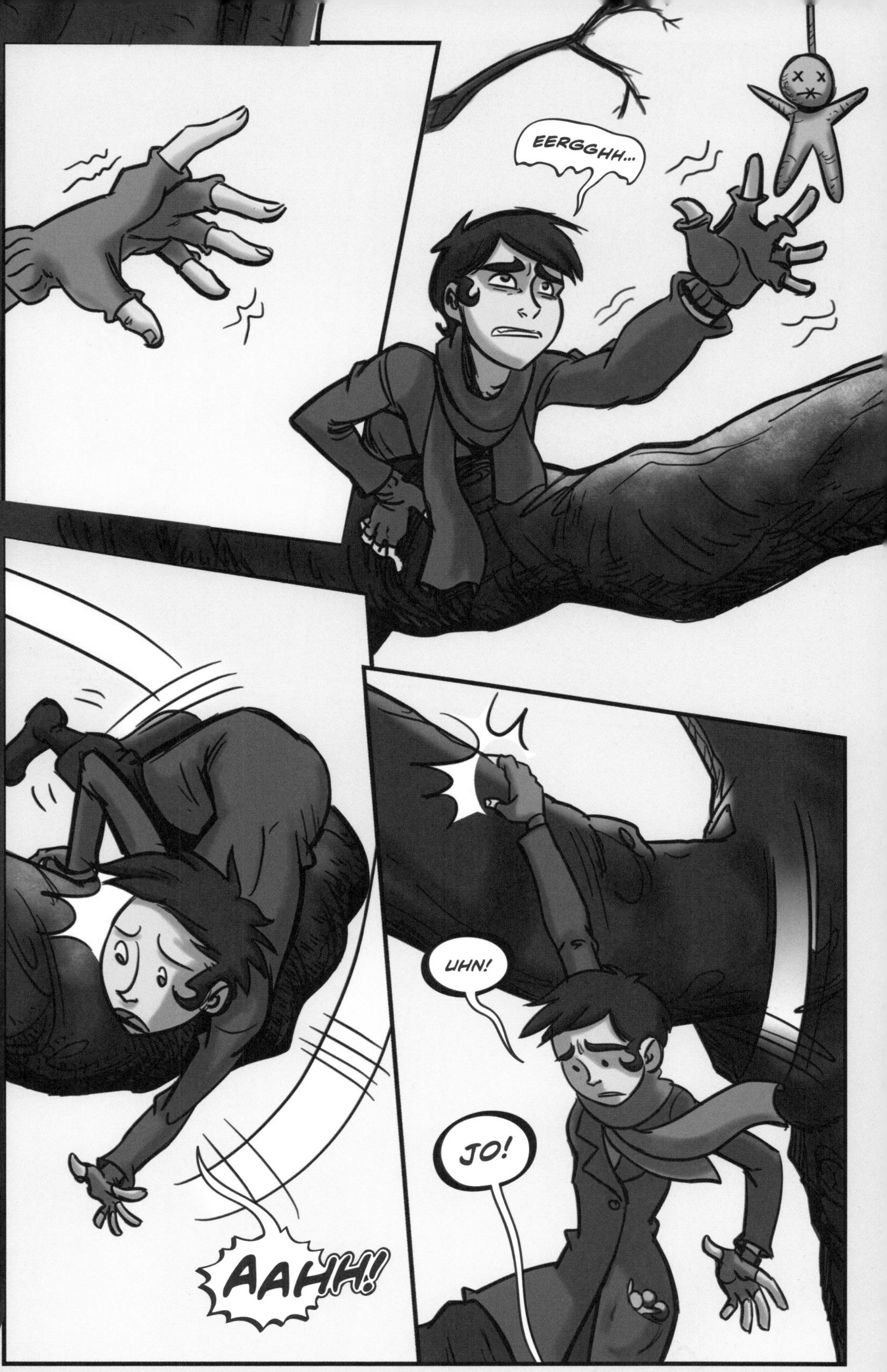
EERGGHH...
AAHH!
UHN!
JO!

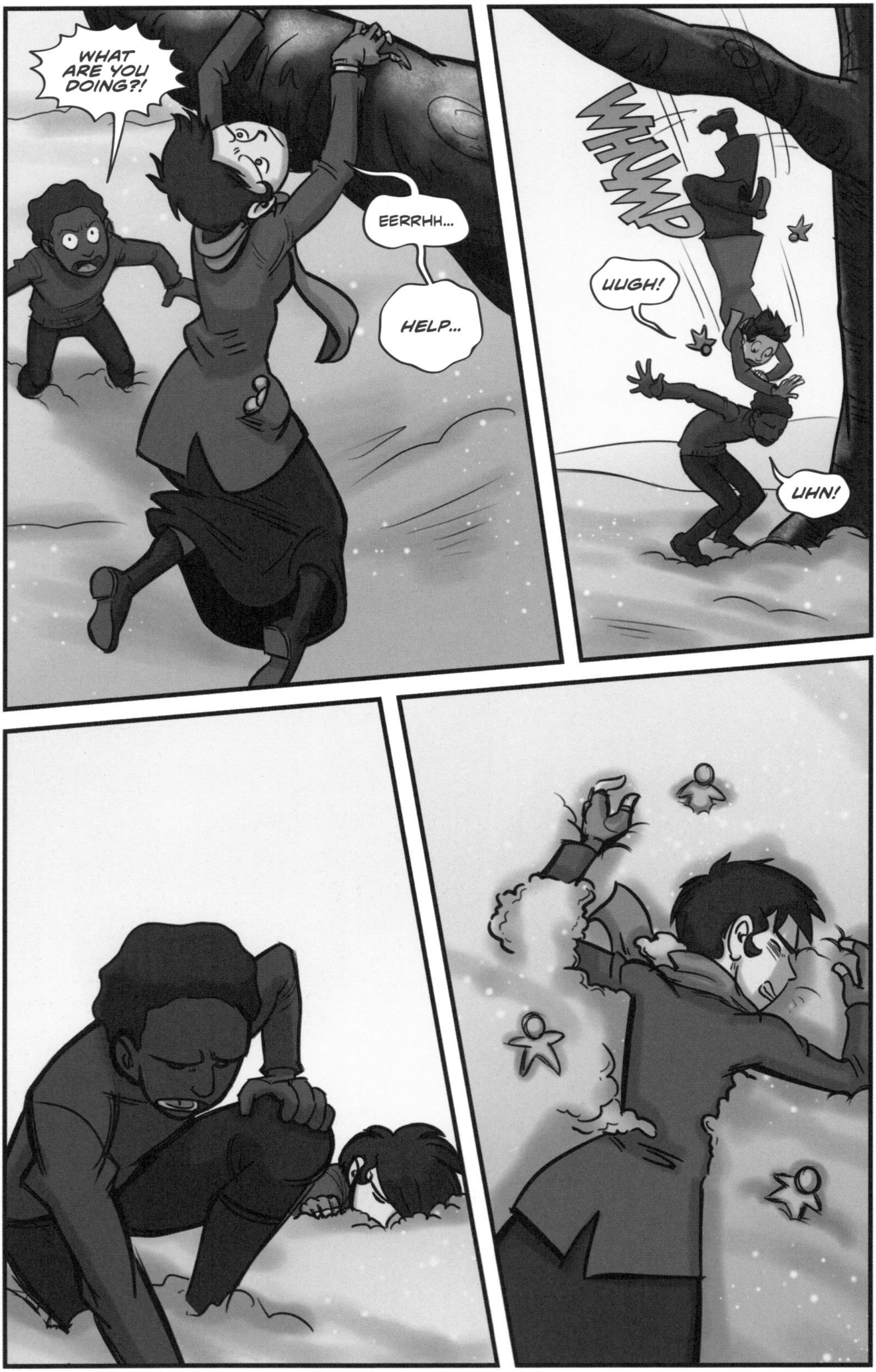
WHAT ARE YOU DOING?!
EERRHH...
HELP...
WHUMP
UUGH!
UHN!

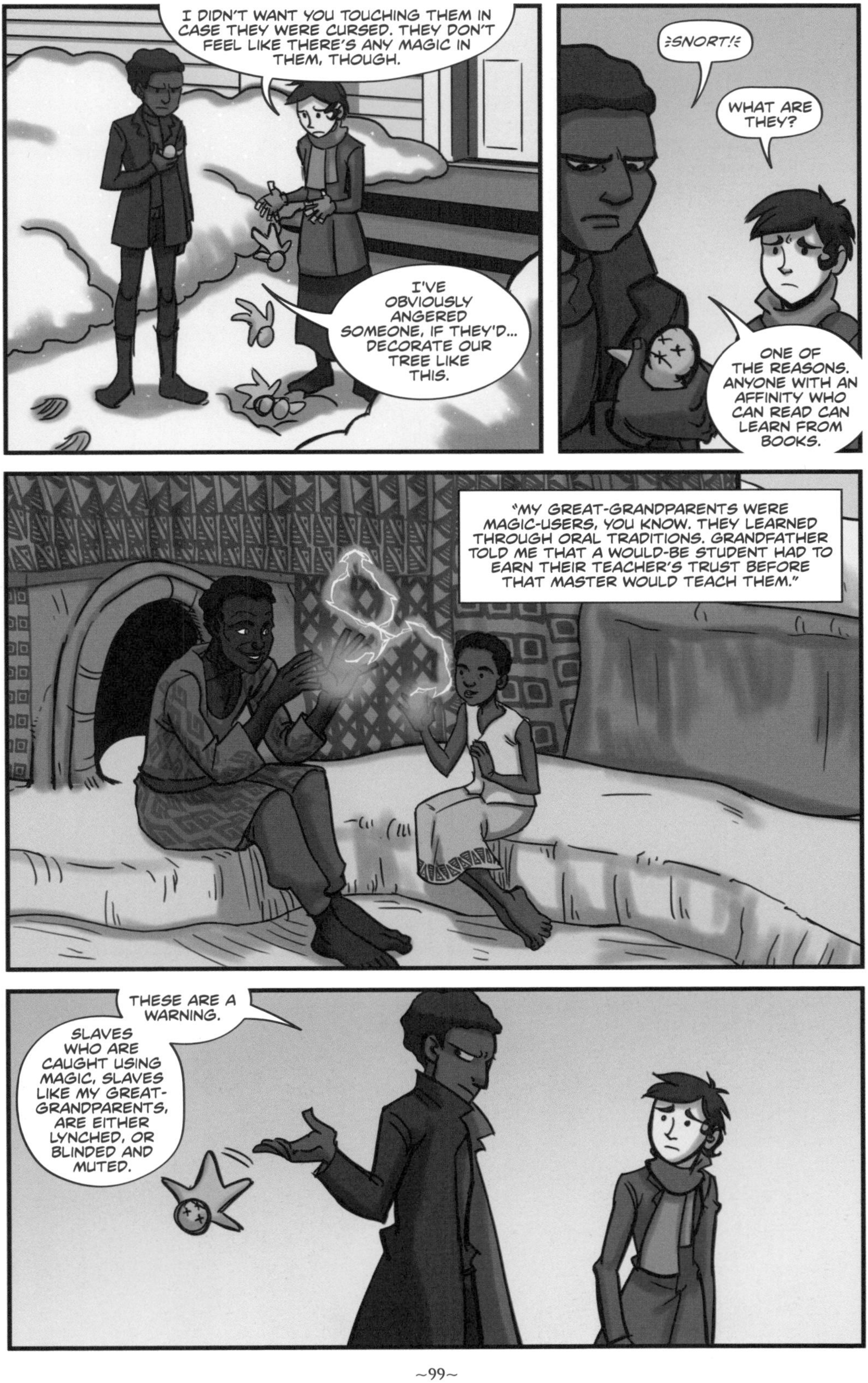
I DIDN'T WANT YOU TOUCHING THEM IN CASE THEY WERE CURSED. THEY DON'T FEEL LIKE THERE'S ANY MAGIC IN THEM, THOUGH.
I'VE OBVIOUSLY ANGERED SOMEONE, IF THEY'D... DECORATE OUR TREE LIKE THIS.
SNORT!
WHAT ARE THEY?
ONE OF THE REASONS. ANYONE WITH AN AFFINITY WHO CAN READ CAN LEARN FROM BOOKS.
"MY GREAT-GRANDPARENTS WERE MAGIC-USERS, YOU KNOW. THEY LEARNED THROUGH ORAL TRADITIONS. GRANDFATHER TOLD ME THAT A WOULD-BE STUDENT HAD TO EARN THEIR TEACHER'S TRUST BEFORE THAT MASTER WOULD TEACH THEM."
THESE ARE A WARNING.
SLAVES WHO ARE CAUGHT USING MAGIC, SLAVES LIKE MY GREAT-GRANDPARENTS, ARE EITHER LYNCHED, OR BLINDED AND MUTED.

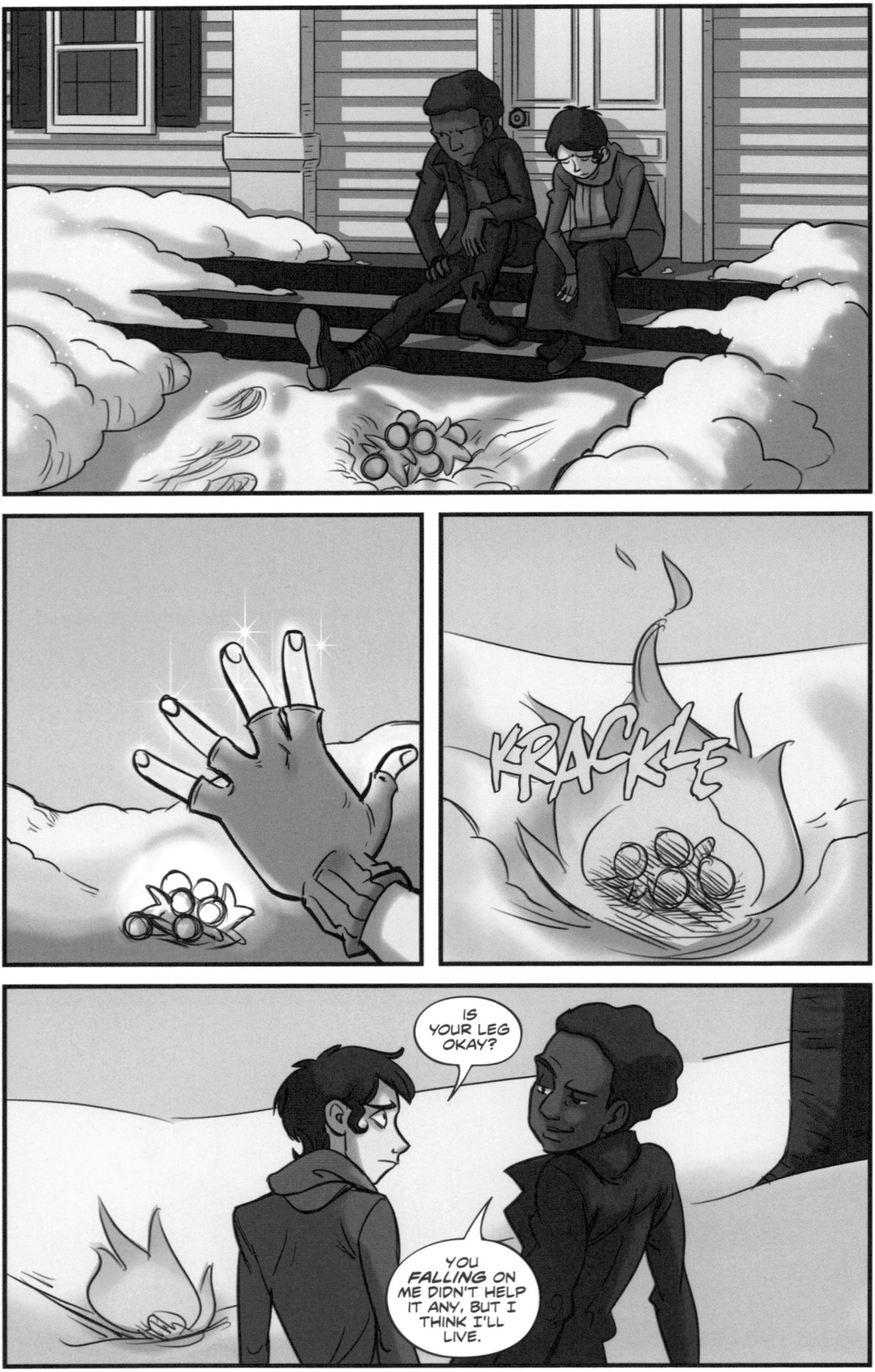
KRACKLE
IS YOUR LEG OKAY?
YOU FALLING ON ME DIDN'T HELP IT ANY, BUT I THINK I'LL LIVE.

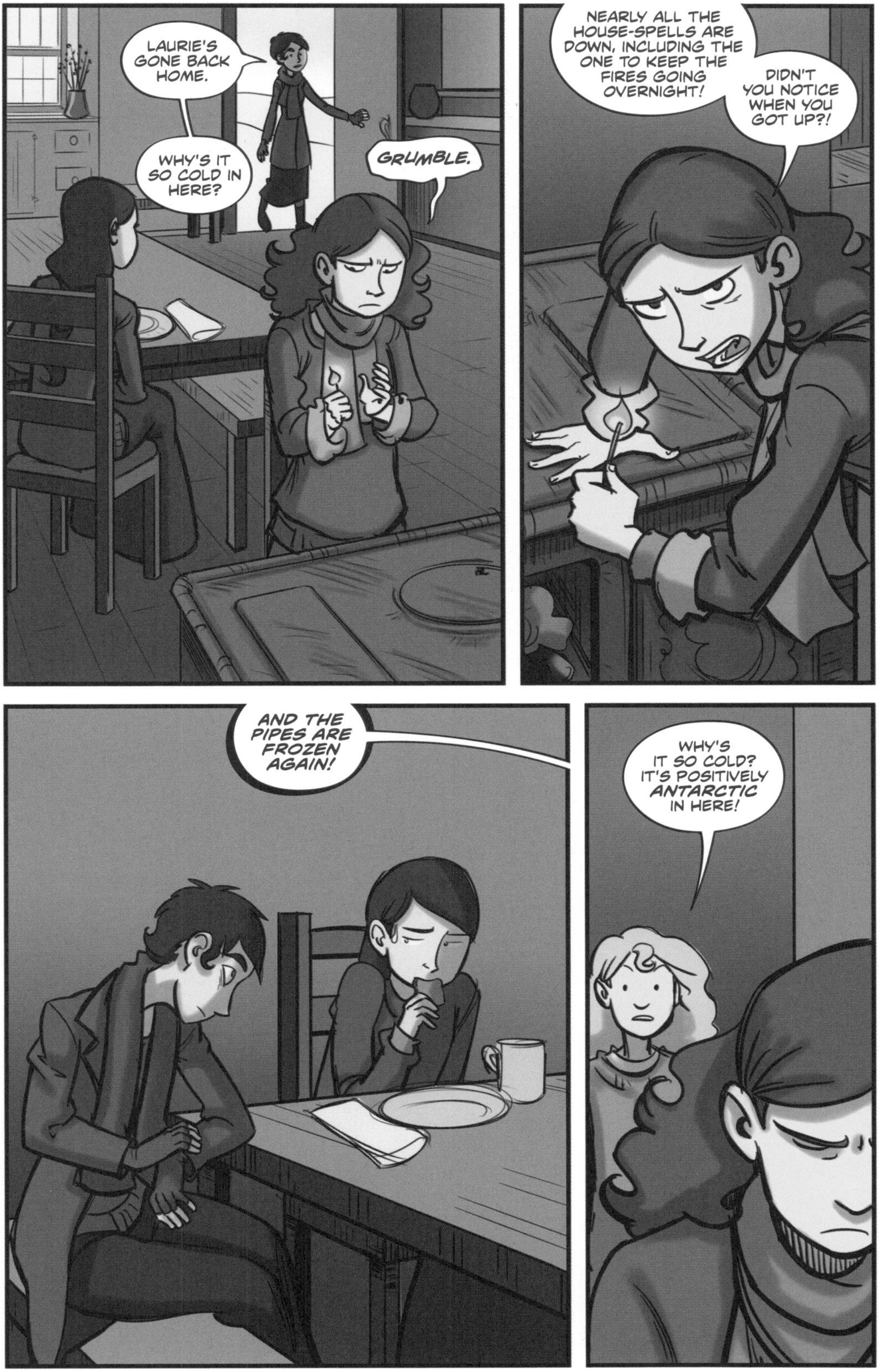
LAURIE'S GONE BACK HOME.
WHY'S IT SO COLD IN HERE?
GRUMBLE.
NEARLY ALL THE HOUSE-SPELLS ARE DOWN, INCLUDING THE ONE TO KEEP THE FIRES GOING OVERNIGHT!
DIDN'T YOU NOTICE WHEN YOU GOT UP?!
AND THE PIPES ARE FROZEN AGAIN!
WHY'S IT SO COLD? IT'S POSITIVELY ANTARCTIC IN HERE!

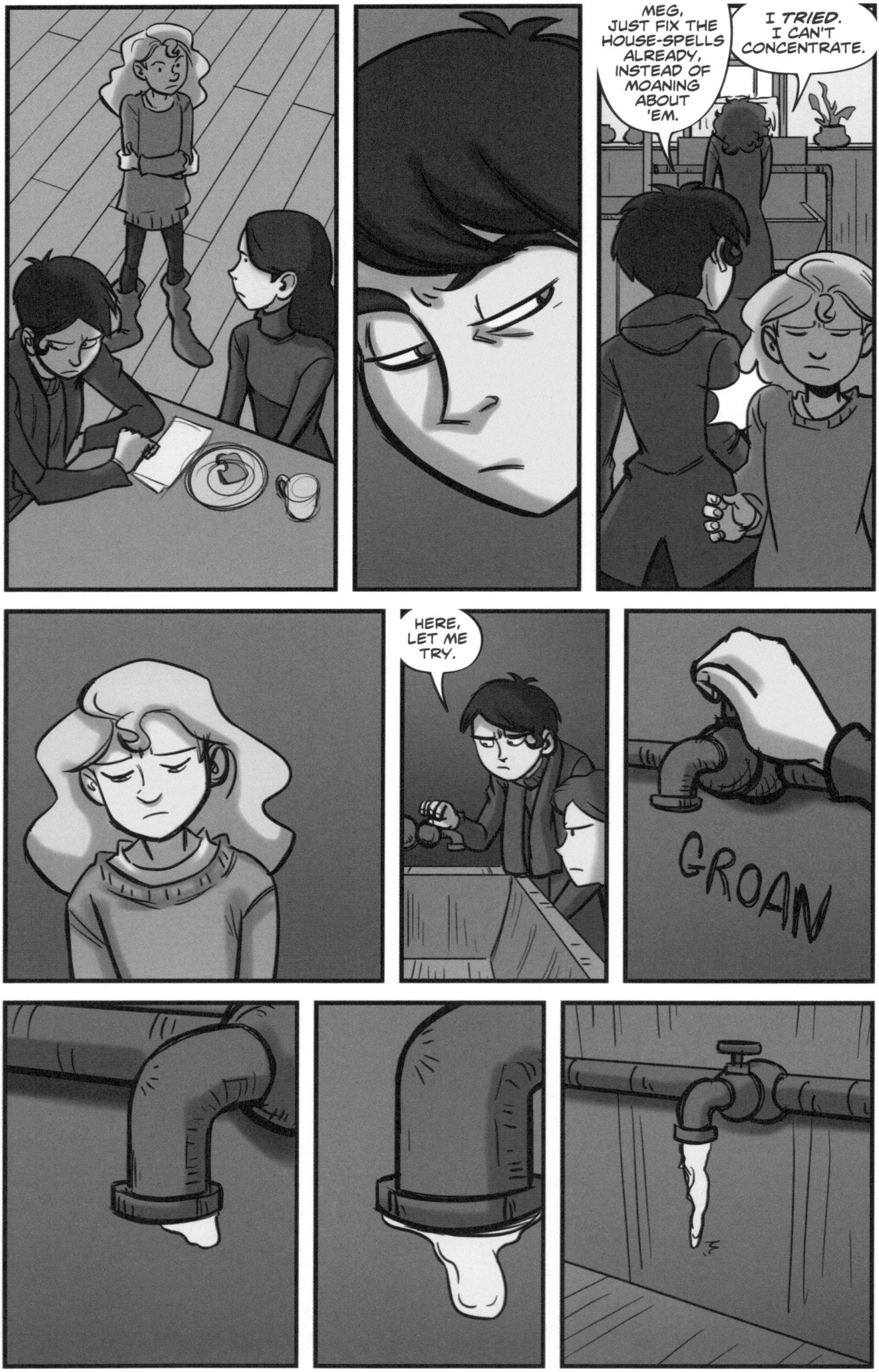
MEG, JUST FIX THE HOUSE-SPELLS ALREADY, INSTEAD OF MOANING ABOUT 'EM.
I TRIED. I CAN'T CONCENTRATE.
HERE, LET ME TRY.
GROAN

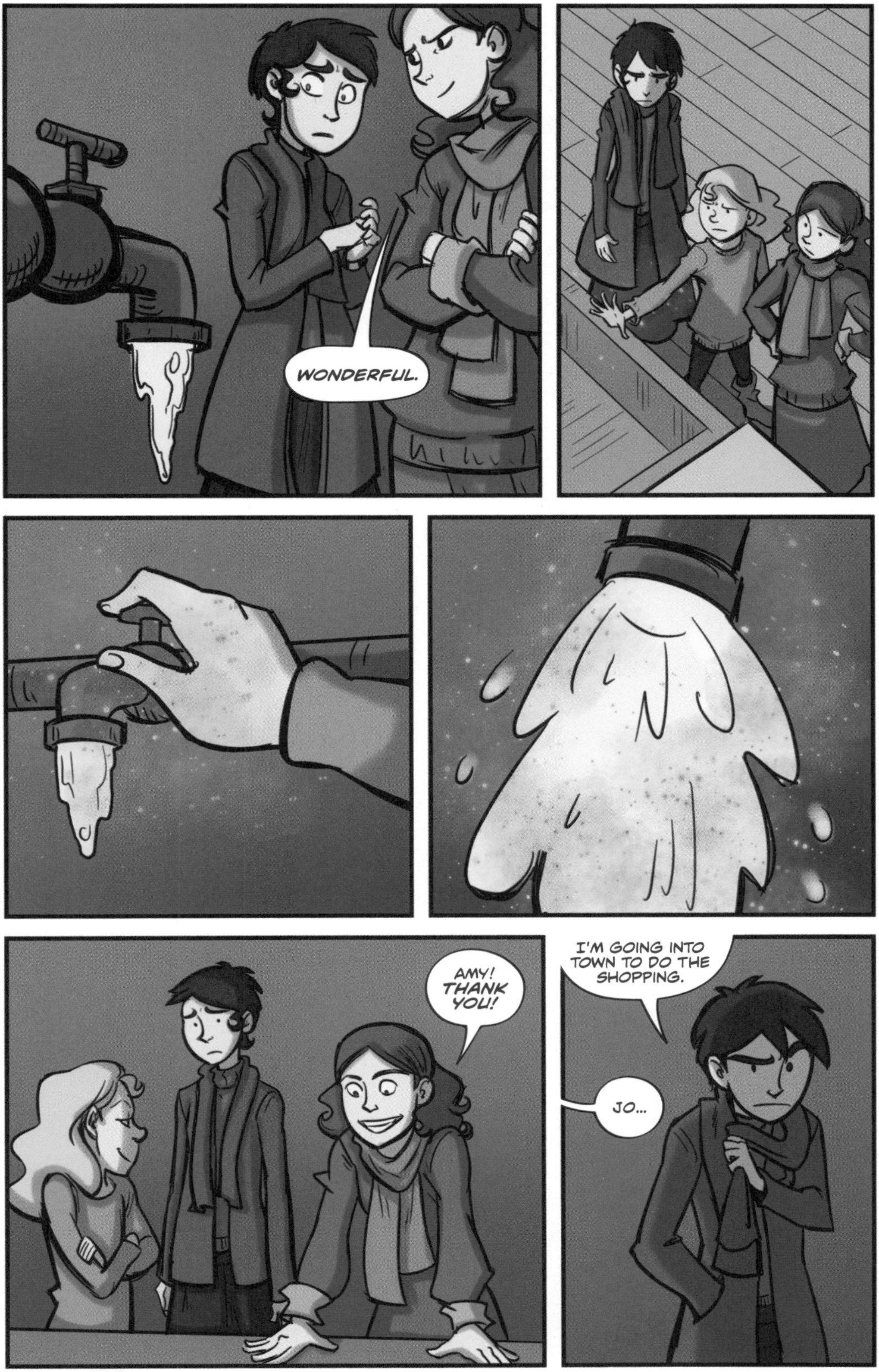
WONDERFUL.
AMY! THANK YOU!
I'M GOING INTO TOWN TO DO THE SHOPPING.
JO...

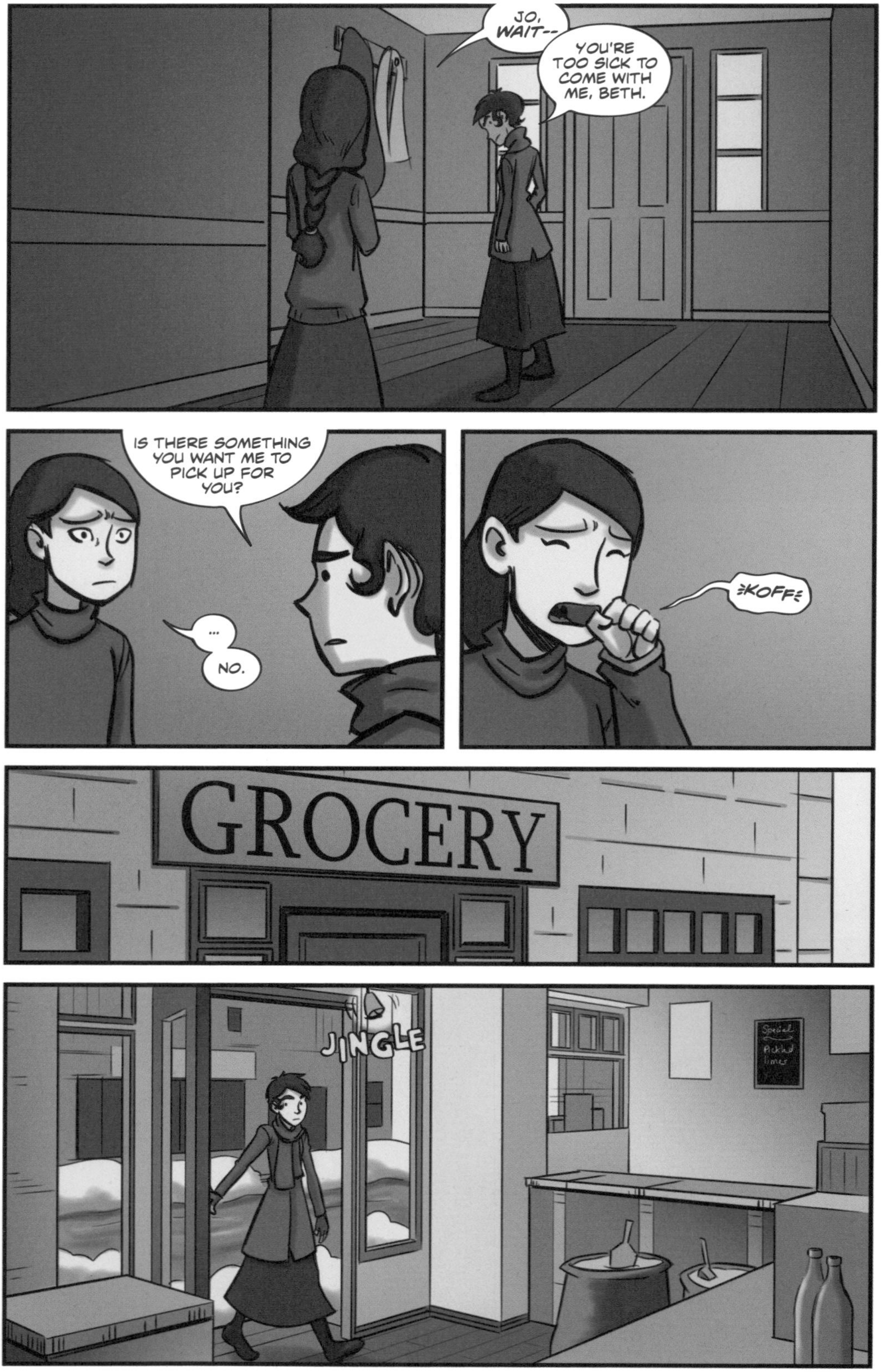
JO, WAIT--
YOU'RE TOO SICK TO COME WITH ME, BETH.
IS THERE SOMETHING YOU WANT ME TO PICK UP FOR YOU?
...
NO.
KOFF
GROCERY
JINGLE
Special
Pickled limes

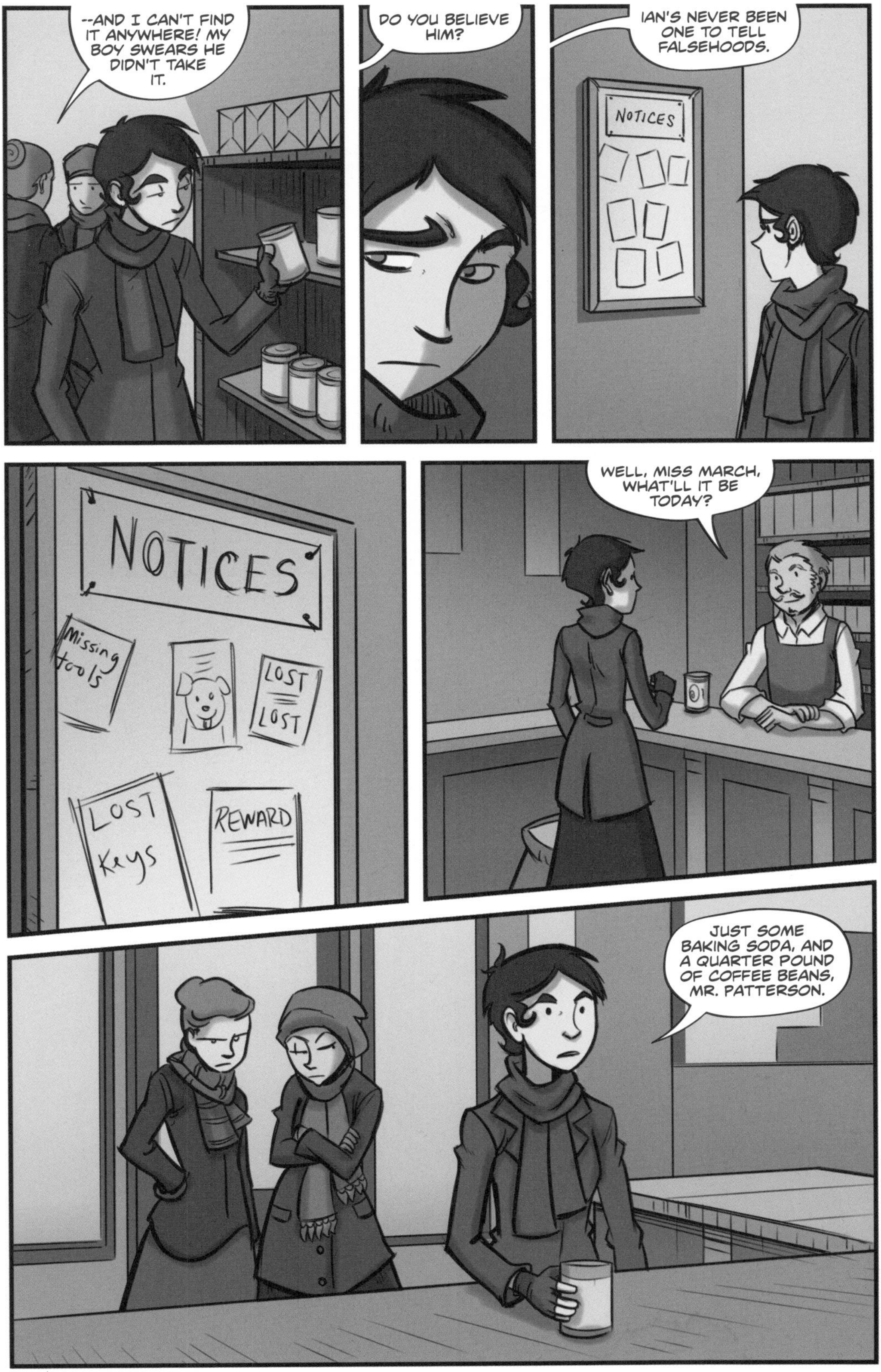
--AND I CAN'T FIND IT ANYWHERE! MY BOY SWEARS HE DIDN'T TAKE IT.
DO YOU BELIEVE HIM?
IAN'S NEVER BEEN ONE TO TELL FALSEHOODS.
NOTICES
NOTICES
Missing tools
LOST LOST
LOST Keys
REWARD
WELL, MISS MARCH, WHAT'LL IT BE TODAY?
JUST SOME BAKING SODA, AND A QUARTER POUND OF COFFEE BEANS, MR. PATTERSON.

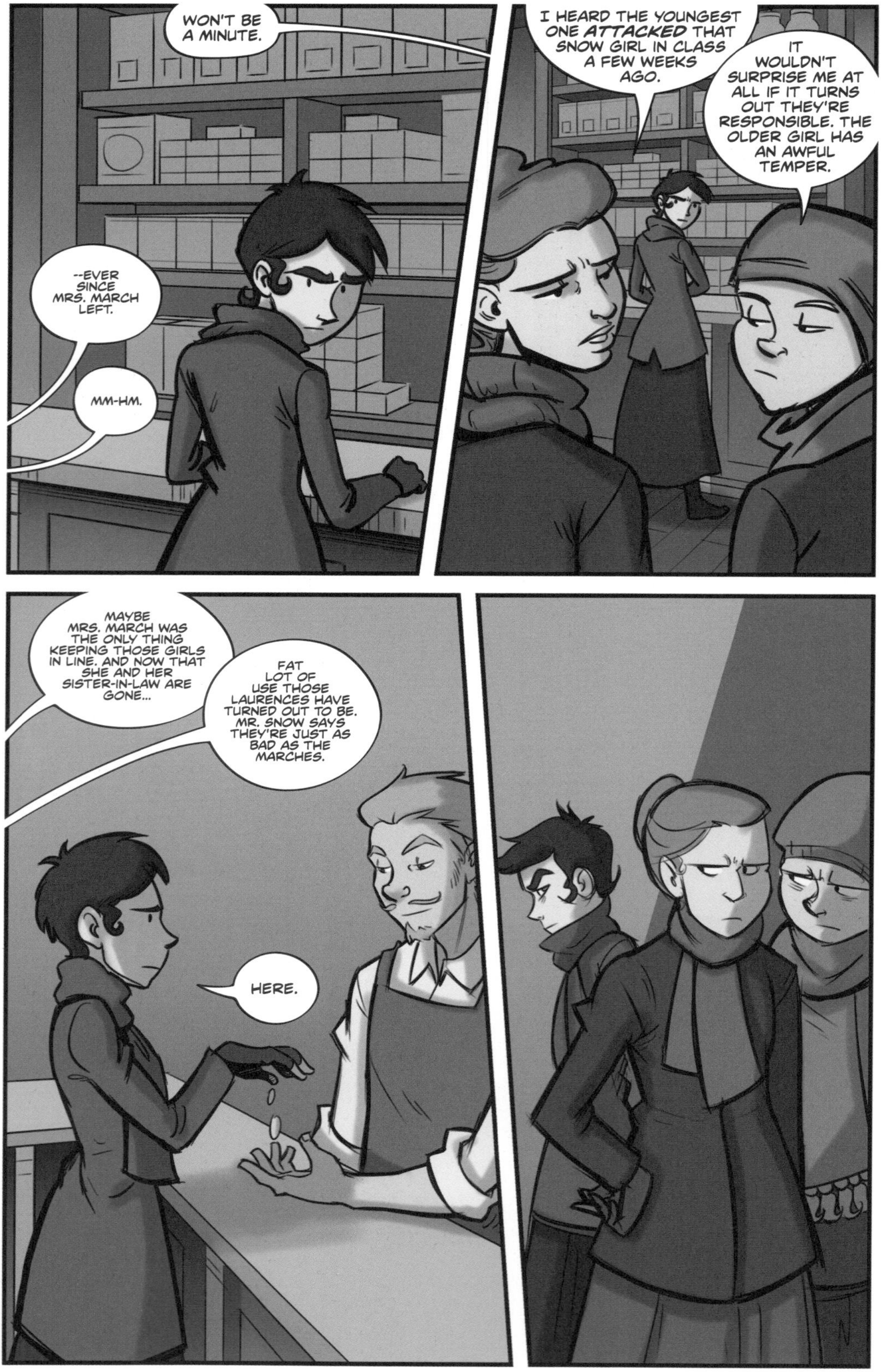
WON'T BE A MINUTE.
--EVER SINCE MRS. MARCH LEFT.
MM-HM.
I HEARD THE YOUNGEST ONE ATTACKED THAT SNOW GIRL IN CLASS A FEW WEEKS AGO.
IT WOULDN'T SURPRISE ME AT ALL IF IT TURNS OUT THEY'RE RESPONSIBLE. THE OLDER GIRL HAS AN AWFUL TEMPER.
MAYBE MRS. MARCH WAS THE ONLY THING KEEPING THOSE GIRLS IN LINE. AND NOW THAT SHE AND HER SISTER-IN-LAW ARE GONE...
FAT LOT OF USE THOSE LAURENCES HAVE TURNED OUT TO BE. MR. SNOW SAYS THEY'RE JUST AS BAD AS THE MARCHES.
HERE.

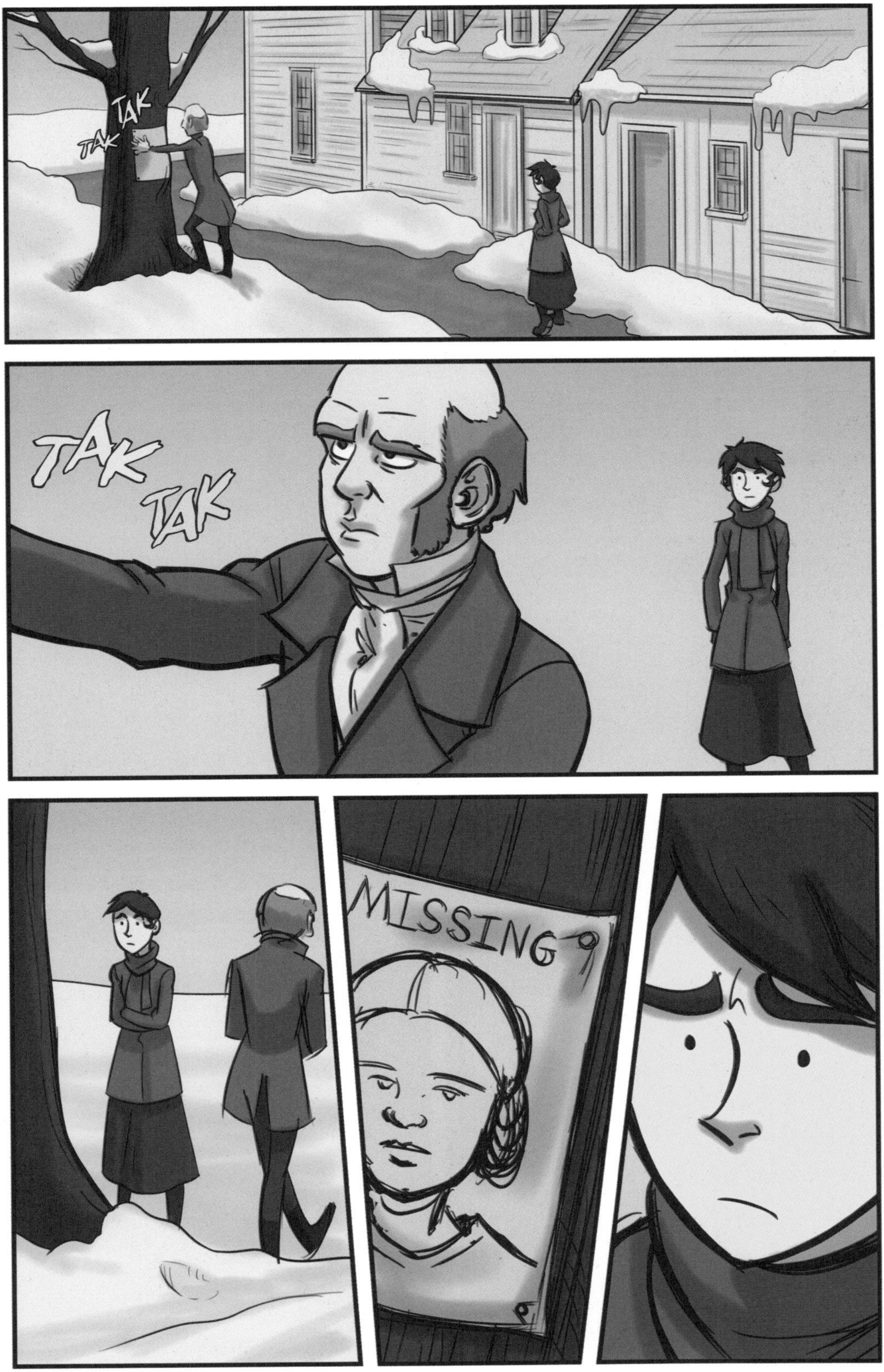
TAK
TAK
TAK
TAK
MISSING

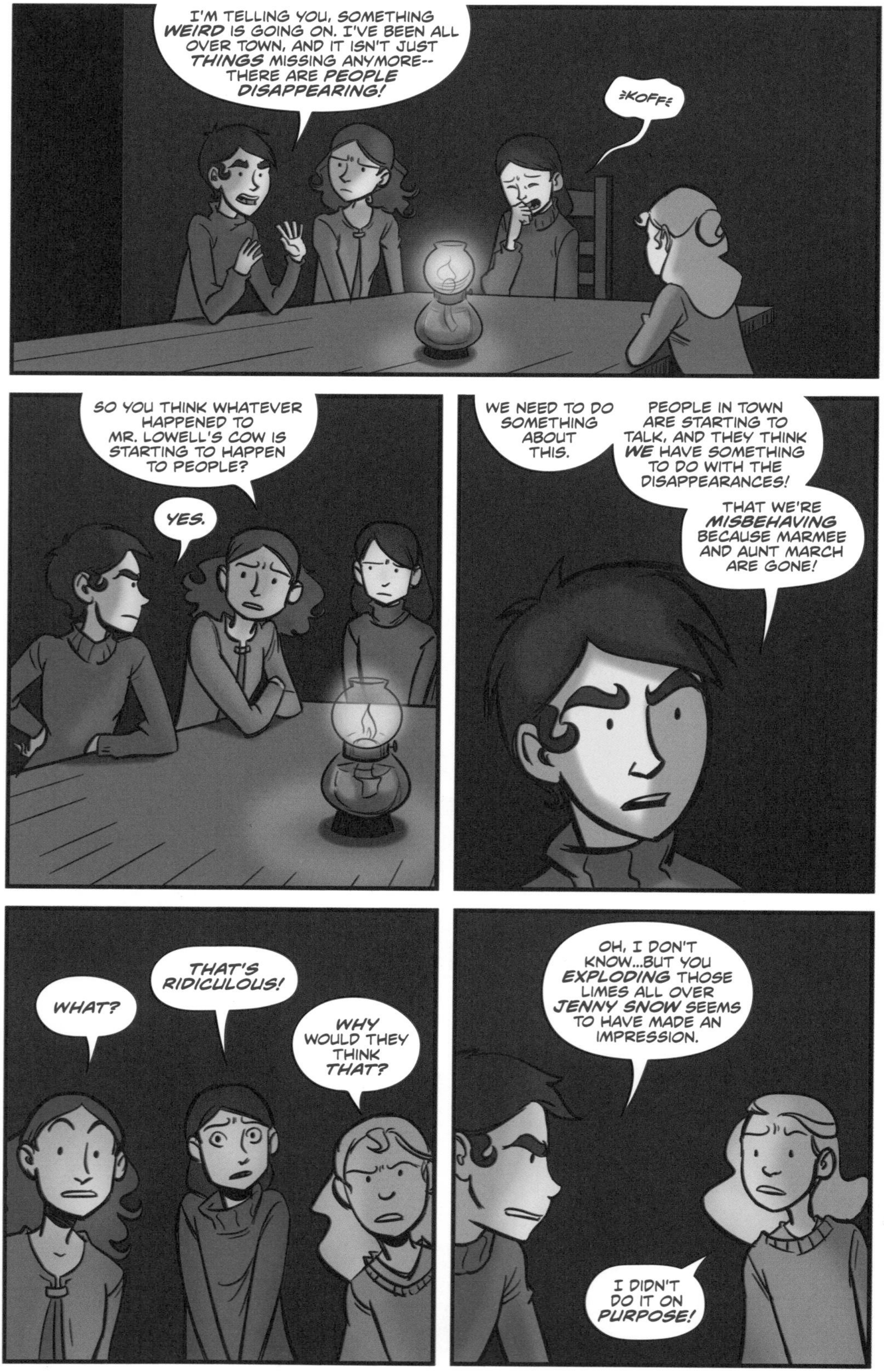
I'M TELLING YOU, SOMETHING WEIRD IS GOING ON. I'VE BEEN ALL OVER TOWN, AND IT ISN'T JUST THINGS MISSING ANYMORE-- THERE ARE PEOPLE DISAPPEARING!
KOFF
SO YOU THINK WHATEVER HAPPENED TO MR. LOWELL'S COW IS STARTING TO HAPPEN TO PEOPLE?
YES.
WE NEED TO DO SOMETHING ABOUT THIS.
PEOPLE IN TOWN ARE STARTING TO TALK, AND THEY THINK WE HAVE SOMETHING TO DO WITH THE DISAPPEARANCES!
THAT WE'RE MISBEHAVING BECAUSE MARMEE AND AUNT MARCH ARE GONE!
WHAT?
THAT'S RIDICULOUS!
WHY WOULD THEY THINK THAT?
OH, I DON'T KNOW...BUT YOU EXPLODING THOSE LIMES ALL OVER JENNY SNOW SEEMS TO HAVE MADE AN IMPRESSION.
I DIDN'T DO IT ON PURPOSE!

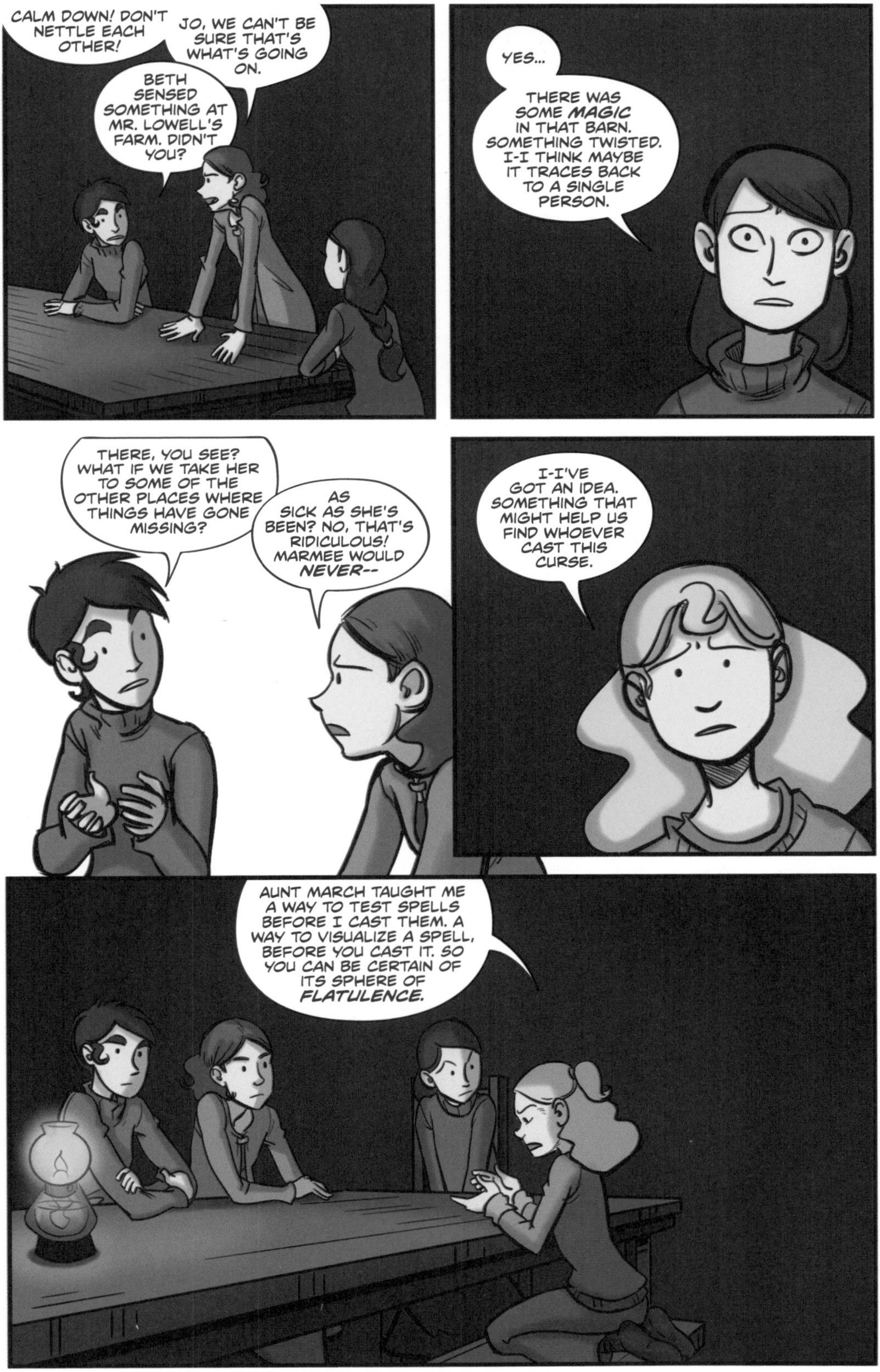
CALM DOWN! DON'T NETTLE EACH OTHER!
JO, WE CAN'T BE SURE THAT'S WHAT'S GOING ON.
BETH SENSED SOMETHING AT MR. LOWELL'S FARM. DIDN'T YOU?
YES...
THERE WAS SOME *MAGIC* IN THAT BARN. SOMETHING TWISTED. I-I THINK MAYBE IT TRACES BACK TO A SINGLE PERSON.
THERE, YOU SEE? WHAT IF WE TAKE HER TO SOME OF THE OTHER PLACES WHERE THINGS HAVE GONE MISSING?
AS SICK AS SHE'S BEEN? NO, THAT'S RIDICULOUS! MARMEE WOULD *NEVER--*
I-I'VE GOT AN IDEA. SOMETHING THAT MIGHT HELP US FIND WHOEVER CAST THIS CURSE.
AUNT MARCH TAUGHT ME A WAY TO TEST SPELLS BEFORE I CAST THEM. A WAY TO VISUALIZE A SPELL, BEFORE YOU CAST IT. SO YOU CAN BE CERTAIN OF ITS SPHERE OF *FLATULENCE.*

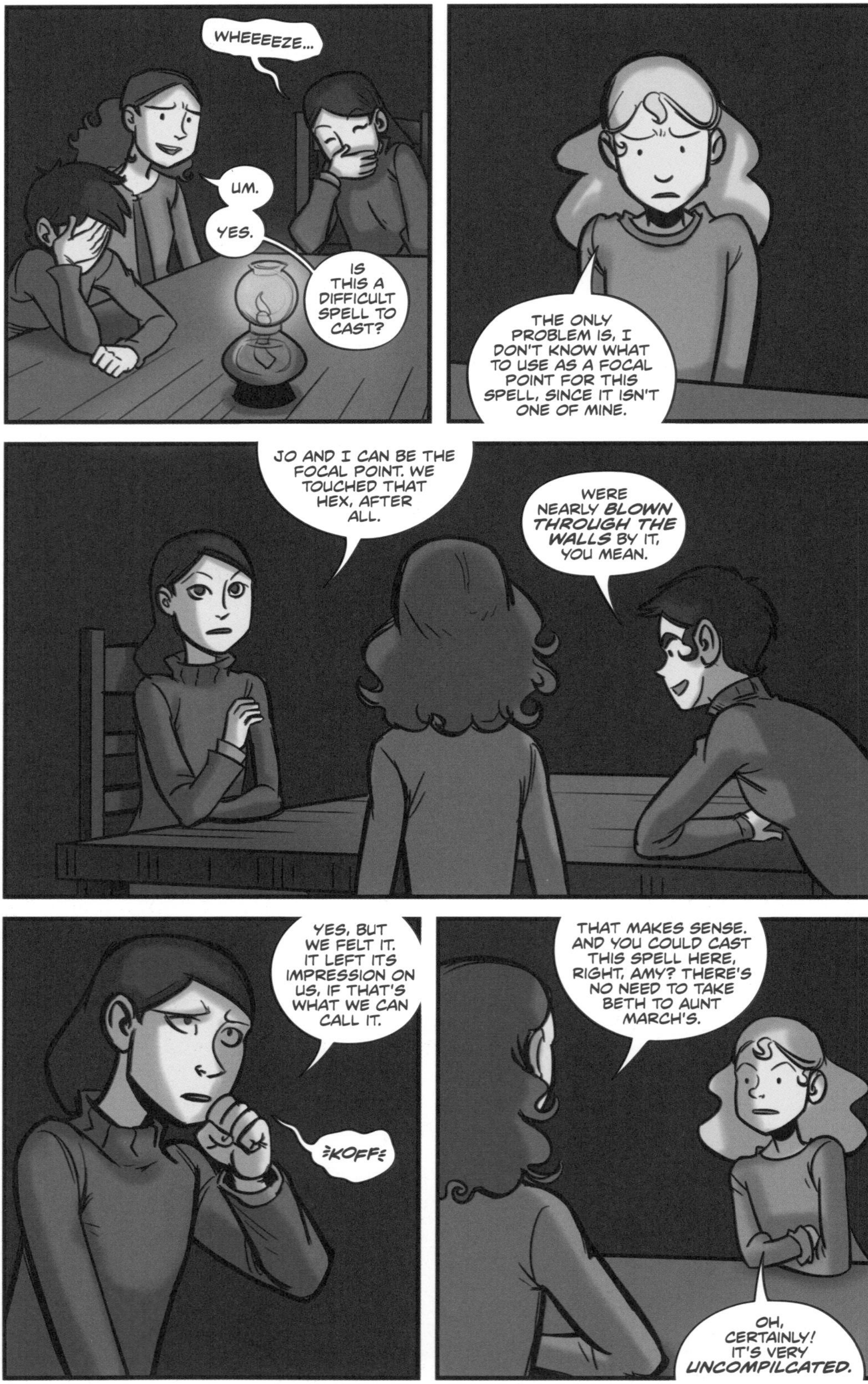
WHEEEEZE...
UM.
YES.
IS THIS A DIFFICULT SPELL TO CAST?
THE ONLY PROBLEM IS, I DON'T KNOW WHAT TO USE AS A FOCAL POINT FOR THIS SPELL, SINCE IT ISN'T ONE OF MINE.
JO AND I CAN BE THE FOCAL POINT. WE TOUCHED THAT HEX, AFTER ALL.
WERE NEARLY BLOWN THROUGH THE WALLS BY IT, YOU MEAN.
YES, BUT WE FELT IT. IT LEFT ITS IMPRESSION ON US, IF THAT'S WHAT WE CAN CALL IT.
KOFF
THAT MAKES SENSE. AND YOU COULD CAST THIS SPELL HERE, RIGHT, AMY? THERE'S NO NEED TO TAKE BETH TO AUNT MARCH'S.
OH, CERTAINLY! IT'S VERY UNCOMPILCATED.

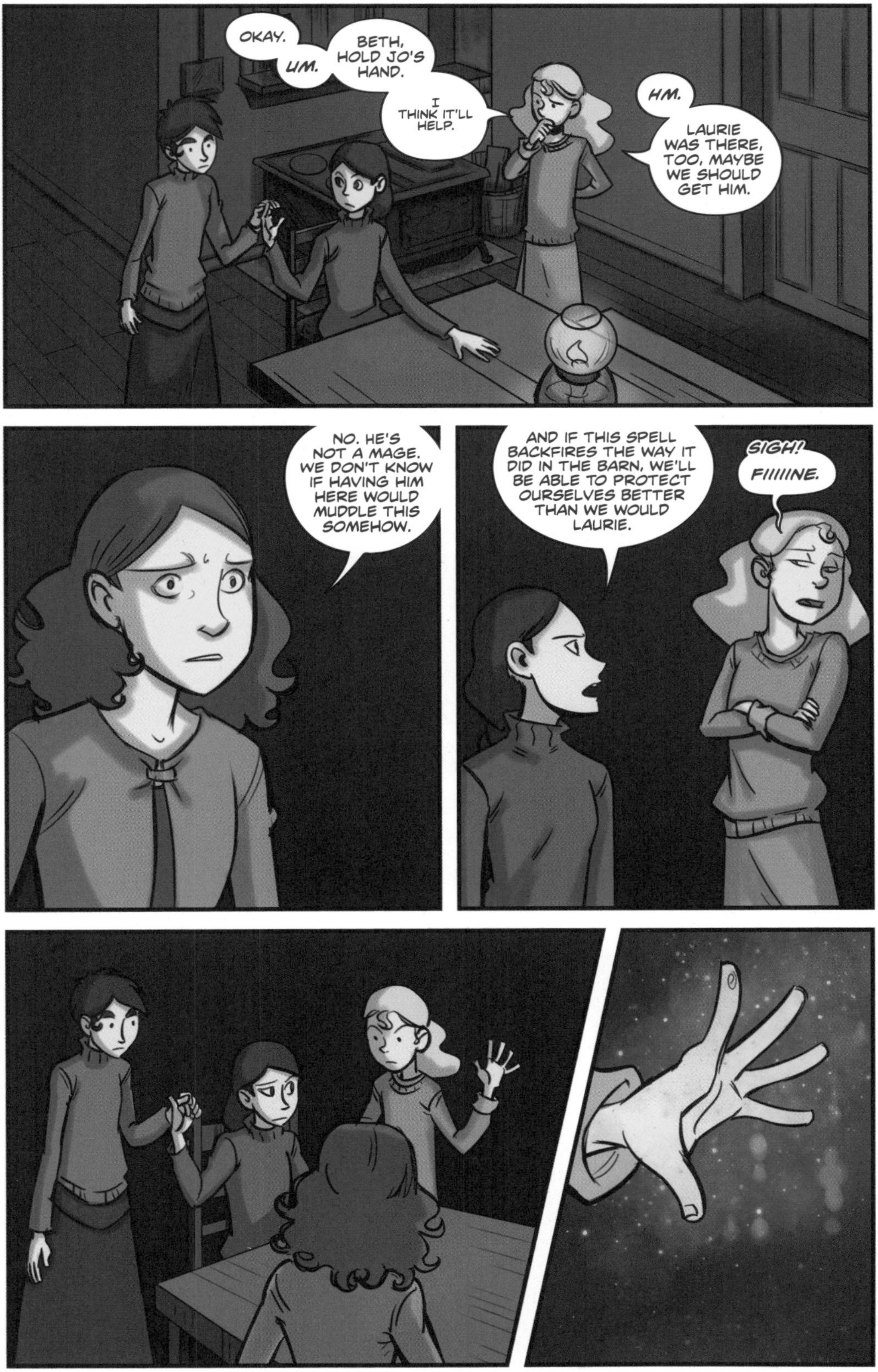
OKAY.
UM.
BETH, HOLD JO'S HAND.
I THINK IT'LL HELP.
HM.
LAURIE WAS THERE, TOO, MAYBE WE SHOULD GET HIM.
NO. HE'S NOT A MAGE. WE DON'T KNOW IF HAVING HIM HERE WOULD MUDDLE THIS SOMEHOW.
AND IF THIS SPELL BACKFIRES THE WAY IT DID IN THE BARN, WE'LL BE ABLE TO PROTECT OURSELVES BETTER THAN WE WOULD LAURIE.
SIGH!
FIIIIINE.

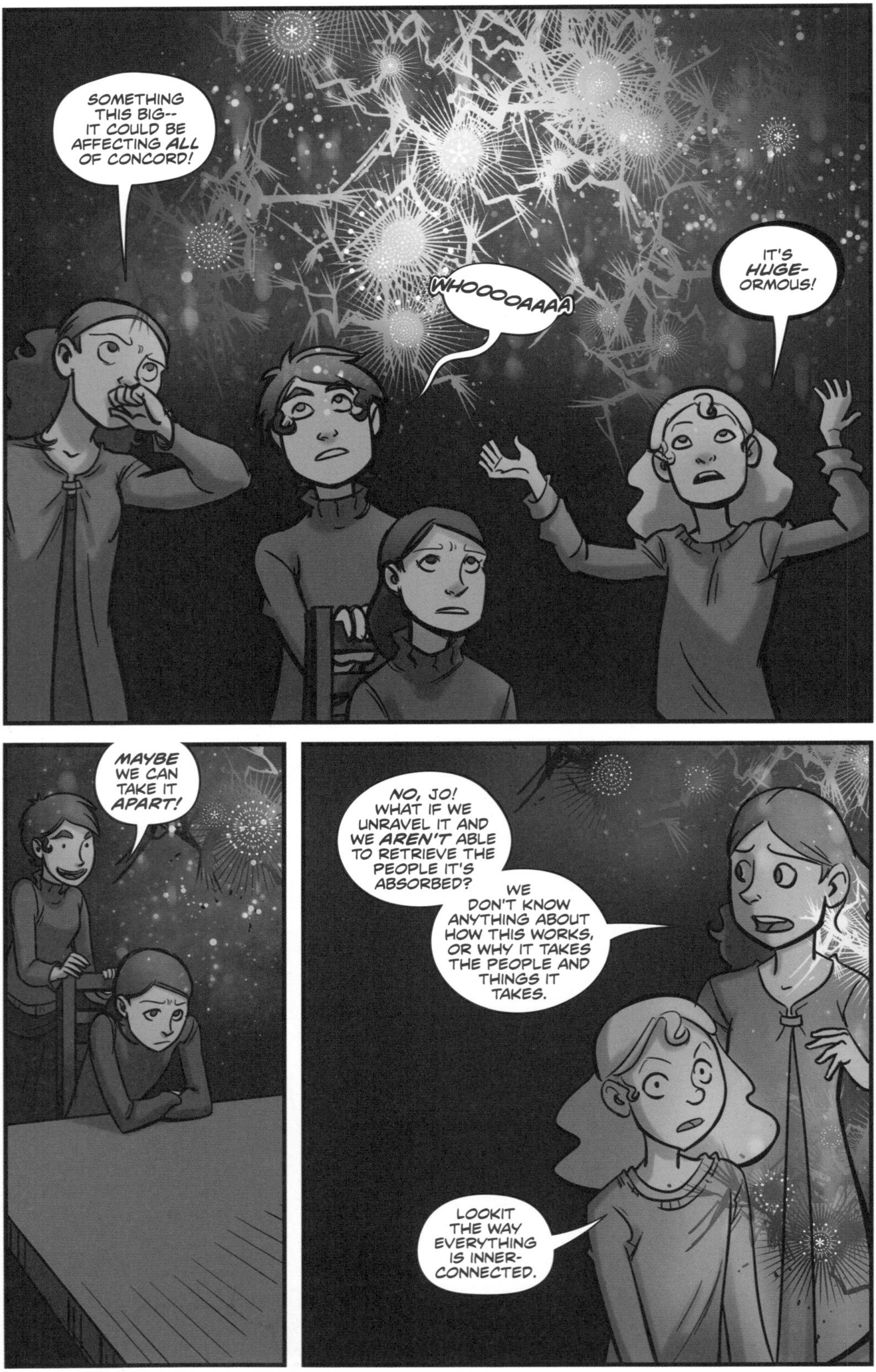
SOMETHING THIS BIG-- IT COULD BE AFFECTING *ALL* OF CONCORD!
WHOOOOAAAA
IT'S *HUGE*-ORMOUS!
MAYBE WE CAN TAKE IT *APART!*
NO, JO! WHAT IF WE UNRAVEL IT AND WE *AREN'T* ABLE TO RETRIEVE THE PEOPLE IT'S ABSORBED?
WE DON'T KNOW ANYTHING ABOUT HOW THIS WORKS, OR WHY IT TAKES THE PEOPLE AND THINGS IT TAKES.
LOOKIT THE WAY EVERYTHING IS INNER-CONNECTED.

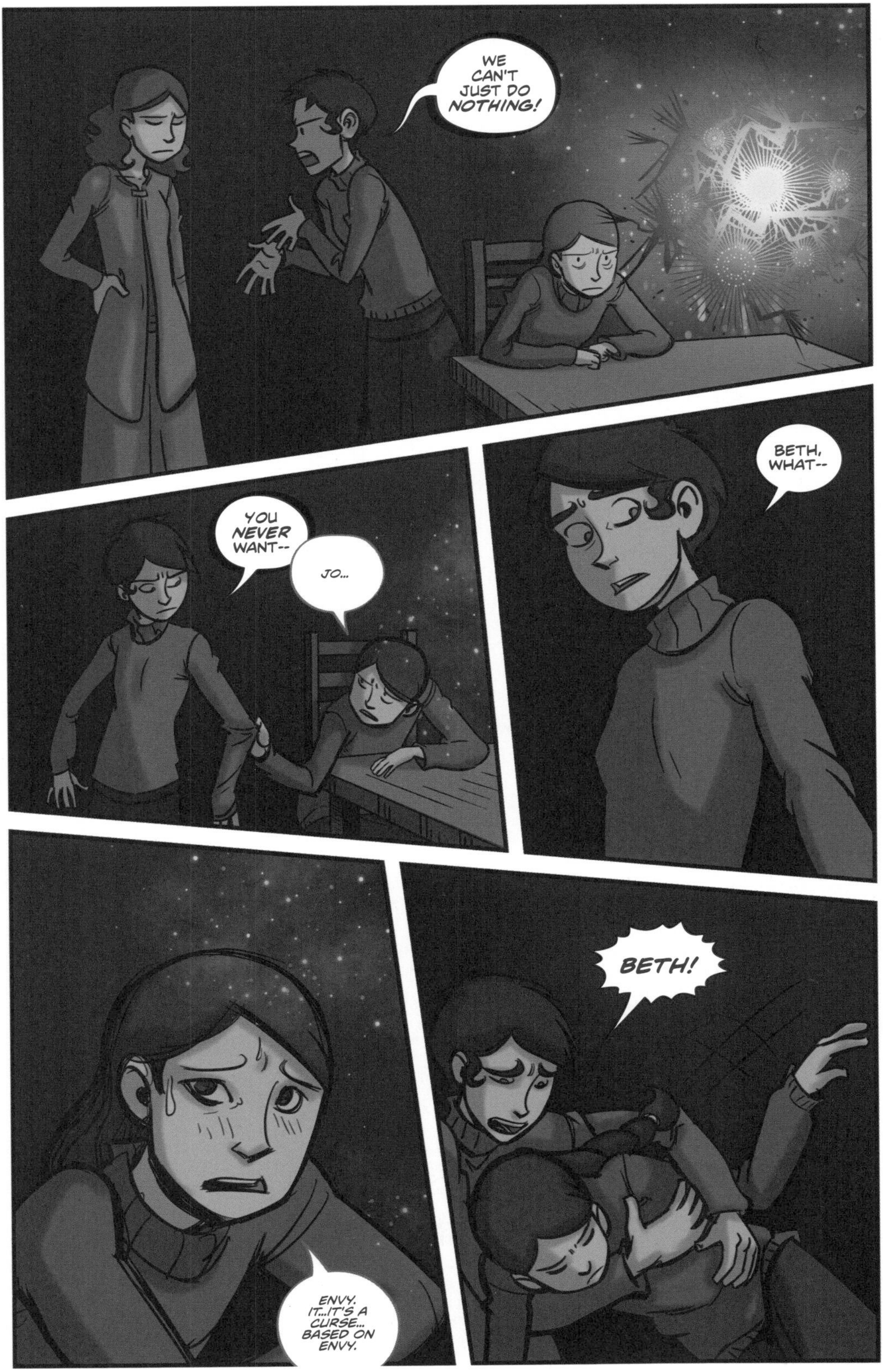
WE CAN'T JUST DO NOTHING!
YOU NEVER WANT--
JO...
BETH, WHAT--
ENVY. IT...IT'S A CURSE... BASED ON ENVY.
BETH!

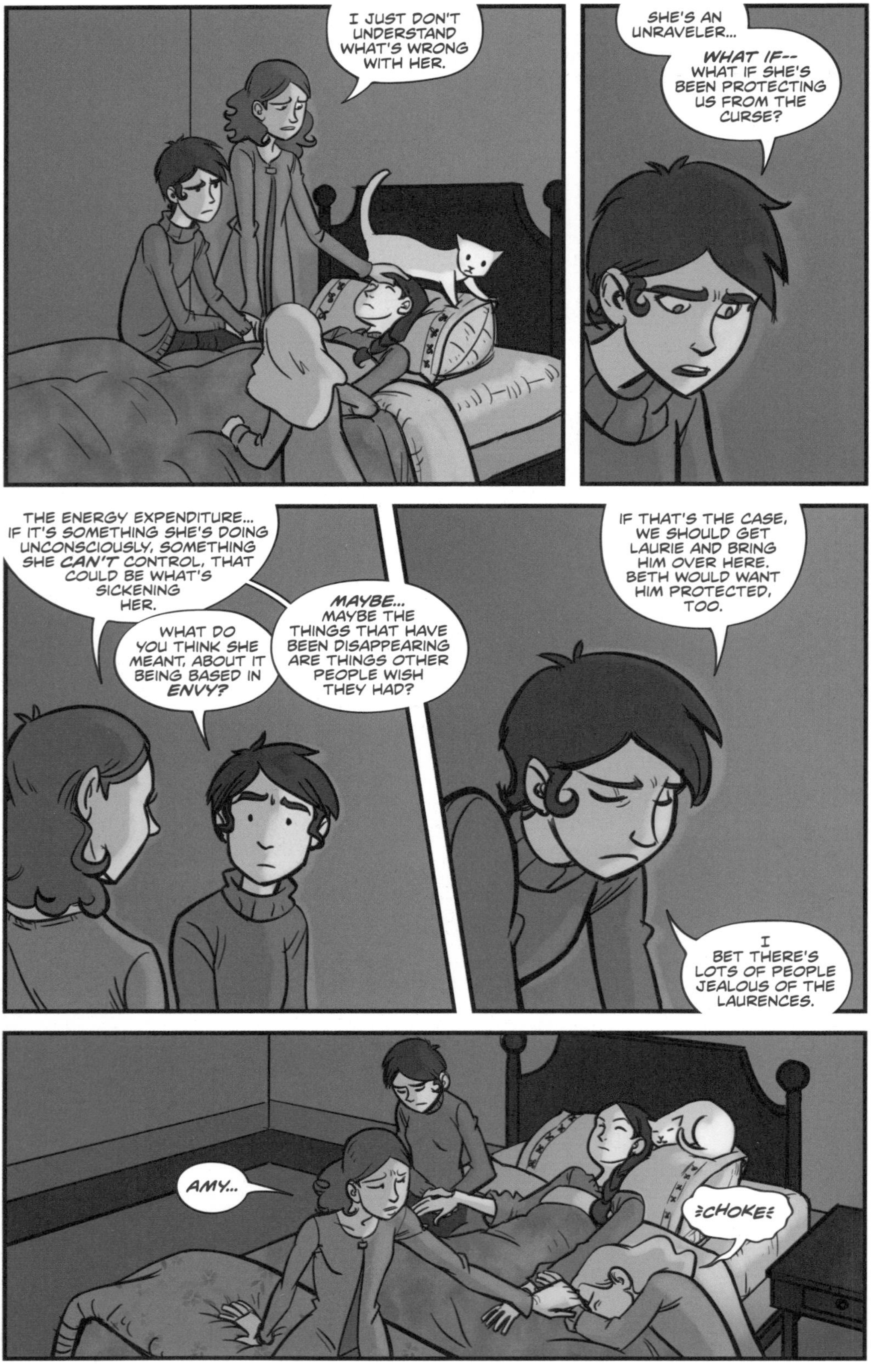
I JUST DON'T UNDERSTAND WHAT'S WRONG WITH HER.
SHE'S AN UNRAVELER...
WHAT IF-- WHAT IF SHE'S BEEN PROTECTING US FROM THE CURSE?
THE ENERGY EXPENDITURE... IF IT'S SOMETHING SHE'S DOING UNCONSCIOUSLY, SOMETHING SHE *CAN'T* CONTROL, THAT COULD BE WHAT'S SICKENING HER.
WHAT DO YOU THINK SHE MEANT, ABOUT IT BEING BASED IN *ENVY?*
MAYBE... MAYBE THE THINGS THAT HAVE BEEN DISAPPEARING ARE THINGS OTHER PEOPLE WISH THEY HAD?
IF THAT'S THE CASE, WE SHOULD GET LAURIE AND BRING HIM OVER HERE. BETH WOULD WANT HIM PROTECTED, TOO.
I BET THERE'S LOTS OF PEOPLE JEALOUS OF THE LAURENCES.
AMY...
CHOKE

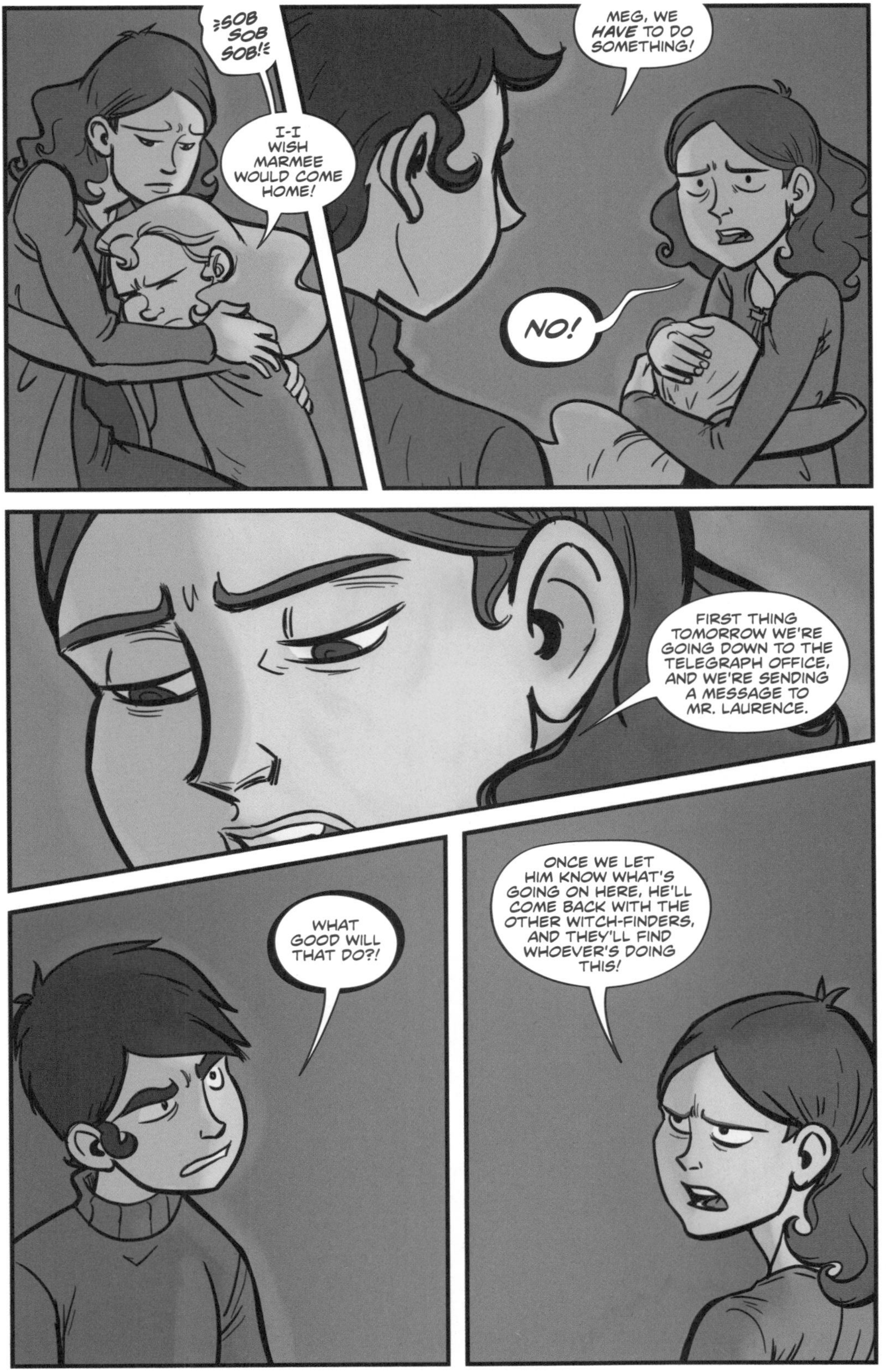
SOB SOB SOB!
I-I WISH MARMEE WOULD COME HOME!
MEG, WE HAVE TO DO SOMETHING!
NO!
FIRST THING TOMORROW WE'RE GOING DOWN TO THE TELEGRAPH OFFICE, AND WE'RE SENDING A MESSAGE TO MR. LAURENCE.
WHAT GOOD WILL THAT DO?!
ONCE WE LET HIM KNOW WHAT'S GOING ON HERE, HE'LL COME BACK WITH THE OTHER WITCH-FINDERS, AND THEY'LL FIND WHOEVER'S DOING THIS!

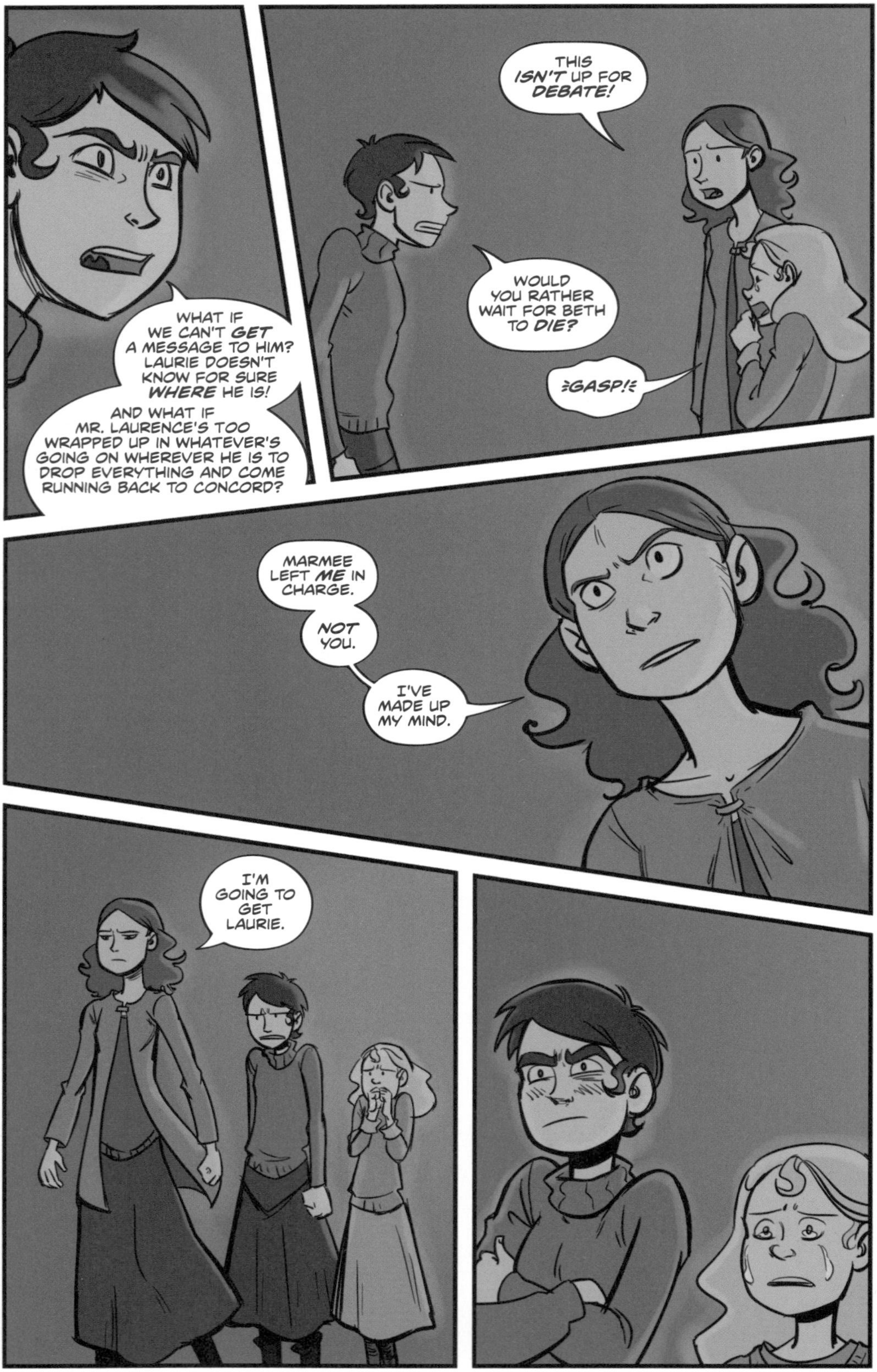
WHAT IF WE CAN'T GET A MESSAGE TO HIM? LAURIE DOESN'T KNOW FOR SURE WHERE HE IS!
AND WHAT IF MR. LAURENCE'S TOO WRAPPED UP IN WHATEVER'S GOING ON WHEREVER HE IS TO DROP EVERYTHING AND COME RUNNING BACK TO CONCORD?
THIS ISN'T UP FOR DEBATE!
WOULD YOU RATHER WAIT FOR BETH TO DIE?
GASP!
MARMEE LEFT ME IN CHARGE.
NOT YOU.
I'VE MADE UP MY MIND.
I'M GOING TO GET LAURIE.

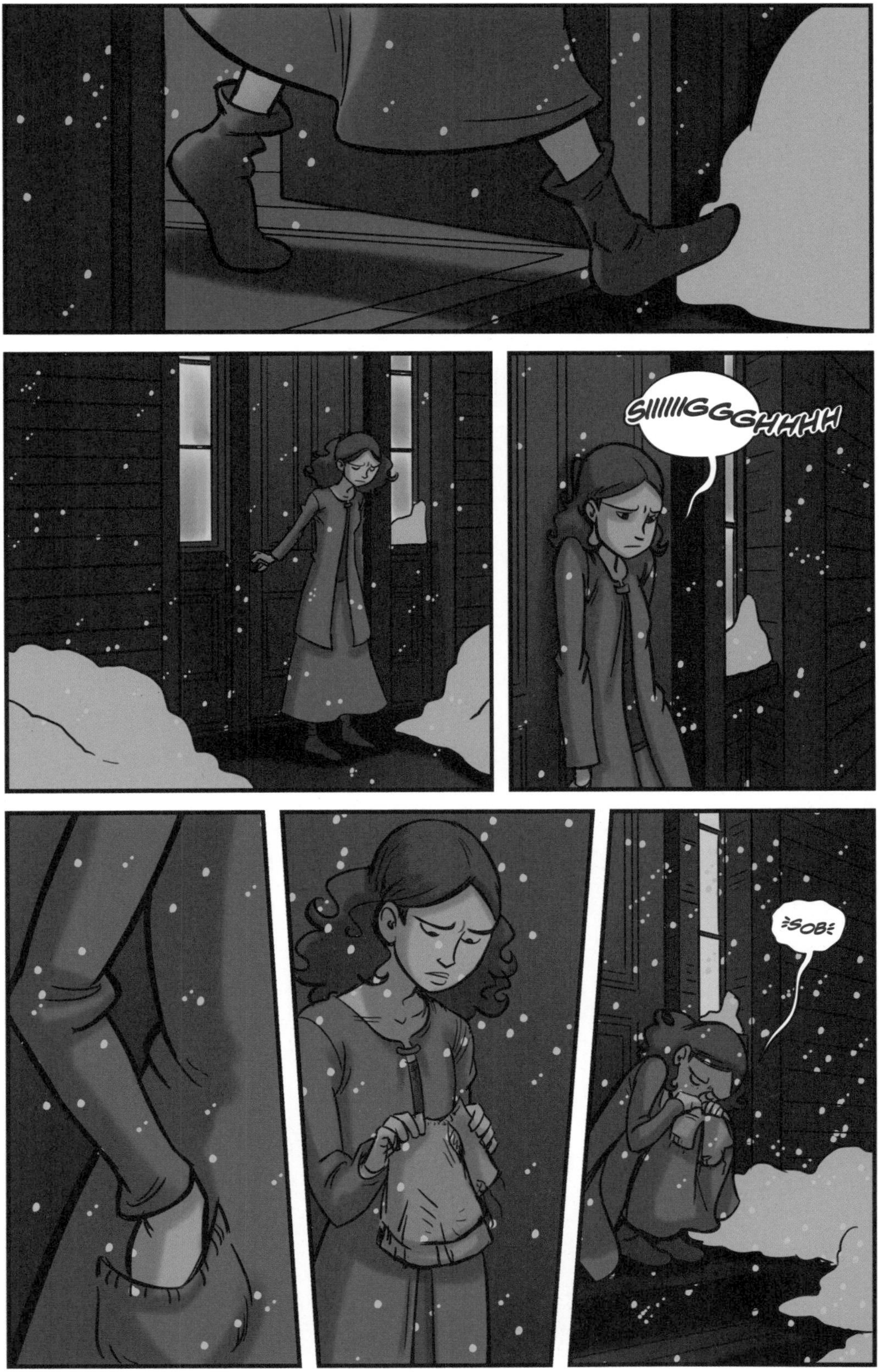
SIIIIIGGGHHHH
SOB

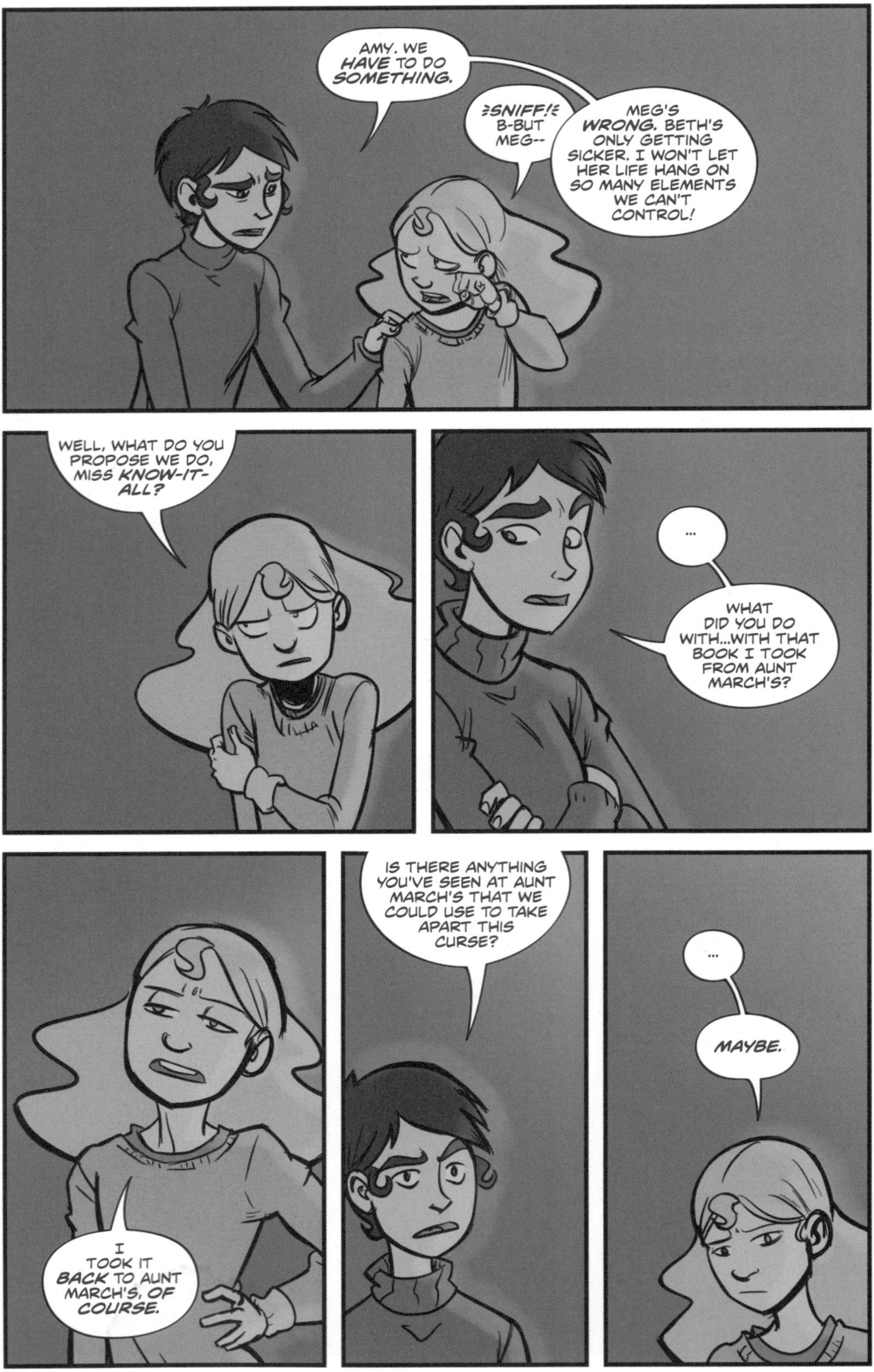
AMY. WE HAVE TO DO SOMETHING.
ᵜSNIFF!ᵜ B-BUT MEG--
MEG'S WRONG. BETH'S ONLY GETTING SICKER. I WON'T LET HER LIFE HANG ON SO MANY ELEMENTS WE CAN'T CONTROL!
WELL, WHAT DO YOU PROPOSE WE DO, MISS KNOW-IT-ALL?
...
WHAT DID YOU DO WITH...WITH THAT BOOK I TOOK FROM AUNT MARCH'S?
I TOOK IT BACK TO AUNT MARCH'S, OF COURSE.
IS THERE ANYTHING YOU'VE SEEN AT AUNT MARCH'S THAT WE COULD USE TO TAKE APART THIS CURSE?
...
MAYBE.

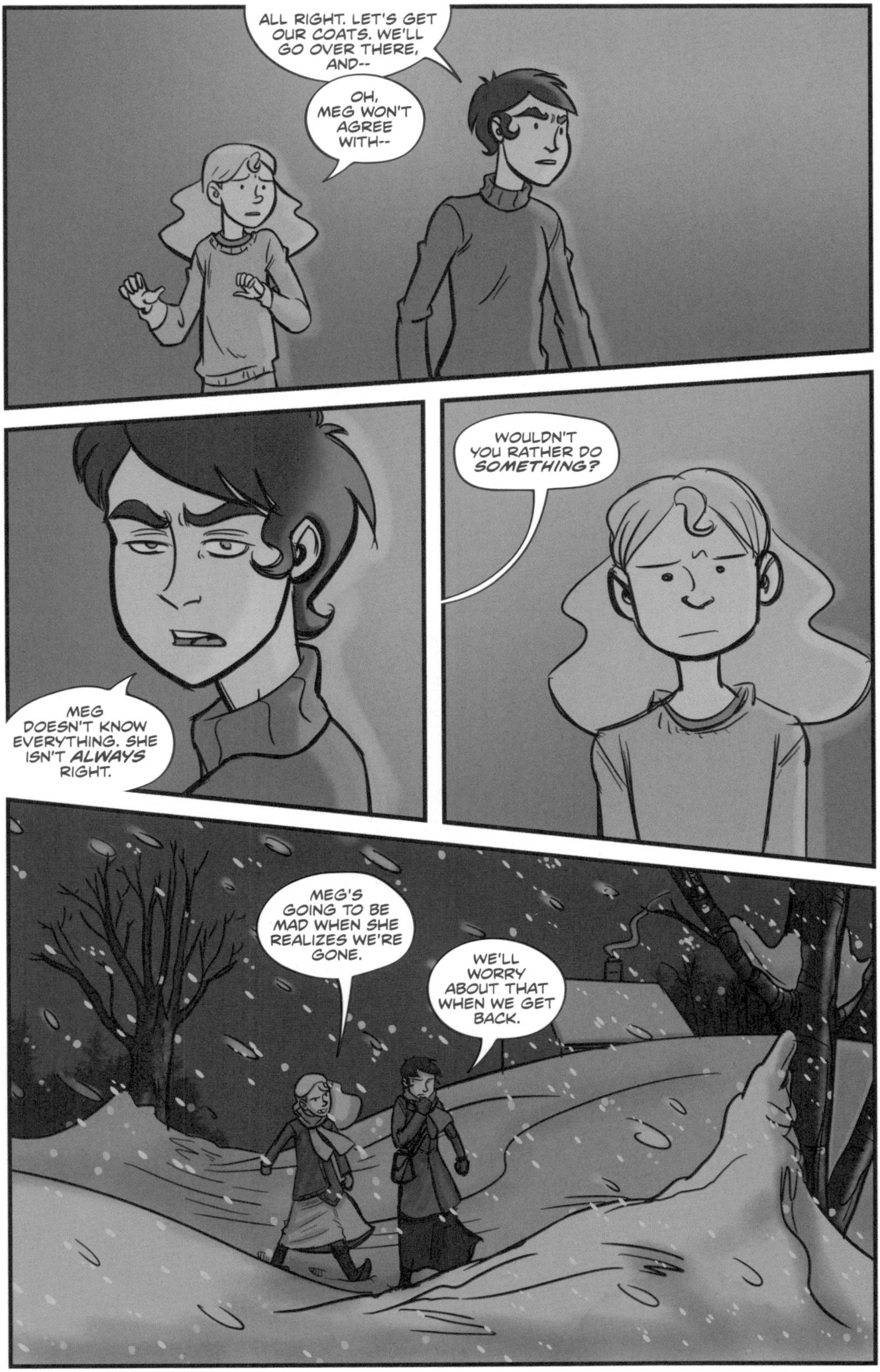
ALL RIGHT. LET'S GET OUR COATS. WE'LL GO OVER THERE, AND--
OH, MEG WON'T AGREE WITH--
MEG DOESN'T KNOW EVERYTHING. SHE ISN'T *ALWAYS* RIGHT.
WOULDN'T YOU RATHER DO *SOMETHING?*
MEG'S GOING TO BE MAD WHEN SHE REALIZES WE'RE GONE.
WE'LL WORRY ABOUT THAT WHEN WE GET BACK.

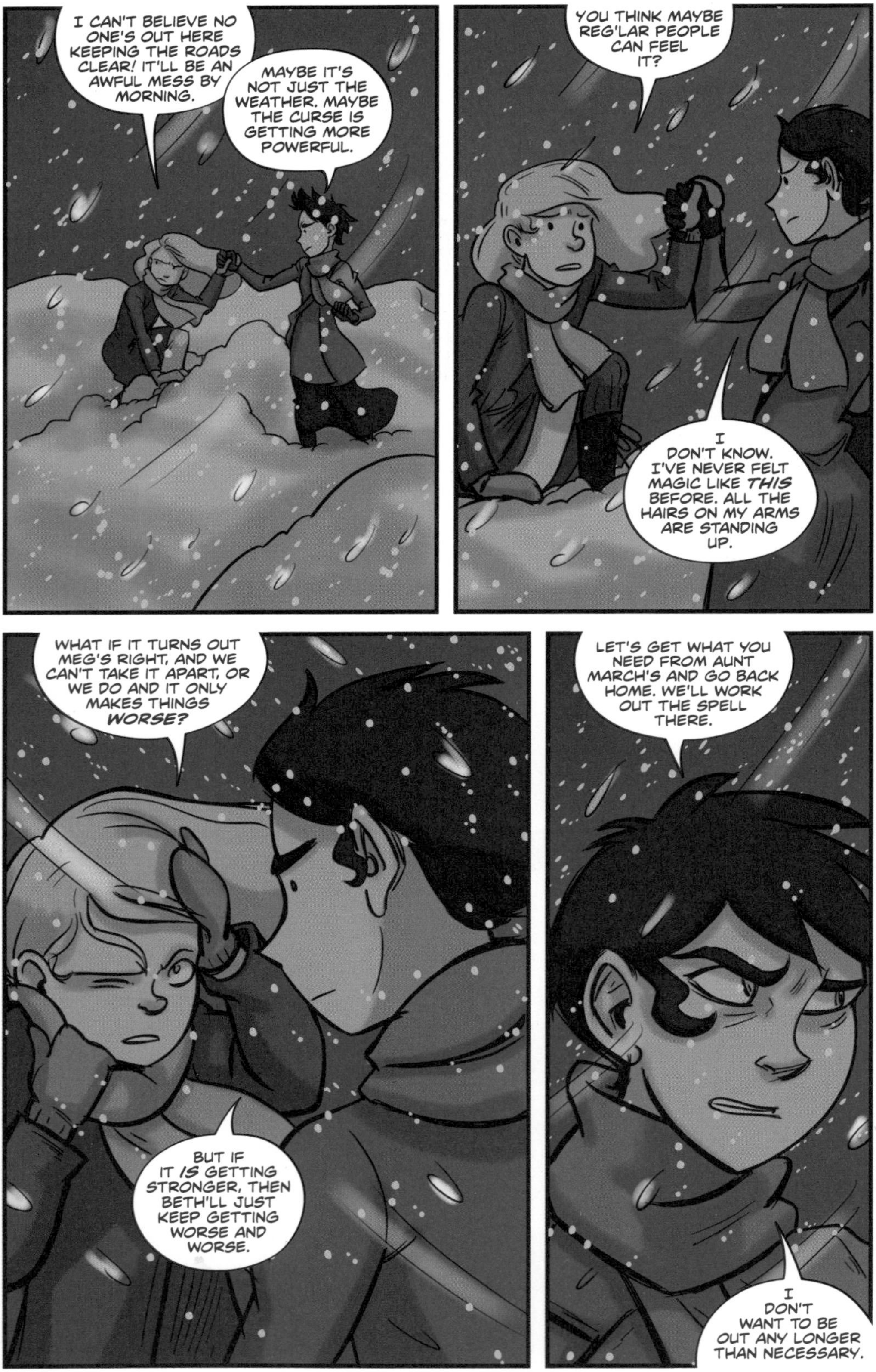
I CAN'T BELIEVE NO ONE'S OUT HERE KEEPING THE ROADS CLEAR! IT'LL BE AN AWFUL MESS BY MORNING.
MAYBE IT'S NOT JUST THE WEATHER. MAYBE THE CURSE IS GETTING MORE POWERFUL.
YOU THINK MAYBE REG'LAR PEOPLE CAN FEEL IT?
I DON'T KNOW. I'VE NEVER FELT MAGIC LIKE *THIS* BEFORE. ALL THE HAIRS ON MY ARMS ARE STANDING UP.
WHAT IF IT TURNS OUT MEG'S RIGHT, AND WE CAN'T TAKE IT APART, OR WE DO AND IT ONLY MAKES THINGS *WORSE?*
BUT IF IT *IS* GETTING STRONGER, THEN BETH'LL JUST KEEP GETTING WORSE AND WORSE.
LET'S GET WHAT YOU NEED FROM AUNT MARCH'S AND GO BACK HOME. WE'LL WORK OUT THE SPELL THERE.
I DON'T WANT TO BE OUT ANY LONGER THAN NECESSARY.

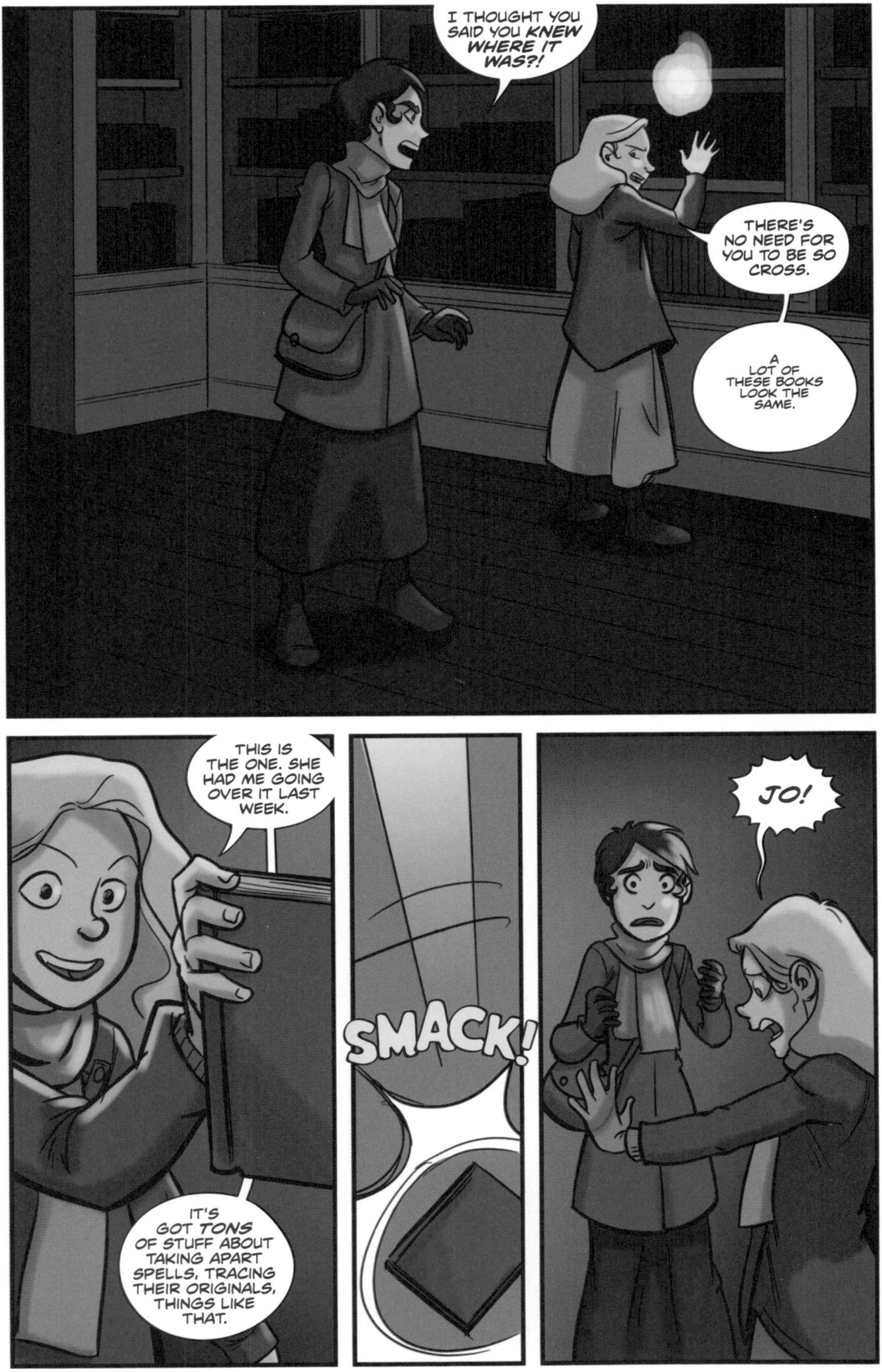
I THOUGHT YOU SAID YOU KNEW WHERE IT WAS?!
THERE'S NO NEED FOR YOU TO BE SO CROSS.
A LOT OF THESE BOOKS LOOK THE SAME.
THIS IS THE ONE. SHE HAD ME GOING OVER IT LAST WEEK.
IT'S GOT TONS OF STUFF ABOUT TAKING APART SPELLS, TRACING THEIR ORIGINALS, THINGS LIKE THAT.
SMACK!
JO!

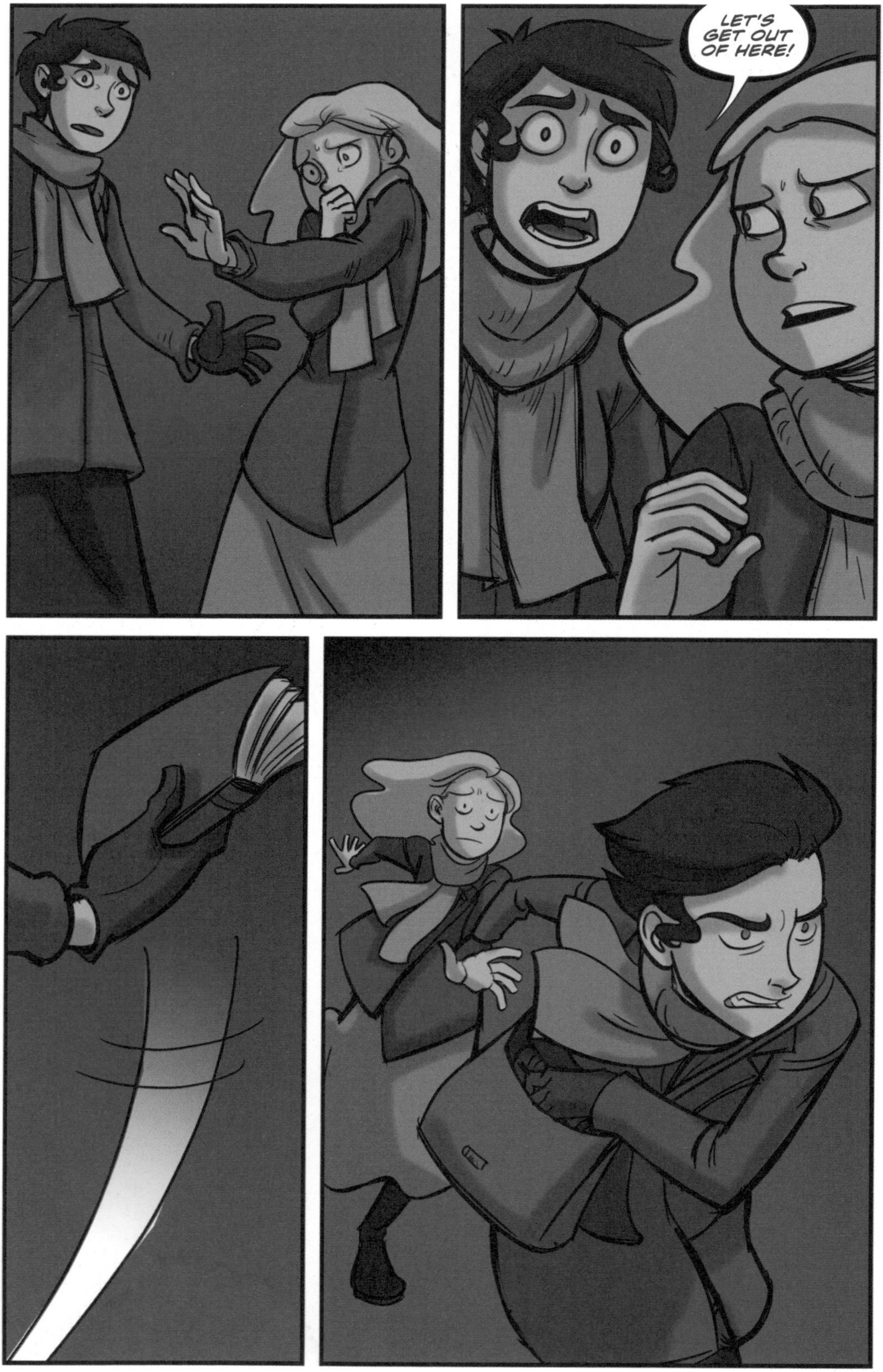
LET'S GET OUT OF HERE!

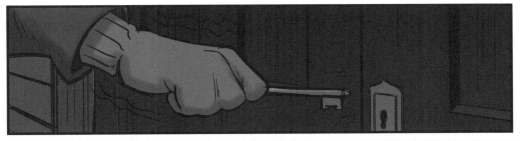

COME ON!

MISS MARCH?! IS THAT YOU?

MR. DAVIS?

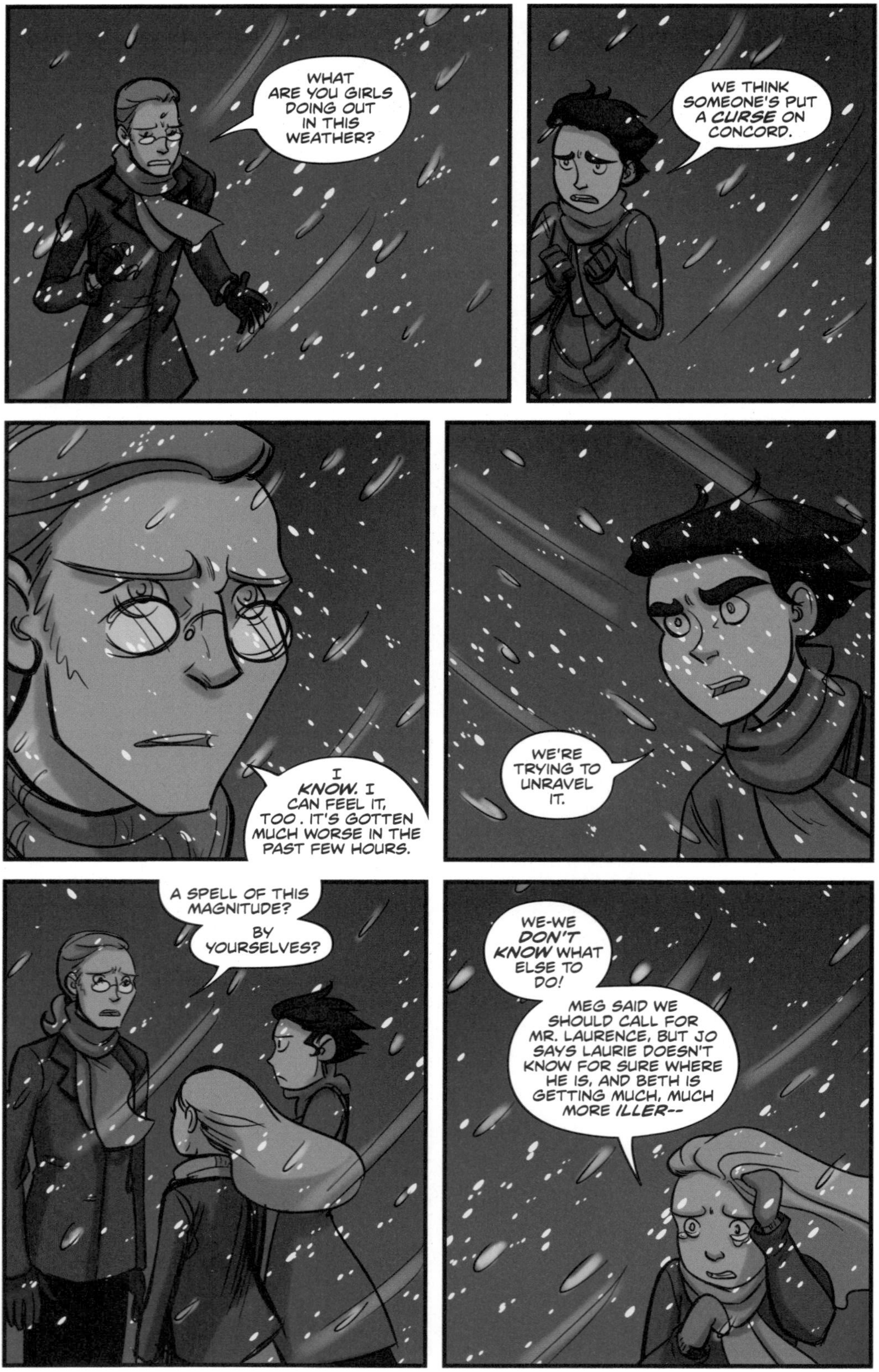
WHAT ARE YOU GIRLS DOING OUT IN THIS WEATHER?
WE THINK SOMEONE'S PUT A *CURSE* ON CONCORD.
I *KNOW.* I CAN FEEL IT, TOO. IT'S GOTTEN MUCH WORSE IN THE PAST FEW HOURS.
WE'RE TRYING TO UNRAVEL IT.
A SPELL OF THIS MAGNITUDE?
BY YOURSELVES?
WE-WE *DON'T KNOW* WHAT ELSE TO DO!
MEG SAID WE SHOULD CALL FOR MR. LAURENCE, BUT JO SAYS LAURIE DOESN'T KNOW FOR SURE WHERE HE IS, AND BETH IS GETTING MUCH, MUCH MORE *ILLER*--

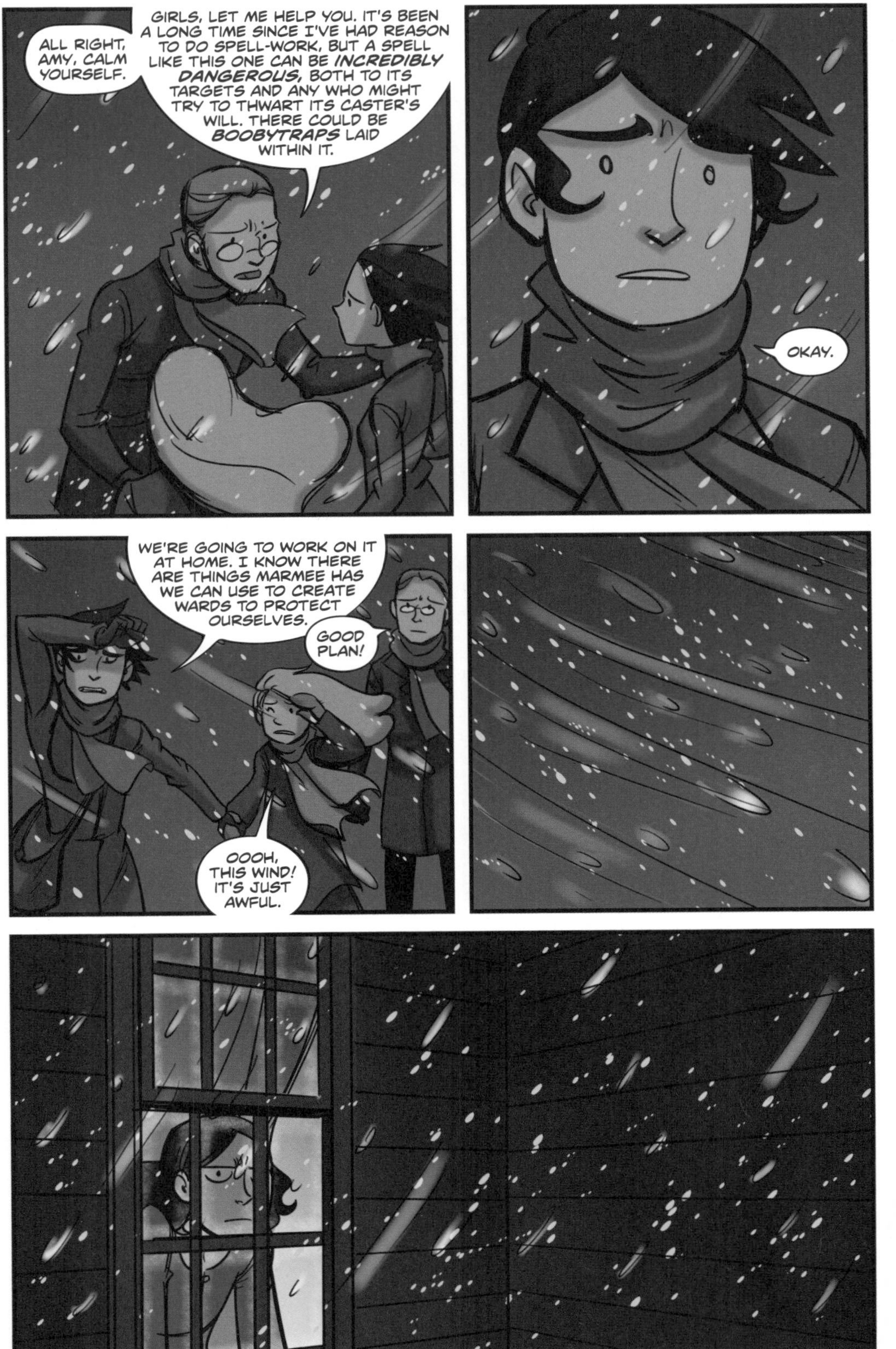

ALL RIGHT, AMY, CALM YOURSELF.
GIRLS, LET ME HELP YOU. IT'S BEEN A LONG TIME SINCE I'VE HAD REASON TO DO SPELL-WORK, BUT A SPELL LIKE THIS ONE CAN BE *INCREDIBLY DANGEROUS,* BOTH TO ITS TARGETS AND ANY WHO MIGHT TRY TO THWART ITS CASTER'S WILL. THERE COULD BE *BOOBYTRAPS* LAID WITHIN IT.
OKAY.
WE'RE GOING TO WORK ON IT AT HOME. I KNOW THERE ARE THINGS MARMEE HAS WE CAN USE TO CREATE WARDS TO PROTECT OURSELVES.
GOOD PLAN!
OOOH, THIS WIND! IT'S JUST AWFUL.

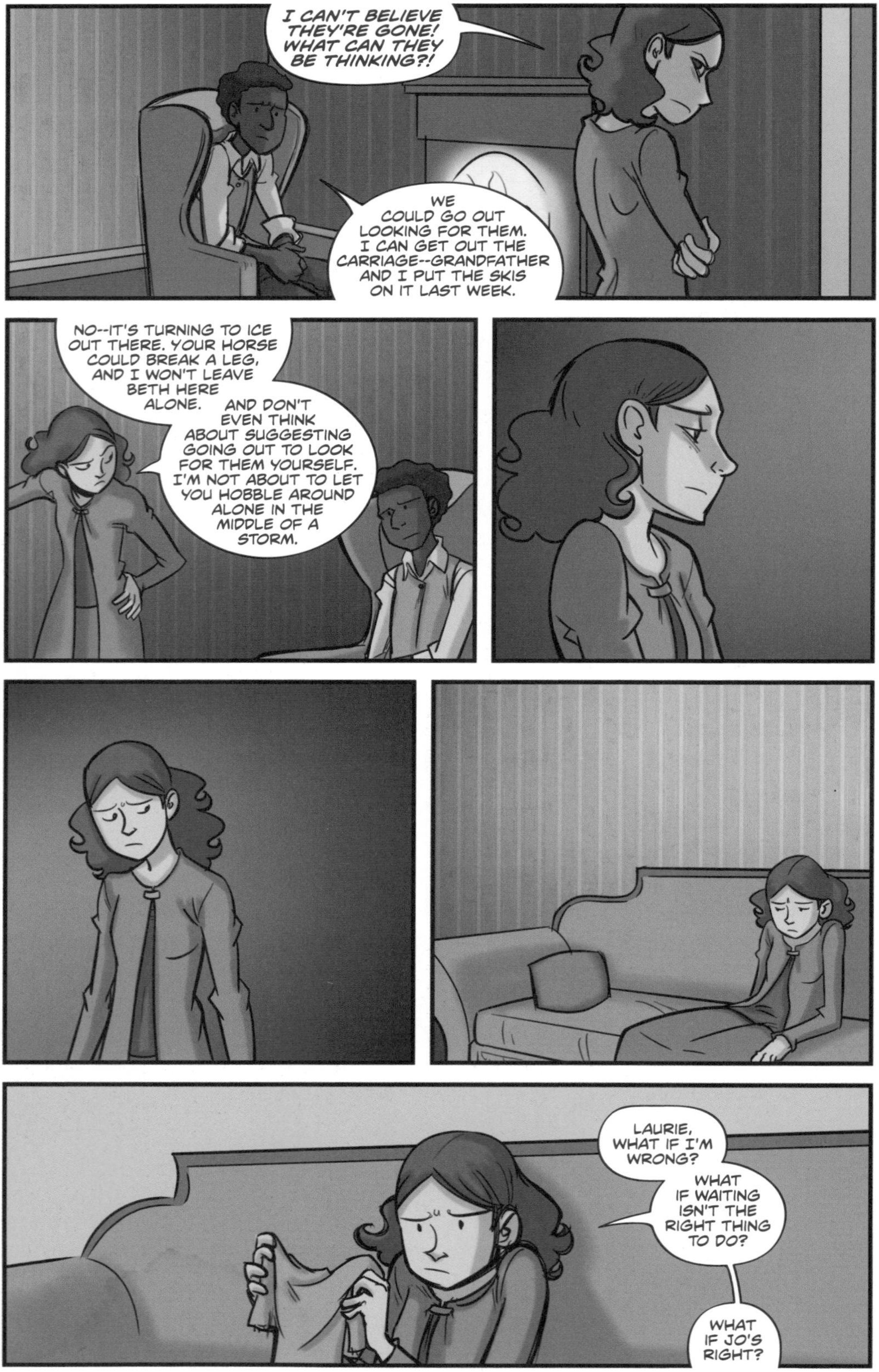
I CAN'T BELIEVE THEY'RE GONE! WHAT CAN THEY BE THINKING?!
WE COULD GO OUT LOOKING FOR THEM. I CAN GET OUT THE CARRIAGE--GRANDFATHER AND I PUT THE SKIS ON IT LAST WEEK.
NO--IT'S TURNING TO ICE OUT THERE. YOUR HORSE COULD BREAK A LEG, AND I WON'T LEAVE BETH HERE ALONE.
AND DON'T EVEN THINK ABOUT SUGGESTING GOING OUT TO LOOK FOR THEM YOURSELF. I'M NOT ABOUT TO LET YOU HOBBLE AROUND ALONE IN THE MIDDLE OF A STORM.
LAURIE, WHAT IF I'M WRONG?
WHAT IF WAITING ISN'T THE RIGHT THING TO DO?
WHAT IF JO'S RIGHT?

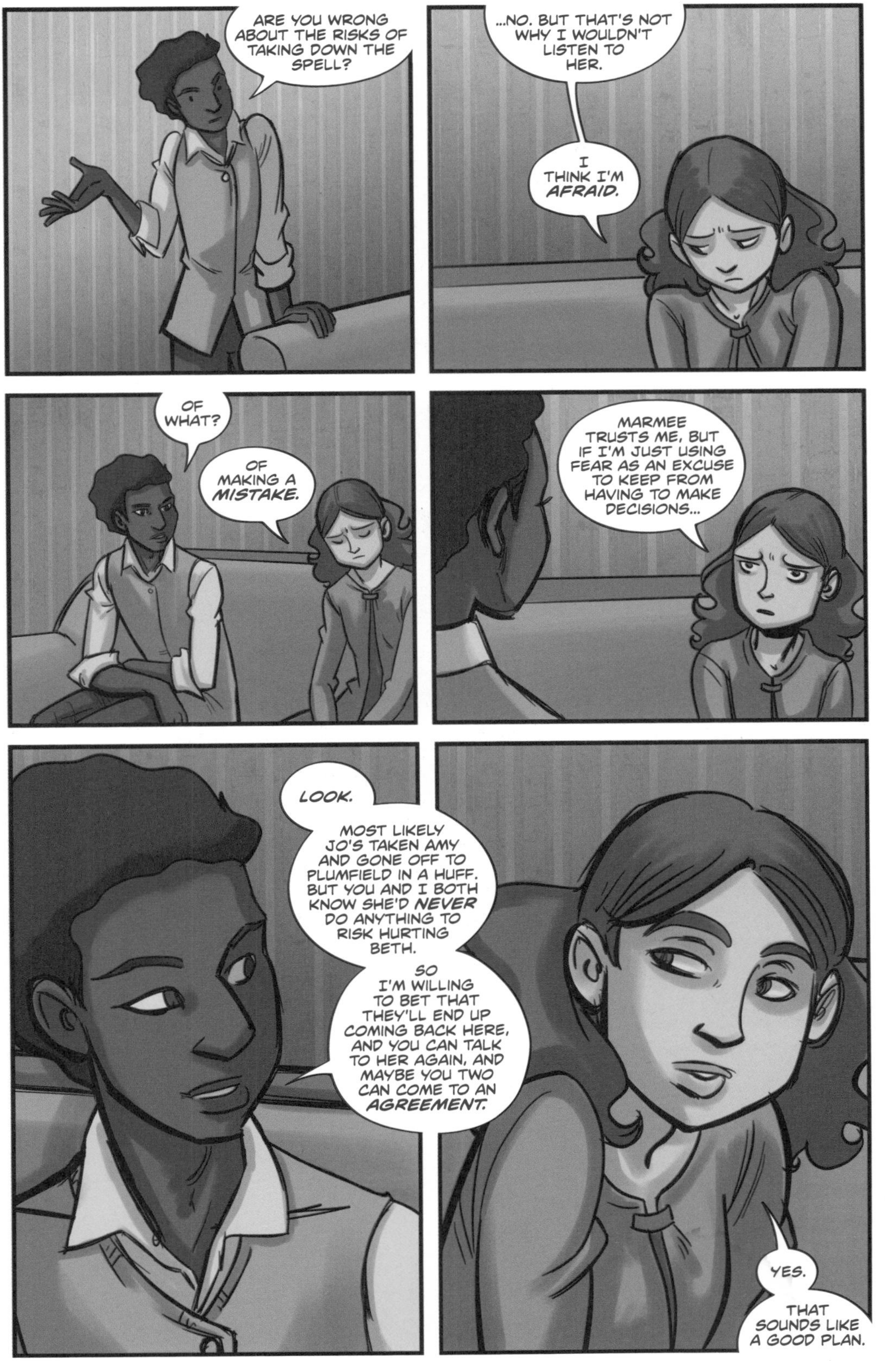
ARE YOU WRONG ABOUT THE RISKS OF TAKING DOWN THE SPELL?
...NO. BUT THAT'S NOT WHY I WOULDN'T LISTEN TO HER.
I THINK I'M *AFRAID.*
OF WHAT?
OF MAKING A *MISTAKE.*
MARMEE TRUSTS ME, BUT IF I'M JUST USING FEAR AS AN EXCUSE TO KEEP FROM HAVING TO MAKE DECISIONS...
LOOK.
MOST LIKELY JO'S TAKEN AMY AND GONE OFF TO PLUMFIELD IN A HUFF. BUT YOU AND I BOTH KNOW SHE'D *NEVER* DO ANYTHING TO RISK HURTING BETH.
SO I'M WILLING TO BET THAT THEY'LL END UP COMING BACK HERE, AND YOU CAN TALK TO HER AGAIN, AND MAYBE YOU TWO CAN COME TO AN *AGREEMENT.*
YES.
THAT SOUNDS LIKE A GOOD PLAN.

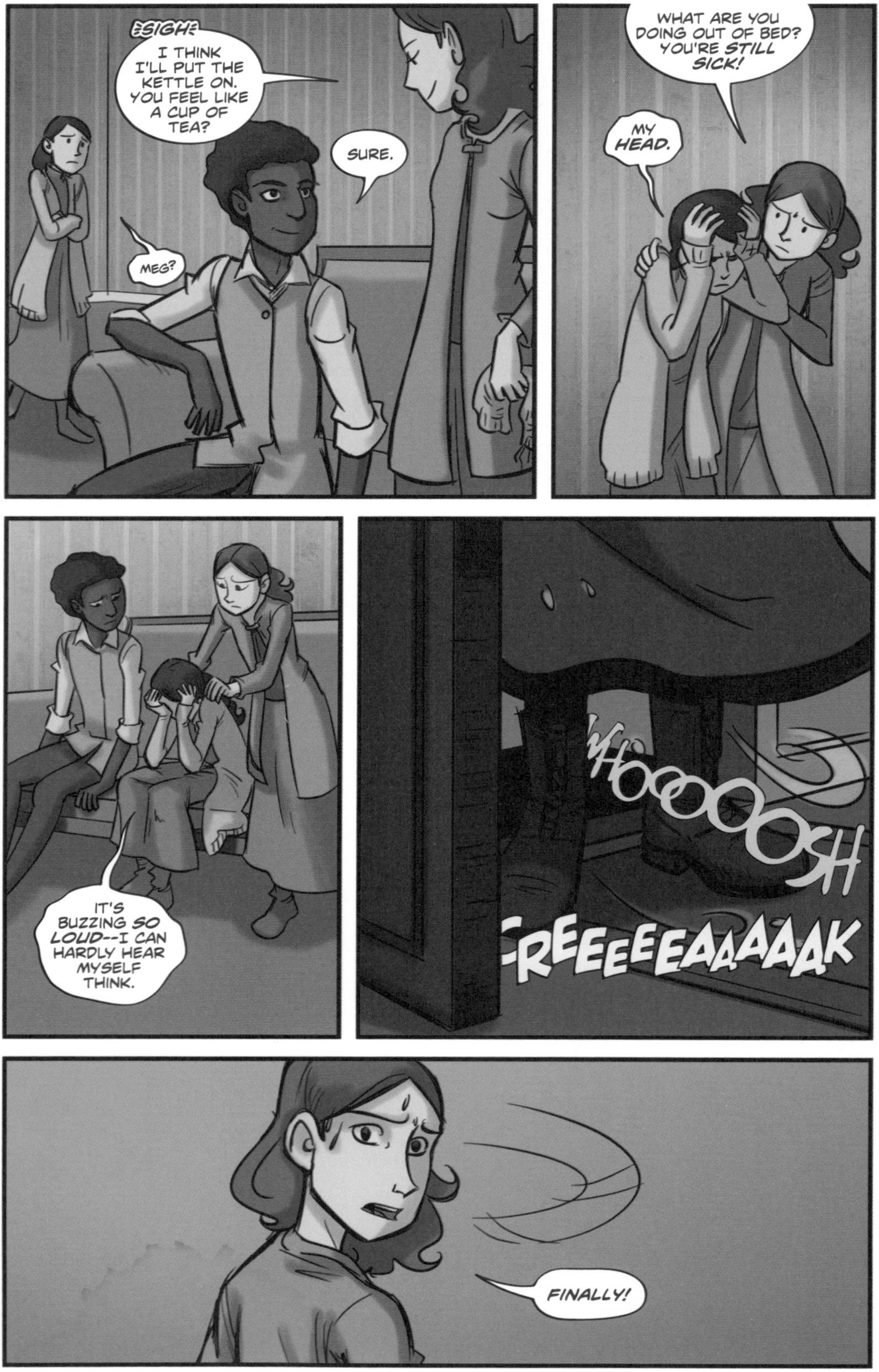
SIGH
I THINK I'LL PUT THE KETTLE ON. YOU FEEL LIKE A CUP OF TEA?
SURE.
MEG?
WHAT ARE YOU DOING OUT OF BED? YOU'RE STILL SICK!
MY HEAD.
IT'S BUZZING SO LOUD--I CAN HARDLY HEAR MYSELF THINK.
WHOOOOOSH
CREEEEEAAAAAK
FINALLY!

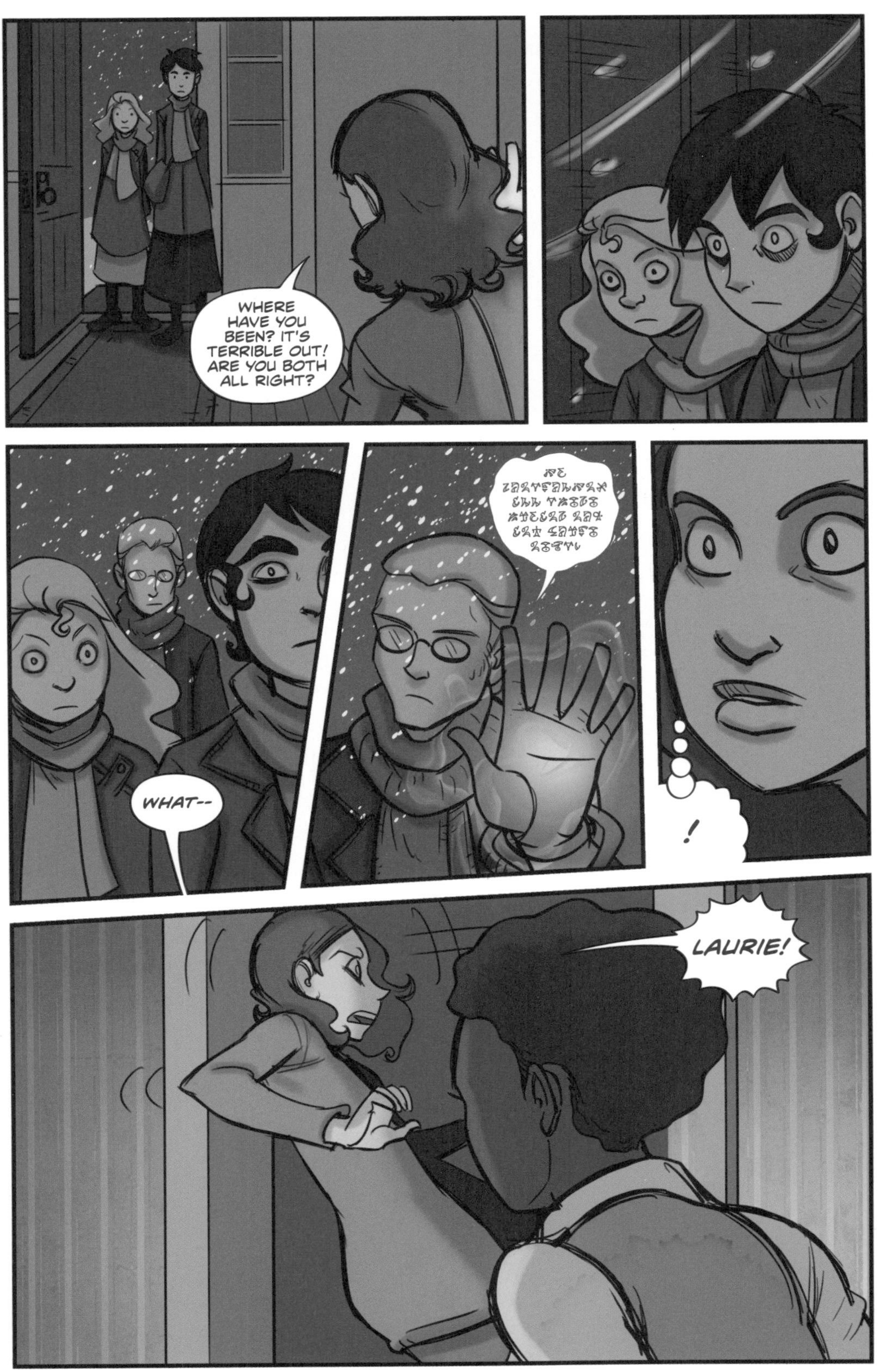
WHERE HAVE YOU BEEN? IT'S TERRIBLE OUT! ARE YOU BOTH ALL RIGHT?
WHAT--
!
LAURIE!

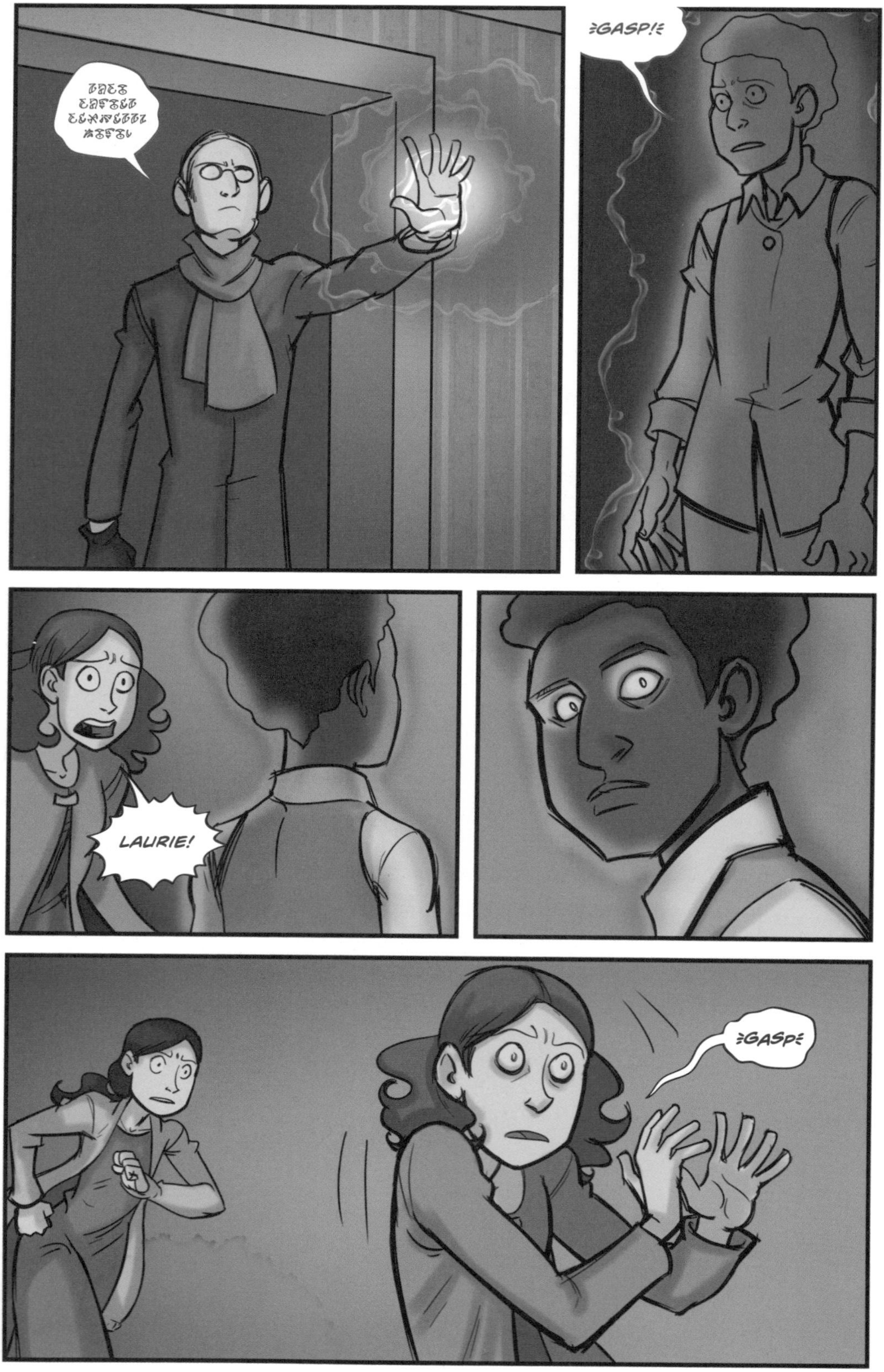

GASP!
LAURIE!
GASP

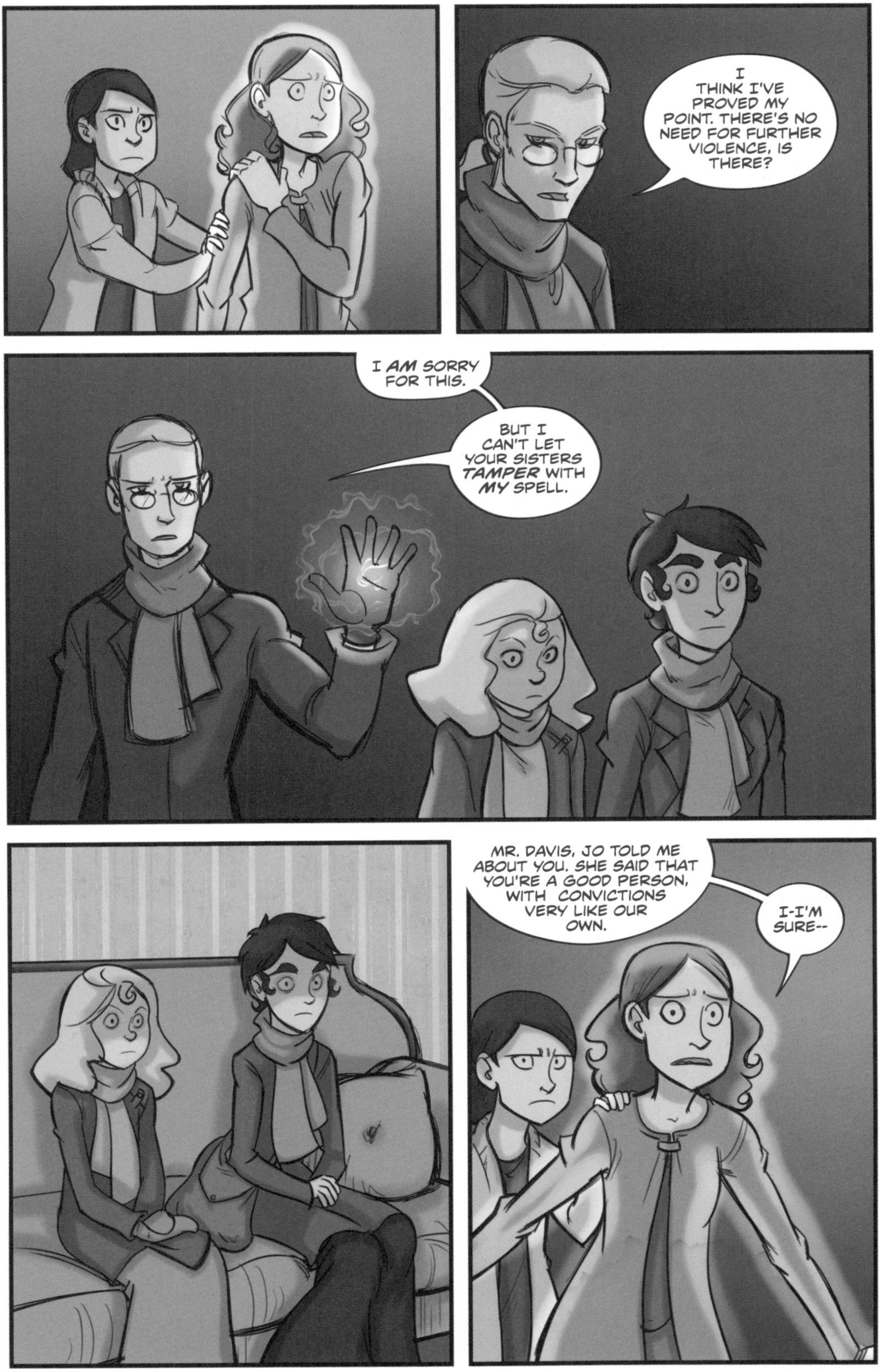
I THINK I'VE PROVED MY POINT. THERE'S NO NEED FOR FURTHER VIOLENCE, IS THERE?
I *AM* SORRY FOR THIS.
BUT I CAN'T LET YOUR SISTERS *TAMPER* WITH *MY* SPELL.
MR. DAVIS, JO TOLD ME ABOUT YOU. SHE SAID THAT YOU'RE A GOOD PERSON, WITH CONVICTIONS VERY LIKE OUR OWN.
I-I'M SURE--

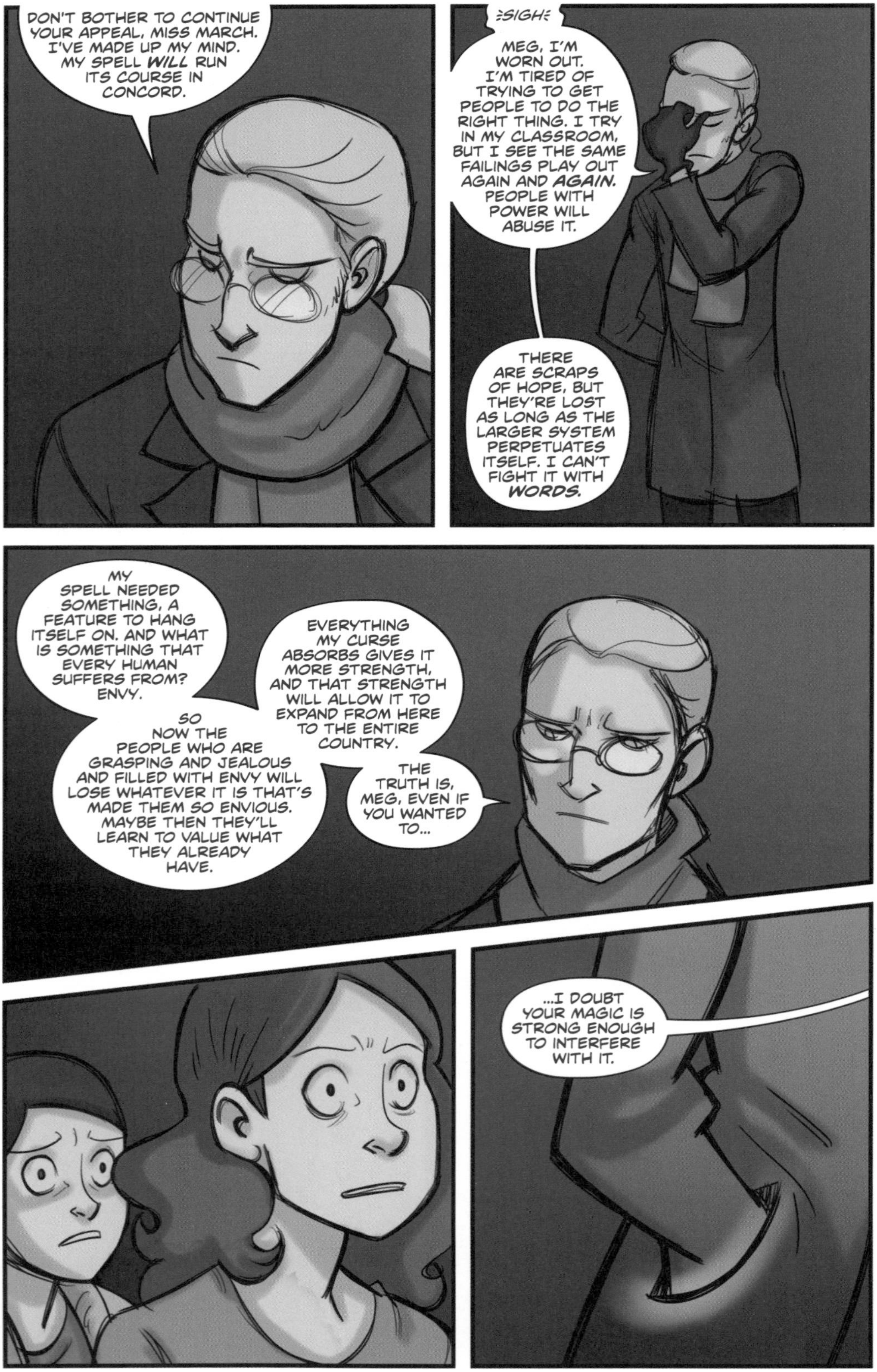
DON'T BOTHER TO CONTINUE YOUR APPEAL, MISS MARCH. I'VE MADE UP MY MIND. MY SPELL *WILL* RUN ITS COURSE IN CONCORD.
SIGH
MEG, I'M WORN OUT. I'M TIRED OF TRYING TO GET PEOPLE TO DO THE RIGHT THING. I TRY IN MY CLASSROOM, BUT I SEE THE SAME FAILINGS PLAY OUT AGAIN AND *AGAIN.* PEOPLE WITH POWER WILL ABUSE IT.
THERE ARE SCRAPS OF HOPE, BUT THEY'RE LOST AS LONG AS THE LARGER SYSTEM PERPETUATES ITSELF. I CAN'T FIGHT IT WITH *WORDS.*
MY SPELL NEEDED SOMETHING, A FEATURE TO HANG ITSELF ON. AND WHAT IS SOMETHING THAT EVERY HUMAN SUFFERS FROM? ENVY.
SO NOW THE PEOPLE WHO ARE GRASPING AND JEALOUS AND FILLED WITH ENVY WILL LOSE WHATEVER IT IS THAT'S MADE THEM SO ENVIOUS. MAYBE THEN THEY'LL LEARN TO VALUE WHAT THEY ALREADY HAVE.
EVERYTHING MY CURSE ABSORBS GIVES IT MORE STRENGTH, AND THAT STRENGTH WILL ALLOW IT TO EXPAND FROM HERE TO THE ENTIRE COUNTRY.
THE TRUTH IS, MEG, EVEN IF YOU WANTED TO...
...I DOUBT YOUR MAGIC IS STRONG ENOUGH TO INTERFERE WITH IT.

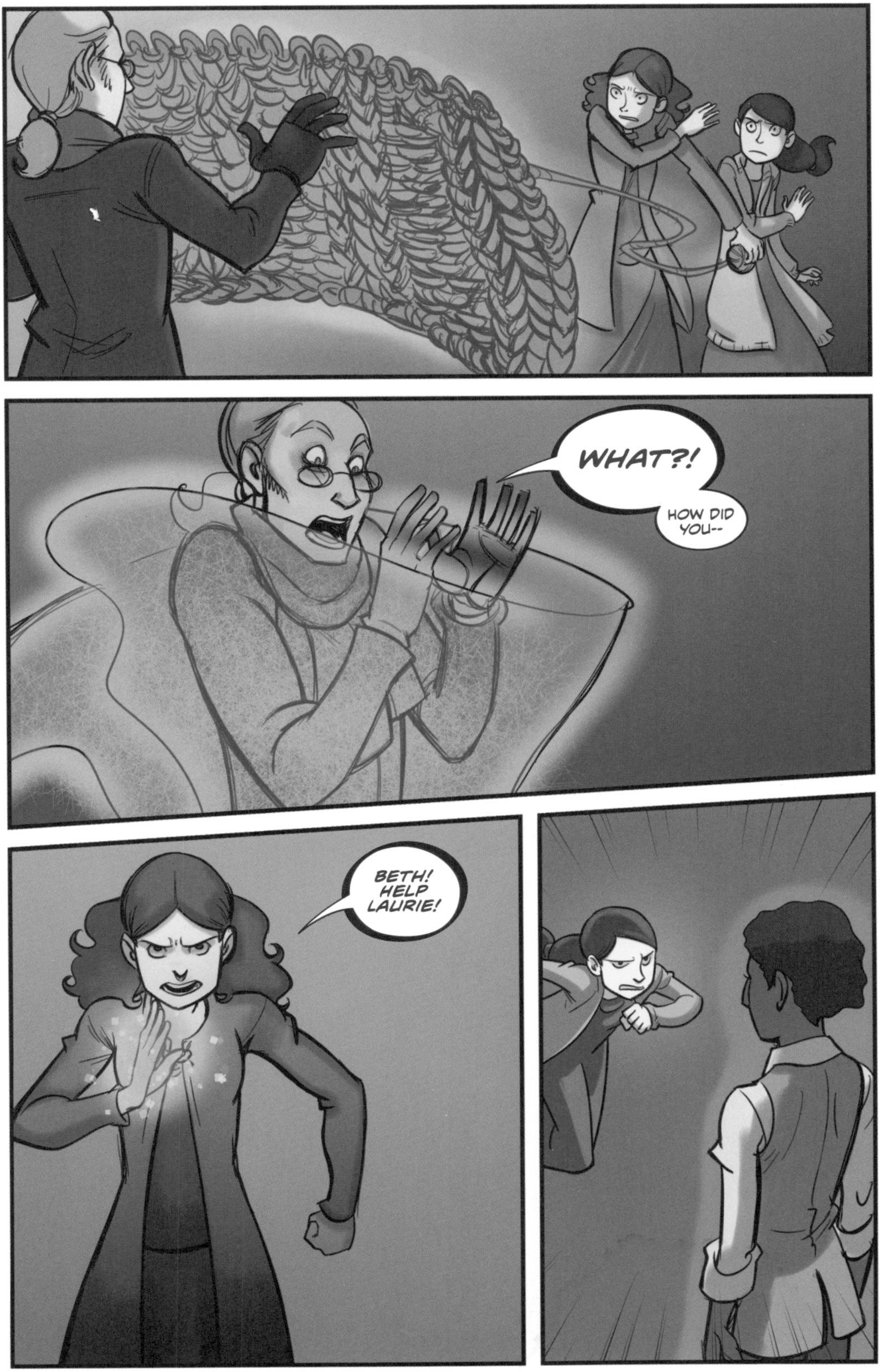
WHAT?!
HOW DID YOU--
BETH! HELP LAURIE!

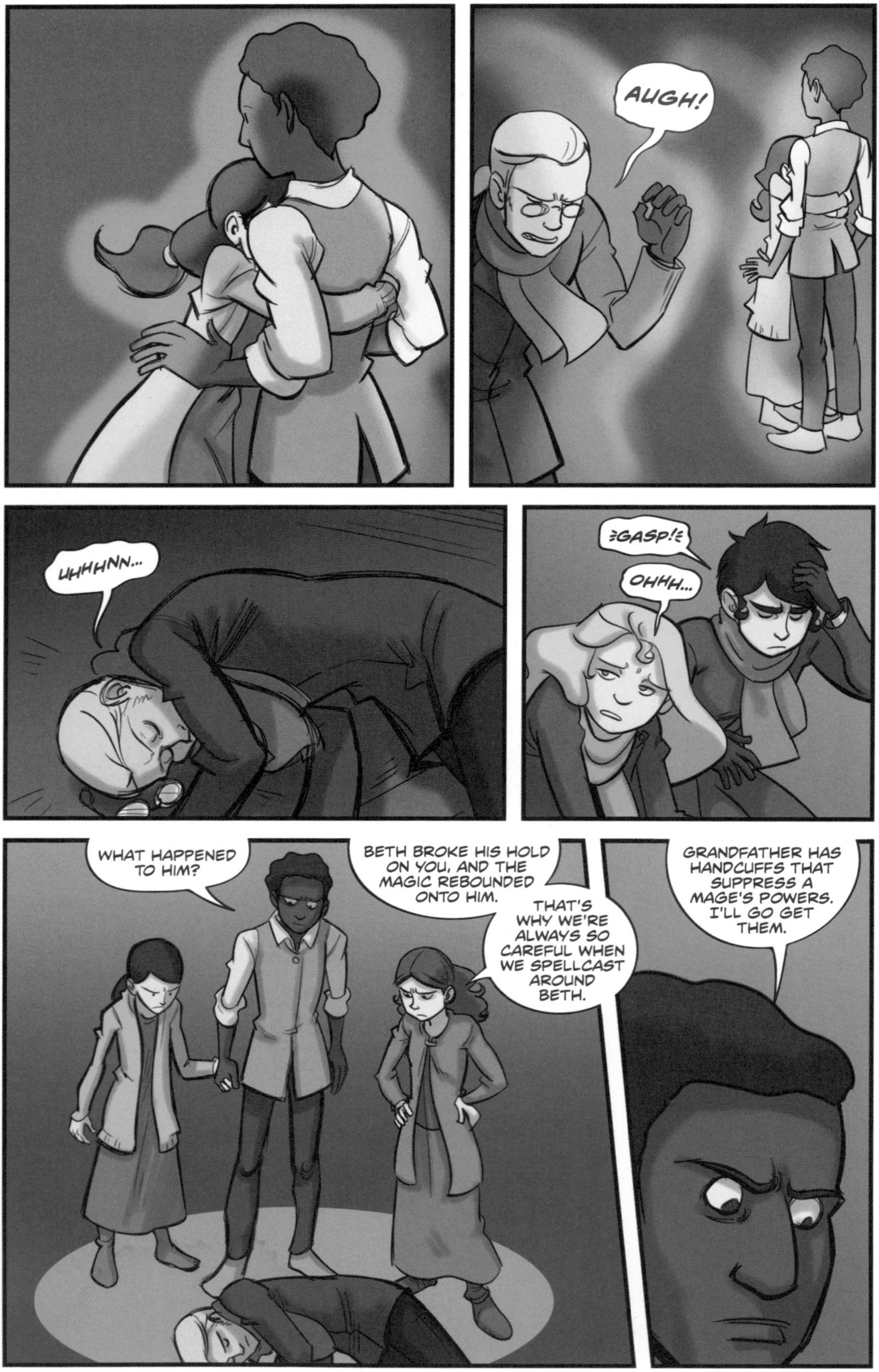
AUGH!
UHHHNN...
GASP!
OHHH...
WHAT HAPPENED TO HIM?
BETH BROKE HIS HOLD ON YOU, AND THE MAGIC REBOUNDED ONTO HIM.
THAT'S WHY WE'RE ALWAYS SO CAREFUL WHEN WE SPELLCAST AROUND BETH.
GRANDFATHER HAS HANDCUFFS THAT SUPPRESS A MAGE'S POWERS. I'LL GO GET THEM.

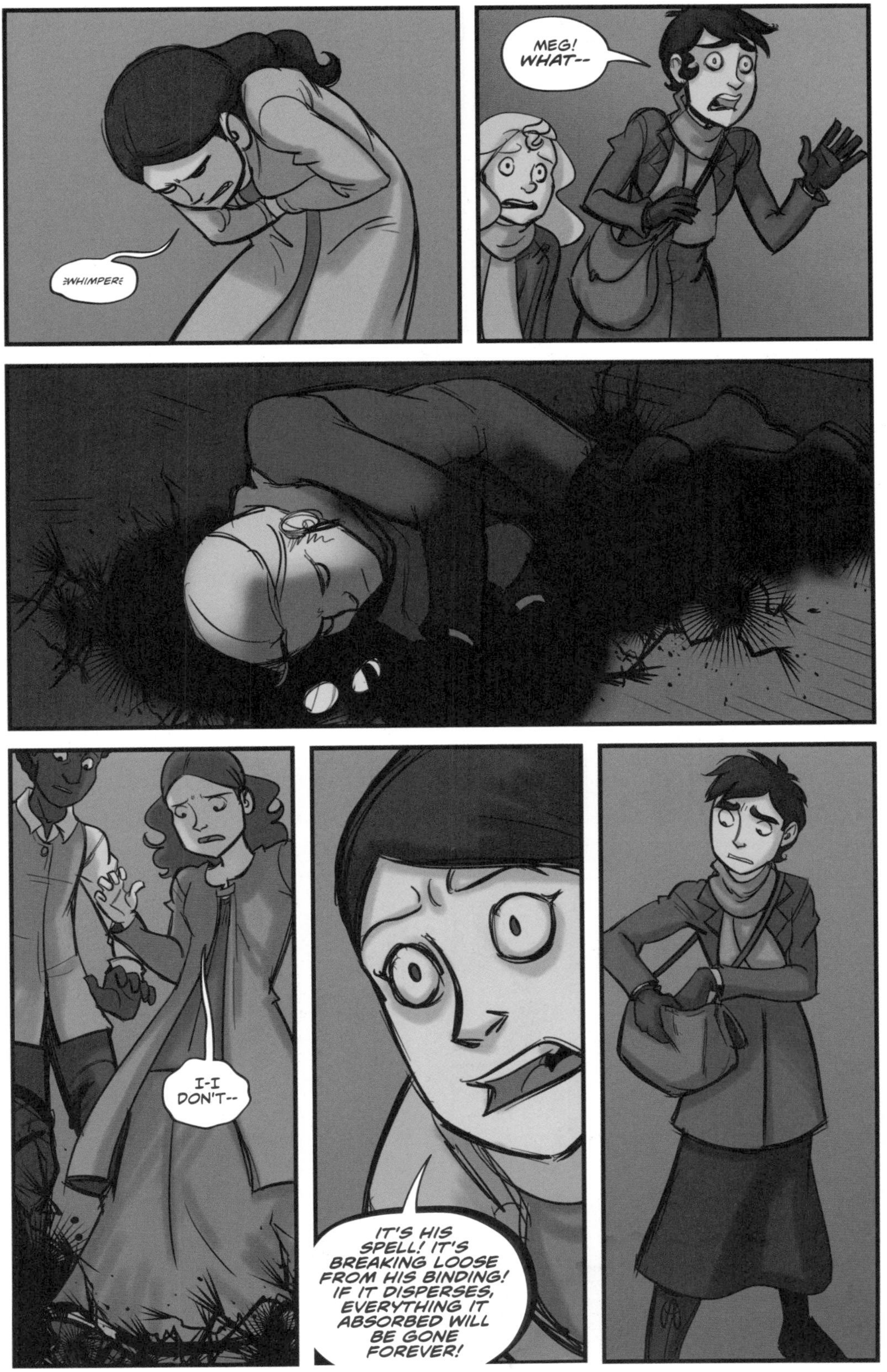

=WHIMPER=
MEG! WHAT--
I-I DON'T--
IT'S HIS SPELL! IT'S BREAKING LOOSE FROM HIS BINDING! IF IT DISPERSES, EVERYTHING IT ABSORBED WILL BE GONE FOREVER!

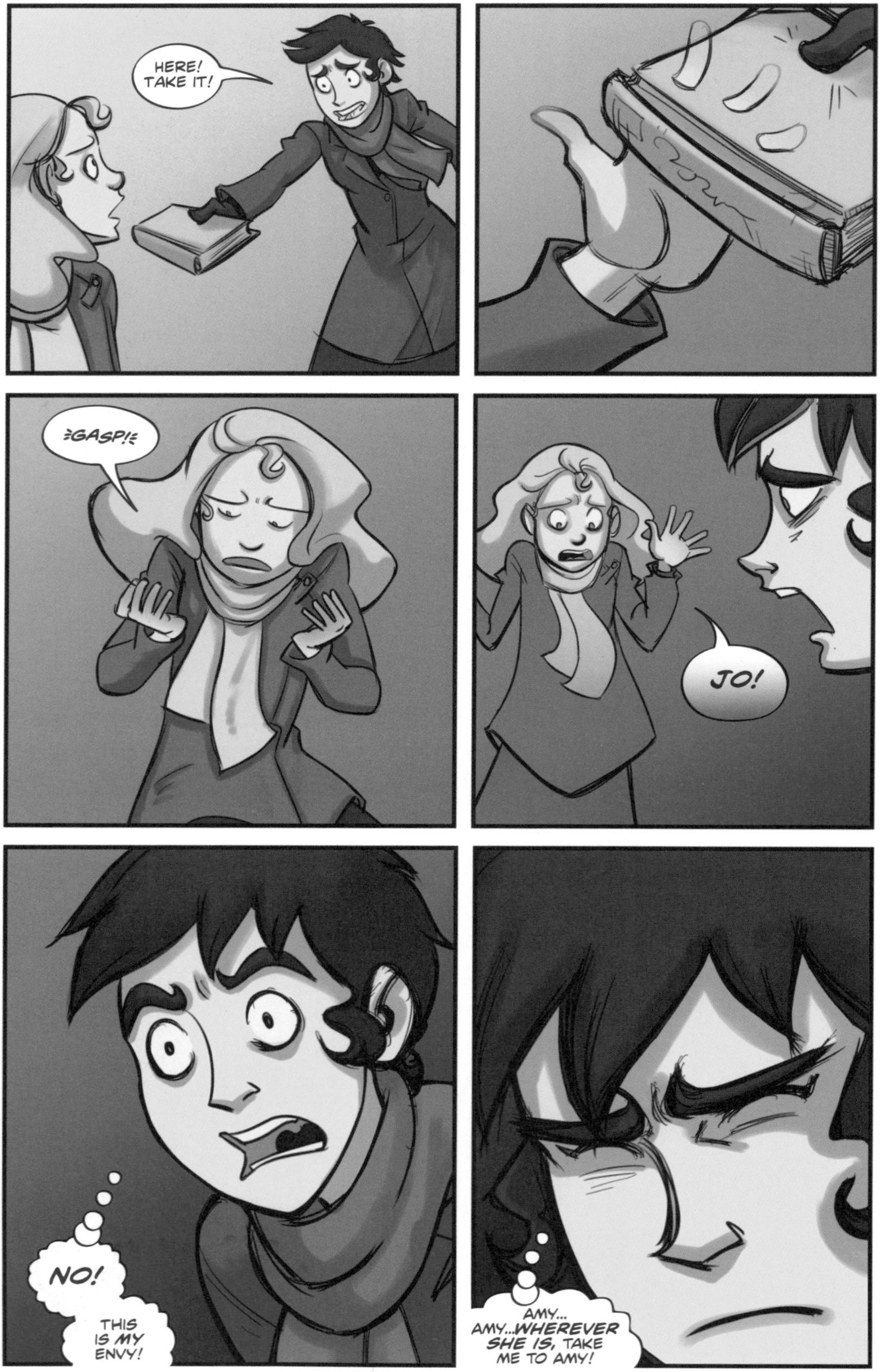
HERE! TAKE IT!
GASP!
JO!
NO!
THIS IS MY ENVY!
AMY... AMY...WHEREVER SHE IS, TAKE ME TO AMY!

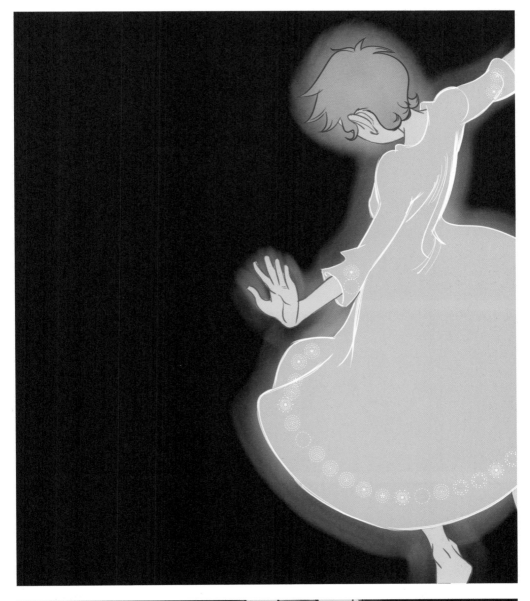

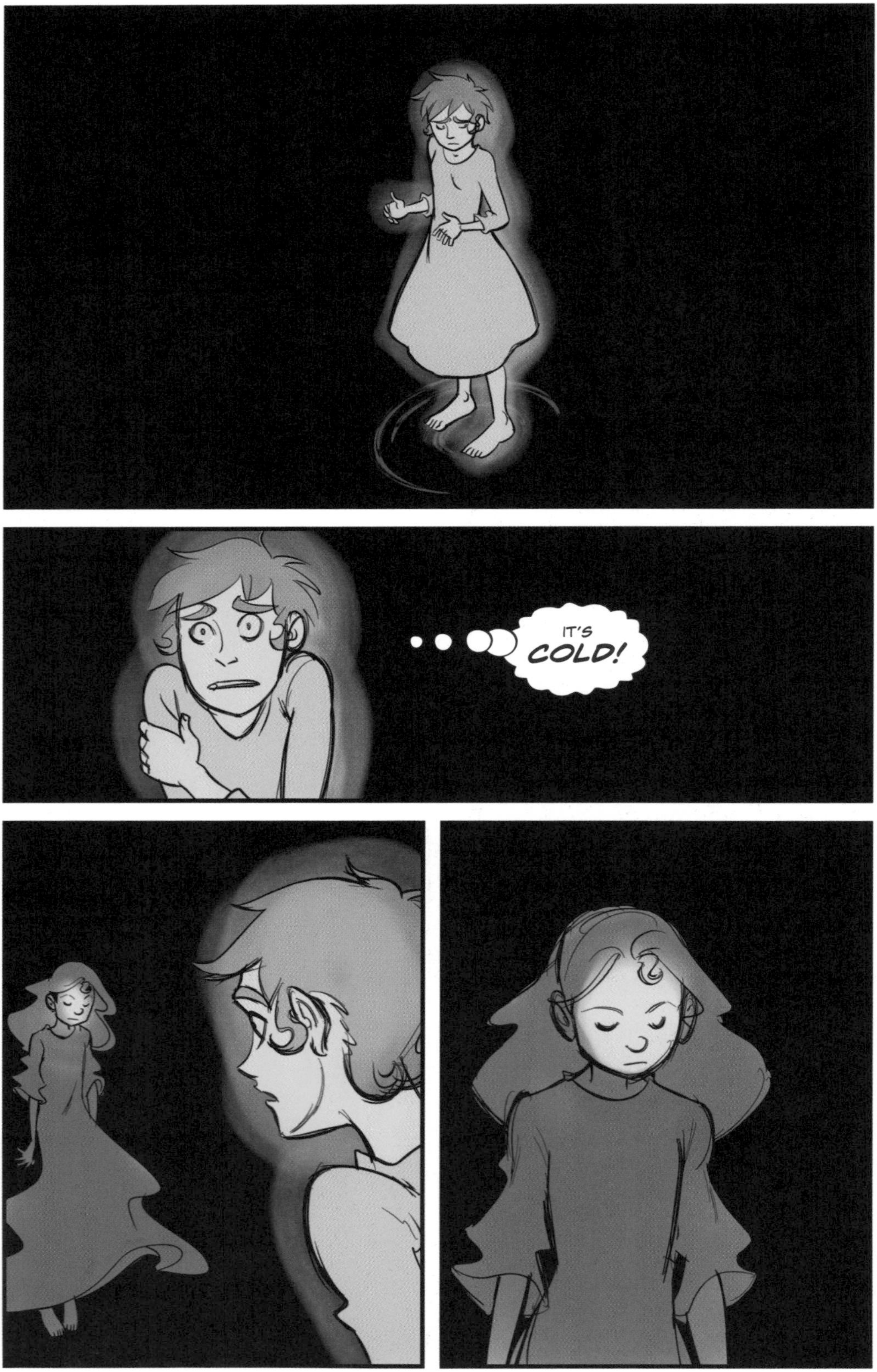
IT'S
COLD!

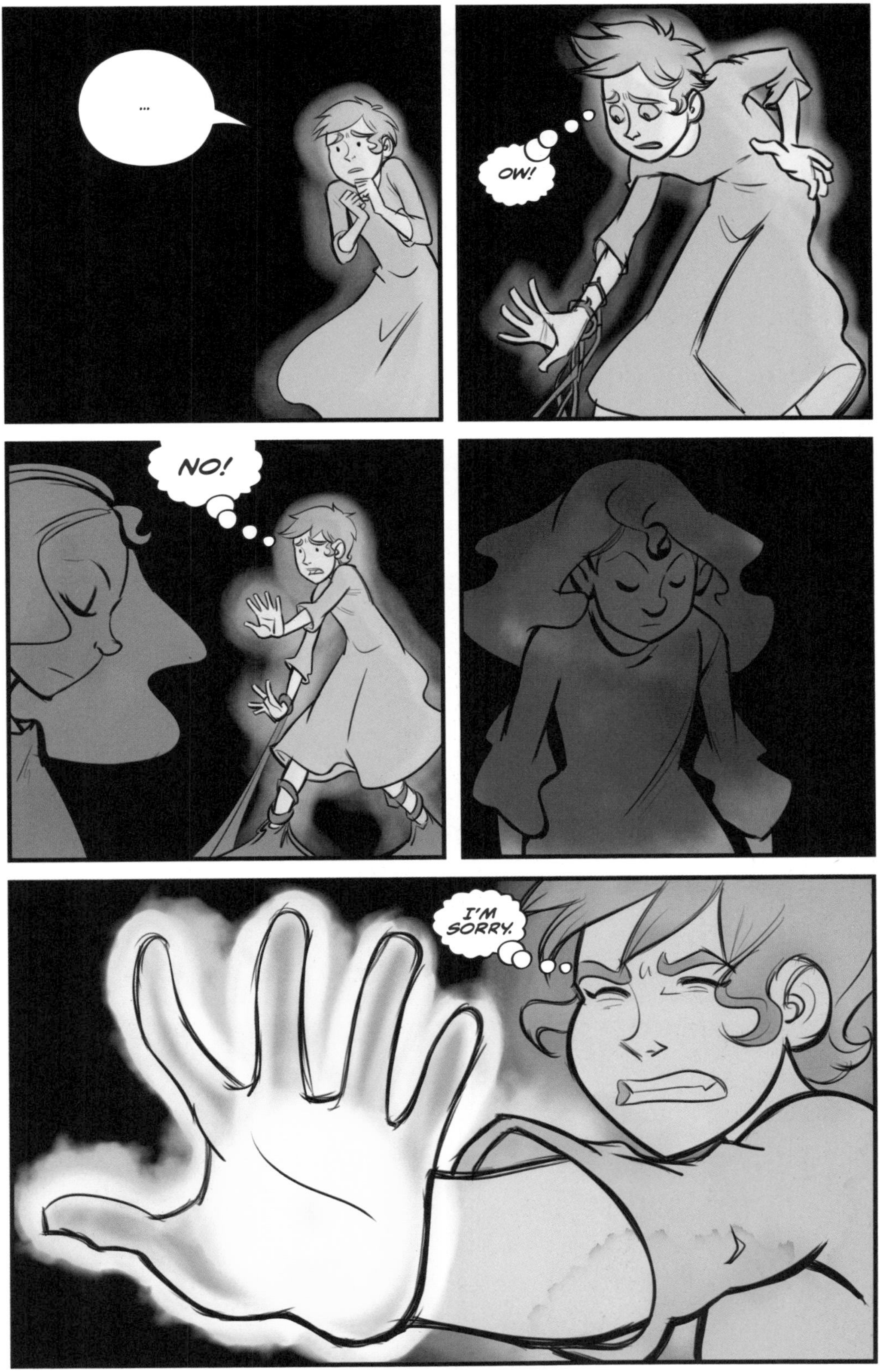
...
OW!
NO!
I'M SORRY.

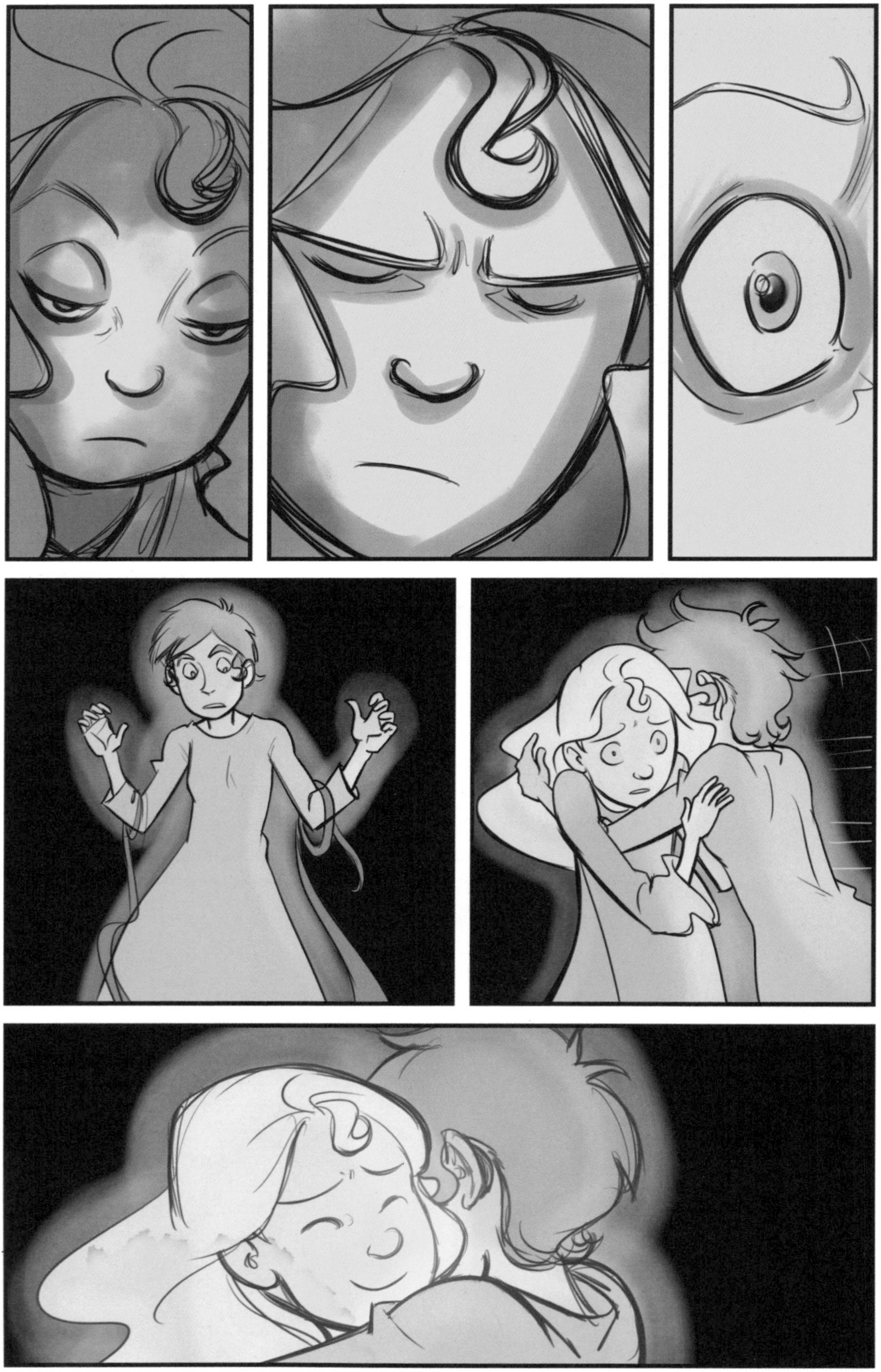

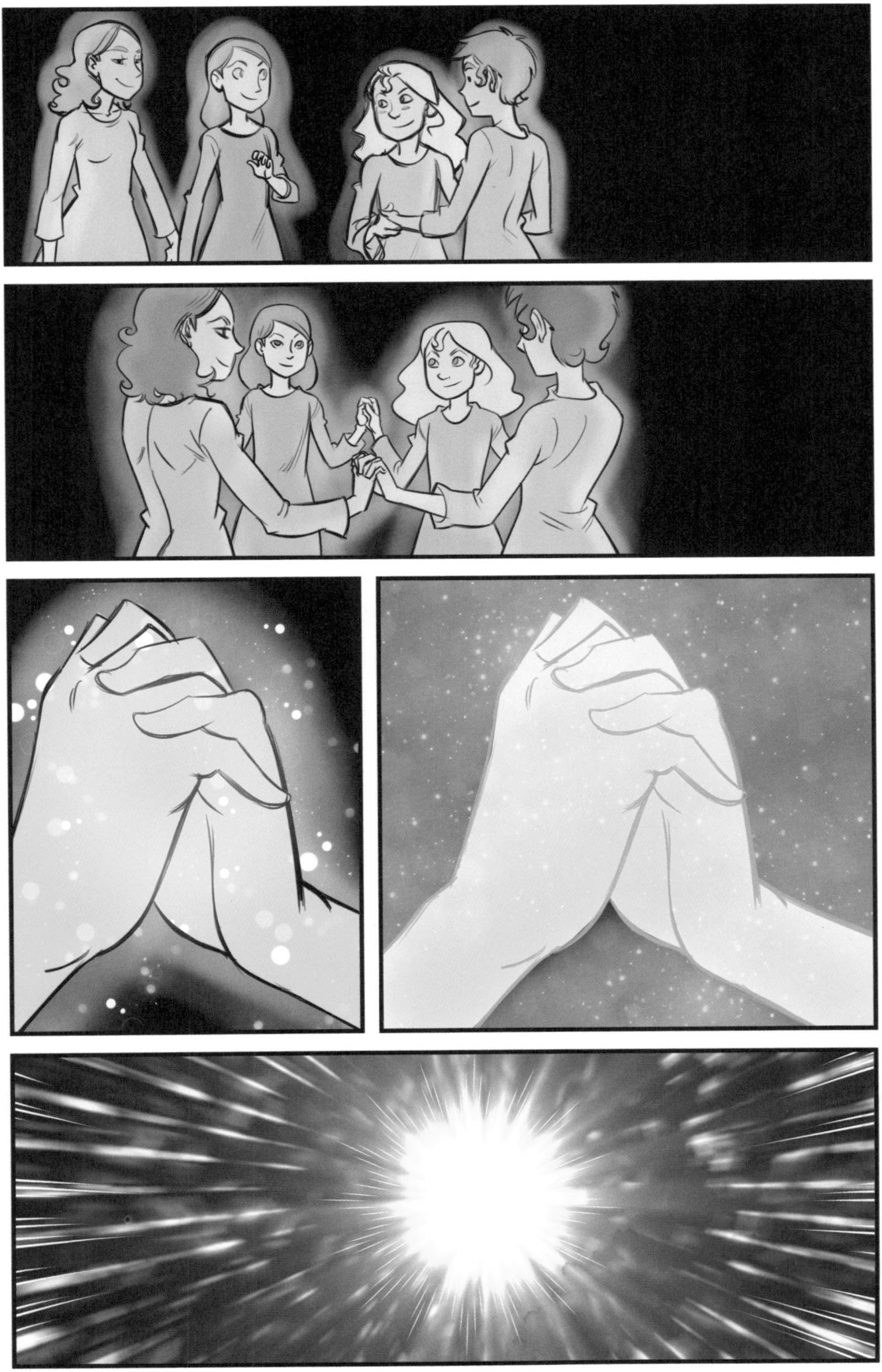

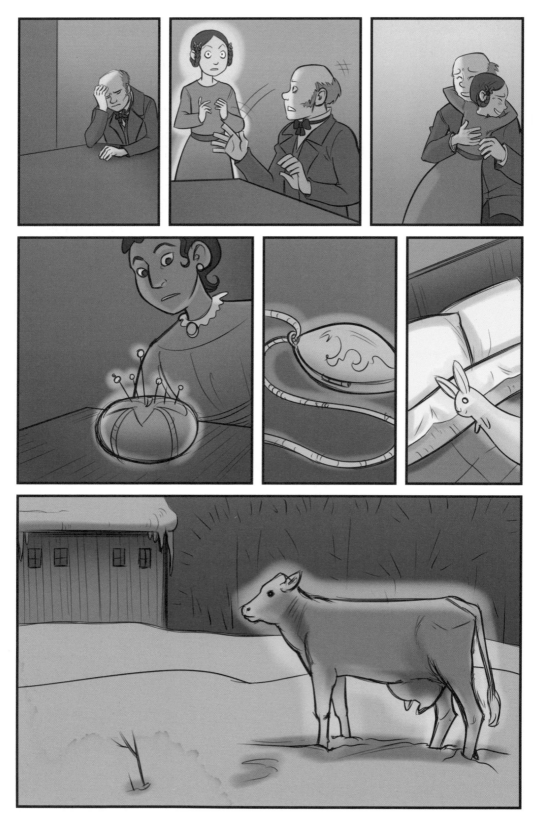

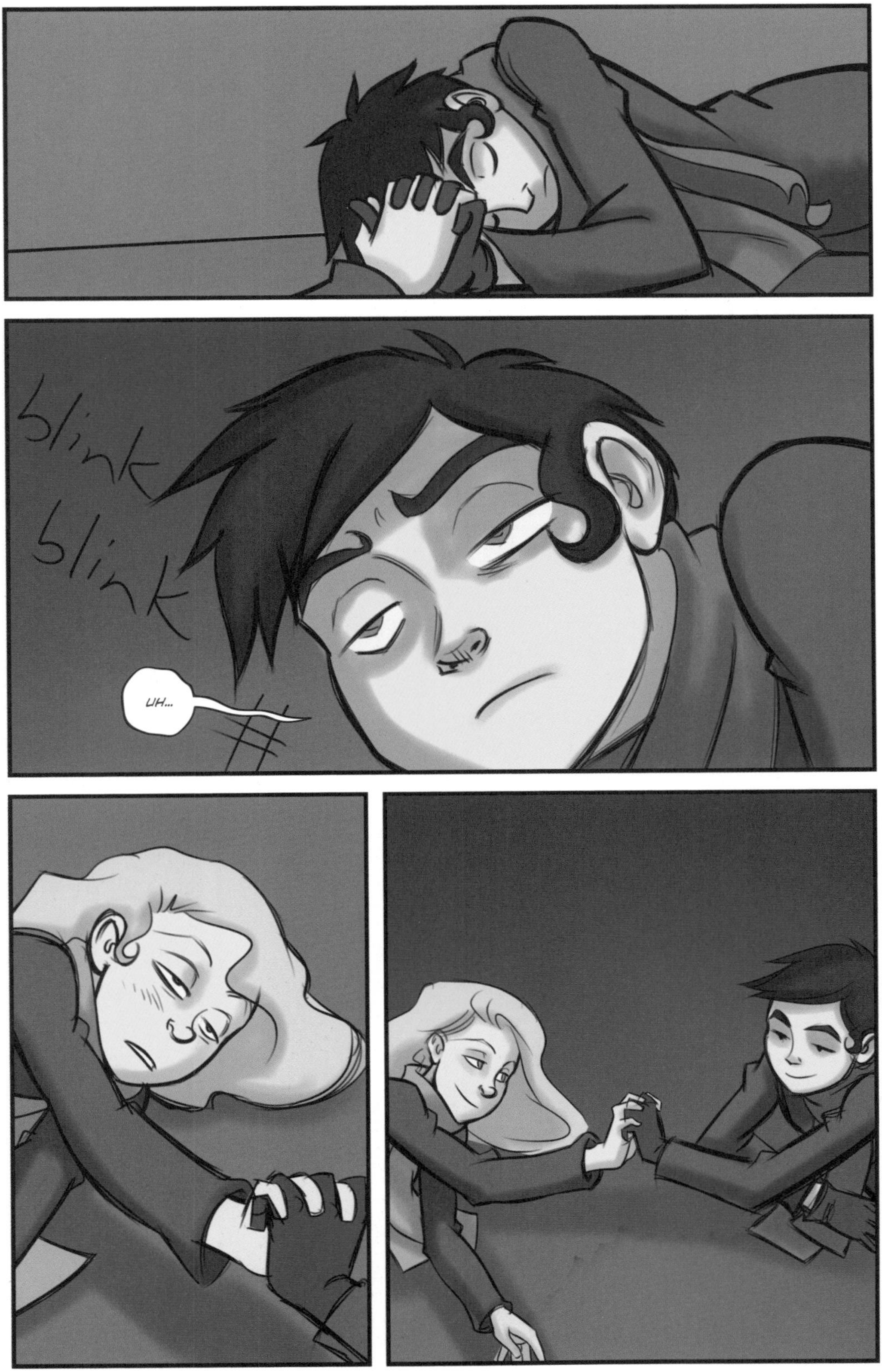
blink
blink
UH...

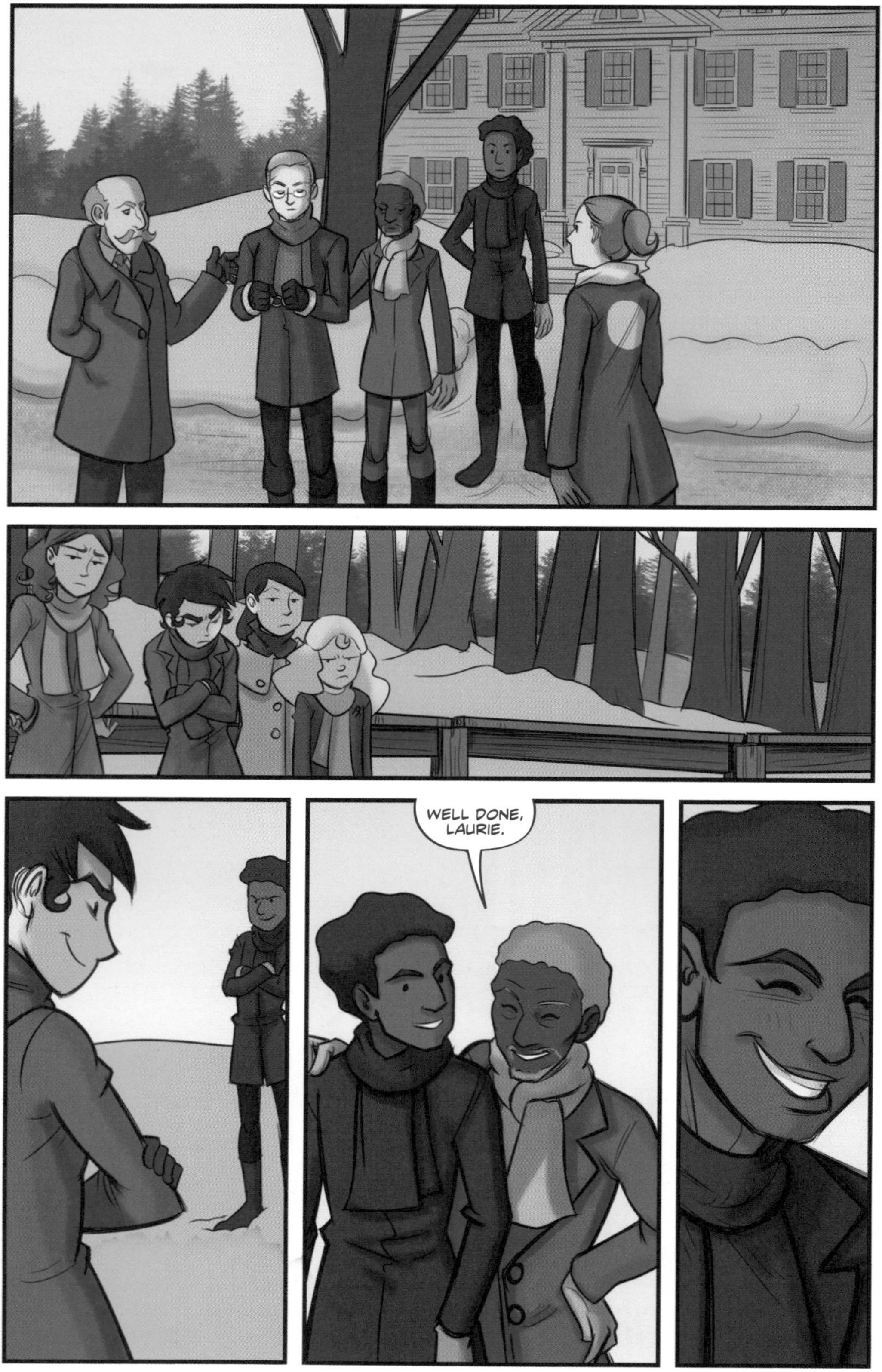
WELL DONE, LAURIE.

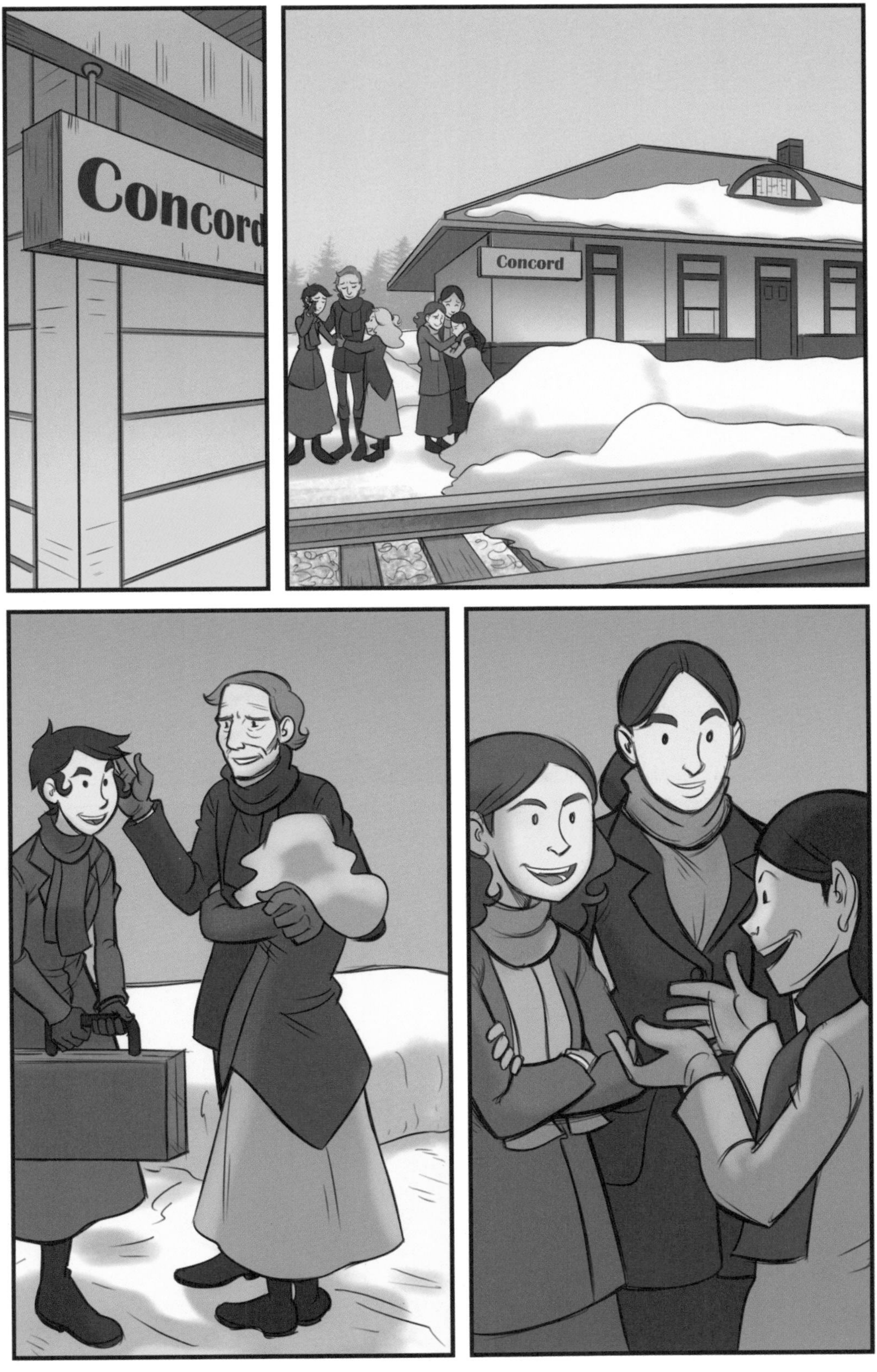
Concord
Concord

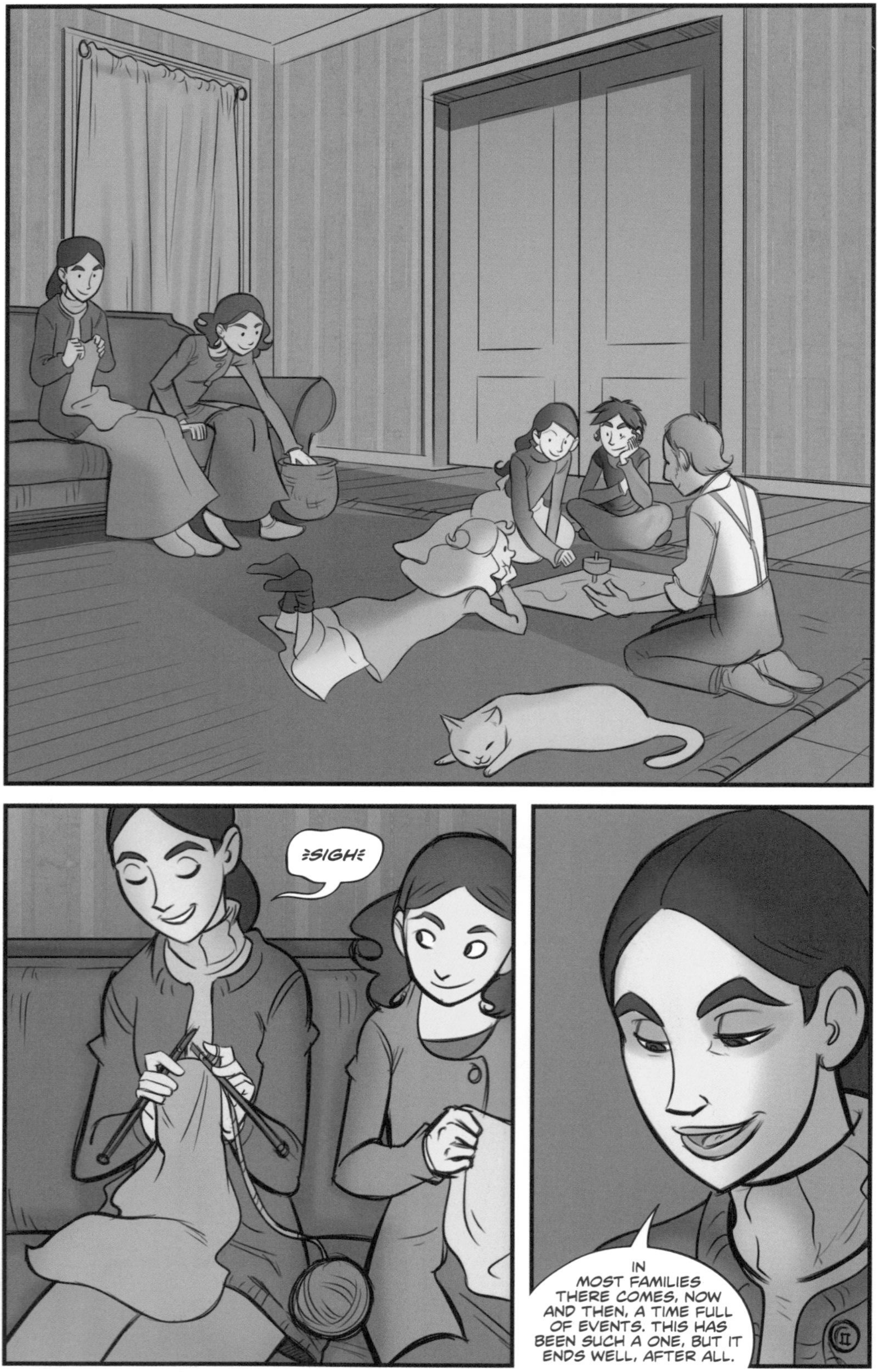
SIGH
IN MOST FAMILIES THERE COMES, NOW AND THEN, A TIME FULL OF EVENTS. THIS HAS BEEN SUCH A ONE, BUT IT ENDS WELL, AFTER ALL.

Little Witches

THE PROBLEM OF TOO MANY PESTS

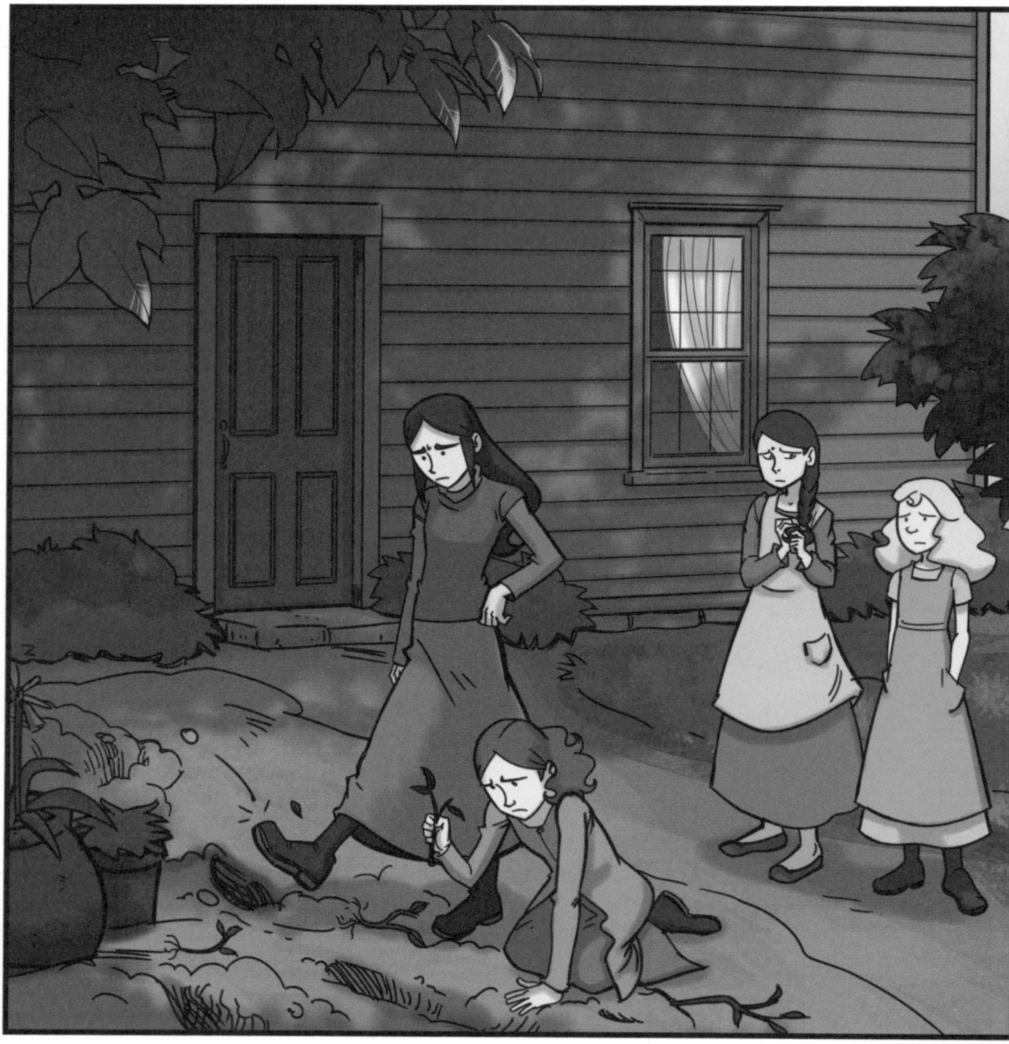

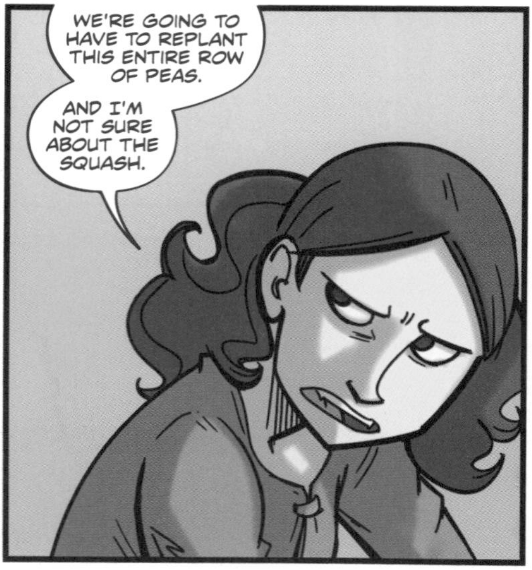
WE'RE GOING TO HAVE TO REPLANT THIS ENTIRE ROW OF PEAS.
AND I'M NOT SURE ABOUT THE SQUASH.

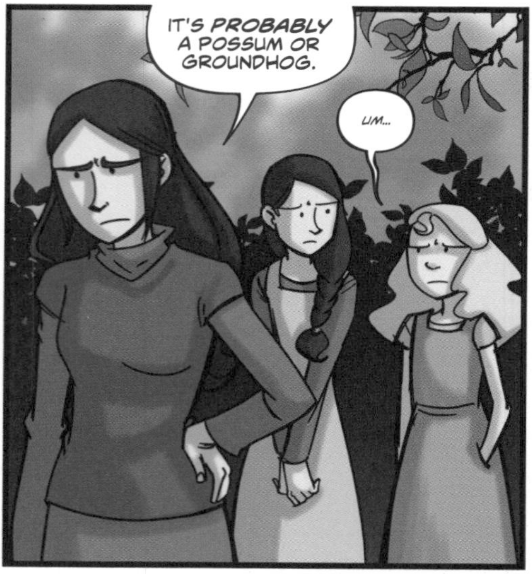
IT'S *PROBABLY* A POSSUM OR GROUNDHOG.
UM...

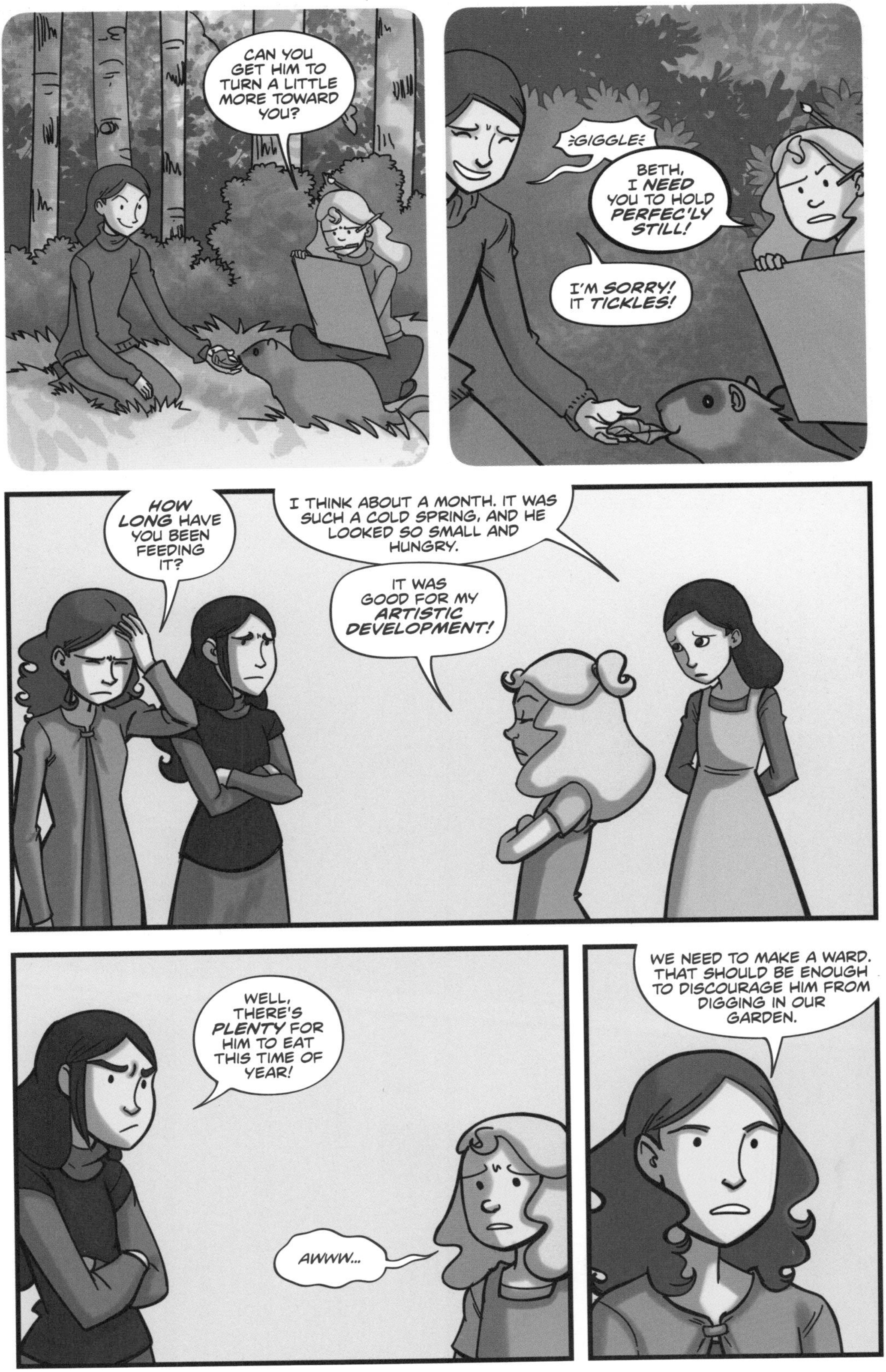

CAN YOU GET HIM TO TURN A LITTLE MORE TOWARD YOU?
GIGGLE
BETH, I NEED YOU TO HOLD PERFEC'LY STILL!
I'M SORRY! IT TICKLES!
HOW LONG HAVE YOU BEEN FEEDING IT?
I THINK ABOUT A MONTH. IT WAS SUCH A COLD SPRING, AND HE LOOKED SO SMALL AND HUNGRY.
IT WAS GOOD FOR MY ARTISTIC DEVELOPMENT!
WELL, THERE'S PLENTY FOR HIM TO EAT THIS TIME OF YEAR!
AWWW...
WE NEED TO MAKE A WARD. THAT SHOULD BE ENOUGH TO DISCOURAGE HIM FROM DIGGING IN OUR GARDEN.

FLIIING

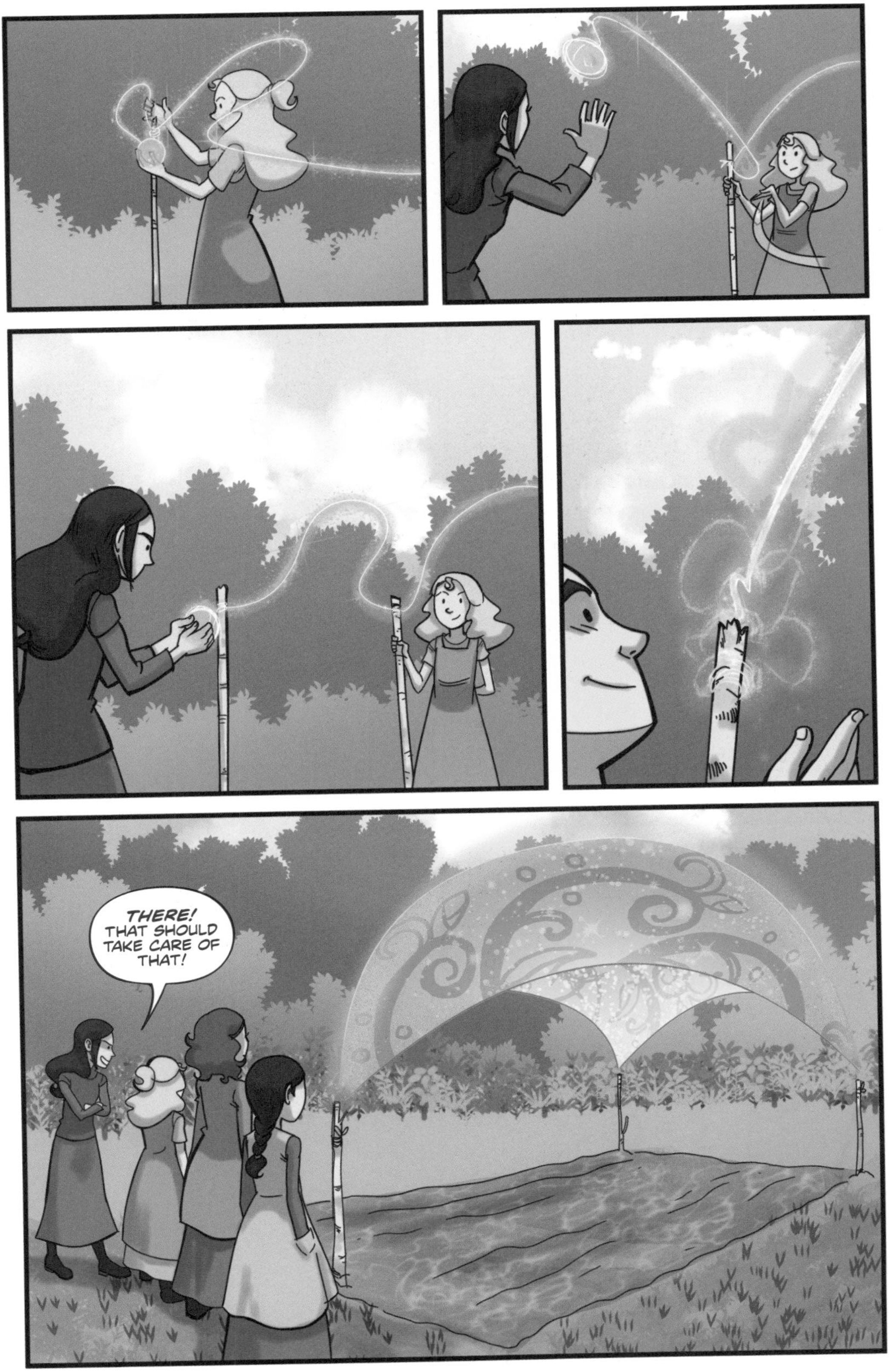
THERE! THAT SHOULD TAKE CARE OF THAT!

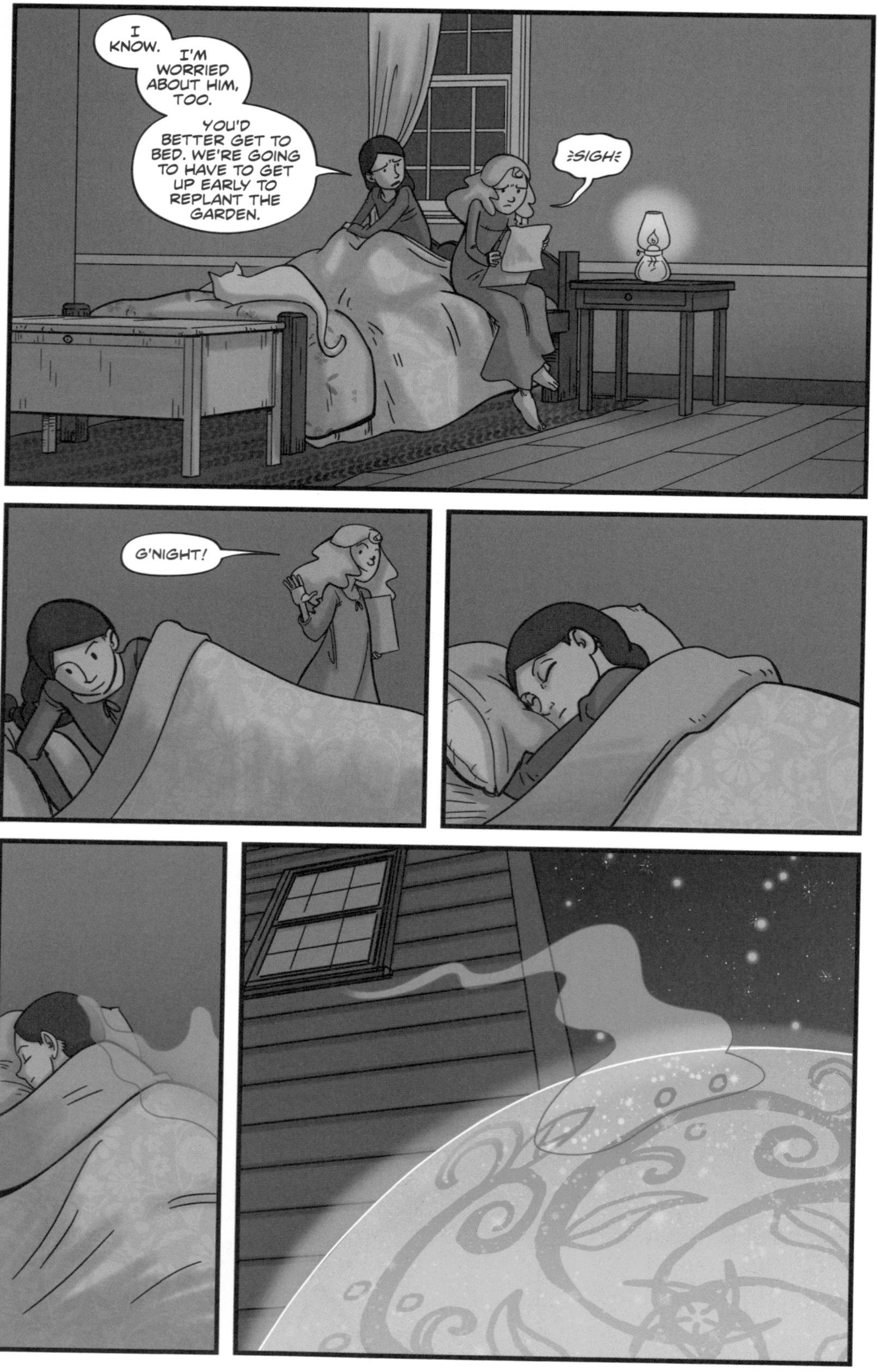
I KNOW. I'M WORRIED ABOUT HIM, TOO.
YOU'D BETTER GET TO BED. WE'RE GOING TO HAVE TO GET UP EARLY TO REPLANT THE GARDEN.
SIGH
G'NIGHT!

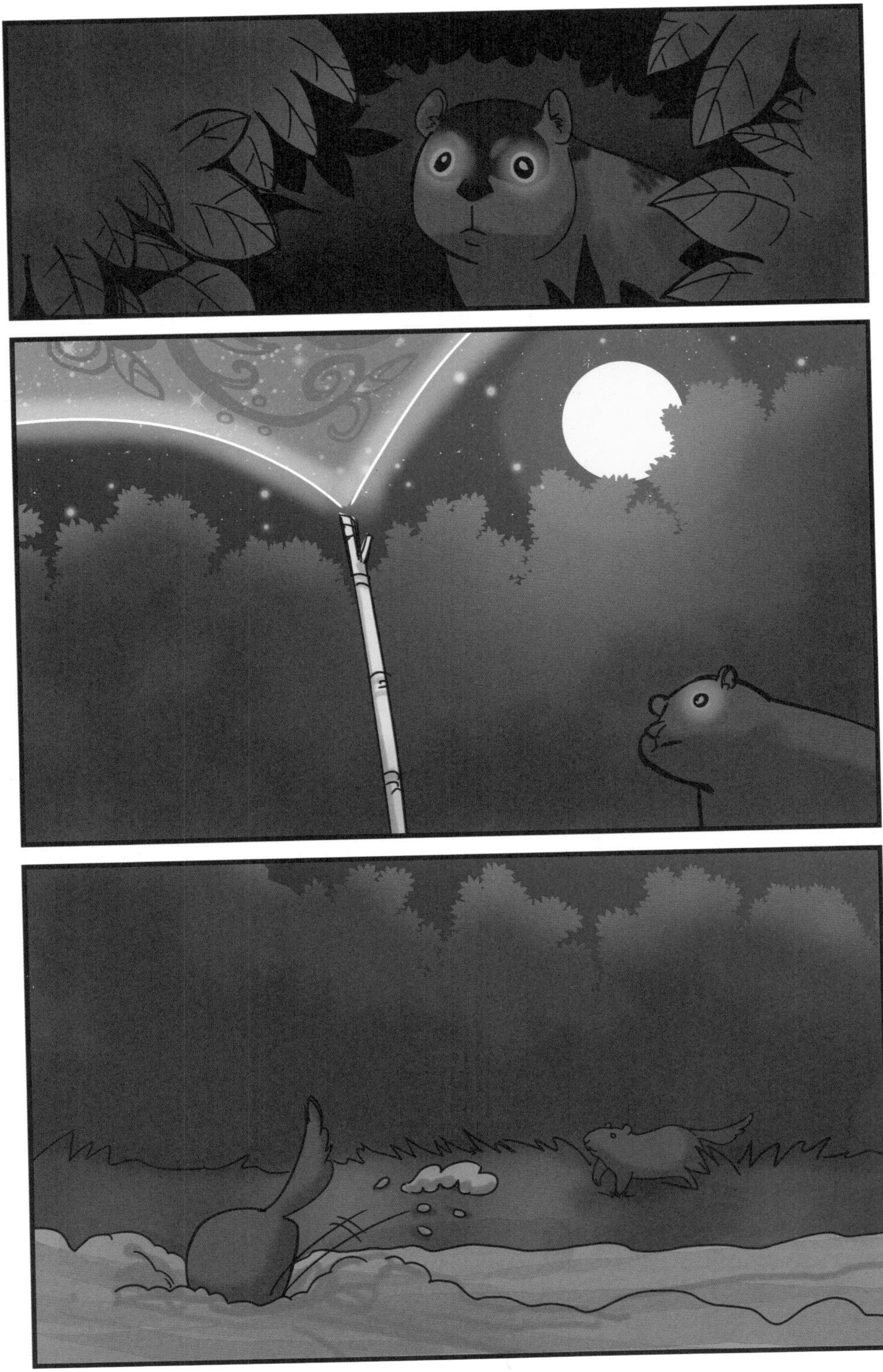

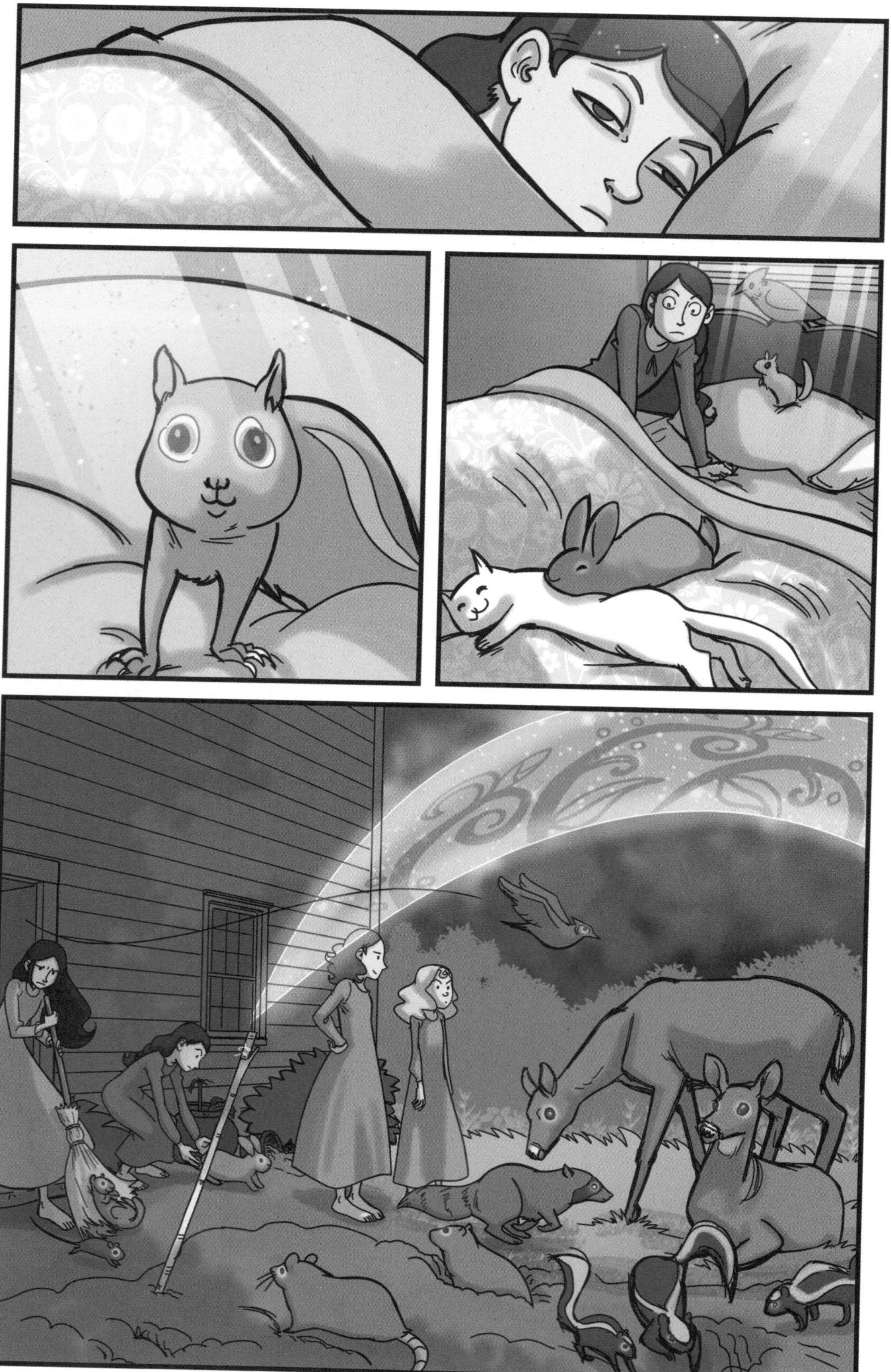

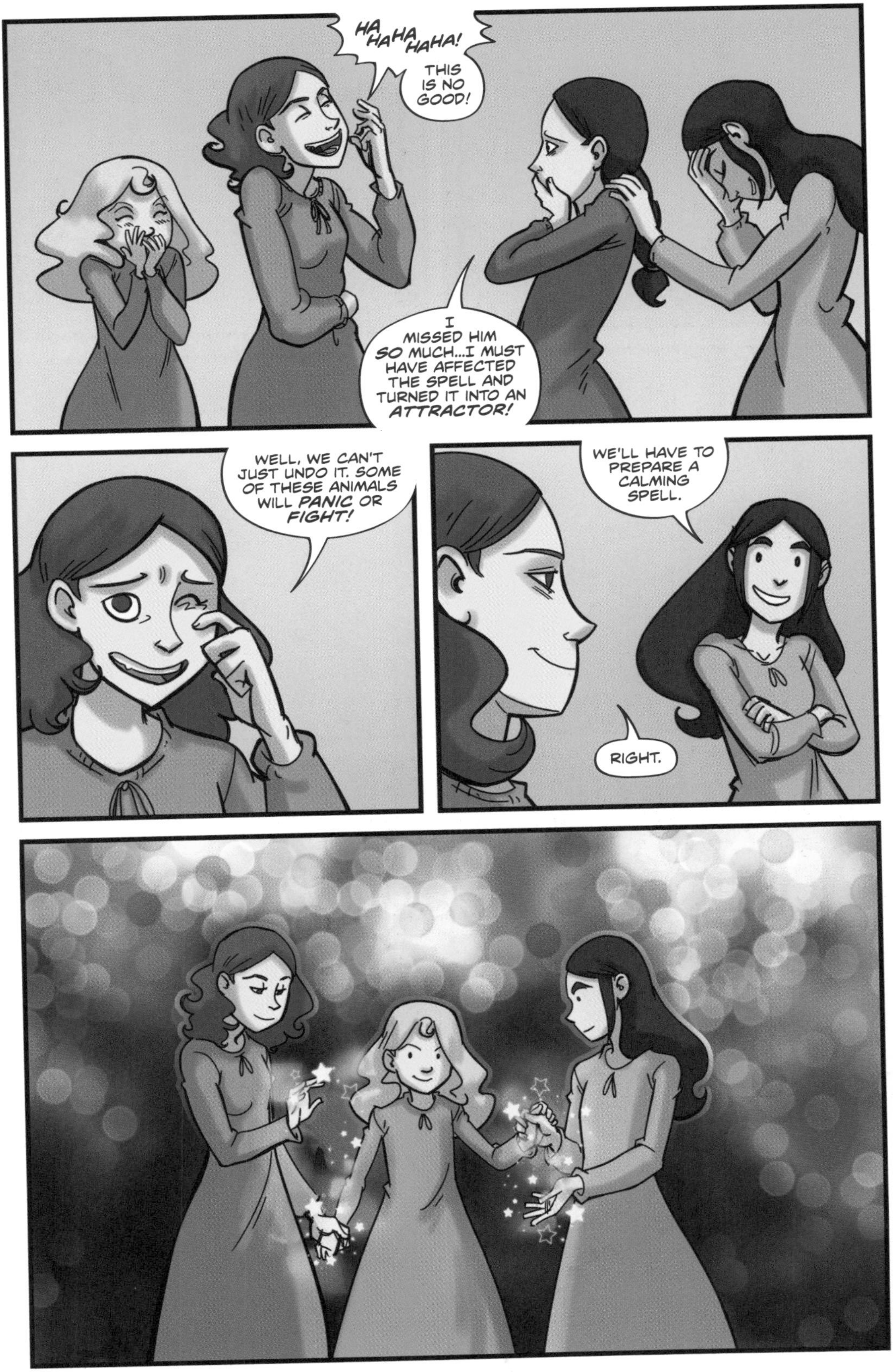
HA HAHA HAHA!
THIS IS NO GOOD!
I MISSED HIM SO MUCH...I MUST HAVE AFFECTED THE SPELL AND TURNED IT INTO AN ATTRACTOR!
WELL, WE CAN'T JUST UNDO IT. SOME OF THESE ANIMALS WILL PANIC OR FIGHT!
WE'LL HAVE TO PREPARE A CALMING SPELL.
RIGHT.

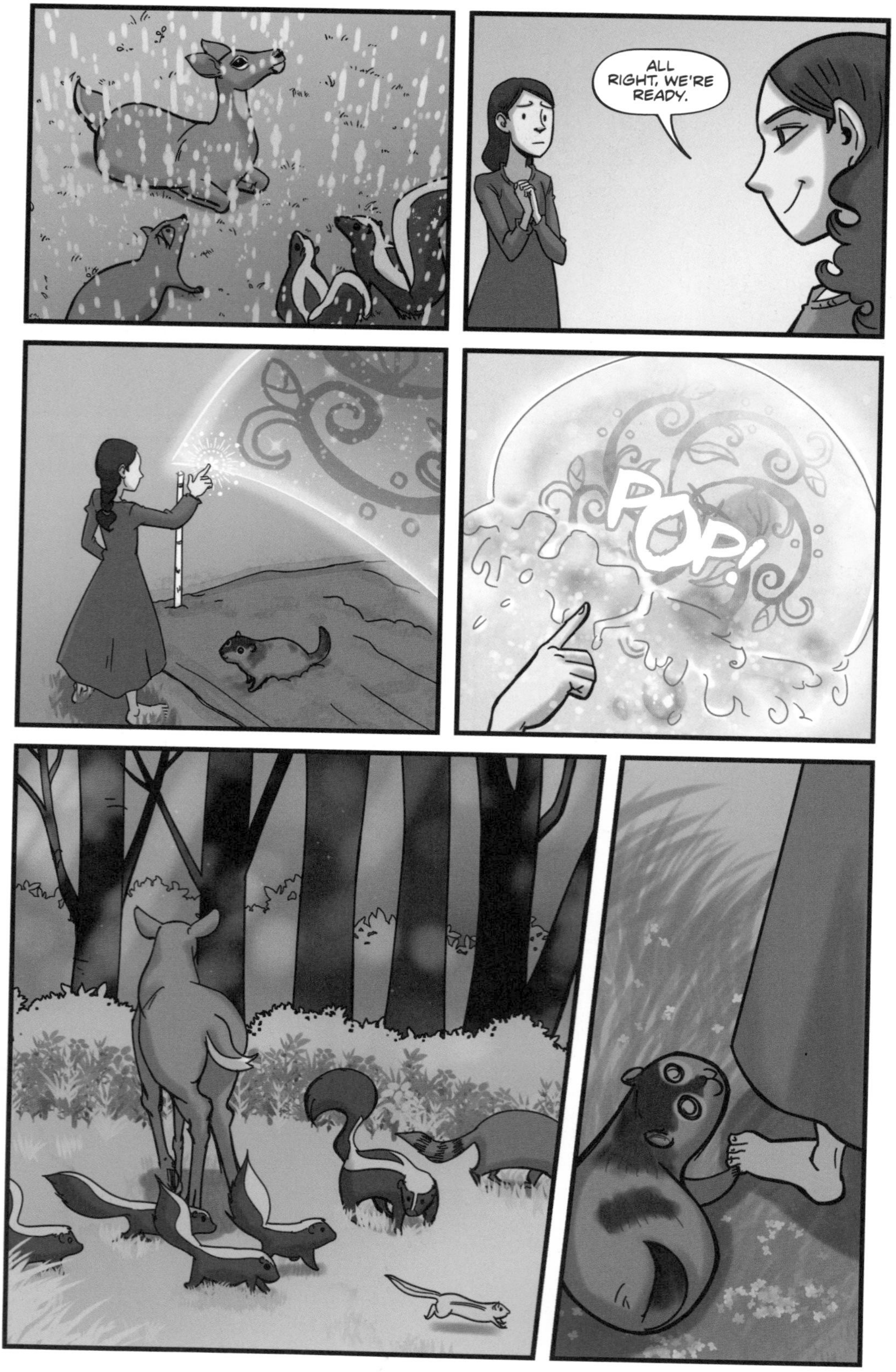
ALL RIGHT, WE'RE READY.
POP!

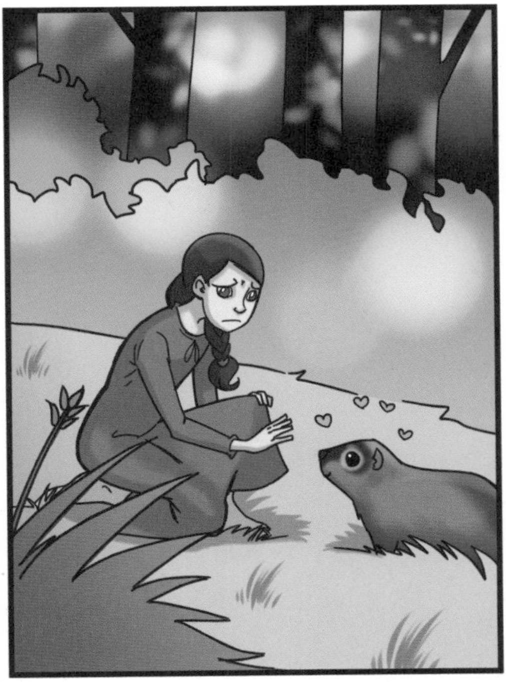

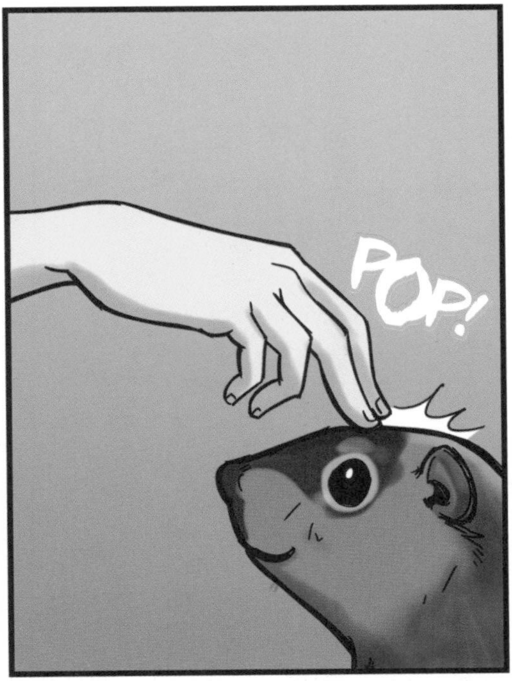
POP!

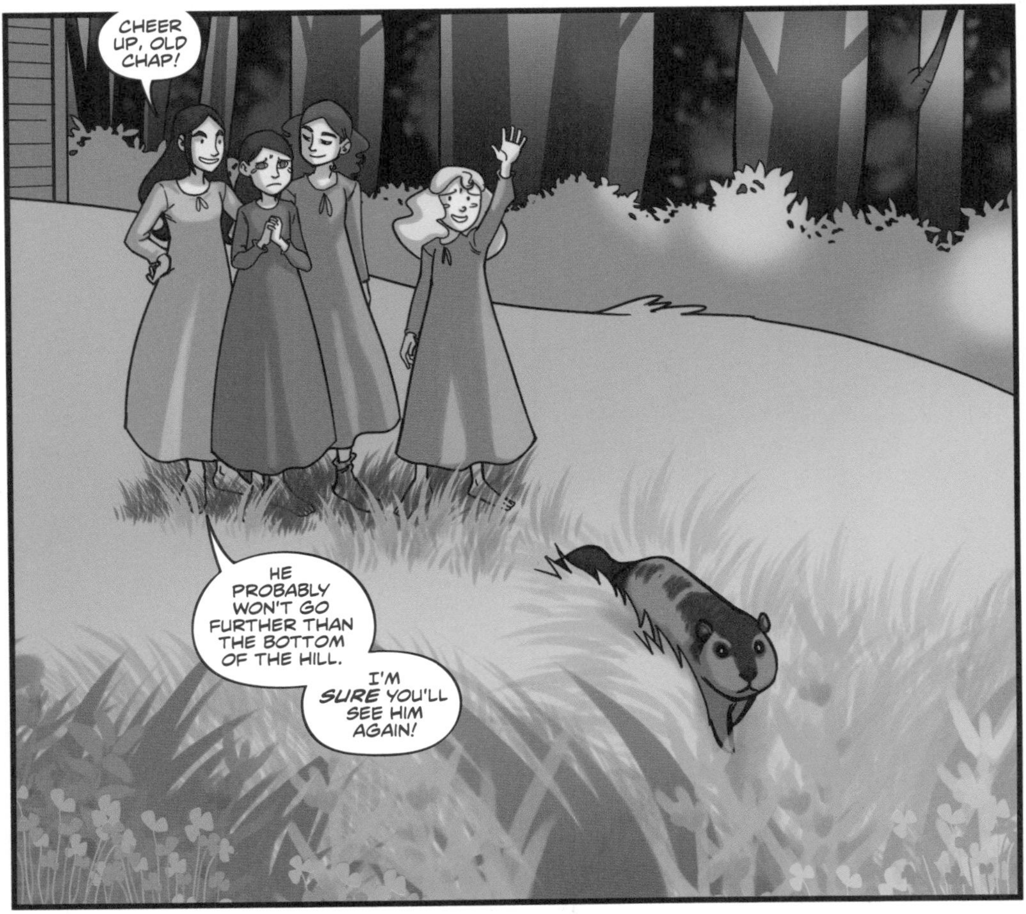
CHEER UP, OLD CHAP!
HE PROBABLY WON'T GO FURTHER THAN THE BOTTOM OF THE HILL.
I'M ***SURE*** YOU'LL SEE HIM AGAIN!

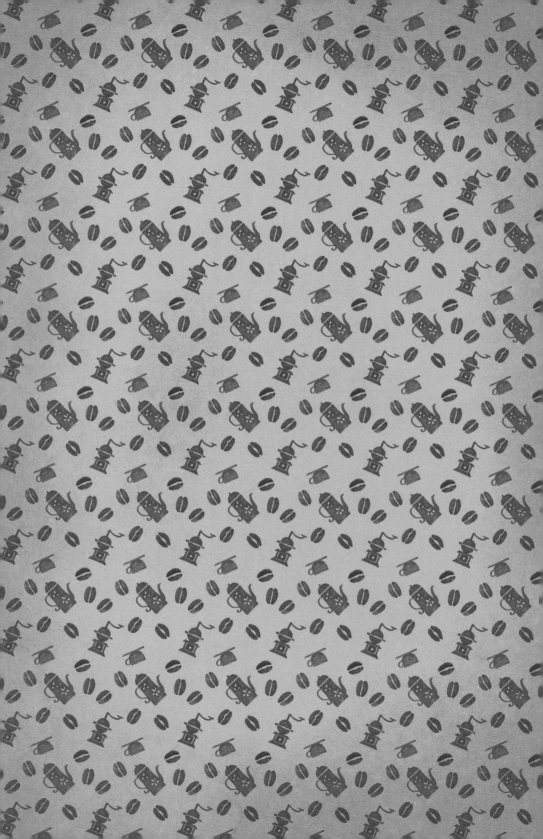

LEIGH DRAGOON was raised in a log cabin in the Adirondacks, where she developed an early love of reading and writing. She became a fan of *Little Women* at age nine, after Beth's demise made her bawl herself to sleep. This led to a life-long appreciation of the book. After years of annual re-reads, she also became fascinated with learning about Louisa May Alcott and her family.

Leigh has several print publications of her own, both graphic novels and prose, through HarperCollins and Penguin. She adapted both Richelle Mead's *Vampire Academy* and Marie Lu's *Legend* series into graphic novel scripts. She also wrote two prose *Adventure Time* novels: *Queen of Rogues* and *The Lonesome Outlaw*, as well as creating original comics stories and scripts for Mattel's *Ever After High* and Disney's *Tangled*.

MORE ONI PRESS BOOKS ABOUT MAGIC AND MAYHEM!

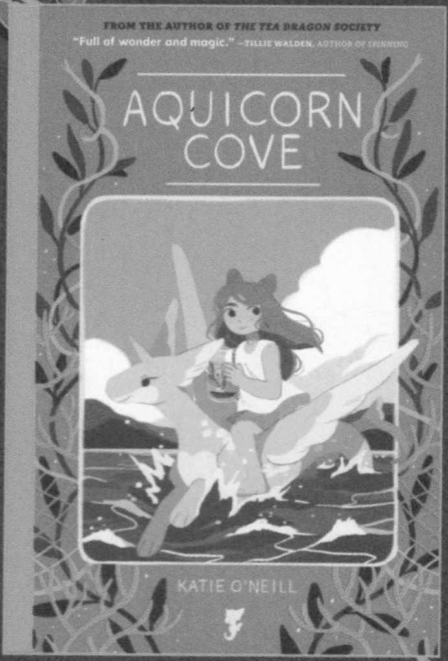
FROM THE AUTHOR OF THE TEA DRAGON SOCIETY
"Full of wonder and magic." —TILLIE WALDEN, AUTHOR OF SPINNING
AQUICORN COVE
KATIE O'NEILL

AQUICORN COVE
By Katie O'Neill

Unable to rely on the adults in her storm-ravaged seaside town, a young girl must protect a colony of magical seahorse-like creatures she discovers in the coral reef.

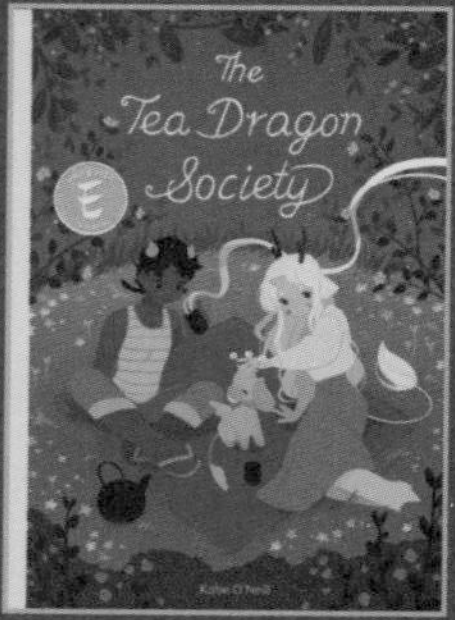
The Tea Dragon Society

THE TEA DRAGON SOCIETY
By Katie O'Neill

When Greta finds a lost creature in the market, she learns about the nearly-forgotten art of Tea Dragon caretaking.

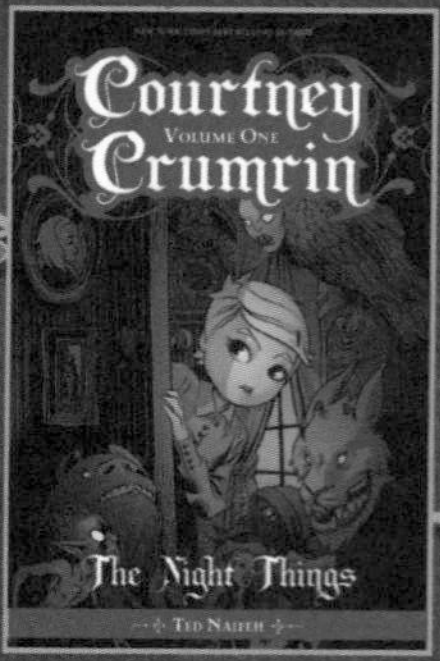
Courtney
Volume One
Crumrin
The Night Things
TED NAIFEH

COURTNEY CRUMRIN VOLUME ONE
By Ted Naifeh and Warren Wucinich

Courtney Crumrin moves in with her uncle and learns there's a complex magical world of warlocks, witches, and fae.

MOONCAKES
By Suzanne Walker and Wendy Xu

When teenage witch Nova's childhood friend, Tam, moves back to town, the two discover a sinister group plotting to harness Tam's werewolf powers for their own gain.

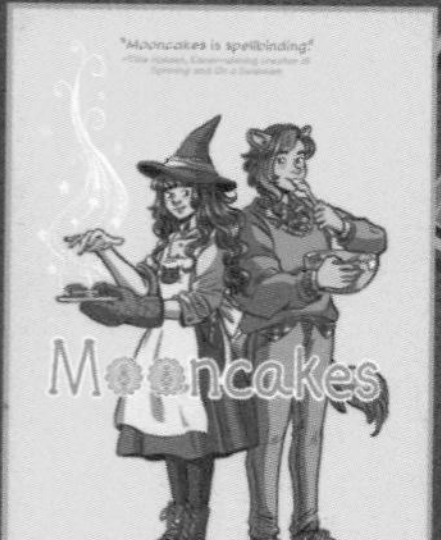
"Mooncakes is spellbinding!"
Mooncakes
Wendy Xu
Suzanne Walker

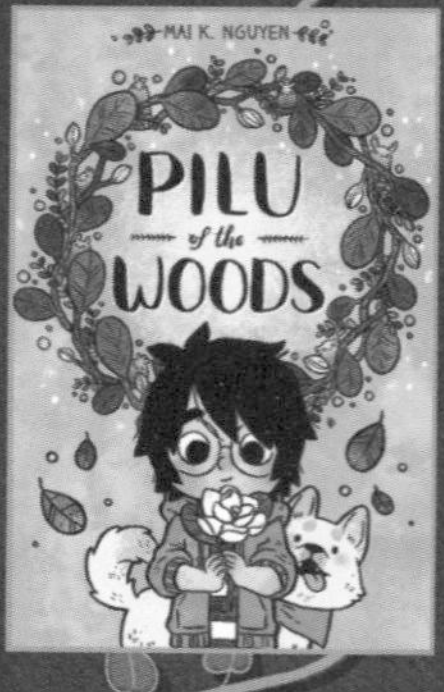
MAI K. NGUYEN
PILU
of the
WOODS

PILU OF THE WOODS
By Mai K. Nguyen

After running away from home, Willow befriends a tree spirit, Pilu, living in the woods near her house.